FINDING HOME

THE ROSE CITY SERIES
BOOK ONE

VALENTINA BURNS

Finding Home is a work of fiction, created without the use of AI technology. Names, characters, places, and incidents are the product of the author's imagination and used in a fictitious manner. Any resemblance to actual persons, living or dead, places, or events is entirely coincidental.

Editing by: Jacqui Nelson

Proofreading by: Elizabeth Vidulich

Cover design by: Books and Moods Graphic Design

ISBN electronic book: 978-1-7389724-7-0

ISBN print book: 978-1-7389724-6-3

For Matt, the love of my life.
My home is wherever you are.

CHAPTER ONE

Hope Morgan thought she learned her lesson on impulse buys long ago. They were almost always followed by regret. If not immediately, then definitely when the credit card bill showed up. But today, Hope couldn't let anything, not even the threat of debt, take the joy out of her most recent splurge.

In fact, as she exited her favorite shoe store in downtown Portland, swinging the chic bag that held her new elegant, yet sexy, stilettos, she couldn't drum up a single ounce of regret.

This wasn't an impulse buy, but a celebratory treat. After a month of diligent online job hunting, resume editing, and pounding the pavement the old-fashioned way, she'd finally met with success.

She walked down the street, smiling as she recalled the interview she had that morning with one of the city's biggest marketing firms. Not only was it her second interview, but it'd gone perfectly.

The first drops of cold January rain landed on her forehead as her phone started ringing in her purse. Sidestepping for cover under the nearest storefront awning, she dug out her phone and smiled when she saw the name of the company she'd interviewed with on the screen.

"Hope Morgan," she said eagerly into the phone.

"Ms. Morgan," came the monotone voice of the HR rep she'd met that morning. "I'm glad I caught you. We didn't want to keep you waiting if we didn't have to."

A loaded pause on the other end of the line caused the first tendril of apprehension to curl in her gut.

"Ms. Morgan, you were an excellent candidate. Your education, professionalism, and experience are what had us calling you for a second interview."

You were *an excellent candidate*. As his words sank in, her stomach dropped.

"Unfortunately..." he continued, confirming her worst fear in a single word.

Her hand holding the phone to her ear shook.

"Unfortunately," he repeated. "We interviewed another excellent candidate, and we've decided to go with him as he has more experience."

Hope said nothing. She couldn't. She was afraid if she opened her mouth, she'd start crying in the middle of a public street.

"Ms. Morgan, are you still there?" Monotone HR guy asked.

She took a deep breath. "Yes. I'm here. I'd like to thank you for the opportunity and the interviews. I'm sorry it didn't work out."

After the world's most awkward goodbye, the call ended. With a sigh, she slumped against the shop window. The chic bag holding the stilettos now weighed her down, and the raindrops had turned into a full-fledged downpour.

Having moved the week between Christmas and New

Year, she'd lived in Portland for over a month now. She'd given herself one month to find a job, one month to start contributing to society.

Four weeks later, she felt no closer to that goal.

Was it too much to ask to finally make her own way? To get a job on her own merits without depending on her wealthy family for support? To submit a resume without listing her influential father as a reference?

Apparently so.

The cold rain now pelted down, reaching her under the storefront's awning, dampening her smart suit jacket and matching pencil skirt. The Pearl District apartment that she shared with her best friend, Ivy, was a twenty-minute walk away. Her heels tapped the pavement as she headed for it. If she kept up this pace, she'd make it in fifteen.

All she wanted was to get inside, go straight to her freezer, and have an indulgent counseling session with her therapists: Ben and Jerry.

Sixteen minutes later, soaked completely through and shivering uncontrollably, she reached the front door of the building she loved. Restored in the last decade, it had a beautiful brick facade. She and Ivy lived on the second floor above the popular street-level bar called Bowie's. Ivy had been here for three years before Hope became her roommate, and Hope felt grateful because in her current state, there was no way she'd be able to afford her own place in the heart of this city.

Still shivering, Hope set down her shopping bag to attack her purse with both hands and reach the bottom where her keys were likely hiding. Just as she hunched over her bag, the front door burst open and nearly bowled her over.

"Oh, hey!" Cathy, the postal worker she'd met a few

times before, sidestepped her to reach the sidewalk. "Sorry, hun, I nearly knocked you over."

Hope scrambled to grab the door and keep it open. "No worries. I was—" She eyeballed Cathy's raincoat with more than a little jealousy, wondering if the woman would be willing to trade it for the shoes she'd just bought. Too late. Cathy was already on her way to the next stop on her route.

Safely inside, Hope trudged up the steep staircase leading to the second floor, still digging through her purse. Where were her damn keys? When she reached her apartment door, she dropped to her knees and dumped the entire contents of her purse on the floor.

Groaning, she rifled through crumpled receipts, an assortment of lip glosses, a mascara wand, a half-eaten Luna bar, two packs of gum, and a long strand of glow-in-the-dark condoms she'd won at the bridal shower Ivy had dragged her to last weekend.

Why she kept them, she had no idea. It wasn't like she needed more reminders of the gaping void that was her sex life. *Priorities,* she reminded herself as she sifted through more random crap living in her purse. Pens, a cosmetic mirror, enough Kleenex to fill an empty box, and the wrapped candies she collected every time she left an eating establishment. All there, strewn on the floor in front of her apartment door, but no sign of her keys.

Slumping against the wall beside her door, she closed her eyes and tried to remember the last time she'd seen them. She drew a blank. That morning, she'd left with Ivy, so she hadn't been the one to lock up. Her keys could be anywhere.

She thunked her head against the wall a couple of times before she dropped her forehead to her knees in sodden defeat. Hot tears pricked her eyes, and she didn't try to fight them this time. It was all too much, and there was no one around to see her display of weakness, so she let loose. This day couldn't possibly get any worse.

From under the cocoon of her huddle, she blindly reached for one of her purse tissues and wiped her nose. At the exact moment she let out a pathetic sounding whimper, she heard heavy footsteps striding toward her. Two very large, very male, Blundstone-clad feet appeared in her peripheral vision.

Scratch that. Her day could definitely get worse.

~

Gabe stared at the woman curled in a ball at his feet. She looked like a wounded puppy. A sniffling one.

Shit, was she crying? *Shit.* He could handle bar fights, drunk-assed adults acting like children, and worse. He could patiently wade through complicated liquor licensing red-tape hell. He would even handle the things that went bump in the night. But one thing he wasn't equipped to handle, and never had been, was a woman's tears.

Women were a complex equation he was always struggling to solve but never quite could. He barely managed the ones in his own family, let alone a stranger. Shoving his hands in his pockets, he shifted uncomfortably from one foot to the other.

He hadn't officially met her since she moved into the apartment across from his, but he'd known who Hope Morgan was the instant he saw her. Not only because she didn't look like your average Portlander with her chic clothes and perfectly manicured appearance, but also because Ivy had given him a pretty good rundown on her friend when she'd asked if it would be okay if she took on a roommate.

Not to mention, Hope came from a rich California family. So rich that even Gabe had heard about the property and construction legend that was her father. Walter Morgan was a self-made zillionaire who started doing odd jobs in construction as a teen and built his own construction empire. Morgan Construction had developed half of the most notable high-end buildings in Northwest California. He didn't know much about Walter Morgan himself, but he admired the man's ferocious work ethic, and respected anyone who could build something successful from little more than nothing. Gabe had been trying to do the same for himself, and he knew the grit it took.

When it came to the man's daughter, however, Gabe was happy to keep his distance. He could imagine the type of woman Hope was, and he always gave women like her a wide berth. Rich daddy's girls whose biggest concerns were their social calendars and matching wardrobes. Superficial women who didn't think twice about tapping into daddy's bank account. Over the years, he'd seen plenty of them go through his bar and had never been drawn to them. The opposite, really.

Women like this hadn't had to deal with realities like putting food on the table or scraping together enough cash to make rent a single day in their lives. He couldn't say he blamed Hope's father for protecting his daughter from the harsher realities of the world. Lord knows, he tried to do the same for his daughter, Ruby. But it was hard not to harbor an underlying resentment knowing that while he worked his ass off for every last thing he owned, this woman—who was likely in her mid-twenties—probably still had her daddy taking care of her every need. It was one thing to make sure your kids had a good life and another to spoil them.

And it wasn't like his presumptions were totally unfounded. The other day he heard her in the hall between their apartments talking in hushed tones on the phone about "dad's money." He hadn't meant to eavesdrop. The doors were flimsy. He'd have to fix that. Anyway, he heard enough to know his assumptions weren't totally baseless. Not to mention the fancy shopping bag that was currently propped beside her bearing the name of an expensive shoe store in town.

Simply put, he hadn't had much doubt that Hope Morgan was just another society princess who existed on her father's money.

Except, apart from the fancy shopping bag, the woman curled up at his feet didn't exactly fit the picture he'd painted. In fact, she looked wrecked, messy, and totally vulnerable.

When he'd come up the back staircase and spotted her, something about seeing her like that had drawn him. Instead of walking past her to his own apartment, which he might have done to give her privacy, his legs took him right to her.

He was a master at avoiding difficult situations. Truthfully, he'd been a master at it for going on seven years. He'd had enough difficulties to last him a lifetime, and he wasn't looking for trouble for the hell of it. But seeing Hope huddled on the floor—soaking wet with her hair falling out of her fancy hairdo from all sides and the entire contents of her purse spread around her like shrapnel—had him going against his usual survival instinct.

"You okay?" he asked as he crouched down so he was level with her.

Her sniffling stopped. She seemed to freeze in place at the sound of his voice. She didn't so much as stir. Didn't appear to be breathing, either. Like maybe if she played dead, he'd go away.

Another time, he might have. But this time, he couldn't —and hell if he knew why.

Slowly he lifted the wet hair that curtained her body. The long golden strands peeled off of the cream-colored blouse that clung to her arm like a second skin. A translucent second-skin. He tried very hard not to notice that the rain had made the material see-through against her flesh, and he definitely tried not to notice the outline of her soft curves through the wet fabric.

When she shuddered, he realized she must be freezing. He might have avoided women like this—hell, most women, if he was being honest—but he hadn't forgotten his manners. He shrugged out of his leather jacket and draped it over her shoulders.

Finally, she lifted her head from her knees and looked up at him. Her deep-brown eyes were a direct contrast to her sunny-blonde hair. Her clothes and the subtle scent of expensive perfume co-mingling with the smell of fresh rain coming off her skin, told him she was normally every inch the stylish aristocrat he imagined her to be, even though, in that moment, she looked anything but.

Mascara ran down her cheeks. Her eyes were red and puffy from crying. Her forehead held a red mark from the pressure of her knees as she'd curled into a ball. And despite all this, he couldn't stop the sudden, unbidden thought that she was the most beautiful thing he'd ever seen.

A hundred emotions shone brightly in eyes so pure and honest, he felt he could read each one. Sadness, worry, anxiety, and—the one that shot him right in the heart—vulnera-bility. Without warning, something uncomfortable and unanticipated bloomed in his chest.

Frowning, he steeled himself against it. Against her. Pulling his internal armor around him, he leaned back, putting distance between himself and her watery gaze.

"Rough day?" he guessed, and couldn't help but crack a smile when he got a very un-aristocratic snort in response.

She wiped a tissue across her nose but said nothing. He waited her out. He wasn't her damn counselor; he wasn't going to probe.

"I got caught in the rain, and I can't find my keys," she said eventually, gesturing to the regurgitated contents of her purse.

Wild guess, but he was pretty sure more was going on. Even so, he nodded gamely, looking at the stuff on the floor around him. His gaze zoned in on a string of condoms that advertised themselves to be glow-in-the-dark.

"Hmm," he rumbled as he ran his finger along the strand. Trying to lighten the mood, he added, "Glow in the dark, eh?"

With a gasp, Hope bolted to her knees and snatched the condoms away from his hand.

"I'll have you know." Her voice took on a haughty edge as she crammed the condoms and everything else back into her purse. "I won those at a party."

Her jerky movements and the blush blooming across her cheeks, told him she was royally pissed and probably a little embarrassed, too.

Mission accomplished. He'd done what he'd intended to do. He'd stopped her tears and interrupted her sadness. He should let it go at that. Let her go. If he valued his life even a little, he would have. But she looked so damned cute—with her pink cheeks and bright, indignant eyes—that he just couldn't.

"Whatever you say, sweetheart," he said with a hint of mocking. He was pushing it, and he knew it.

Sure enough, she stopped what she was doing and slowly looked up to meet his gaze. Her eyes darkened with a fury that screamed *oh-no-you-didn't,* but he could tell her good breeding was keeping her from making an equally rude retort.

Instead, she huffed a disgusted breath as she scrambled to her feet and faced him toe to toe as he rose along with her.

Gabe was a full head taller than her, but her killer heels brought her almost to his eye level. Her eyes were blazing. Blessedly, empty of the sadness and vulnerability he'd seen earlier. She stared him down as good as any tough guy he'd ever had a throwdown with—and in his field of serving alcohol to those who often didn't know their limits, he'd stared down plenty of tough guys.

He could tell she wanted him gone, but the thing was, she was still stuck, key-less. The ball was in his court, and by the look in her eyes, she hated that fact.

With her eyes flashing and cheeks blazing, Gabe thought again that Hope Morgan was the sexiest thing he'd seen in a long time.

Had he misjudged her? The woman in front of him clearly had grit. She stood her ground, arms crossed, silently glaring at him, daring him to call her sweetheart again.

Interesting. Maybe the privileged little rich girl could hold her own, after all.

A smile tugged Gabe's mouth, an unfamiliar sensation these days. He reached into his pocket for the key ring that held the key to his apartment, the key to the bar, and the master key to the rest of the doors in the building—including Hope Morgan's.

Her body tensed as she eyed the keys dangling in front of her. "Let me guess. Now I'm going to owe you a favor."

She said it so deadpan that he couldn't mistake it for the bad joke he'd hoped it was. What the fuck? What did she think? That he'd suggest they put those condoms to good use as a thank you? Christ, did he really come off like such an asshole?

"No. Jesus." Gabe turned to the door as he found the right key. "Why would you owe me a favor for opening your damn door?" An unsettling thought entered his head. "What kind of assholes do you usually run with?"

At her silence, he gave her a sideways glance. She stood very still beside him, watching with great interest as he turned the key in the lock and opened her door. He pushed it open and stepped aside to give her plenty of room to enter.

As soon as she was inside, she spun to close the door, but before she slammed it in his face, as he was sure she would have liked to, she kept a crack open and said, so softly he almost didn't catch it, "Thank you."

Then she shut the door, leaving him standing alone, wondering what the hell just happened, and who the hell Hope Morgan really was. Because she sure as shit wasn't who he'd thought she was.

CHAPTER TWO

He is not your type. Stay away from him, do you hear me? He is not your type. Hope tapped her forehead against her apartment door and repeated her mantra over and over, hoping that it would stick.

She'd been here for over four weeks and never met her landlord, but she'd known it was him—and not because no one else would have a reason to be on the apartment level of the building but him. The second she looked up and met his intense dark-green gaze, something had clicked inside her, and she'd just *known.*

Not only that, but her heart had gone wild, and butterflies had erupted in her stomach as if she were a naive schoolgirl coming face to face with her first crush. Except Gabriel Walsh was nothing like the clean-cut quarterbacks she'd had the hots for in high school.

Her landlord was the opposite of clean-cut. He was handsome enough, with his tall, broad-shouldered body built like a football player. But the five o'clock shadow he sported gave a dark edge to the square cut of his jaw and added ruggedness to his other sinfully delicious facial features. His hair, a dark brown, was two missed haircuts too long, which should not have been sexy, but annoyingly was. Then there was the hint of a tattoo snaking up his bicep, the allure of which should have been criminal.

He was as far removed from the clean-cut, blonde Californian Ken dolls she'd become used to as a man could get.

As far as first impressions went, Hope had run the gamut from annoyed to pissed off to aroused in the span of five minutes. Which was not in any way okay because she had no business feeling attracted to someone who clearly viewed her as a disaster. And, if nothing else, Gabriel Walsh had made it clear he believed she was that at the very least.

It didn't matter, she told herself, and besides, he was NOT her type. Not to mention the fact that she was on a dating moratorium, finding it safer to avoid men altogether. Until she had her life in order, she had no intentions of starting a relationship with anyone. Especially not a man like that.

"Ugh," she groaned as she shoved away from the door and headed to the shower. "He needs a haircut."

It wasn't until she started undressing that she realized she was still wearing his jacket. "Of course." She shrugged it off her shoulders, immediately catching a whiff of him.

As his scent flooded her nostrils, her hormones took over and, against her better judgment, she pressed the jacket to her face and inhaled deeply. *Oh. My. God.* No person had any right to smell this sexy—ever. His scent went straight through her, and she went instantly damp between her legs. She dropped his jacket like it was on fire and took a full step backward.

Nope, this was not good. Not good at all. Any man who could fry all of her brain cells with his scent alone was one she needed to avoid.

She quickly stripped and sought the heat of her shower, reliving the highlight reel of her incredibly crap-tacular day, starting with how utterly defeated she'd been when she didn't get the job, and ending with one Gabriel Walsh finding glow-in-the-dark condoms in her purse.

With a groan, she let the day's humiliation pour over her like the water washing over her body.

What would her father think of her now? How was she supposed to face him? Or her mother? She couldn't avoid their calls and emails much longer, and the last thing she wanted was for them to show up in Portland and see the mess she'd made of her life. Another flood of desolation swamped her. She was still so angry, and she didn't want to care what her parents thought, but she did. And that made everything feel worse.

Finishing her shower, she tossed on a pair of gray leggings and a black cami. Then she went into the living room where Ivy had helped set up her little oasis. Her easel and paints faced the light of the window looking down onto the busy street below, and a huge potted palm blocked her view of the rest of the apartment, so that when she dove into her painting, she saw only the easel in front of her, the view of the city beyond that, and the green of the plant in her periphery.

For her cluttered mind the blank slate in front of her was freedom. It was what she loved most about art. It started from nothing. It waited for her to unleash everything inside her. Things she couldn't communicate in any other way.

"Alexa, play 'When the Party's Over,'" she told her best non-human friend. As the opening chords filled the room, she put brush to canvas and lost herself, leaving behind the horrible memories of the day.

Only when she heard a thud on the apartment door,

then a muffled curse followed by the jingle of keys, did she leave her trance and look at the time on her phone. She gasped when she learned nearly four hours had passed.

A heartfelt "Oh, for fuck's sake" came from the other side of the door before it opened a crack and a yoga mat, exercise blocks, and a huge duffle bag slid through. Then Ivy squeezed inside, carrying a box piled to capacity with the tools she used as a physical therapist. Under her arm was a bottle of wine, and in her mouth were envelopes that Hope guessed were their mail. As soon as she was inside, she dropped everything but the wine and kicked the door shut behind her. Spitting out the mail so that it fluttered to the floor, she sagged against the door and swiped her arm across her brow.

"Fuck me, that was harder than the six miles I ran at the ass crack of dawn."

And just like that, Ivy Harrington was home.

Ivy had been Hope's best friend since they met on their first day in college. Saying they'd been to hell and back together since then would be an understatement. Hope couldn't imagine life without her.

Ivy was on the shorter side of average, with pale skin that stood out against hair that was the color of seventy percent chocolate. The dark tresses normally fell in a straight line to her shoulders, but today was pulled back into a stubby ponytail, the strands that had come loose sticking to her sweaty brow. After three years of diligent training at the gym where she also worked as a PT, Ivy was lean, toned, and, most importantly to her, strong. Thanks to her assiduous training with the gym owner, Sean Thompson, she also had some pretty fierce kickboxing skills.

However, anyone looking at Ivy was always drawn in first by her crystal-blue eyes. They held the kind of icy clarity that made you feel like you could see right through them. But as Hope well knew, that was an illusion. No one saw through or inside Ivy. Her eyes might be clear as blue glass, but they hid a world of secrets and pain that only a handful of people knew about.

Hope was one of those people. Knowing what Ivy had not only survived but risen from had cemented their bond even more. They had become transparent to one another. Hope could see what lay beneath that crystal-blue gaze, and Ivy saw through Hope's carefully curated exterior.

As Ivy seemed to be doing now. "Oh, Christ," she said, scanning Hope from head to toe. "What happened?"

Hope blinked. "What makes you think anything happened?"

"Well, for one, you're standing there braless, in yesterday's leggings, with paint smeared across your face." Ivy gave her a knowing look. "And if that wasn't clue enough that your day was shit, I see that you let your hair air-dry. Air-dry, Hope." Ivy arched an eyebrow as if to say *any other questions?* Then she flopped down onto the couch and patted the cushion beside her.

"Spill."

Hope blew out a breath and sat.

"I didn't get the job," she murmured.

Rather than say anything, Ivy got up and grabbed two glasses to go with the bottle of pinot noir she'd wrestled home. She didn't speak until she was seated next to Hope again and uncorking the wine.

"You're not a failure just because you didn't get one stupid job you didn't really want in the first place. You know that, right?" Ivy poured two generous glasses and handed her one.

"Right," Hope said unconvincingly as she indulged in a

long sip. "And what makes you think I didn't really want that job?"

Ivy gave her an impressive eyeroll. "Puh-leeze, Hope Morgan. You no more want to be pushing paper and crunching numbers than I want to be friendly to strangers." Ivy cracked half a smile, then nodded in the direction of Hope's easel. "Everyone and their dog knows that creating art is where your heart really lives."

Hope contemplated the painting she'd begun hours before, the colors colliding with each other as the image took shape. Since she was a little girl, all she wanted was to paint and draw and make things. Still, she knew that wasn't going to pay this month's rent. Or the next. And even though Ivy had been after her for months to open an Etsy account so she could put out feelers for interest in her art, Hope had focused on pursuing the more traditional employment route. Get a job on her own educational merits that her family would be proud of and start living and paying for her own life. Independence.

It was a huge part of the reason she'd come to Portland. However, she thought with a dejected sigh, it was all backfiring on her. Big time.

"Also, I bought a pair of Marc Jacobs shoes that I had no business buying, but at that point I was convinced I had the job in the bag." Twirling the stem of her glass, Hope lowered her gaze. "And my dad wants to e-transfer me this month's rent money," she admitted, feeling the familiar heat of shame work its way across her face.

Ivy nodded quietly. Understanding, without judgment. After a long pause, she said, "Show me the shoes."

Hope gave her a sidelong glance, then pulled the bag from under the coffee table. She took out the box and lifted the lid. With a gasp, Ivy raised one stiletto as if it were the

Holy Grail. The shoe was delicate with a four-inch heel, slim ankle strap, and an ultra-feminine bow looped along the side, all in a classic sleek black. Ivy drew her fingertip reverently along the pretty bow.

For a long moment, they were silent, sipping wine and admiring the shoes.

"I've got rent covered this month," Ivy finally said.

"No. No way," Hope declared vehemently. "God, I don't want to be that person, Ivy. The pathetic rich girl. The lost cause who needs immediate bailing out when she tries to make it on her own."

Frustrated, Hope took another swig of wine and rose to pace the room. "I've been here a month, and I'm already failing!" She thrust her glass into the air for emphasis. "I don't want to live on your charity forever. I want to find a job on my own, pay my own way. To prove that I can. To show everyone that I have the brains and guts to make it in this world without having to hide behind my daddy every time the going gets tough. I have a business degree for chrissake. No matter how much I off-roaded to get there, I got there on my own, didn't I? And I graduated with honors, too. Honors!" This time when she thrust out the glass, wine sloshed up to the rim and almost over. To prevent spilling, she took another deep sip.

"At this point I think I just need to take anything. I'll serve coffee if I have to." Finishing her glass, she sank back into the couch. "I just can't go back and take that cushy office next to Joel's on the top floor of my dad's building knowing that the only reason I'm there is because my dad feels guilty and saved a spot for me."

Hope dropped her head in her hands. "I'm not one of them, and I'm tired of everyone pretending I am. I want to find out who I am and get ahead on my own."

And wasn't that exactly how she ended up here in Portland? Determined to forge her own path, to find out who the real Hope was—away from the facade of the Morgan family pedigree.

After being served the biggest lie of her life, all she'd wanted was the space and time to figure out who she really was.

Because she knew who she wasn't—a real Morgan. At least not a to-the-blood one she thought she'd been her whole life. Every time she reminded herself of that, which was often, a familiar hit of grief struck her gut.

Theoretically, she found out on the evening of her sweet sixteen birthday party. Her cousin, Beth, had been jealous that the much-coveted high school quarterback, Luke Bradley, was paying more attention to Hope than to her. Beth had screeched and flung cruel words at Hope in front of everyone at the party, doing her best to humiliate her, ending it all with the words Hope would never forget.

"I don't know why he likes you, anyway. You're not even a real Morgan."

Hope hadn't understood.

And Beth, seeing Hope's genuine confusion, had told her the cold truth with twisted delight. *"You're adopted, Hope. You're not one of us."* Then, with gleaming wide eyes that mocked innocence, Beth had said, *"Oh my God, you didn't know. That's so cute."*

It was like a scene right out of *Mean Girls*. Except it hadn't been a teen movie, it'd been Hope's life. And it hadn't been a mean girl from school, it'd been her cousin, her flesh and blood—or so she had thought up until that moment.

It had only taken one sentence, and life as Hope knew it had changed course.

She hadn't wanted to believe Beth, but there was something about the cruel words that had sunken in and taken root. By the time Joel had intervened, having heard the shouting, shock had immobilized Hope, stunning her speechless. Joel had calmed everyone down, as he was always able to do, and sent Beth home, but for Hope, the night had been ruined.

Later, while she'd been sobbing into her pillow in her bedroom, Joel had come in. He sat on the side of her bed and stroked a hand down her hair. "It's not true," he reassured her. "You're a Morgan through and through, Hope. Don't listen to her. She's always been jealous."

With Joel's reassuring presence and steadfast reasoning, Hope had finally accepted his logic. There was no way it could be true. If it were, her big brother would definitely know. Joel knew everything, and he wouldn't lie to her. He'd never lie to her.

And so, she'd convinced herself that her parents would never keep such a big secret from her either, and tried to brush it off. But looking back, she realized that the damage had already been done. Whether it was subconscious or not, she spent years thereafter internally tallying every difference and similarity between her and the rest of her family. From the opposing shade of their eye colors to the slight differences in their personalities. A seed of doubt had been planted, and she hadn't been able to stop it from growing.

Without realizing it, or even intending it, a void between her and her parents had started to grow. When she turned eighteen, she'd left home for college, hoping that the physical distance would close some of the emotional distance her doubts had created. Absence made the heart grow fonder, and all that.

Besides, once she started questioning her identity, the desire to figure out who she really was, independent of her family, had become all-consuming. For a blip in time, she wanted to be out from under the Morgan umbrella, even if it meant getting wet.

Well, she had gotten wet alright. No, she'd gotten drenched, nearly destroyed by the storm that she'd been caught up in. And four years later, before the end of her senior year, she'd been forced to return home under the weight of scandal and accusations she couldn't shake off, not even with the power of her family name behind her.

When she'd arrived home, stunned and traumatized, the comfort and familiarity of her family had been the balm she needed. She'd finished her degree at a local college and fallen into a comfortable rhythm where she could pretend her past hadn't happened. After everything that had transpired while she was away at college, it had been easy to let go of the niggling doubt over her identity and cocoon herself in the safe bubble of being a Morgan.

But soon enough, that nagging doubt was back. Maybe it was working at her father's company alongside Joel, who was competent and efficient and so damn natural at all things Morgan Construction that it made her feel more acutely out of place than ever before. Or maybe it was just time passing and the tally she'd subconsciously kept in her mind growing longer on the "not a Morgan" side.

Until, finally, last Christmas, she gifted her parents one of those popular do-it-yourself DNA kits. Was it underhanded? Maybe. Could she have confronted her parents honestly about what her cousin had said way back in high school? Probably. But she hadn't. She'd done this. And the truth had finally spilled out. Everything Beth had said, everything Hope had dreaded, her most secret nightmare, was true. She was adopted, and her parents had hidden it from her. Her entire life.

Walter and Audrey Morgan had made excuses for keeping the truth from her. She was a daughter to them, they'd said, as real as any biological child could be. They'd meant to tell her, but as time passed, so did the opportunities. Blah, blah, blah. She hadn't wanted to hear it then. She still wasn't sure she was ready.

She'd been made to look like a fool—at her sweet sixteen birthday party and who knew where else—by the two people she'd trusted most in the world. Her parents.

That night, a few weeks ago, when the truth had been confirmed, the numbness of denial she'd felt for years melted into a painful awakening, as if she'd looked down to find a gaping wound in her chest but was only just realizing she'd been taken down.

That was why she left home right after Christmas. She needed space and distance to sort it all out. To heal and regroup until she understood what it all meant.

The day she moved to Portland was so different from everything she'd ever known. She felt a palpable sense of relief. Like a heavy coat had been removed from her.

Here, she was free to work through her conflicting feelings at her own pace. She had distance from her parents' forlorn and guilty looks. From her brother's watchful eye and practical reminders that things could be so much worse (thank you Joel, but not a helpful assessment when the rug had been pulled out from under her).

Here, she didn't owe anyone anything. In Portland, sharing this apartment with Ivy, she could be her own person. Credit card debt and all.

The gentle rub of Ivy's hand on her back pulled Hope out of her broody trip down memory lane. She hated memory lane. Too many of her memories were either bad or built on a lie.

"First of all," came Ivy's voice out of the fog, "you've got more guts than anyone I know, and if anyone wants to challenge that, I invite them to try. Second, you've never hidden behind your dad. The one time I recall him bailing you out, it was because I called him. And technically, even then, it was Joel who came."

Hope lifted her head. "Ivy—" she started, not wanting her friend to dig up their painful shared past, but Ivy ignored her interruption.

"And third, you've been here for just over a month. This is one job in a zillion you've applied for. Be patient. Good things are coming."

Ivy rose to her feet and padded down the hall toward her bedroom. "Get your hair iron and a cute skirt. We're going down to the bar."

The mention of the bar brought its owner, Gabriel Walsh, to mind. The possibility of seeing him again made her heart flutter excitedly. She ignored it—or tried to. A night out wasn't the best way to cure her dwindling bank account. She hadn't gone down to the bar for that very reason. She couldn't afford to drink her sorrows away. Immobilized by her melancholy, she continued sitting on the couch with her new shoes in her hand. God, self-pity was a slippery slope.

But before she knew it, Ivy was standing in front of her, hands on hips, wearing a vintage Rolling Stones t-shirt tucked into a red leather mini skirt in a way that only Ivy could make look both cool and sexy. Her hair was tousled in a just-woke-up-after-a-good-fuck way, with her bangs falling over her eyes. She blew them aside.

"Wear the shoes, Hope." She stabbed her finger at the shoebox on Hope's lap. "If you make them worth it, then they're not an impulse buy anymore." She paused with a mischievous grin. "They're a necessity."

Ivy bent to don her black thigh-high leather boots. "Besides, everyone knows that shoes make the outfit. And if you look good, you feel good. And if you feel good, you slay. Therefore," she said as she straightened to stand a few inches taller in her boots. "All shoe purchases are necessary purchases."

Fifteen minutes later, Hope had squeezed herself into her black pleather skinny pants, a loose silky tank that flirted with her waistline, and her necessity shoes. Ivy had tamed Hope's hair and insisted she wear the cherry red lipstick she'd given her as a moving-in gift.

Studying herself in the mirror, she had to agree. Looking good did make her feel better.

When she got her purse from the closet, she saw Gabriel's jacket hanging there. She stared at it for a moment, remembering his scent when he crouched so close to her, the feel of his skin when he touched her face, his sexy half-smile when he found those damn condoms on the floor.

Not your type. Not your type. With a stifled groan, she grabbed his jacket and reached for the door.

"What's that?" Ivy asked, pointing at the jacket in Hope's hand. "Actually, *whose* is that?"

"Gabriel Walsh's," Hope said in what she hoped was a casual voice, but Ivy knew her too well.

"And why do you have *Gabriel's* jacket clutched to your chest like a security blanket?"

Hope raised her chin as she considered how she could explain with as few words as possible. "Because I got caught in the rain coming home from my crappy day, and I forgot my keys, and he kindly let me into the apartment."

"I see," Ivy said. "And he gave you his jacket because...?"

Hope narrowed her eyes, waiting for Ivy to finish her own sentence so she wouldn't have to.

"Because," Ivy drawled. "You were wet?" She grinned diabolically.

"And cold. Wet AND cold," Hope emphasized as she opened the door. "Can we go now, please?"

"Interesting."

"What?"

"You're blushing. You like this guy, who is our landlord and who also owns the bar we are about to go to."

"Stop it! I barely know him. I *don't* know him," she stressed.

Ivy looked at her with a full-on grin now.

"Can we go?" she asked in her haughtiest voice.

Ivy shrugged. "Hey, don't get mad at me. You're the one clutching the man's jacket like a life preserver." And with that, Ivy strutted along the hall to the back staircase, leading Hope down to their irritatingly alluring landlord's bar.

CHAPTER THREE

Gabe scanned Bowie's, the bar he'd owned for over seven years now, with bittersweet satisfaction. It had taken hard work and brutal hours to transform the place into a reliably popular hangout for Portland's local hipsters and millennials, who craved the modern-downtown-bar-meets-neighborhood-dive vibe, but he could now admit, as he observed the crowd, that he'd been successful. Given what it had cost him, he wouldn't accept less.

Sundays to Thursdays had a more relaxed vibe, with people milling in for after-work drinks, food and good music. Friday and Saturday heated up with crowds that wanted to let loose and drink off a long week at work.

Tonight was a typical Friday night. A local band played indie rock in the corner while people gyrated on the dance floor and others lounged at cozy tables.

Gabe stood behind the bar getting drinks for thirsty customers. Beside him his best bartender, Carter, mixed Moscow Mules for two women who leaned so far over the bar they were in danger of spilling their goodies out of their shirts. Carter, professional as always, kept his gaze locked on their faces, while he smiled and flirted his way through their order.

Huffing a laugh, Gabe went back to pulling a craft beer for the guy in front of him. Out of all his bartenders, Carter was the most popular. He was charming, witty, and had enough confidence to indulge in the attentions of women and men alike. He was basically a fresh-faced Casanova who knew how to work a room with his pretty-boy face alone.

The opposite of Gabe, whose pretty-boy days were long over, if they'd ever existed. He might only be thirty-two, but he sometimes felt ninety. A weathered old man who'd seen too much of life's rough side.

"Look alive, dude," said the guy sitting on the barstool in front of him. His best friend, Sean, took a long sip from the beer Gabe had handed him and rolled his eyes. "You know, it wouldn't kill you to smile. It'd probably get your tips looking a lot more like Carter's." Sean jerked his head in the direction of the mason jar that sat on the bar next to Carter's station, which was overflowing at only nine in the evening. Early hours in the bar life.

Gabe flipped him the bird then wiped down the counter and nodded at the next guy in line, who ordered an old fashioned. He grabbed the bourbon and set to work.

Sean chuckled. "You should come to my kickboxing class tomorrow. Let off some steam. 6 a.m. on the back mats."

Sean owned Thompson Kickboxing. Initially focused on the martial arts, his business had grown over the years to attract all kinds of fitness enthusiasts. Sean was a certified trainer and taught most of the martial arts classes, in addition to the personal training he did.

And he was right—Gabe did need to decompress. A certain blonde had gotten under his skin, and he couldn't seem to shake her. Gabe kept recalling his encounter with Hope in the hall this afternoon. Her wide dark eyes, red and wet from tears, were burned into his memory. She'd looked so vulnerable and sad that it had taken all his willpower not to go back to check on her. He wanted to know what had caused her misery, and more than that, he wanted to fix whatever it was. The intensity of his concern had thrown him.

Distantly, he heard Sean going on about his latest idea for an MMA class geared toward women, when his chest tightened and his neck muscles tensed. Like his thoughts alone had conjured her, he caught sight of Hope following Ivy into his bar.

She was dressed like a man's hottest wet dream in tight-ass pants that clung to her like a second skin and a loose top that exposed her belly button when she moved. Her shoes raised her willowy frame a few inches, and the way she walked in them made the blood rush to the wrong parts of his body. But the fact that she was covering some of her sexy ensemble with his jacket had his whole body tightening with desire. She looked good enough to eat. Like a candy bar he wanted to unwrap and devour. He wanted to taste her. Everywhere. Preferably right here on his bar top. The feeling was unfamiliar and primitive, but God help him, he couldn't shake it.

He probably needed to get laid. It had been a while. A long fucking while.

"Huh." Sean's single judgment-laden word yanked Gabe out of his sex-hazed trance.

"What?" he demanded, a little too defensively, his gaze snapping back to find his friend's eyes lit with amusement.

Sean glanced at Hope, then back at Gabe. "You got a thing for Ivy's roommate." Not a question.

"What?" Gabe snorted, trying to sound appalled. "Not my type, man. Not even close."

"Yeah?" said his soon-to-be-former best friend who was now grinning like a Cheshire cat. "Then why is she wearing your jacket?"

He knew it was primitive, illogically possessive, but seeing her in his jacket, knowing that other people were seeing her in it too, knowing she now smelled like him, filled him with satisfaction... and hunger.

And just like that, his traitorous brain imagined hoisting Hope up onto the bar wearing nothing but his jacket and those fuck-me shoes, spreading her thighs wide so he could make room for himself between them.

Christ, when had he turned into a sex-crazed macho-assed caveman?

Before he could come up with any kind of retort to his friend, Ivy and Hope had arrived at the bar. Ivy hopped up on the bar stool next to Sean, while Hope leaned against the bar top, eyeing him strangely.

"Sup, hotties," Ivy said by way of greeting. She eyed Gabe deliberately as she gestured to his jacket on Hope's body. "I've been informed that you met my new roomie this afternoon so I won't bother with introductions."

"I did." He replied and turned to Hope with a nod of acknowledgement. "Hope." She offered him a polite smile in return.

Ivy, meanwhile, grinned like she knew something he didn't before she proceeded to take Sean's beer out of his hands for a long swallow.

Sean let her. He always let her. He was such a sucker for Ivy it almost made Gabe feel sorry for him. It was so obvious to everyone except Sean. And maybe Ivy herself.

Gabe could only shake his head. Those two had the

oddest chemistry. To those who didn't know her, Ivy often appeared sullen and standoffish. Most men gave her a wide berth, respecting her don't-fuck-with-me-I'm-the-original-ice-queen vibe. But when Sean was around, two things happened. One, Ivy lost some of her edge and relaxed, just marginally. And second, Sean, who was typically easy going and laid-back, suddenly got into protective alpha mode.

Ivy stayed close to Sean, and he kept her close. Both seemed oblivious to this inevitable gravitational pull. Gabe was used to it now, but still never understood why his friend hadn't made an actual move.

"What can I get you, ladies?" Gabe asked.

Ivy ordered a beer of her own, while Hope opted for a vodka soda.

"Make hers a double," Ivy said, jerking a thumb in Hope's direction. "Our girl's had a rough day."

Dumping a lime and two healthy shots of his best vodka into a glass and filling the rest with soda water, he pushed the glass along the bar toward her. Hope took the glass and sipped immediately.

While she drank, Gabe studied her. She'd fixed her drowned-rat look, but she still appeared tired. Downright weary. Her elegant features seemed a little pinched, and the shadows under her eyes betrayed her stress and worry. Whatever was wrong had been wrong for a long time, and Gabe had an unfamiliar urge to draw her in, hold her close and promise her no matter what she'd be okay. He'd make sure of it.

He gave himself a mental slap. A girl like Hope Morgan didn't have problems, not real ones, anyway. And if by some slim chance she did, she sure as hell wasn't going to turn to a guy like him for help. What had gotten into him?

The answer hit like another slap. Their encounter in the

hall. Their first encounter, and it had only lasted minutes, but it had felt... real. In those few minutes, Gabe had an onslaught of feelings he hadn't experienced in years. She'd provoked him, challenged him, and captivated him all in one. She'd left him rattled all day. Then she'd walked through the door of his bar, wearing his jacket, and just the sight of her had settled him.

It was insane. And unnerving.

Preparing Ivy's drink, he tilted his head until he caught Hope's gaze. "Your afternoon didn't get any better after you got back into your apartment?"

Hope dipped her head, and a pretty blush crept into her cheeks as she tugged his jacket tighter around her, like she was trying to wrap herself in it. Hot damn, she was enthralling as hell.

"It was fine," she murmured. "I'm fine."

Ivy snorted. "Say it one more time and we might believe you."

Hope rolled her eyes. "Everyone has bad days. Today was mine. But I'm fine."

Gabe didn't believe her. They all stared at her, waiting for her to elaborate.

Then Sean grinned his million-watt smile that had the power to melt the panties off any girl and slung his arm around Hope's shoulders, drawing her onto the bar stool next to his. "Right. We're all human, all on the same ocean of life," he said philosophically, sounding like an inspirational Hallmark card. "Some days, life sucks. Then you wake up the next day, put yourself together, and get on with it." He tugged her a bit more, until she leaned against him. "But if you can't for any reason, remember you got friends who have your back. You don't have to do life alone. Right?"

Sean knew a little something about bad days. And he

was right. Sometimes you needed to be reminded that you didn't have to tackle life alone.

When the shit hit his own fan six years ago, there was no way he could have gotten his act together without Sean or his sister and father. Hell, there'd been a stretch when he wouldn't have remembered to feed himself if it hadn't been for the intervention of family and friends.

"Right," Hope said, snuggling in for one of Sean's trademark one-armed hugs, but not looking altogether convinced. "I appreciate the sentiment, and that you count me as a friend considering we've only hung out a few times at your gym, and both times you were kicking my ass in class, which didn't feel particularly friendly." She matched Sean's smile with one of her own.

"Any friend of Ivy's is a friend of mine," he countered with a charming wink.

Hope chuckled, then drew herself up straight on her stool.

"It's all going to work out. I know it," she said, her tone confident.

The way she said it, Gabe knew she was the glass half full kind of person. Optimism. Personally, he was allergic to it. Couldn't afford it in his life. But a woman like Hope was made of it. For her, life had probably always worked out— one way or another. Coming from a rich-ass family had to help in that regard.

Finding for the second time that day that he just couldn't let it go with her, and more than a little curious to know what kind of problems a beauty queen from the right side of the tracks could possibly have, he heard himself asking, "So what exactly made your day so bad?"

She gave him her best *as if you don't know* look.

"Other than the getting-caught-in-a-rain-storm and locking-yourself-out-of-the-apartment bits?"

"You locked yourself out during the rain?" Sean asked with a wince of sympathy.

"Yep." Ivy on the other hand was wearing a gleeful smirk. "And none other than our very own Gabriel Walsh came to the rescue. A right gentleman he was. Gave up his coat so that our poor Hope wouldn't freeze to death in the heated hallway of our building."

Gabe didn't miss the sarcasm.

"That's why she's wearing your jacket," Sean said, slapping a hand on the bar top for emphasis. "I knew there was a story."

Gabe ignored his friends and kept his gaze steady on Hope. She avoided eye contact with everyone, clearly wanting a subject change. There was definitely way more to her story, and it didn't take a rocket scientist to see that. He'd bide his time, wait her out. He'd find out what he wanted to know, eventually. Though why he wanted to know anything about her, he didn't have a damn clue.

"No story really," he told his friends nonchalantly, turning to pour pretzels into a couple of bowls, hoping that if their mouths were full, Ivy and Sean might shut the fuck up.

When he turned back, Hope had slipped out of his jacket and draped it over the bar. He tried his best to ignore the sharp sting of disappointment that arrowed through him.

"I just wanted to say thank you again, Gabriel." Her somewhat sheepish tone surprised Gabe.

He didn't often experience women being timid around him. The women in his life never treated him with anything less than confident bossiness. Then again, the women in his life consisted of his sister, his daughter, and Ivy. He hadn't expected a show of humility from someone like Hope, and he wasn't sure what to do with it.

"Gabe," he said. When she looked at him blankly, he clarified, "Everyone but my father calls me Gabe." He added a shrug to make it casual. He didn't need things feeling more personal with her than they already did.

"Gabe," she said slowly, and damn if he didn't feel the sound of his name on her lips right in his cock. "I'm grateful for your help today," she continued quietly. "You saved me several uncomfortable hours loitering outside my apartment." She gave him a half-smile that had his heart doing a slow flop in his chest. Christ, this woman.

Struggling not to overanalyze his reaction to her, Gabe busied himself pouring a second bowl of pretzels. "No problem," he mumbled and shoved the bowl toward her.

Jesus, what was he, an inept teenager having his first real conversation with a girl? Nah, he mused, just a widowed single father who hadn't experienced anything beyond a casual interest in a woman in six years. Fact was, Hope was stirring something in him. Something that hadn't stirred in a long time, and it was throwing him off balance.

Before he could pull his head out of his ass long enough to find something more intelligent to say, a loud crash hit the floor beside him, followed by a string of profanities. One of the women who had been chatting Carter up had boosted herself onto the bar, but she must have given herself too much lift because she had sailed right over and crashed into Carter on the other side. Now she lay sprawled, none too elegantly, on top of his best bartender, along with shards of broken glass and spilled drinks.

Gabe carefully lifted her up to her feet. Holding her steady, he gave her a once over, assessing if she was injured.

She seemed fine until she giggled flirtatiously and ran her hand down Gabe's chest. Her unsolicited familiarity was totally *not* fine. He released her immediately.

"Ooops!" She giggled, then hiccupped loudly. Her eyes went wide as she covered her mouth with her hand, flashing her fire-engine red, inch-long nails. She burst into another fit of giggles, looking totally wasted and probably thinking this was the funniest thing ever.

"Oh, my gawd, Amy!" shrieked her friend from the opposite side of the bar. "I told you showing the bartender your thigh tattoo would be a bad idea."

Christ Almighty. Sometimes Gabe wondered why he got into this business. Shaking his head, he turned his attention to Carter, who was sitting on the floor holding a bar towel to his forearm. It was smeared with blood.

Gabe gently peeled the towel from Carter's arm.

A two-inch gash ran along the inside of his forearm, looking deep and nasty.

His voice betrayed his alarm when he exclaimed, "Holy shit, did she stab you?"

Carter looked pale and clammy, but he still managed to say, "Got cut on some glass."

His blood was pouring out steadily. "Okay, hold still. Let me get some help."

Sean had already come behind the bar, and together they helped Carter up and took him into the back with Ivy and Hope following them. On their way Gabe signaled Nala to take over the bar.

"I can't leave Nala alone long," Gabe said to Sean. "She's a hell of a waitress, but she's only tended bar a couple times."

After they'd settled Carter into a chair, Gabe fished out his first aid kit.

"He's going to need more than a first aid kit." Ivy said as she inspected the bar towel that Carter still pressed to his arm. It was soaking through. "Let me take him to urgent care."

"I'll go with them," Sean added, his tone serious.

Gabe regarded them both. Then Carter, who was starting to turn gray and ashen. Gabe nodded. "Take him in. Keep me up to date." He gave Ivy a hard glare. "I mean it."

Moments later, Ivy and Sean, with Carter between them, went out the rear door of the bar. Gabe stood in the kitchen, Hope at his side. He scrubbed a hand down his face, wishing it could erase the last twenty minutes. Hell, maybe the last hour. Hope put a hand on his arm, giving it a gentle squeeze, and damn if that sense of calm didn't come over him again.

"He's going to be okay," she said reassuringly.

Gabe locked onto her eyes. Those sweet, optimistic eyes that made him want nothing more than to lose himself in them, in her, and never be found. He took a deep breath and closed his eyes for a moment.

"I need to relieve Nala. She can't bartend to save her life."

Hope's eyes brightened. "I can!" she said, sounding very excited.

CHAPTER FOUR

"**E**xcuse me?"

"I can bartend!" Hope ignored the look of amused disbelief on Gabe's face. "I'm a great bartender. I tended all through college." Hope paused, remembering that it wasn't quite *all* through college. Her thoughts darkened at the memory, but she pushed it back. She was good at pushing the bad stuff as far back as it would go. "Almost all through college. Anyway, the point is I was good at it." Meeting Gabe's increasingly speculative gaze with a determined pride, she added, "*Very* good at it. Gabe, let me help you. I promise you won't be disappointed."

She pressed her hands together prayer style, and offered Gabe a smile, which she hoped was both charming and convincing without coming across as desperate. She needed him to give her this chance. If she could prove to be an asset behind the bar, he might give her a job until she got herself on her feet.

"You bartended through college," he repeated, sounding like he wasn't buying it for one minute.

Hope nodded emphatically. "To help pay my tuition."

She crossed her arms indignantly at his raised eyebrows. "Not only was I good, but I could make Coyote Ugly look like amateur hour."

He snorted. "Is that so?"

"Yes, it's so. Let me prove it to you. Half an hour," she pleaded. "And if you don't want me after that, I promise I'll go."

Gabe stood there, arms crossed over his broad chest, assessing her with amused eyes. She felt like he was looking right into her, trying to gauge her level of authenticity. She'd seen that look plenty of times over the years. People knew her father and thought that placed her firmly in the *spoiled rich kid* category. She knew that Gabe probably thought she was a privileged wealthy girl who never had to lift a finger in her life, and she was itching to prove him wrong.

If she could do this for him tonight, she could kill two birds with one stone. Get a job *and* wipe the judgmental expression from his face.

Suddenly, proving him wrong meant more than anything. More than possibly landing a job, more than earning her share of this month's rent, more than never having to mooch off her parents for another day in her life.

She was here to prove something to herself and her family. She came to Portland to start building her own identity and find her own way. And maybe, while she was at it, she could show everyone that she was more than just her family name. That she could exist without it.

Her spark for independence had been struck at her sixteenth birthday, and by the time she was accepted into the University of Southern California she had been set on paying her own way with the partial scholarships she'd secured and money from various part-time jobs for the rest.

Her parents hadn't fully understood it, but she had been adamant.

That's how she ended up bartending for her three years at college. And she'd loved it. Loved making her own way and depending on herself.

Circumstances beyond her control had forced her to return home and give up the independence she'd gained, but if anything good had come out of that experience followed by the genetic-test kit she'd given her parents, it was that it had led her here. To a fresh start, where she could be anything and anyone she wanted.

And now that she was here, she refused to lose her chance again. To lose *herself* again. She had only gotten a taste of who she really was and who she could be. If she could only convince the broody man in front of her that she was worth this one small chance, then maybe the dream of getting back on track to building a life for herself wasn't that far off after all.

Hands still pressed together, Hope hadn't realized she was holding her breath until Gabe blew out his in a long stream of air, turned on his heel, and walked away from her, disappearing behind a door she assumed was his office. Probably to call in a more appropriate replacement for Carter.

Hope released a disappointed sigh and closed her eyes as she rode yet another wave of discouragement over yet another cool dismissal. She considered herself a positive person, but it was getting harder and harder when at every turn she came up against a wall of rejection. Was she really only worth something if she used her family connections? What would she be if she didn't have her family name behind her? Oddly, having her adoption out in the open had made her think about this acutely. Who was she, if she wasn't a Morgan?

A fraud. A nobody. The words whispered like the haunting echo of her worst fears.

The sting of tears behind her eyes snapped her out of her pity party. No way in hell was she going to cry twice in one day. Nor was she going to admit defeat. Not yet.

Gabe Walsh had no clue who she truly was. No idea what she was made of, or how hard she was willing to work to prove herself, and she wasn't going to let him make up his mind about her based on misguided assumptions and judgements.

With a new determination, she strode to the closed door and lifted a hand to the knob, ready to walk right in and demand he give her a chance. Before she could turn the handle, the door flung open, and she stumbled across the threshold and into a brick wall inside.

Wait—not a brick wall, but Gabe's very large and very hard chest. He caught her by one elbow and stepped forward, guiding her backward until he could close the door to his office tightly behind him.

When he didn't immediately move to release her, Hope's hands had no choice but to brace against his chest. For balance, she told herself. Taking in his gloriously chiseled, perfectly built strength, she tentatively ran her fingertips over his t-shirt, spreading her fingers across the planes of muscle. Muscles that she would have sworn quivered, then tensed under her touch.

He continued to keep her close, so she gave into the sheer pleasure of being this close to his powerful body, pressing her right hand against his hard left pec, feeling the strong beat of his heart beneath her palm.

Between them, heat sizzled, scorching her like a bolt of

electricity that made her shudder. Did he feel it too? Because she was most definitely feeling parts of her that she hadn't felt in a long time come to life and sing hallelujah.

Somewhere in the distant recesses of her brain, her logical side tried to call a time out. She needed to pull away. This guy probably thought she was not only a daddy's girl but a ditz. Nothing more than a blonde airhead. She should be running away from him, not feeling him up like some sex-starved hussy.

The other side of her brain, the side that reminded her that she hadn't had a man touch her in years, told her to lean up and inhale the skin on his neck to see if he smelled as delicious as his coat had earlier.

Totally helpless and completely riveted by their closeness, she did just that. Leaned right in and ran her cheek up along the length of his neck, inhaling as she went. Sure enough, he smelled like sex personified. She wanted to lick him there. Well, she wanted to lick him everywhere really, but she could start with there.

Between them, Gabe reached up, covering her hand with one of his own, and for one thrilling second she thought he was going to lift her fingers to his lips. Instead, he gently removed her hand from his chest and dropped her arm to her side, effectively tearing her out of the sexual haze and returning her to her reality of humiliation and rejection.

Stunned, and a little dizzy by all the sensations that had suddenly collided inside her, she blinked up at him.

He stared down at her, his green eyes lit with laughter. His sexy mouth quirked into what she was beginning to realize was his signature smile.

Did he think this was funny? Was he laughing at her? Heat flooded her cheeks and embarrassment rose hot and burning up her neck. She opened her mouth to tell him where he could stick his amusement, but he waved something black in front of her, directing her attention away from his ridiculously sexy grin and her rising temper.

"If you're going to go all Coyote Ugly on me, you're going to do it in my t-shirt." He held up the black fabric, letting it fall open.

It was identical to the one he wore. The one all his staff wore. A basic black tee with the Bowie's logo over the breast.

Gabe waved it at her again, one eyebrow up. "You in?"

Hope could see that part of him was giving her the option to bow out gracefully. But Hope didn't bow out—not anymore—so she grabbed the t-shirt.

"I'm in."

CHAPTER FIVE

Gabe wasn't sure what he expected after he handed Hope the staff shirt, but he certainly hadn't expected what he was witnessing now.

Beside him at the bar, Hope was wielding bottles of Jack and vodka with utter confidence, total control, and unprecedented skill. She'd been at it for over an hour and hadn't needed to ask him how to mix a single drink. Hope mixed, poured, and served whatever order she received with easy efficiency.

He tried to focus on his own end of the bar, but it was hard not to notice her at the other end smiling and chatting up customers as if she'd been born to do this. Awareness coursed through his body from head to toe, annoying him. The last thing he needed right now was his body betraying him by lusting after Hope Morgan.

She laughed at something one of the male customers said, and he looked over to catch her throwing back her head, her long blonde hair, which she'd tied up into a high bouncy ponytail, falling down the length of her back. She was still wearing those bloody heels, and they were still distracting him out of his mind, but more now that he was acutely aware of how fucking uncomfortable they must be after standing in them for hours. He watched her pivot, bend, and turn as she worked in her space, seemingly undeterred by the fact that she was balanced on four-inch chopsticks.

Hope's throaty laugh floated over to him again. A scowl etched his face as he watched her full red lips spread into a toothy smile, her eyes brighten with laughter. And as she handed over the beer she'd poured, the sonofabitch had the nerve to slip a small card into her fingers.

Gabe knew the move like the back of his hand. Happened all the damn time. He was willing to bet his own goddamn bar that little piece of paper had that guy's number on it. He was about to drop the whiskey bottle he was holding and march over to yank that fucking piece of paper out of her hands and shove it up the guy's ass when he saw Hope wink at the jerk, then lean in slightly as she tossed the paper in the waste basket below the bar without the guy being the wiser.

Ok, not her first rodeo, he conceded, and hell if he didn't admire her for holding her own without causing a scene like he'd been about to do.

Growling under his breath, Gabe went back to mixing a whiskey sour. This woman confused the hell out of him, tied him into knots, and turned him on all at the same time. Worse, he had no idea what to do about it.

In the last hour alone, she had shattered nearly every assumption he'd made about her. If he was being honest, she'd been blowing his assumptions out of the water since their encounter this morning. And when they'd collided in front of his office and he'd touched her... Christ, he had to stop thinking about it, or he'd humiliate himself by getting a hard-on right here behind the bar.

He'd been reliving the moment when she leaned into him and ran her face along his neck, all but inhaling him, since it happened. He'd nearly lost it. Same as he was nearly losing it now. His reaction didn't just shock him, it was scaring the bloody daylights out of him. Never in his entire life had he experienced such an instant and blinding attraction to a woman. Then again, Hope was proving to be unlike any woman he'd ever met before.

In fact, Hope Morgan was proving to be none of the things he assumed her to be, and for reasons that both irritated and intrigued him, this pulled him into her stratosphere even more. He was feeling things he hadn't in years, and it was unsettling.

So, Gabe responded to these unsettling feelings like he always did—with a bad attitude and a scowl.

If his clientele noticed, they didn't say anything, and the evening went on as most Friday nights did—in a blur of activity, loud music, and energy. He lost himself in the pulsing beat of it all and tried his damnedest not to think about Hope for the rest of the night.

They closed at 1 a.m., but by the time the last of his employees had left, it was nearly two.

Gabe came out of his office and through the kitchen to find Hope alone in his bar, wiping down tables. Propping his shoulder against the doorway separating the bar from the back rooms, he crossed his arms and watched as she reached across a table to wipe up a spill. He tried and failed to take his eyes off the way her skintight pants stretched across her amazing ass. Her feet going up to her toes as she leaned forward to give him a million-dollar view of her milelong legs. He felt like a jerk—worse than a jerk, he thought in disgust. He felt like a horny, sex-starved weirdo who hadn't had a woman in way too long.

Which maybe wasn't so far from the truth.

Sean was right: he needed to get a life. Maybe it was time he put himself out there for more than a one-night stand, before he was forced to live off of fantasy alone.

She must have sensed his presence because she straightened and caught his gaze. Her smile slipped a bit when she caught his look. By the scowl he could feel etched on his face, she likely thought he was staring at her in disgust. Fine, that was probably better than having her know what he had really been thinking.

Shoving off the wall, he grabbed a towel and moved behind the bar to give everything a final wipe. Together, they worked in silence. It felt easy, effortless. She didn't need small talk or constant instructions. She simply moved in tandem with him doing what needed to be done, all the while swaying her hips in gentle rhythm with the music that now played low over the speakers.

Finally, at 2:30, he called it.

"You weren't lying," he said, walking up to her and tugging the towel she'd been using out of her hands, signaling that they were done for the night. "You know your way around a bar."

A smug smile lifted her lips, and it was all he could do not to drag her into him and wipe it right off her mouth with his own.

"I'm not in the habit of lying," she countered, her deep-brown eyes sparkling with humor. But no sooner had he absorbed the way her face lit up than something shifted in her eyes, her gaze dipping to the floor, her pretty smile faltering.

Okay. His earlier curiosity niggled back to life. Something was definitely up there. The urge to probe was strong. Fuck, why did she have to be so intriguing?

"So, you worked at a bar in college?" he asked, caving under the weight of wanting to learn more about her. If he could admit he was wrong about her, then he at least wanted to know her truth.

She looked back into his eyes. Whatever moment she'd had with the floor was over. "Yep. Three years at a bar near the campus. Helped subsidize my partial scholarships."

Gabe held her gaze, tilting his head, assessing. He deliberated his next question carefully, then, deciding he wanted it out there between them, he said, "Your dad is Walter Morgan, isn't he?"

As he predicted, Hope's back went up. Literally. She straightened to her full height, which was above average for a woman, and because he was no shrimp himself, she came right up to his chin.

Her eyes glittered, battle ready. "Yeah, so?" She crossed her arms in a defensive gesture and took a big step backward, closing herself off from him.

Not so fast, sweetheart. He took a deliberate, but slow step toward her. She held her ground, which he took as a good sign. She could turn her back on him, tell him to go to hell, mind his own business, fuck off, any number of things really, but she didn't. She stood rooted in place, eyes blazing.

It impressed him. *She* impressed him.

"So, it seems strange to me that a man like Walter Morgan, construction and business genius, would let his precious daughter sling liquor bottles so she could pay tuition."

After a brief pause, Hope bit out, "If you must know, he wasn't on board with the idea. In fact, both my parents hated it. But..." She shrugged like it was an insignificant part of her past, which Gabe had the distinct feeling it was not. "I was determined to make it on my own." She raised her chin and said with utter resolve, "I still am."

Then her pretty lips spread into that wide smile, the fire in her eyes softening into a sweet, pleading, melted-chocolate look. The overall effect hit him square in the chest with a blast of heat that went directly south.

"Which is why I need a job," she said. "Bartending. For you."

Gabe stared at her, waiting for the punch line. When her smile stayed plastered in place, he realized she wasn't joking. He let out a hard laugh and turned his back on her—and the smile he was damn sure many a man couldn't and didn't resist. "No," he said firmly, as he walked around the bar to start his lock-up routine.

Her hand came around his forearm with an impressive grip, and he stopped what he was doing to look at where she touched him. Heat sizzled from his arm to his groin. Christ, this woman might be the end of him.

"I'm sorry," she said, removing her hand quickly, completely unaware of how his body had responded to her touch. "I shouldn't have grabbed you like that." She sighed heavily. "Look, I know you think that I am the spoiled princess daughter of a wealthy man who is going through her wild disobedient phase."

Now it was Gabe's turn to cross his arms, not liking at all that his judgments of her had been so easy to read, but not ready to admit she wasn't totally off base either.

Hope rolled her eyes. "I've seen the way you look at me—like you can't be bothered to give my charmed little rich life the time of day."

Then you're not looking hard enough, princess. Because

more and more he was looking at her like he'd be happy to give her a lot of his time of day—and night.

"I get it. You think we're worlds apart. But we're not, Gabe. I'm actually a lot like you."

He snorted at that. *Not likely*. She was sweet, vulnerable, kind to the bone, and optimistic. He was her opposite on all four counts. And more.

"I am," she insisted. "I want a chance to prove to my family, but mostly to myself, that I can take care of myself. That I can build a life for myself without needing to depend on anyone." Her warm brown eyes melted into his. "Can you understand that?"

Damn it. Yes. He could. More than she realized.

His mother died when he was eleven. After that, his sister, Lori, who was five years older, swept in and took over the role of caretaker. His dad worked his ass off to keep a roof over their heads and food on the table. Together, his sister and father made sure they had enough of their shit together so that Gabe's teen years could unfold as normally as possible. He had thanked them by being the biggest pain in the ass he could be. He remembered, vividly, the fights with Lori over his general disobedience. The long looks of disappointment and weariness he'd get from his dad while they'd have a fight, which usually ended with Gabe slamming the door and taking off for hours without anyone knowing where he was.

His sister and father just wanted to make the best life they could for him in the absence of a nurturing maternal figure. But what they couldn't see was how all their hovering and rules and regimens only made him miss his mom more. And in turn made him act out more. Looking back at how he'd behaved, he didn't know why his father and sister still talked to him.

By the time he turned eighteen, he was so sick of his sister's mother-hen routine, and his dad's quiet but watchful eye, that all he wanted to do was break free and have a life of his own. He moved out, took odd jobs for a while, got up to a lot of no good, then eventually took a few business classes at the local college and got it into his head to buy the bar and make a living out of its success.

What he hadn't realized was how much work would go into making it a success, or how much it would ultimately cost him. Never in a million years would he have guessed he'd be in the situation he was in right now, but one thing he did know was that he could relate to wanting to make a life for himself, to hell with what anyone who loved him had to say about it.

It hadn't ended well for him on most counts, but it could for Hope. Still, the truth was that he didn't need another bartender. "Carter will be back soon, Hope. He's not out for good."

The look in her eyes told him that she knew that, but still she persisted. "Look, if I let them, my parents would happily live my life for me. They would make all of my decisions for me and finance them without even thinking twice about it." She took a long breath. "I know this, because for a long time that is exactly what I let them do, without any real thought to who I truly was or what I wanted."

She fell onto the nearest chair, as if the weight of this conversation was taking too much energy. Almost subconsciously, she reached down and rubbed her feet, which were still trapped in those shoes that could have doubled as a weapon as far as Gabe was concerned. They must be killing her.

She looked up at him, a fresh sadness in her eyes that tugged at a long untouched part inside him.

"My parents are good people," she said quietly. "My parents, my brother, they're fixers, caregivers. It's deeply ingrained into the very footprint of their beings to provide, save, fix, care for. I know it all comes from a place of love."

The way she said it, Gabe wasn't sure if she was trying to convince him or herself.

"But I decided a while back that I didn't want them making the decisions they think are best for me anymore. I took back control of my life. And part of that meant breaking away from my father's empire, being on my own and not feeling like I have to live my life a certain way because he paved the road and paid for it."

He wanted to know what happened "a while back" to make her think this way, but he kept his mouth shut, mostly because his interest in her was starting to feel far more personal than anything he was ready to take on at the moment, and also because she looked so raw and exposed, he didn't want to make her feel any more vulnerable than she already was.

"Do you know what I mean?" she asked after his prolonged silence, her eyes shining with emotion, her voice a soft whisper in the empty bar.

He nodded, because he really did know. He watched her release a shuddering breath, an unmistakable relief filling her features.

Aw hell, he didn't stand a chance against her shimmering doe eyes, and he was done kidding himself for this evening at least.

Dragging out a chair, he took a seat in front of her. Moving on instinct, he lined his knees up so they touched hers. The now familiar electricity hummed between them. Without breaking eye contact, he lifted one of her ankles to cradle her foot in his hands. At the skin-to-skin contact, the electricity turned into an almost palpable pulse. This desire, this feeling he had every second he spent around her, it made no fucking sense.

He'd only met her today, but this inescapable chemistry that insisted on heating between them was something he'd have to work out. The trouble was that he wasn't sure he had the emotional capacity to do it tonight. Or ever.

He watched Hope's chest rise and fall in quick little pants as he undid the thin strap around her ankle and took the shoe off her foot, dropping it on the floor beside him. Purposefully, he pressed his thumb into the arch and slowly rubbed up, then down. A low groan rumbled out of Hope's throat as her head fell back and her eyes closed. He repeated the motion with her other foot.

They stayed like this for a while, a quiet intimacy building between them in the empty, silent bar. As he rubbed her feet, he let his own body relax. His tension drained in tandem with hers.

"Hope," he said after some time, and watched as she unhurriedly opened her eyes, gradually coming out of her blissed-out trance.

The swamping emotion that had filled her eyes earlier was replaced by a darker look that he recognized because he was pretty sure it matched his own. It was a look that reflected need. Desire. Lust.

"Better?" he asked, his voice husky in his own ears.

With a hooded look, Hope nodded slowly.

She lifted her feet off his lap, then shifted closer so that now their legs were interlocked. His knee. Her knee. His knee. Her knee. Her lips parted enough for her tongue to dart out and moisten her lips.

God, she was going to kill him.

He opened his mouth to say something, anything to

interrupt this collision course they were on, but no sound came out. Instead, he felt himself lean forward, until their lips were a whisper apart. Hope's scent intoxicated him, wrapping around them like a mist that set them apart in another world. Her thigh twitched as it edged closer to his. Her lashes fluttered as her lids lowered. That fucking pretty mouth parted ever so slightly. Invitingly.

And not even a dead man could have resisted her.

Fuck. He was going to kiss her. He *had* to. If he had the choice between his next breath of air and a kiss from Hope Morgan, he was going to take the kiss, hands down.

This is insane, was his last coherent thought before he closed in on the space between them. Nothing, not even an earthquake would have stopped him.

Nothing, that is, except one voice saying one word.

"Daddy?"

Fuuuuuuck.

Hope shoved off of him so quickly she nearly knocked him out of his chair. She leapt to her feet in confused shock, wild eyes searching for the source of the interruption.

Shit. He hadn't seen this coming.

Grappling to switch gears from lover to father, Gabe scrubbed both hands down his face before rising on surprisingly unsteady feet. Attempting to inconspicuously readjust himself in his pants was another hurdle.

Christ. Perfect timing.

"Hey, sweetie," he said, moving toward his daughter. Ruby, who looked sleepy and adorably tousled, melting his heart on sight.

She'd been asleep on the couch in his office because his babysitter had bailed for the third time this week, and he couldn't get anyone short notice to watch her while he was working that night. He'd disappeared every five minutes over the evening to go check on her, and last he'd checked, she'd been tucked in with her pillow and blanket sound asleep and had been since eight o'clock.

He kicked himself for not even considering that Ruby might wake up. But why would he have? His girl slept like a log once she was out. Not even the thumping sounds from the bar caused her to twitch. She slept so soundly he could normally carry her up to the apartment and tuck her into bed without so much as a flutter of an eyelash. So having her interrupt him now felt like the universe playing a cruel joke.

Or trying to tell him something.

Whatever the case, his baby girl was slowly walking into the empty space now, holding her favorite stuffed bunny in one hand and rubbing her eyes sleepily with the other. To his relief, it did not appear as though she had caught him almost kiss a beautiful woman in his bar.

Meeting her in the middle, he scooped her up and held her against his chest, her legs dangling from his waist. She was getting so big. He nuzzled her soft pillowy cheek with his, and she responded by burrowing her face into his neck. He cuddled her for a moment, soaking up the sheer unbelievability that this beautiful little human belonged to him. He absolutely did not deserve her.

"I had a bad dream." Ruby spoke in a muffled murmur. "Can we go home now?"

"Of course, sweetie." Gabe said, rubbing her small back.

He turned to find Hope standing in the spot where a moment ago they'd almost had their tongues down each other's throats. She seemed completely bewildered, and it dawned on him she must not have known he'd had a daughter.

Not totally unsurprising since he kept Ruby the most

precious and tightly guarded part of his life. He wasn't really open to sharing Ruby with many people. But standing there in the middle of his bar with his daughter in his arms, the only thing that settled over his heart watching Hope watch them was an unfamiliar sense of peace.

Not that Hope looked peaceful. She looked surprised and shocked as hell. Reminding Gabe how little she really knew about him. And how much he really did want her to know him... and Ruby.

Which was exactly why tangling with her in any way was a bad idea.

CHAPTER SIX

He had a child. A daughter.

How had she missed this fact? She hadn't seen any evidence of a child. Had she been so absorbed in her own tumultuous world that she'd never noticed an adorable little girl living across the hall? Probably. Crap. Someone should have told her! Why had Ivy never mentioned there was *a child*?

A horrifying thought suddenly entered Hope's mind. If there was a daughter, could there be a wife? A girlfriend? A partner, lurking in the shadows?

Hope quickly surveyed the room, as if a wife might suddenly jump out from behind the bar, swinging a bottle of vodka at her head.

If that had happened, she wouldn't blame her. After all, she'd just spent the better half of the evening lusting after this man who was standing in front of her now, looking ridiculously hot as he cuddled his daughter close to him. Not to mention the fact that a minute ago she was about T-minus ten seconds from tearing every piece of clothing off his body.

In less than a day, Hope had allowed herself to feel something for Gabe that she hadn't in a very, very long time. Attraction. It didn't make sense. She couldn't explain it. But the second he wrapped his coat around her shoulders, and she'd inhaled his scent, she had begun a losing battle against this insane pull toward him.

Then, she spent the evening working beside him and those feelings amplified. As soon as he'd given her the okay to work the bar, he'd shown total faith in her. He didn't make a point of checking in on her every two minutes or second guess her ability as a bartender. Once he decided to give her a chance, he left her to it. He'd trusted her.

His faith in her had been a bigger turn on than his irresistible smell or watching him move as he worked his end of the bar, sexy forearms and biceps straining in all the right places as he maneuvered bottles, poured drinks, and lifted heavy trays of glasses.

By the end of the evening, she'd had half a dozen fantasies about him. One of which had been seconds away from playing out.

But now he was standing in front of her holding a child, possibly in a relationship with someone else. Guilt slammed into her chest like a cold, hard fist. Guilt and apprehension.

He must have picked up on her distress because he slowly came toward her and brought his free hand up to tuck a strand of hair behind her ear. The same way he had this afternoon in the hallway.

The small smile he gave her caused a fluttering sensation to erupt in her heart. And then she knew. No other woman lurked nearby. He wasn't that guy.

"You look exhausted, too." Gabe said to her. "Why don't we all call it a night?"

The little girl who'd tucked herself into her father's side

lifted her head and, with eyes the exact same shade of green as her father's, stared down at Hope.

"Who are you?" came a sleepy voice, and Hope couldn't help but smile into the sweet face as her heart melted a tiny bit more.

"My name is Hope. What's yours?"

"Ruby."

"Hi, Ruby. It's nice to meet you." Looking pointedly at Gabe, she added, "Your dad never mentioned you before."

Ruby rubbed her chin up and then down Gabe's stubbled jaw, making Hope wish she could do the same, and gave a shy smile. "Yeah, Daddy says I'm special. Too special to share with everyone at the bar when he's working."

Hope looked at Gabe. "Is that so?"

He gave her a little shrug, which she returned with her best *you have some explaining to do* look.

Shifting Ruby in his hold, he nodded to the door. "Let's get you two ladies upstairs and into bed."

Into bed? Her eyes flared wide at the thought of getting into *his* bed.

He winced, obviously realizing what he'd said and how it had sounded. "I mean Ruby." He tried again. "Let's get Ruby to bed and see Miss Hope to her door. Okay?"

Amused, Hope nodded and walked behind them to the back door that opened to the stairs that led up to the apartment level.

Instead of turning right to her own place, she turned left with Gabe and followed him to his front door. Without seeming bothered by the weight of a little human in his arms, he reached into his pocket and took out keys, shoving one into the lock. Pushing the door open, he turned and looked at Hope.

"We need to talk," he said, surprising her because she'd

been sure he was going to tell her to go home and mind her own business.

She nodded but didn't move. Sighing, he caught her hand in his and tugged her into his apartment.

"Give me a minute," was all he said before he let go and disappeared down the hallway.

Standing alone by the door, she took in his apartment at a glance. The small entry way opened into a spacious living room that had a kitchen off to the side. A similar layout to hers and Ivy's, which probably meant it also had two bedrooms on either side of the hallway where Gabe had gone.

She moved into the living room and took in the night view. It was a corner suite, like hers, but faced west, to the water. She walked to the window. At her own place, this corner was her dedicated painting space. Here, in Gabe's space, he'd constructed a workout area, complete with a weight bench and rack. Looking at the setup, she surmised a single father who ran a thriving bar wouldn't have much time to hit the gym, even if his best friend owned one. Glancing out the window into the darkness, she considered how far apart their two worlds were. The hard-working single father, and the construction heiress who had no clue who she was or what she wanted.

"In the daylight, there's an awesome view of the river." Gabe's deep, rough voice came from behind her, interrupting her thoughts.

She shifted to face him. Under the soft glow from the streetlights coming through the windows, she noted the shadows under his eyes, his mussed hair, like he'd recently run both hands through it, and the stubble darkening his jaw. Somehow, he looked a lot less tough and impenetrable, and a lot more... human.

Her heart did a slow roll in her chest, and she tried her best to ignore it.

"So, you have a daughter?" she said, cutting to the chase.

Nodding, Gabe crossed the living room to switch on a lamp next to the couch.

"Ruby." He jerked a head in the direction of the hallway. "She's out cold again in her room." He sank down into the couch, looking completely exhausted.

Hope sat down beside him. He looked at her but didn't say anything.

Ok, so it was going to be twenty questions then.

"How old is she?"

"Six."

"She's very cute."

He gave a single nod. Apparently, it was also going to be like pulling teeth.

"Why did you never mention her?"

"It never came up." Hope raised her brows to that, so he lifted one shoulder and added, "Also, I guess I thought you knew. You know, from Ivy or someone."

Fair enough. But he clearly didn't know Ivy very well, because if anyone could keep a secret, it was that girl.

"Why was Ruby sleeping in your office?" Hope asked.

Gabe inhaled deeply. "Her babysitter has been..." He paused, as if searching for the right word. "Unreliable, lately."

Hope nodded. "So, she sits in your office all night, alone?"

She clearly hit a nerve because Gabe's eyes got a defensive edge she'd never seen before. "I check on her, and she watches movies, and the staff pop in and bug her all the time. She's hardly alone, but I can't bring her into the bar. And it's only been a few times while I find someone who I trust who can watch her up here." He ran his hand through his hair again, shoving his already tousled hair from one side of his head to the other. Which only made Hope want to run her own fingers through the strands. To smooth them out, of course.

"I work six days a week. Sometimes seven. And most nights I don't get home until at least 2:30 a.m., so it's been hard finding someone who's willing to give up that much of their time to watch her. Especially on weekends. My sister helps out sometimes, but she lives on the other side of the river and has her own kids and family, so I hate to take advantage of her too much," he said, confirming there was no wife or ex around to help.

Gabe met her gaze and said in a defeated sounding tone, "I've been through four nannies in two and a half months."

Hope shrugged casually, the solution obvious to her. "I'll do it."

Gabe stared at her. She sat where she was, turned sideways, and waited him out, while he clearly tried to determine if he'd heard her correctly.

Or maybe he thought she hadn't heard him correctly because he repeated what he'd said before. "I don't get home until 2:30, Hope." Glancing at his phone, he added, "Tonight it's three."

Yes, it had been a long night. A busy night. She knew how busy a bar on a Friday night could be. She assumed Saturdays were just as busy, if not more so. But from her memory, the rest of the week wasn't usually too crazy.

She also knew Bowie's had weekend hours and weekday hours, so she knew that the late nights would only be two or three days a week tops.

Admittedly, she didn't know Ruby, but she knew she loved kids. She always had. She loved their adventurous spirits, their unflappable optimism, their limitless creativity. She loved how they taught her patience, resilience, and self-giving.

Since she was a little girl, playing with her dolls, she'd dreamed of the day she could replace them with real babies of her very own.

Even as a teen, she'd loved children, babysitting neighborhood kids and enjoying every minute. She'd never spent time with a child and left feeling unfulfilled. In fact, it had always been the opposite. There was a fulfillment in childcare that called to her heart.

For as long as she could remember, before her life fell down around her like a house of cards, she'd dreamed of being a mother. She had wanted to give to her own children what she had been given growing up. A life of love, security, and adventure. Her parents had made it look like the very best job in the world. And she wanted exactly that same job for herself one day. That, and to be an artist.

That had been the dream.

Reality looked more like working at Morgan Construction—her father's legacy. The finish line of her career accomplishments. It was why she'd studied business, why she'd applied only to business administration jobs, and why she only painted as a hobby and never tried to sell anything.

Because all roads led to Morgan Construction.

Joel was primed and on track to take over as CEO. He lived and breathed their father's company. In the last few years, almost obsessively, as if he had nothing beyond the company in his life. But for her, it had always felt like a forced fit. Like she was doing it because it was what she'd been raised to do. Like Prince William groomed for the throne. As if he had a choice to do anything else. As if King

Charles would simply smile and nod if his son chose to be a dentist instead.

That was the problem with a family business. It set you on a predetermined track, and while her parents had always been loving and supportive of her other interests, the expectation had always been clear.

Shifting in her seat, she reminded herself that things were different now. Finding out a few weeks ago that her years of suspicion were true, that her parents had hidden the truth of her adoption from her for her entire life, had put a kink in her sense of loyalty. So if she wanted to sign up for a job as a nanny, why the heck shouldn't she? It would certainly be more fun than the jobs she'd applied for so far.

Besides, beggars couldn't be choosers, and her half of the rent needed to be paid.

So, she met Gabe's gaze with what she hoped was a serious one of her own.

"Thursdays, Fridays, and Saturdays are probably your busiest nights. So those are the nights you will be the latest. Every other night, it won't be as late. Also, I don't mind late nights as evidenced to you this evening. And," she said, lifting a finger to silence him when she saw his mouth opening. "I live right across the hall, so I'm here, anyway."

"Hope—"

"Oh, come on, Gabe. You checked my references when I moved into your building, but I can give you more. Run a criminal record check on me if you want to." She turned fully, looking directly into his eyes. "Please, Gabe. I'm good with kids, I promise. I'll show you and Ruby. You'll both love me in no time."

The second the words came out, she wished them right back in. She sounded desperate, and worse, pathetic. Poor little, adopted, rich girl begging for a chance to be loved.

"That came out wrong. I meant…" What had she meant? God, it was way too late in her day to have a job interview. Her third of the day, if she was counting. Her second with this man, who had already told her once that he was not interested in hiring her.

"You know what? Never mind." Shaking her head, she stood and headed for the door. She was partway there when his warm strong fingers grabbed her wrist and stopped her.

"Hope, wait."

She turned to find Gabe, who looked rumpled and worn out. Her heart softened, despite itself.

"You keep taking me by surprise. I can't keep up."

She didn't say anything, finding that he often did most of his talking when she wasn't doing any herself. So she waited until he spoke again.

"It's not that I don't want your help. It's just that…"

In the silence, she stared at him, brow arched.

He shrugged. "When it comes to Ruby, I am protective. I don't make spur-of-the-moment decisions. I deliberate, and over think, and then deliberate some more." Gabe shoved his hands into his jean pockets, glanced down at the floor, then back at her, his eyes more open and honest than she'd seen them yet.

"I don't trust many people with her. She's my…" He paused. "Everything. If anything happened because I made one wrong decision…" Gabe's voice drifted off, and she could tell he was wrestling with emotions he clearly wasn't comfortable with.

She resisted the urge to ask him a million questions, about himself, Ruby, their story… her mother.

Pulling his hands out of his pockets, he took her hands in his again. Flipping both of them over, he stared at her palms like they might have all the answers. He rubbed his thumbs in circular motions on the base of her wrists, over the delicate veins there, in a way that made her entire body stir to life. Finally, he lifted his gaze to meet hers. "I don't know what to do with this." He paused, his green eyes holding hers. "It's been a strange day."

No kidding. But because she knew exactly how he felt, she tried to reassure him. "I only want to help you, Gabe." She added an eyeroll because they both knew she had an ulterior motive. "And, okay, I also really need a job. Badly."

This got a small smile out of him, and she relaxed a bit as the tense emotions in the air shifted. Which she was relieved about because she was nowhere near ready to deal with the level of emotion he brought up in her.

They stood like that another moment, fingers interlocked. Eventually, he stepped away, letting her hands fall to her sides.

"I drop Ruby off at school just after eight in the morning. Then I have some errands to run, but I can meet you in my office at eleven. We can go over Ruby's weekly schedule and what I would need from you in terms of hours. Pay, of course, and... we should go over both of our expectations, so we're on the same page."

Hope nodded, the memory of their almost-kiss coming to mind. Definitely wouldn't want to confuse their expectations.

"I'll see you tomorrow at eleven," she said. Then, because she'd been wanting to since they'd broken apart downstairs, she ran her palm along Gabe's jaw. "Get some sleep, okay?"

With that, she turned and walked out the door, across the hallway, and into her own apartment.

CHAPTER SEVEN

Hope woke to the smell of strong coffee that seemed to waft up in delicious smelling ribbons of steam right under her nose. She cracked an eye open and flinched when she realized there was indeed a cup of coffee being held close to her nose.

Groaning, she yanked the covers over her head, blocking out the steaming mug in Ivy's hands.

"Oh, come on!" Ivy said in an obnoxiously alert voice. "You didn't actually think that I'd go to work and not see you all day without getting the deets of your night working the bar with our hot, single landlord, did you?"

Hope responded with another grunt, but Ivy gave a persistent bounce on her bed.

"Just be grateful I didn't wake you up *before* I went on my morning run."

Ivy was her best friend. The sister she never had, and they'd been through a lot together. But that didn't mean that Hope had to be happy, or even obliging, when Ivy invaded her bedroom at some ungodly hour to discuss her personal life.

Even if she did come bearing heaven's nectar. No one brewed coffee like Ivy did.

"Come on," Ivy repeated. "It's 6:15. I have to be at work in forty-five minutes, and I haven't showered yet," Ivy said with another bounce on the mattress. "Spill."

Resigned, Hope threw the covers off her face and grabbed the cup.

Ivy watched her with a smirk as she gulped down the coffee. Over the rim of her cup, she contemplated her best friend in return. What the hell was she was going to tell Ivy without her seeing right through it? Deciding there was nothing she could say that Ivy wouldn't call bullshit on, she opted to buy some time and change the subject.

"How's Carter?"

Ivy pointed a finger in Hope's face. "Evading will get you nowhere. But he's good. Needed eight stitches and said he's not serving booze to vixens with thigh tattoos anymore, but he'll live and return to work tonight."

Ivy bounced on the mattress again. "Soooooo. What was the rest of last night like? I didn't hear you come in. You must have stayed at Bowie's till closing."

"I did." Hope sighed. Best get it over with. "*It* was good." She took another long swallow from her cup. "Gabe offered me a job," she finally admitted.

"No shit! At the bar?"

Shoving the covers and Ivy aside, Hope jumped out of bed and rummaged in her closet for workout gear. "No, as a nanny." She dug out her black Lululemon running pants. "For his daughter."

Hope turned around and met Ivy's dropped jaw. She would have laughed if she didn't empathize with her friend's total shock. She swapped her pajama pants for her leggings. "I know. I was shocked to learn he had a daughter, too."

Ivy's mouth snapped shut, then opened, then shut again. After her impression of a guppy fish, she blinked a few times.

"Hope, it's not that. I *knew* he had a daughter, but he guards Ruby like she's the long-lost Russian princess. He doesn't talk about her, doesn't parade her around. In fact, most people don't even know she exists."

Ivy moved to Hope's dresser, found a bright-pink workout top, and tossed it at her.

"Why would he hide her? She's the sweetest little thing. And watching them together, I could tell they have a close relationship."

Ivy waved her hands erratically. "Oh my God! Oh. My. God. You *met* her!" She grabbed Hope's shoulders. "Hope, it took me a whole year before he let me see her. And another year before he'd let me babysit her. Even now, I only get to watch her when he is one hundred and ten percent desperate—which he has been more lately since his sitters have all been unreliable flakes."

"So, why did you never mention her?"

Ivy shrugged and headed to the bedroom door. "It never came up." She sauntered out and down the hall toward her own room.

"Oh no," Hope called after her. "You don't get to walk off all cryptic."

Ivy stopped and turned to Hope with a serious look. "If Gabe is introducing you to Ruby *and* hiring you to watch her after this short of a time, then he's telling you he trusts you —in a big way. To him, you're clearly different from the rest of us. I'm not interfering with this."

Hope snorted. "Now you don't interfere? When I actually want you to?"

"Ruby is Gabe's story to tell. Not mine."

Hope said nothing to that, since she knew Ivy had a story of her own that Hope had kept quiet for three long years. She was well aware of the importance of allowing people the freedom to narrate their own stories. Or not.

Returning to her room to finish getting dressed, Hope wondered how and if she'd find the courage to tell her own.

Half an hour later, procrastinating about going for a run, Hope decided to check her financials. Taking out her laptop, she figured that she'd rather do some banking now so she could burn off the stress of it on her run after.

Pulling up her bank information, she braced herself for an all-time low, but her stomach dropped when she saw an unfamiliar number, one with several zeros after it, pop up in her checking account.

Hope pressed a few buttons to backtrack her account activities and froze when she saw that last night a large sum had been transferred into her account. Before she could even log out, she tossed her laptop to one side, her fingers hitting speed dial on her phone.

Joel answered after one ring.

"Get rid of it," she ordered before he could even say hello.

"Well, good morning to you too, sweet sister." The velvety voice that could make women the world over drop to their knees lazily rolled through the phone line.

But this woman paid no heed to it. Hope adored her brother, had even idolized him as a child, but she never fell to his feet for anything. If anyone did the bidding in their sibling relationship, it was Joel who did hers.

She couldn't remember a time when he'd refused her anything. And although they had had typical sibling squabbles, he'd only ever been there for her, which was why she called him.

"So help me God, Joel, if you don't get rid of it in the next half hour, I am going to lose my colossal shit. And you know how ugly that is."

"Whoa, can you chill for one minute and tell me what you're even talking about?"

Hope took a deep, shaky breath and tried to rein in the uncharacteristic fury that was reverberating through her.

Teeth gritted, temper rising, she explained. "I checked my bank account this morning. There's money in it. Lots of money. Money I haven't earned, seeing as up until last night I've been unemployed."

When silence reigned at the other end of the line, she continued, "Someone has set up a monthly automatic deposit into my account and since I know you wouldn't risk your life transferring money into my personal account without discussing it with me first, I am going to assume it was Dad, who I am way too angry to talk to at the moment, so I need you to make it stop. Reverse the funds, send them back, whatever you need to do, just make it go away." All this came out in one long rush of frustrated air.

"Now," she added with emphasis when her brother still said nothing.

Her brother's ongoing silence was unnerving. And annoying. She could hear him breathing, so she knew he hadn't hung up on her. Good sign. But she could tell he was frustrated—it was palpable even through an electronic device. If it was with her or the situation she didn't know, but because she loved him, she let him have time to collect himself.

"Ok, first of all, take a deep breath," were the words he chose to follow the silence up with.

Okay, so maybe he did want to die after all.

"Oh hell no. Do NOT tell me to take a deep breath like I

am some out-of-control toddler, Joel." Her voice cracked with emotion. "You know how important this is to me. I don't want him to interfere. He's been interfering my whole life, and I am sick of it." The first hot tear leaked down her cheek, and she was grateful Joel couldn't see it. She knuckled it away with a rough fist, because the only thing worse than sounding like an out-of-control toddler was acting like one. "He needs to stop making decisions for me."

Joel must have heard the emotion in her voice, because his took on a soothing, coddling tone that only made her temper spike. "Look, you're my sister and I love you, but we are talking about Dad here. His providing instincts go deep, and the thought of you out there on your own—struggling to make ends meet because of some stupid decision he and Mom made when you were a baby—is killing him." He sighed placatingly. "It's not going to be so easy for me to make him stop taking care of his little girl. Whether you're done being angry with him or not."

Joel was right, of course. Damn him. And Hope knew it was unfair to keep dragging him into the middle of her emotionally-charged interactions with their parents. Yet, she knew Joel was the only one she could count on to stand up for her when it came to them or anyone.

By all accounts, Joel was the superhero of big brothers, and she owed him many times over. Still, this situation was triggering her deepest pain, so she couldn't stop herself when she mumbled, "We both know I'm not really your sister."

Which, obviously, was the wrong thing to say.

"Fuck that, Hope," Joel returned emphatically, his voice rising. He never yelled at her, and certainly had never sworn at her, so she reared back on the other end of the phone, shocked. "Don't you dare start with that shit. You are my sister, down to the soul, and I'd do anything for you." And not so long ago, he had. "So don't go there. Okay?"

If it had been possible for tension to physically leak through phone lines, she'd have sworn it was happening now. She could feel her brother's fury rise to meet her own, and she could imagine Joel running a frustrated hand through his undoubtedly perfectly cut hair. His handsome face would be furrowed with barely contained anger—and probably a good deal of hurt.

It was knowing that she had hurt him that got her. Of everyone who had hurt her over the course of her life, Joel hadn't been one of them. He'd been the soldier of support at her side all this time, and if she had any relationship with her parents left at the moment, it was because of him. Since the bottom of their family had fallen out over Christmas, it had been Joel who mediated between them all. The only reason she still communicated with her parents was because of him.

"You're right," she whispered. "That was unfair, and a shitty thing to say. I'm sorry."

In the echoing silence that followed, Hope reminded herself that whatever had happened to her had happened to him as well. The illusion of their perfect family had shattered for him as well when the truth of the adoption came out. She needed to remember that she hadn't been the only one hurt by the lie.

"Joel—"

"I'll talk to Dad," he interrupted in a tight and cold voice. "But for the record, they love you. Both of them do. When things got hard you ran away, and now no one has closure. They don't know how else to get through to you. Mom's a wreck every time I talk to her. I think you're being completely unreasonable and... a little unfair and—"

"Unfair?" she said, cutting him off because what she did not need right now, on top of everything else, was to feel guilty about the suffering she'd caused their mother over the last few weeks. "Joel, they didn't tell me I was adopted for *twenty-six* years. Our cousin knew the truth and I didn't. *That's* unfair."

But many things were unfair, including how her reaction had hurt her parents and caused stress on her brother. And because the bubble of hurt and betrayal that had lodged in her throat was now being joined by an unavoidable weight of regret, she mumbled, "Look, I have to go. Love you." And hung up.

CHAPTER EIGHT

Hope wasn't a seasoned runner like Ivy. In fact, she was a horrible runner. But she was feeling restless after her encounter with Gabe last night, and her conversation with her brother this morning had only made it worse. She needed to get a good sweat on, so she put on her sneakers and decided she'd see how far she could get before she collapsed.

She took off through the city streets for a while before turning down Couch Street and heading toward the water so she could run along the waterfront.

It was the first of February and absolutely freezing outside, and it only felt colder once she was by the water, but she didn't mind too much. She wore gloves and a cap, and the chilled air against her face made her feel alive and went a long way to clearing the noise in her head.

As she jogged, she tried to lose herself in the view of the river on one side, the park on the other, and the path ahead. She passed dog walkers, other joggers, and people walking to work.

In the last several weeks, she'd come to feel at home in

this city. Portland was small enough to feel comfortable, but large enough to feel like she could be anonymous if she wanted to be. Which, incidentally, she did.

Other than Ivy, no one really knew her here. Her father's name wasn't plastered on construction sites all over the city. Her friends didn't try to hit her up for rental deals in the newest high-rises built by Morgan Construction.

In Portland, she wasn't Hope Morgan, Walter Morgan's daughter. She was just Hope, a normal twentysomething figuring life out on her own.

She had just passed the Oregon Maritime Museum, which was basically a giant ship docked against the river's edge, when her lungs gave out. She staggered to the nearest bench, where she collapsed and dropped her head between her knees, heaving breaths.

She didn't know how far she'd run, but judging by the way her breath was sobbing in and out, it had to be farther than she'd managed yet. Maybe even as far as Ivy. No, scratch that. Ivy never ran less than five miles a day. There was no way Hope had run that. She'd be lucky if she'd run a quarter mile, which felt like a marathon for her. Ivy would be proud.

She still had her head bent between her knees, trying to regulate her breathing when she saw a pair of Nikes come to a stop in front of her. Judging by how her heart rate picked up again, she had a pretty good idea who they belonged to.

"I wasn't expecting to see you until eleven," came the sexiest voice she'd ever heard.

Lifting her head, she squinted against the February sun —and found Gabe.

A long-sleeved running shirt hugged his superbly toned chest and a beanie revealed his just-a-touch-too-long hair curling under it. He gazed down at her with the lopsided smile that she'd learned last night had the power to simulta-neously stop her heart and wet her panties.

Seriously, being this hot should be illegal, or at least punishable by fine. He could cause an accident, distracting innocent joggers from watching where they were supposed to be going. They could run into a pole or the river or, even worse, knock over a child in a stroller or something. Honestly, did no one care about the safety of innocent pedestrians anymore?

Without waiting for an invitation, he dropped down beside her on the bench and stared at the water.

"I didn't know you were a runner," Hope said.

"I'm pretty sure," he replied without looking at her, "there's a lot you don't know about me."

Wasn't that the truth.

"Do you do that on purpose?" she asked.

That got her a look. His green eyes narrowed and his brow furrowed as he observed her. "Do what?"

"Keep your life so tightly guarded."

"Maybe," he said with a shrug. "I guess I got used to it over the years. I'm not good at sharing myself with people. I learned pretty early that the less people know about you, the fewer people get close to you. And the fewer people you have in your life, the less likelihood you get hurt."

His revelation struck her, mostly because it was so unex-pectedly raw and honest. She shifted her gaze from his face to the water. As sad as his words sounded, she could under-stand them and had to agree. In theory, if the people you loved the most were the ones who could hurt you the deep-est, it made sense to have less of them in your life. Except in practice it wasn't working out for her in the way she'd imagined.

"And how's that been working for you?" she asked Gabe, truly curious.

He looked at her. "It's been working great. Never thought about switching it up." Then he turned to look back out over the water. "Until recently." A little smile tipped his lips upward.

Oh-kay. What did *that* mean? Her heart started to pound again, her cheeks heating. But she couldn't bring herself to reply. He couldn't possibly be referring to her. They'd only met yesterday. People didn't change their life philosophy after one meeting. Did they?

They sat in silence, and Hope's breathing finally returned to normal range.

Just as she was settling into their companionable silence, Gabe rose to his feet. "Come on," he said, taking her hand and pulling her up from the bench.

She almost succumbed to total humiliation when her rubbery legs nearly buckled under her.

"What are you doing?" she asked.

Sauntering beside her along the river, he smiled, the first all-out smile she'd seen on him, and she just about melted into a hormonal puddle. Was he *laughing*? Unashamedly staring now, she took him in, admiring his stunning look of joy. He really was a beautiful human when he smiled outright like that.

Her admiration fizzled when she realized he'd picked up their pace. Once again, she was jogging along the river.

"Well, I figure since we are both here now, we might as well go a little farther to the donut shop I know a few blocks away. We can discuss what we need to about Ruby over coffee and a maple-bacon donut."

Maple-bacon donut? Was that a real thing?

Resigned to going farther than she'd anticipated, and

too proud to beg him to stop, Hope kept pace with him—even as her screaming muscles had her plotting all the ways she might shove him over the riverbank without anyone being the wiser.

~

Gabe had to hand it to Hope. Even though she was clearly a novice runner, and probably reached her limit three city blocks ago, she kept up with him. Her breaths came in quick little gasps, crystallizing in front of her like puffs of smoke. He probably shouldn't be pushing her, but the look of utter determination on her face was the cutest thing he'd seen in a long time. She hadn't complained once, or asked him to stop, and he admired that. She had grit, and it was sexy as hell.

As they continued jogging, they said nothing, probably because she didn't have any extra air for talking, but Gabe wanted to talk, so he slowed to a walk. Beside him, he thought he heard a muffled "Thank God" but when he looked over, she only matched his stride and smiled up at him.

There it was again, her optimism. Her unapologetic determination to make the best of every situation. Even though her skin was sweat slicked and she still hadn't caught her breath enough to speak. Running clearly wasn't her jam, but she was looking at him like she was happy just to be walking beside him. Gabe couldn't remember the last time anyone other than Ruby had made him feel this wanted. Or the last time he'd allowed himself to feel this wanted.

A few minutes later, they were sitting on bar stools by

the shop window, with two steaming mugs of coffee and a couple of donuts between them.

Gabe had never been good at small talk, so he got right to the point. "I'll be honest. I've always had a hard time passing Ruby off to a babysitter. I don't do well with handing over control like that with anything, but especially not with her."

The last time he thoughtlessly surrendered control the worst had happened, and there was no way in hell he'd ever let it happen again. But out of sheer necessity there was no way he could get around his childcare issue any longer. Whether he liked the idea or not, he needed to trust other people to care for Ruby when he couldn't.

Up until now, he'd only trusted three people with his daughter: his father, his sister, and Sean. Because, first of all, they knew his past and had been with him every step of the way. They knew his trauma, his fears, his triggers. They knew how to deal with him and Ruby accordingly.

Second, they were all family. Sean might not be a blood brother, but he was as close as one could get without sharing DNA. Gabe's dad, for all his own pain and faults, had come to bat countless times after Carrie died. Regardless of what had passed between them before the accident, Gabe had let it go when his dad had shown up at the hospital and sat with him for the three long days they had been there. As for his sister, Lori, she'd taken over the mother role the day their mom had died. She'd mothered him to within an inch of his life, and when Carrie had passed, she swooped in on him and Ruby like a fierce mama bear determined to make sure they had everything they'd needed.

Apart from those three people, and on occasion out of desperation, Ivy, he'd never really let anyone fully into their lives. Which made it hard to secure a reliable, trustworthy caregiver for his child. It was hard to expect trust and reliance when you weren't willing to give it yourself. And he hadn't been willing. Still wasn't. But he knew he had to change that, otherwise he'd keep running into the same problem of rotating through one babysitter after another without any continuity—or security—for Ruby.

When Hope had offered to help, his first thought was *hell no*. But the more time he spent with Hope, the more he suspected she might be a good fit for Ruby. She was calm, but joyful. She had a sense of fun and energy—even if she couldn't run worth shit. She was tenacious, something he absolutely had not expected from her. She was determined to work hard, for whatever reason, because God knew the daughter of Walter Morgan didn't need to lift a finger unless she wanted to. And mostly, she was optimistic. Her cup was half full, she saw the pot of gold at the end of the rainbow, and Ruby could use a lot more of that in her life.

He had judged Hope harshly; he knew that now even if he wasn't quite ready to admit he was totally wrong about her. However, he conceded that she was so much more than he'd originally thought, and he was willing to give her a chance with his daughter, mostly because the guilt of forcing a six-year-old to spend her evenings locked inside his office was killing him.

"You're right," he said, as she sat beside him silently. "Ruby can't spend every evening sleeping on the couch in my office. So..." He met her gaze.

Her deep-brown eyes stared back at him hopefully.

"You're hired."

A smile broke out over her face so wide and genuine he couldn't help but smile back. "Don't get too excited," he warned, when she let out a little squeal of glee. "Ruby is six, she has a ton of energy, and she's nearly impossible to tire out. She'll go all day if you let her."

"No problem," Hope said confidently. "I'm a pro at coming up with creative ways to entertain kids. It'll be great! I'll come over tonight before you go down to work, and I'll make dinner. Is there anything she doesn't like to eat?" Before he could answer she went on. "Then I thought we could do some finger painting. You can make the cutest little birds out of thumbprints. But then again if the weather holds, it might be nice to get some fresh air. If you have a car, I could borrow it and drive her out to—"

"No driving." The words came out immediately, harshly, before he could stop them.

"Oh, but I'm a good driver. Never had an acc—"

"I said, no driving." Gabe bit out with cold finality.

Hope's smile froze in place, then confusion crept across her features.

Guilt tugged at him. She had no idea what had happened in his past, and here he was behaving like a massive jerk because she'd offered to do something lovely for his daughter. He took a breath and tried again.

"No one drives with Ruby except me." He attempted to sound casual this time, less crazy, but he knew it was too late. She'd caught him off guard, and he forgot himself. "It's non-negotiable. You can take her anywhere you can go by walking, the bus, or street car, but no driving."

"Understood," she said quietly, then busied herself by picking up her donut and taking a bite. She paused midchew, then closed her eyes and moaned. The sound shot southbound through his body.

"Oh. My. God," she whimpered, licking glaze from her lips.

Relieved that the tension had broken and to have an

excuse to change topics, Gabe smiled at her and took a huge bite of his own donut. "Good, right? They're the best in the city."

"So good," Hope said. "Better than s—" She stopped abruptly, blushing.

She looked so cute and embarrassed Gabe laughed. "Uh-uh, nothing is better than that." He dipped his head so he could catch her eye. "And if it isn't, then you haven't been doing it right, princess."

Her cheeks bloomed into an even deeper shade of pink, and she choked a bit on her *better-than-sex* donut. Remembering how his body nearly exploded simply from the prospect of kissing her, Gabe couldn't help thinking what it would be like to have her under him, naked and writhing, moaning his name as he showed her exactly how much better than donuts sex with him could be.

Taking a deep gulp of coffee, he shook the thought from his head, reminding himself he was in no place to be thinking those things about her. He had nothing to offer a woman like Hope Morgan, except a job. Which brought him to his next thought—he needed to broach the topic of the almost-kiss.

"Hope, look, what happened in the bar last night—"

"Don't worry about that," she said, shaking her head and licking sugar crumbs off the top of her lip. His eyes dropped to her tongue and followed the movement. Fuck, she was mesmerizing. "We were caught up in the moment. It was a long day, lots happened, high emotions all around. Obviously, it was a mistake."

Shooting his gaze back to hers, he narrowed his eyes. The word *mistake* didn't sit right with him. He had wanted to kiss her. He still wanted to kiss her. And he was pretty sure she wanted to as well, but she was about to work for him, and he couldn't muddy the waters with their mutual lust.

"I was going to say that I really wanted to kiss you last night." More than he'd wanted to kiss anyone in a long time. "But given our new arrangement I think it's best if we just keep this about Ruby." It was the right thing to do. And he really needed to do the right thing here. For both Ruby and Hope.

"Absolutely. Ruby is the priority," she agreed, nodding excessively. "There will be absolutely no more talk about kissing." As if to prove that the matter was closed, she started to nervously sweep crumbs up on their table with her napkin.

He had more he wanted to say on the topic. Like that he needed her to know that last night had meant something to him, that he wasn't the type who almost-kissed beautiful blondes in bars and then acted like it was nothing. He wanted to explain that, for reasons he could not decipher, he'd been drawn to her from the moment he saw her huddled in the hallway. That the idea of her taking care of his daughter both excited and scared him in a way he could not describe.

But Hope didn't seem to need or want further explanation, so he followed her lead and let the matter drop. For now.

They spent the next half hour going over the details of Ruby's daily schedule. The hours he'd need her. What he would pay her, which made her eyes bulge a bit.

"Gabe, that's way too much for babysitting a sweet little girl like Ruby," she'd said.

He shook his head, adamant. "This is more than babysitting, Hope. You'll be cooking for her, getting her ready for bed, helping with homework, giving up most of your weekend evenings. Trust me, what I can pay you probably isn't enough."

She was quiet about it after that, but he could tell she wasn't convinced.

They agreed she'd start that afternoon. They'd give it a couple of weeks, then see how they were all getting along. If need be, they'd reassess the arrangement then.

Although tempted, Gabe didn't make Hope run home. Instead, they walked back to the Pearl District, and as they did, he listened to Hope talk about herself, finding himself absorbing every little morsel of information as if she was telling him all her secrets.

"Do you miss San Francisco?" he asked after she'd explained how her brother lived in one of the more recent Morgan Construction penthouses downtown, while her parents still lived in Oakland in the family home she'd been raised in that her father had designed and built.

Listening to the life she described, Gabe couldn't help but wonder if this city, *his* city, known for its hipsters and local breweries, would be enough for her.

"No." Her reply came swiftly. "I mean, I miss my brother, Joel. He's kind of been my sanity." She huffed out a laugh. "He's kind of been everyone's sanity. So, it's been hard not having him nearby, but I don't miss the city. Morgan Construction is everywhere there. Everywhere I turn I see my family embedded in one high-rise or another, and it reminds me..." she trailed off, walking for a few steps in silence. "It reminds me why I needed the distance."

Gabe nodded, noting how her normally cheerful tone took on an edge of melancholy. There was more than she was telling him, but she didn't elaborate. And he didn't push, understanding all too well what it was like wanting to keep the past in the past. He hated talking about his own, so he'd never force someone else to talk about theirs.

Besides, she changed the topic by peppering him with questions about Portland for the rest of their walk. Her ability to evade and deflect was impressive.

When they got to the building, Gabe walked her right to her door. "See you at 3:30 then?"

She nodded, her eyes locking and holding with his for a long moment, then she let herself into her apartment leaving him alone in the hallway. And for the first time in a long time, being alone didn't feel as familiar as it once had.

CHAPTER NINE

As Hope smoothed her pink knee-length skirt over her thighs, her damp palms caught on the soft fabric. Why was she nervous? She was spending the evening with a six-year-old. There was no reason to be anxious. Heck, up until this moment, she'd been excited about the prospect.

Taking a deep breath, she told herself this was just new job jitters and had absolutely nothing to do with her surprising attraction to Ruby's father, or the deep-seated desire to have both father and child like her. It would be dangerous to start overthinking all these feelings or why they were popping up in the first place. For now, she'd chalk it up to feeling lonely for family since hers blew up in her face.

Picking up her giant shoulder bag, which she hoped rivaled that of Mary Poppins, she left her apartment and crossed the hallway to Gabe's.

With one last fortifying inhale, she knocked. A squeal, a thump, and the soft but unmistakable deep rumble of Gabe's voice came from within the apartment. Then the door whipped open and a tiny girl lunged through the opening.

"Hi!" Ruby exclaimed, beaming up at her with a big smile that revealed a missing front tooth and dimple in her cheek. Her bright green eyes sparkled with excitement.

Looking at that face, the last of her nerves, and a little piece of her heart, melted away.

"Hi," she said, offering a friendly smile of her own.

Ruby grabbed her hand and pulled her into the apartment. Well, at least this Walsh family member wasn't afraid to get close to people.

"I was showing Daddy my dance. We're learning a new one in dance class. Do you dance?" Ruby said all at once as she pirouetted into the living room, releasing Hope's hand and twirling without concern until she toppled onto the couch and broke out into a fit of giggles.

"Ruby, careful! One of these times you're going to crash into something much harder than the couch," Gabe said, striding into the living room from the kitchen. He was wearing a t-shirt, jeans, no socks—and had a dish towel slung over one shoulder. Casual and in dad-mode, but still absolutely mouthwatering.

"She's been at it since we got home. Apparently the new dance is very exciting."

Hope set her bag down, removed her ballet flats, and made her way into the living room to join them. Ruby bounced off the couch and ran to meet her halfway. She looked up at her intently, head tilted, green eyes focused, like she was studying a rare painting at a museum. Hope tried her best not to squirm under the scrutiny of this six-year-old pistol.

"You're pretty," Ruby announced after a moment. Then

once again, she grabbed Hope's hand and tugged. "Come on, I want to show you my room."

Gabe swooped in, lifting Ruby clear off her feet, cuddling her to his chest like he had last night. "Hold on there, wildcat, give me a minute with Hope. I want to go over a few things with her before I leave for work." After one more squeeze, he set her down and, holding her by the shoulders, turned her in the direction of her bedroom. "You head to your room, and I will make sure Hope follows as soon as I'm done with her."

Ruby rushed off, and Hope's gaze collided with Gabe's. A shiver ran down her spine at the thought of some of the things she'd love to have him do to her and it satisfied her deeply to see his eyes heat in the way she was now luckily becoming more and more familiar with. The way that mirrored hers.

This wanting without even really knowing each other was the oddest sensation. In hindsight, it would have been prudent to put a few more guards up, but she hadn't anticipated this... this connection between them.

Not that any of it mattered, because they had agreed there would be no more talk of kissing. And for her that had to include putting an end to her near-constant lusting and daydreaming.

"She likes you," he said, shoving his hands in his pockets and drawing her attention to the flex of his biceps.

"You were right about her energy," she said with a laugh, striving to ignore the thrum of awareness that somehow took over her entire body the moment she saw him. "I think I am going to find her eagerness very entertaining."

Gabe snorted. "More like very exhausting. Trust me. By the end of an evening chasing after her, you'll be ready to collapse into a dead sleep."

He collected a sheet of paper from the small table by the door and handed it to her. "I wrote out a loose schedule. You know, dinner, homework, bedtime routine." He moved toward the kitchen, and she followed. "There's left-over spaghetti from last night that you can heat for dinner." He opened the fridge and gestured to a large Tupperware. Then he closed the fridge door and crossed to a wall of cupboards. "Or you can root through these to see if there's anything you prefer." When he turned abruptly to face her, Hope realized she'd been following him too closely.

She collided with the solid wall of his chest. He reached out to steady her, his hand lingering on her arms. His fingers were warm against her bare skin, and her heart quickened in her chest at his nearness. After a moment, he released her and took a small step back, clearing his throat.

"While you're here, I want you to make yourself at home. Feel free to use or eat whatever you like. Ruby knows where most everything is, but if anything comes up, you can call me." He pointed to a number on the paper he'd handed her. "That's my cell. Put it in yours and use it whenever you need." He bent a little to stare directly into her eyes. "If you need anything, Hope, I'm right downstairs. Don't hesitate, okay? I can be up here in thirty seconds."

She nodded, but he continued to watch her intently. "I'll call if I need you," she promised.

He was trusting her with the most important thing in his life, and she was going to make sure she warranted that trust by not doing anything stupid, like not calling him when she knew he'd want her to.

Apparently satisfied by her answer, he straightened and moved off toward the hallway. "I have to get ready. I promised Carter I'd be down in the bar by four. But I'll return and check on you both before Ruby's bedtime."

He pointed down the hall in the opposite direction of where he was headed. "She's in her room at that end, probably painting on the walls."

Hope grinned. "Perfect, that's my favorite activity."

Gabe grimaced, and she laughed.

"Don't worry. I won't let her paint on the walls. I brought special paper for that."

"Hope," he said, more seriously, his eyes softening as he leveled her with a grateful and relieved look. "Thank you."

And then he was gone.

~

Hope's evening with Ruby flew by in a flurry of activity, energy, and color. Donning sparkly pink tutus and feathery purple hair pieces, they played dance class (Hope was the student, Ruby the instructor). Then they moved on to painting and Hope made Ruby's day when she opened her Mary Poppins bag and gave Ruby the tubes of rainbow watercolors to use instead of her standard set of primary shades. Ruby had fun squeezing drops of turquoise, canary yellow and magenta onto a tray, also from Hope's magic bag of wonders, and mixing them into a vivid kaleidoscope that ran the gamut on the color wheel.

After dinner, Ruby wanted to go swimming, but since that wasn't in the cards for the night, Hope whipped out a puzzle with puppies on it, which did the trick of occupying the little girl until bath time.

At 7 p.m. sharp, Ruby was out of the tub but still wrestling herself into her pajamas when the sound of a key turning the lock made both of their gazes snap to the direction of the front door.

Ruby spun to Hope, her eyes wide, her mouth shaped in

a tiny O of excitement. Then she squealed, "Daddy!" and sprinted down the hall with one arm in her pajama top and one arm out.

Hope was halfway down the hall when Gabe pushed open the door and caught Ruby, who had taken a flying leap up into his arms.

He grinned as she locked her arms and legs around him like a monkey. "Hey, sweet pea. I came to say good night. Did you have a good evening?" he asked his daughter, but his eyes sought out Hope, and when they locked on her, they filled with humor. "Keeping Hope busy, I see."

With great effort, Hope kept her eyes level with his and refused to give in to her compulsion to smooth her rumpled skirt or tame her hair, which nobody had to tell her looked like a rat's nest by this point of the evening. She was very aware that she had water splotches all over her shirt—and probably a spaghetti stain or two. But the truth was, despite her appearance, she'd had the time of her life with Ruby, and she opened her mouth to tell Gabe exactly that.

Ruby beat her to it, though. "Daddy, we had the *best* night ever! We played dance, and I cooked dinner, and then Hope let me use her special paints, and I made you a picture!" She wriggled out of his grasp and ran to the dining area to carefully pull a still damp paper off the table. She walked like she was on a balance beam back to Gabe and showed him the image she made of him and her in a garden of flowers.

He crouched to her level to view her artwork.

"See. Hope even let me use sparkles, and now the flowers look glittery, like they are in Mommy's garden in heaven."

Wait, what? Shock punched through her, knocking the

wind out of her. Had she heard right? Ruby's mother was dead?

Her heart started to palpitate. A chill cloaked her body. Her knees went weak.

Gabe slid her a look, then refocused on Ruby, wrapping his arm around her, drawing her and the painting into the curve of his big body. He studied her creation as if it was the most precious piece of art in the world.

"These are the most beautiful flowers I've ever seen," he whispered.

"Yeah," agreed Ruby solemnly. "They are."

Father and daughter stayed like that, heads drawn close, staring without speaking at the painting they cradled between them.

Feeling like a voyeur in a private moment that wasn't hers, Hope crept down the hall to the bathroom, where she busied herself draining the bathwater and setting the tub to rights.

Several minutes later, as she straightened and turned to hang a towel, she gasped in surprise when she caught Gabe nearly filling the bathroom doorway. With arms crossed, he watched her. Silent and assessing.

She pressed her hand to her heart, which was racing, and not only because he'd surprised her. A dull ache lingering there since Ruby had referred to her mother's death.

"You startled me," she said quietly, unsure of herself given this new revelation. What was she supposed to say now?

He didn't move.

And as always, when she was in close proximity to him, the butterflies awakened in her stomach. "Where's Ruby?" she asked.

Uncrossing his arms, he stepped into the bathroom. He shut the door silently behind them, so they were in the small space together.

Instinctively, she retreated, her calves coming up against the cool tile of the bathtub. Her heart lodged itself in her throat, clogging half her airway, then started to beat there frantically. He watched her, curiosity in his eyes, but he came no closer.

"Ruby passed out on a stack of books on her bed before she could even read them," he said. "You did a good job burning her energy."

Hope nodded, not sure what to say in light of the bombshell revelation she'd just heard. She'd given some thought to why a man like Gabe might be single, but she had never considered this. She'd assumed divorce. She'd assumed there'd be an absolutely typical story of two people growing apart and lives moving on in separate directions. She hadn't expected death.

He was so young. Ruby was a child.

He was a widower. Ruby was motherless.

And she was the square peg trying to fit into the heart-shaped hole in their lives.

Suddenly, the room felt too small. Heat flooded her whole body. Her chest tightened. She couldn't breathe. Emotions she couldn't name churned inside her like a storm she could've never predicted and wasn't prepared for. Before Gabe could say or do anything else, she darted around him, intent on getting out of there.

But he had the reflexes of a jackrabbit. She'd barely touched the doorknob when his hand came over her head and pressed against the door, keeping it closed.

"Hope, wait. We need to talk."

Oh God, he was right behind her. His long torso

brushed her back, his heat wrapping around her like a blanket. A warm blanket. A protective one. It had always been that way with him. From the first moment he'd appeared beside her in the hallway, his heat had settled over her like a cloak of peace and soothed her. She felt safe with him. Always.

With a sigh of surrender, she let her forehead drop against the closed door.

Gabe was right. This was a conversation she couldn't run from. Her brother's words echoed back to her. *When things got hard you just ran away.*

"I'm sorry," she murmured, emotion filling her throat. "I didn't know. I shouldn't have been..." She paused, not knowing what to say that could make up for her unexpected invasion of his privacy. "Gabe, I didn't know," was all she could offer in the end.

A low sound rumbled from deep in his chest. Was he frustrated? Angry? Confused? Sympathetic?

The warmth of hands enveloped her shoulders and turned her to face him. The inescapable draw that existed between them had her eyes moving to meet his. Standing this close to him, she clearly saw all the different green and golden-brown flecks that collided in the kaleidoscope of his eyes. She let herself drown in them—and paradoxically, this calmed her.

"Talk to me," he said, his voice deep and steady.

When she dropped her gaze to avoid the request, he curled his fingers around her chin and tilted her face up, so she was forced to meet his gaze. "Hope, what's going on in that beautiful mind of yours?"

She wasn't totally sure, so she told him what was hurting her heart the most. "I didn't know Ruby's mom had died."

And just like that, a shutter came down over his eyes and

he let go of her. Shivering from the sudden loss of his heat, she wrapped her arms around herself.

"I'm sorry. I should have told you. It's just—not something I'm used to talking about."

Dragging a hand through his hair, Gabe seemed to weigh his next words carefully.

"Ruby was six months old when Carrie died," he finally admitted. "She doesn't remember her mother."

A darkness passed through his eyes that Hope recognized as regret. And pain. Inside her chest, her heart squeezed with a similar sensation.

"But lately she's been talking more about Carrie. Asking questions about her. To be honest, I don't really know what the hell I'm doing, or if I'm giving her any of the answers she needs. Every single day for the last six years, I've felt like I've been winging it, praying to God that I don't screw this up. I've no idea if I'm doing right by Ruby. Or Carrie. They both deserved better than this." His eyes shuttered again and his mouth formed a grim line, as if this story was physically painful.

She knew exactly how hard it was to talk about your rawest pain and decided in an instant she couldn't make him say more. She wouldn't be the one to torment him. Not when they owed each other nothing. Not when she wouldn't be able to return the favor.

She traced her fingertips along his tight, unsmiling mouth. For a moment she simply took him in, every angle and plane of his face, every stress and frown line. It was like a map to all the pain he'd experienced, all the devastation he'd accumulated in his short lifetime.

It was as her fingers brushed the stubble along his jaw that she made the decision not to press him for more. Even though she was desperate to know, even though she had a million questions backlogging in her brain, she wasn't going to push him anymore tonight. She could sense he'd already shared more than he probably had in a long time, and the fact that he'd trusted her with that was enough for now.

"We don't have to talk about it," she said, looking into his eyes, willing him to know she meant it.

Gabe held her gaze, then he reached for her hand, lifting it until her palm rested against his lips. He let his eyes close, and to her surprise, he brushed his lips across her fingertips. The sensation shot down her arm, and straight to her heart.

After a few seconds, he opened his eyes and drew her fingers away from his mouth.

"Thank you," he said, his voice rougher and deeper than before.

Swallowing hard didn't help move the lump that had formed in her throat. As they stood together, staring into each other's eyes—parts of them touching, other parts itching to—the familiar heat built between them.

It felt wrong.

It felt right.

It felt... inevitable, Hope thought as her breathing quickened.

Only a day had passed since their encounter in the hallway, but it might as well have been months, years even. The effortless intimacy that existed between them had been there from the first moment.

Now Gabe was looking at her mouth with hungry eyes. Her lips parted in anticipation of what she instinctively knew was coming.

"Hope," he rasped. "I think I'm about to kiss you."

At his words, her pounding heart knocked the last of her breath out of her throat in a soft exhale. She wanted that kiss. She wanted it so bad. But that's not what they'd agreed on in the donut shop.

"What about keeping things just about Ruby?" She managed to ask with the reserve oxygen in her lungs. Her voice came out as a squeak.

Gabe tipped his forehead towards hers, as if seeking the contact. Guilt flashed in his eyes, and she could see—he was waging the same internal battle as her. Conscience against need. Duty against desire.

"You're right. This is wrong." His gruff whisper was steeped in regret. Hope drew closer to him because of it. He'd done nothing wrong, expressing his needs. They matched hers. She wanted him to know.

"It doesn't feel wrong." She was near enough now that they were sharing the same air. When her breath released, his drew it in. "It feels right."

"Then maybe it is."

In one fluid movement, he closed the gap between them. His lips descended on hers, hot and firm, and moved across them with a single mindedness that made her melt against him in seconds.

Feeling powerless to resist and, more alarmingly, not even sure she wanted to, Hope opened her mouth, allowing Gabe to deepen their connection. When his tongue found hers, the kiss detonated, causing a needy moan to release from deep within Hope's throat. After that, it was all devouring, exploring, and tasting.

She pulled him in by the front of his t-shirt, drawing his tongue deeper into her mouth, relishing the sensations firing all the way down to her toes. His fingers tangled in her hair, tugging her closer as well. She could feel the vibrations that came from his throat low in her belly. Everything that came from him poured into her, and from her to him. As though their kiss was a living, breathing thing.

Eventually, only the need for air broke them apart.

"I don't—know—what this is," he said between hard breaths, his eyes, laced with confusion and desire, burning into hers.

She didn't know what this was, either. And even if she'd known what to call this insatiable attraction between them, she had no idea what to do about it. All she knew was what her body was telling her, and it was telling her to take whatever he was offering her and give back as good as she got. Right here. Right now. They could comfort each other.

On instinct, she let her hands glide up his chest, then ran them back down, digging in her nails a little as they raked across his solid abs, past his navel, to the waistband of his jeans. He released a low, very male sound that told her he liked that. Liked it very much.

He pressed his big body into hers, and she could feel every hard plane and ridge of him. "You make me want things, Hope. Things I haven't wanted in a long fucking time."

"What things?" she asked, in a voice she didn't recognize. Low, husky, wanton.

He groaned again and bent his head, his mouth trailing kisses up her neck before stopping under her ear. A shudder ran through Hope's entire being.

"Things that involve you. Naked. Under me." He licked the shell of her ear. "On top of me." He crushed his torso to hers so that her breasts flattened against him. "In front of me. Christ, I want you any way, Hope. Every way. I have no fucking idea why, but I want you." His words liquified her, and she clung to his shoulders as he pushed her higher up the door so that she came up to her toes. He pinned her there, his hips grinding into hers, showing her just how much his body wanted hers.

Rocking her hips into his, she set into motion a primal rhythm that soon had her hovering on the verge of orgasm. It usually took at least twenty minutes to get her anywhere near the vicinity of an orgasm, but this man had her on the edge of the cliff within a minute, *and* they were fully clothed.

"Oh my God!" she gasped. "Gabe!"

"I know," he ground out, slipping his hand under her skirt and up her inner thigh, only to stop at her panties.

Urgent, desperate, she whimpered beside his ear, thrusting the hottest part of herself towards his hand. She was behaving completely shameless, totally out of character, but she was beyond caring, beyond reason. She was frantic for his touch. Mindless.

Finally, his fingers slipped under her panties, and she thunked her head on the door. Sweet Lord, this felt so good. He felt *so good*.

"So wet," he murmured, his tone full of awe, like he was as surprised by their insane attraction as she was.

"For you," she panted as he stroked her.

He seemed to know exactly where and how to touch her. Her body shook under his ministrations, all of her muscles tensing with anticipation. And when he delved into her core, she released a sob of satisfaction.

"That's it," he coaxed, with that sexy rumble of a voice he had.

Hope dropped her head into the crook of his neck and then, because he smelled so good, she bit lightly into his flesh there. The groan that tore from Gabe's throat went right through her.

He cursed roughly into her hair as her desire slicked his fingers even more. Curving two of his digits deep inside her, he reached some ultra-sensitive spot she'd only read about in books.

She went off like a firecracker on the Fourth of July, riding his hand as a tsunami of sweet pleasure washed over her. She would have cried out, was crying out, but he covered her mouth with his, swallowing her sobs as wave after wave of ecstasy consumed her.

It was only afterward, when he was cuddling her to his chest, their breath regulating in tandem as he stroked a hand over her hair, that the grim realization hit her: she'd nearly screamed out loud during the most powerful orgasm in her entire history—with a six-year-old in a room down the hall. Snapping back to reality with a hard jolt, she wiggled out of his embrace and covered her mouth with her hand.

"Oh my God," she whispered, horrified.

Gabe gave her an amused, if not a little smug, look. "Actually, that was all me, sweetheart," he said cheekily as he stepped toward her again. She glared at him, holding her hand out, palm up, to stop him. He caught her hand in one of his and brought it to his mouth, smiling against her fingertips.

He found this funny, the brute.

"Ruby," she growled in a tone that hopefully made it obvious why they both should be freaking out.

The amusement in his gaze intensified, and she was going to have to hit him if he started laughing at her right now. But he didn't. He took a slow step back and helped her smooth her rumpled clothes, then he tucked a strand of her hair behind her ear in that special way of his.

"It's okay, Hope," he reassured.

But she felt anything but okay. The warmth of her orgasm-induced buzz was quickly being replaced by shame and horror. What had they just done?

"I don't think that can happen again while I'm here," she said adamantly, deciding on the spot. "If we had woken her — " She closed her eyes against the horrible thought. "I didn't think that through. I'm sorry." When she opened her eyes, her gaze collided with his.

The amusement was gone from his green eyes, replaced with a cold, remote look that she hoped was awareness of how truly appalling this situation was.

For a long moment, Gabe said nothing. Then, as if he had decided something in the quiet of his mind that he wasn't going to share, he reached behind her and opened the door.

"Obviously we have more to talk about. But this isn't the time. You should get back to Ruby," he said as he gestured for her to go out ahead of him. "And I should return to my bar."

Hope didn't hesitate, she fled down the hall to Ruby's room, where she quietly opened the door and found the six-year-old asleep on top of her covers, surrounded by books. Her face was serene in sleep, like a carefree doll.

With a sigh of relief, Hope sagged against the wall. Ruby hadn't heard them.

Heard me, she amended.

But it still didn't erase the fact that whatever was happening between her and Gabe had to end immediately. It might have felt right, like it was the most comfortable and natural thing in the world to be in his arms. But she couldn't risk this kind of recklessness. It was completely inappropriate. A child's trust was at stake. She couldn't mess with that, not when she knew first-hand what it felt like to have adults in her life who had been careless with their child's trust and faith in them.

If she was going to care for the man's daughter, there was no way she could be in his arms at the same time. No matter how good and right it felt.

CHAPTER TEN

"Well, why the hell not?" Ivy demanded.

Hope was lying on an exercise mat panting after a particularly brutal set of crunches, while Ivy hovered nearby untangling resistance bands. They were in the section of Sean's gym that Ivy had set up as her physical therapy clinic, and Hope had just finished announcing that there was no way there could ever be a repeat of what happened between her and Gabe last night.

She'd gotten back to her apartment at 2:30 that morning. Gabe had come home from the bar, looking exhausted and more than a little wary. He also looked more tempting than sin, but instead of jumping him like her body was begging her to do, she bolted like the coward she was.

She proceeded to toss and turn the rest of the night until she gave up on the prospect of sleep and got up early to follow Ivy into work. At the gym, she exercised herself into exhaustion by running on the treadmill until her legs gave out from under her.

Now, collapsed on the mat, drenched in sweat, and reliving every hot and humiliating moment of last night,

Hope lifted her hands to cover her face, shame seeping back into her cheeks. Her body still tingled when she remembered what it felt like having his hands on her.

"Because," she reiterated as if Ivy was slow on the uptake, "there was a little girl a bedroom down the hall." She sat up abruptly, her eyes wide with panic. "What if she'd heard us? What if she'd come looking for us!?" Horrified all over again, she dropped her head to her knees and wrapped her arms around them, trying to escape into her self-made ball.

"Jesus Christ, Hope, will you get a fucking grip?"

Hope peeked out of her ball in time to see Ivy toss the knotted mass of rubber strip bands aside with a frustrated sigh.

"What do you think other couples who have kids do?" Ivy crossed her arms. "I mean, for chrissake, do you honestly think your parents never had sex again after they had kids in the house?"

From the safety of her human ball, she said, "Yes!"

Ivy let out an exasperated sigh. "And I thought I was the prude."

"Who's a prude?" Sean's deep voice boomed from somewhere above Hope's head.

"Hope is. She's refusing to have sex with our hot landlord because he has a kid."

Hope came out of her ball and gasped. "Ivy!"

Her so-called best friend shrugged. "It's not like Sean isn't going to hear about it from Gabe sooner or later. They gossip more than a bunch of teenagers at a slumber party."

"Actually," Sean said, leaning his towering, dark, and muscled frame against a pillar. "Getting Gabe to talk about anything remotely personal is like pulling teeth. With tweezers."

Ivy blinked at Sean, then swiveled her head to Hope. "Oops."

Hope groaned and flopped back down to her mat.

Sean's face appeared above her, grinning. "You and Gabe are sleeping together?"

At the same time, Hope said, "No!" and Ivy said, "Pretty much."

Hope covered her face with her hands and groaned again.

"She's in denial," Ivy said to Sean. "They kissed in his apartment while Ruby was sleeping, and now she has it in her head that it was some dirty, shameful thing that can never happen again." Ivy gave Hope a meaningful once over when she dropped her hands from her face. "I'm trying to convince her otherwise."

Sean nodded in sympathetic understanding, then offered his hand to Hope, which she took, and he hauled her up in one swift pull. When she tumbled forward, he caught her shoulders gently. With his imposing height, chiseled muscles, and immense strength, he should have come across as imposing, even dangerous, but Sean's eyes gave him away every time. A few shades lighter than his coffee-colored skin they were always alight with kindness and genuine warmth.

Those melted-chocolate eyes studied hers now, and she knew her number was up. Sean saw right through her. She was running scared and he knew it. He was going to call her on it any minute now.

"You know how many women I've seen go through Gabe's life in the last six years?" he asked conversationally. Before Ivy could give a smart-ass guess, he said, "Zero." He side-eyed Ivy with a brief but warning glance, then looked back at Hope. "His wife died six years ago."

Hope nodded. Hadn't she found that out the hard way?

"And since then, he hasn't so much as alluded to even the possibility of including a woman in his life."

Ivy snorted, and Hope knew she couldn't help herself. Ivy's opinion of men was unfavorable at best, and with good reason.

"Puh-leeze. As if any man could keep it zipped up for that long." Ivy followed up her gross generalization by rolling her eyes so hard they almost popped right out of her head.

Sean glared at her, and something tightened in his features. It passed before Hope could decipher it, but she sensed an underlying frustration.

"You'd be surprised," he muttered under his breath, then he said more loudly to Hope, "I'm not saying he hasn't been laid in six years, although if he has, he hasn't told me about it. What I am saying is that if he's starting something with a woman like you, in his own house, with his daughter in the other room, then he's not messing around." Hope must have looked as uncertain as she felt because Sean drew in a deep sigh before he continued. "Look, I'm not going to get into all the shit he's been through, or the scars that shit left behind. But if he's decided he's ready to move on after all this time, and it's with you, then this is the happiest day of my life because I can't think of a better guy getting a second chance with a better woman."

She wasn't sure she could live up to the expectations of being a better woman. Not when she was hiding so much of herself from Gabe. Things that he might never understand. Feeling like a fraud, she wrapped her arms around herself.

Gabe probably thought he had her figured out, but he had no idea. Her family life was a mess. And she was beginning to feel like she was contributing more to the problem than the solution. How could she ever explain those details to a man who valued and protected family as much as Gabe did?

Then there was the Ivy thing. She glanced at her friend, who was back to fidgeting with the rubber bands.

It was *the thing* that she'd sworn never to talk about with anyone, but it affected her nevertheless. Despite Ivy's smaller than average stature, she appeared so strong standing there, a woodland warrior pixy ready to take on the demons of the forest, one who'd traded her armor and arrows for yoga pants and exercise bands.

But Hope knew better. Behind the tough exterior was a frightened and vulnerable woman who'd probably never trust another man again. And Hope would never risk the fragile veneer or the newfound strength Ivy had built during the last three years by divulging secrets to anyone, including Gabe. Even if it would help him understand the events that had molded her into the person she was today. A person who was nowhere near ready to be the woman he moved on with after six years alone.

If this could be a fling—just a couple of no-strings-attached tumbles to release the sexual tension constantly brewing between them—she might have been convinced to get on board. Lord knew she could use a good affair to take the edge off the stress in her life. But people who did the things they had done in the bathroom the night before with a child down the hall did not have no-strings tumbles. Sean had said it—Gabe deserved a second chance, and she wasn't second chance material. He wasn't a no-strings kind of guy.

No. It wouldn't work. He'd want more. He and Ruby *deserved* more.

If she was being honest, she would have loved to be the one who might give them everything they deserved. She'd always wanted a partner in life, a companion, in the bedroom and out. She wanted a family of her own. Children. Maybe a dog, or at least a cat. A routine, and a family vacation, and a house that was home. She wanted everything she'd had as a child.

But that life wasn't for her, at least not right now. She was too messed up at this point, had too much baggage to sort through. Not to mention her commitment to Ivy.

She wasn't the right woman for Gabe. Or Ruby. Especially Ruby.

"Want my advice?" Sean asked, oblivious to the torrent of thoughts flying around in Hope's head. "Don't think so hard, Hope."

Okay, maybe not so oblivious.

"Go with what feels good," he added. "With what feels right."

But that was the problem. What felt good and what felt right were two different things. And because of that, there was really only one thing to do: she had to quit being Ruby's nanny and focus on finding another job.

CHAPTER ELEVEN

Several weeks later, well into the month of March, Hope still hadn't quit. Of course she hadn't. She'd meant to, had even planned what she would say to Gabe, but in the end she didn't.

The truth was that she was not only enjoying her time with Ruby, but her time with Gabe as well. Over the last few weeks, she'd slowly gotten to know him better, and not just the obvious things like his ability to run his whole life on approximately four hours of sleep and 3 liters of coffee a day, but the little things, like he seemed to have an aversion to wearing socks when he was home, and the fact that he lifted weights daily in his mini home gym right before work so by the time she arrived he was freshly showered and smelled like an intoxicating blend of cedar and fresh male skin.

Most evenings now, they'd gotten into the habit of sitting down at the small dinner table together chatting about the evening while he wolfed down whatever leftovers she'd saved for him. Which is why, she now knew, he absolutely hated potato skins and left a sad empty husk behind anytime she'd made a baked potato with dinner. Sometimes she'd make him one on purpose, because watching him meticulously scoop out the guts then moan about how good it tasted did something inexplicably delightful to her insides.

She'd discovered he was a basketball fanatic and caught up on NBA highlights every night before he went to bed no matter how late he'd gotten home.

Even his preference for nineties rock music was starting to rub off on her, and she caught herself humming *Wonderwall* in the shower more than once now.

But no matter how many new things she learned about him every day, her favorite was still witnessing the sweetness and devotion he had for his daughter. His protective love for Ruby melted her. So much so that she was starting to forget why walking away had made so much sense in the first place.

Besides, what had happened with Gabe in the bathroom hadn't happened again and showed no signs of happening again. As if a silent agreement had been struck between them, they didn't talk about it, and they didn't try to recreate it. Whatever attraction continued to simmer had been successfully ignored by both of them.

By Saturday morning she'd resigned herself to the way things were, convinced it was for the best all round. She'd spent most of the morning painting and now stared at the hues of color that had collided on the canvas. Rich greens and browns, smudges of yellow where light shone through. Pinks, purples, and blues to accent.

She imagined walking through a forest. Her path unfolding into the light beyond. It spoke of faith, and trust, and hope. All the things she felt were always just out of her reach.

Why couldn't it be that easy? Follow a path and come out into a beautiful meadow, where everything was colorful and fragrant and soft. Her childhood had been a meadow. Perfect and safe. Innocent and comfortable.

When she'd found out about the adoption, her first reaction had been numb shock. Hurt and humiliation immediately followed. Her world had been blown to pieces. Her meadow destroyed.

Checking the clock, she saw it was already 2 p.m. She'd have to be at Ruby's soon. Wiping her hands on a rag, she moved to her bedroom to get changed. On her bedside table, her phone vibrated spasmodically. Glancing at it, she saw her mother's name flashing back at her.

Once upon a time, she and Audrey had had an enviable mother daughter relationship, but her cousin's announcement at her sixteenth birthday party had made her start to question everything. By the time she'd presented her parents with the genetic test kit this past Christmas, the closeness she'd once shared with her mother had dwindled. The kit had been a formality. A final nail in the coffin.

But it had been the nail that hurt her parents the most. The devastation on Audrey's face when she unwrapped and saw the kit, and the tears that immediately sprung to her eyes when Hope had said, "I want to know where I come from" — it had been horrible and awkward enough to make Hope believe there might never be any coming back from that moment.

Yep, she'd done a pretty bang-up job of ruining Christmas and blowing her family apart. But damn it, didn't she have a right to know about her own life? Knowing they had kept it from her for so long made it feel like it was some dirty secret. Like *she* was some dirty secret, and that knowledge had clung to her like a stain.

She watched the phone buzz until it went silent. She hadn't answered a call from her mother in a long time.

She'd pulled on a pair of jeans and sweater when the buzzing started again. And if ring vibrations came with emojis attached, this one would have had the red, angry face.

Joel's name appeared on her call display. Perfect. When she didn't answer, her mother must have called him. Again.

She never could ignore the brother, who'd put everything on the line for her more than once, so she steeled herself and hit the answer button.

"Mom's trying to call you," Joel growled by way of greeting. He sounded exasperated. Tired. Annoyed. Worried. The usual.

"Was she?" she replied in her most innocent voice.

"Hope," Joel bit out through what sounded like clenched teeth. "You know I can't keep doing this, right? I have too much on my plate to also play the go-between for you and Mom."

More guilt crashed over her. She knew Joel was busy. He had been groomed to take over Morgan Construction all his life, and now, as their father was slowly stepping back, he was coming into that role. Truthfully, he all but sat at the head now. It was her father's dream to see Joel and Hope at the helm, but she'd shattered that dream when she turned her back on the fancy position and the fancy office her father had been holding for her last Christmas.

So now Joel had all his balls in the air, including hers, and while he was a more than competent juggler, she knew it wasn't fair to keep throwing him in the middle of her personal crisis with her parents.

"She wants to touch base with you about the hospital

fundraising gala," Joel continued. "Have you forgotten about it?"

Of course she hadn't. It was an annual event that her family had taken part in for years.

She heard someone talking to him in the background, another phone ringing in the distance, papers rustling. He was at work, and likely swamped, yet he still took the time to call her. Joel didn't ignore anyone. Not his mother, not his sister, not his responsibility. He wasn't built that way. He was a Morgan through and through.

And he was right. She had an obligation to help the hospital that she wouldn't ignore. "Okay," Hope said. "I'll call her."

"Can I count on it?"

Ouch. "Yes, you can," Hope replied, her tone clipped.

"Good," came his equally curt reply. "We need to work through this, Hope. This can't be the end of our family. I won't let it be." And with that, he hung up.

Joel's words hung in the air. She hated that he resented her way of dealing with the situation. Hated that he was willing to move on, and she wasn't.

She scrolled through her phone to her mother's number.

Audrey answered after the first ring. "Darling?" she asked in a soft, tentative voice.

Darling. The term of endearment Audrey had used to address Hope her whole life. It was hard hearing it, because a whole lot of complicated emotions collided inside Hope's chest whenever she did. An overall uncomfortable, confusing feeling. Precisely why she avoided these phone calls. "Yes, Mom. It's me. Sorry I missed your call earlier." Or the last dozen calls before that.

"How've you been?" her mother asked. In another lifetime, Audrey Morgan had known exactly how her daughter was. These days, she didn't know when Hope had so much as a cold.

"Good," Hope said, then after a moment added, "I got a job."

"Oh, darling, that's wonderful! Is it with that marketing firm you interviewed with a while back?" There was a brief silence before she admitted, "Joel mentioned you'd applied."

Of course he did.

"Um, no." She sat on her bed, feeling awkward and hating it. She hadn't yet admitted to anyone in the family that she'd veered off the expected path of business, however temporary it may be. "It's more in the childcare field. I'm watching a little girl whose single father works late shifts." She bit her lip and waited for a silence loaded with disappointment to follow. To her ultimate surprise, it didn't.

"Oh, how wonderful!" Audrey exclaimed excitedly. "You're so good with children, Hope, a natural."

She wasn't sure why this sentiment surprised her. Her mother wasn't naturally one to judge anyone's career choices. Still, Hope had always felt a lot of pressure to pursue the family business, and being a nanny was so far removed, she wasn't sure how her mother would react. She hadn't expected praise.

It caught her off guard, and before she could think about it, she found herself opening up. "Actually, I really love it. Ruby is sweet and creative. She's always on board for any project I bring over. And her father, Gabe, well, he's—" What? Hotter than hell? Sexually potent? Increasingly irresistible? "He's also been great. He's been generous and kind to me." She hesitated for a moment, then admitted, "I feel like I don't deserve it."

"Oh, darling, of course you do!" Audrey exclaimed. "You are a gift to any family. Believe me, I know. I—" She broke off and inhaled an unsteady breath. "And I know things between us have been..." Her mother's voice wavered, making Hope's heart squeeze uncomfortably. "Strained, but I hope you always know that no matter what, you are a blessing in our lives. So, believe me when I say, you do deserve it. You deserve everything."

Tears stung her eyes, and she blinked them back furiously. She hadn't had a personal talk with her mother in a very long time, and she hadn't realized until this moment how much she'd missed it. She missed the unfailing support and the affirmation, but the hurt from her parents' deception still burned so brightly. There were so many questions she wanted to ask her mother that she'd never asked at Christmas, like, "Why didn't you ever tell me?" or "Why did my freaking cousin know I was adopted and I didn't?" She hadn't asked them then because she'd been afraid of what the answers might be. Now she avoided asking because she wasn't ready to confront the emotions those questions, or answers, brought on. Instead, she changed the subject.

"So, Joel said you wanted to discuss the gala?"

"Right." Audrey cleared her throat. "You're still coming, aren't you? You've never missed one."

Hope pressed two fingers to her temple and rubbed at the tension headache she felt coming on. Her mother organized the annual hospital fundraiser, and Hope had always supported both the cause and her family in this regard. The last few years she'd given the opening remarks, and she knew she was expected to do so again.

Except the gala was six weeks away, and she'd been hoping to avoid going this year. More accurately, she hoped to avoid going home altogether. She still needed... space.

"Well, Mom—"

"Hope," her mother interjected. "You have to come. You simply can't not be there."

"It's just that I started this new job, and it's not a good time to leave, and..." She paused, remembering Joel's words. How had she gone from being the one who'd been hurt to the one who was doing the hurting? Her tension headache was now a full-fledged roar in her head. "I'll get back to you, Mom," she finally managed. "I promise."

About two minutes after she'd hung up, her phone buzzed with an incoming message. Turning it over, she read the screen. It was from Joel.

You're coming to this fucking gala if I have to drag you there myself.

Three bubbles hovered ominously over her screen, then disappeared, taking whatever else he was going to say with them.

Because there was nothing left to say. She already knew how he felt. She had to make the decision: either forgive and move on, or walk away and lose the only family she'd ever known.

Countless times since Christmas, she had wished she could just get over it, that she could will her heart into submission and move on from the fact that her parents had hidden her adoption from her until she'd basically forced them to reveal it. At the very least, she'd wished she could fake it until she made it, so to speak, and just continue on as if it were no big deal until maybe one day it wouldn't be.

She hated coming across like the villain who was unfairly holding a grudge. But the hurt that she felt whenever she thought of the hundreds of times over the course of her childhood that they could have told her—it was unstoppable, like a train barreling down, and no amount of brakes she applied could stop it. It just freaking hurt her heart every time she thought about it.

Flopping back on her bed, she pulled a pillow over her eyes and groaned. A tumultuous storm of doubt and uncertainty—plus hurt and guilt—churned in her heart.

At 3 p.m. sharp, Gabe heard a knock on his door and— just like one of Pavlov's dogs—his heart kicked up a notch and bounced around in his chest like an overly enthusiastic puppy.

Annoyingly, this happened every damn day when Hope arrived to babysit Ruby. He was starting to feel like a sweaty-palmed teenager whose crush was coming over for a private study date. It was sad. And exciting. And, he realized, as he opened the door, he looked forward to 3 p.m. every single day.

As always, she was gorgeous in that subtly regal way of hers, and he had to school his body not to outwardly react. She was perfectly dressed in an outfit he could never dream up, with her sunny-blonde hair falling over her shoulders and her lips glossed with something that made him want to lean in and lick it off. She looked edible.

This afternoon, however, something was off. Her dark-brown eyes were darker than normal, stormy, and she wasn't smiling. Her brows were knit together so slightly that he shouldn't have noticed, but since he noticed everything about her, he saw the lines of strain that marred her usually flawless features.

"What's wrong?" he demanded.

"Nothing." She sounded normal as she tried to push past him into the apartment.

"Like hell. *What* happened?" If someone hurt her, he was going to—

Ruby chose this time to come barreling down the hall, skidding to a stop in front of them. "Hope! Come see what I built in my room. I set up all my Barbies." She tugged Hope's hand. "Come on, you can be the one that looks like you!"

Without taking his eyes off Hope, Gabe crouched down to Ruby. "Baby, I need to talk to Hope about something. You go back to your room, and I'll send her over when we're done. Okay?"

Ruby glanced between him and Hope. Then with a shrug of assent ran back to her room. Gabe rose and cupped Hope's chin, tilting it up until she was looking at him.

"Talk to me?" he asked, keeping his voice gentle this time.

She tried to lower her gaze, but he held firm to her chin so she couldn't move away from him. He'd come to realize that she was good at hiding, avoiding, or diverting depending on the situation. He'd seen her do it plenty of times. Had *let* her do it plenty of times. But today she looked shattered, and he wasn't going to let her be alone with whatever was bothering her.

"Really, Gabe, it's nothing."

He loved it when she said his name. So intimate and warm, like the connection he imagined growing between them was real.

"Crazy family stuff," she added. "That's all."

"Your family can't be crazier than mine, Hope." He had a pretty hard time believing the Morgans were any kind of crazy. But he let that go, and said, "Trust me, I can deal with crazy. So tell me. What's up?"

Her eyes rolled upward, and she blew out a breath. "I

had a phone call with my mom. It didn't go so well. Then my brother texted afterward to tell me off and made me feel like a colossal asshole, so—" She shrugged, like it was nothing, but he could see what had been said had hurt her. "You know. The usual."

"Actually, I don't know," Gabe said, looking into her eyes. "You haven't talked about your family much." It reminded him how much more he wanted to know about her. These little pockets of time before and after his shift didn't give him nearly enough time with her. And the scary thing was, he wanted more time with her. Much more time.

He ran his hands down her arms, enjoying the way she quivered under his touch. Yeah, there was still something between them. Something they both wanted, something he didn't intend to let go of. But this wasn't the time to go after it, not when she was clearly still reeling from what her mom and brother had said to her. "Keep talking to me, Hope. Tell me exactly what's up."

She gazed at him then, her deep brown eyes fathomless and so full of emotion he felt like he could stand there and read them for hours. She opened her mouth, and he was sure she was going to say something, open up to him in a way she hadn't yet.

But, of course, Ruby chose that moment to once again come out of her room and interrupt them.

"You guys done talking?" she demanded, impatiently tapping her foot.

Hope laughed, her eyes warming, and she turned from Gabe to face Ruby. "I'm all yours," she said, walking away from him. But as she went down the hall, following his daughter, she glanced over her shoulder and said, "Thanks."

"For what?" He'd done nothing; she hadn't given him a chance to.

Hope shrugged. "For caring," she said, before disappearing into the bedroom to play Barbies with his daughter.

Shaking his head, he stalked toward his own room to change from his dad gear to his bar gear. He didn't know if he'd ever understand women, wasn't sure there were many he wanted to understand, but when it came to Hope Morgan, he was finding it harder and harder to pretend that he wasn't interested. He wanted to know what made her tick, what made her laugh and cry, what made her hot—he really wanted to know what made her hot—and just what made her, her.

And he hadn't wanted that with a woman since Carrie.

Knowing what that signified was scary as fuck, and he wasn't ready to dig deep into the emotional implications of his growing feelings for Hope. So, instead of dwelling, he shoved any thoughts of her to the back of his mind and stripped out of the shirt he'd been wearing all day. Pulling on a black Bowie's t-shirt, he reminded himself that his priority was Ruby, and if he kept focused on that, he'd be safe from whatever threat Hope Morgan was posing on his heart. And his soul.

CHAPTER TWELVE

Later that night, Hope was sitting with Ruby at the dining room table. Over the last week and a bit, they had fallen into a nice little routine. Much to their mutual delight they'd discovered they shared an intense love for drawing, and they spent the time between dinner and bedtime sitting at the dining room table with sheets of paper spread out between them, drawing all the things their imaginations could come up with.

Tonight they were working on people, and Ruby was bent over her paper with her tongue sticking out the way it always did when she was concentrating. She was practicing drawing noses.

"Mine doesn't look like yours," she declared. "Mine's ugly." Ruby shoved the paper away from her and crossed her arms.

Hope continued shading in the contours of the face she was drawing with an HB pencil. "You know," she said, "if you are going to be a good artist, then there is probably one very important secret you should know."

Taking the bait, Ruby dropped her frustrated posture

and turned to Hope. "Really?" She sounded uncertain but hopeful.

The beauty of children, Hope thought, smiling. They could be pessimistic and optimistic at the same time. They could be swayed either way. They didn't commit their personalities to only one side. They were fluid, ready to accept change, flexible and resilient in a way that was lost in adulthood. It was a gift.

She knew that whatever she told Ruby now would be accepted as truth without question, and she didn't take that kind of blind trust lightly.

Turning to Ruby, who was gazing up at her with those bright green eyes that she was finding harder and harder to resist in both man and child, she bent to Ruby's eye level.

"Yes, really. Once you know the secret, your art will always be beautiful, no matter what you create. You see, the most important thing about art is that..." She watched Ruby lean closer, her eyes widening with the anticipation. "It's impossible for art to be ugly," she finished in a matter-of-fact tone, a simple statement of certainty. "It's literally impossible. If it is art, then it is always beautiful, and you will always find someone who thinks so."

Ruby's eyes narrowed. "That's not true. Art can be ugly. I've seen it."

Hope turned back to her drawing. "No, it can't. It's *literally* impossible. Even if you aren't happy with what you created, or someone else thinks it isn't good, I promise someone, somewhere, is going to love it." She slid her gaze to Ruby, who was staring at her now, totally riveted. "Of course, you have to share your art for that to happen."

Reaching across the table, she slid the discarded paper forward with one finger. "If you toss it away or hide it, you'll never know who it is that loves your art and thinks it's beautiful."

Ruby frowned down at her drawing. "It's impossible for this to be ugly?" she asked with a healthy dose of skepticism.

"Literally."

"What if I scribble on it?"

"That's called abstract art, and it's one of the most popular kinds."

"Oh." Ruby leaned closer to the drawing, assessing her work.

Hope did as well. It was a picture of three people. A man, a shorter girl, and a taller woman. The man had an interesting blob in the center of his face, which Hope assumed was the *ugly* nose. It was quite *abstract,* to say the least, and Hope swallowed a giggle.

"Why don't you tell me about this picture?" she suggested.

Ruby wiggled in her seat, sitting a little taller, looking proud. "Well, this is my dad," she said, pointing to the man.

Yep, so it was, shaggy hair and all.

"This is me." She pointed to the little girl that was sporting pigtails. "And this," she said, her voice softening. "Wait, it's not finished." She hunched over her drawing once more, and Hope's heart squeezed painfully in her chest as Ruby carefully drew a wing on each side of the woman. "This is my mom."

The lump in Hope's throat clogged her airway, making it impossible to speak even if she had the right words. What was she supposed to say to this six-year-old who had just drawn an angel for a mother? She took a shallow, aching breath and said reverently, "She's beautiful."

"Yeah," Ruby agreed. Then she cocked her head up at Hope. "I have a real picture of her. Do you want to see it?"

With the emotion of the moment threatening to take over, she decided to buy herself a minute and nodded. Ruby hopped off her chair and ran down the hall into her bedroom.

Pressing the heel of her hands against her eyes, she took a deep breath and reminded herself that for Ruby, this was normal. Tragic as it was, her mother was gone and had been since before she could remember. She was sharing her reality, and she didn't need Hope's emotions to make the moment uncomfortable or sorrowful when it wasn't those things for her.

By the time Ruby bounded back into the room carrying a box, she had collected herself. Ruby opened the box and took out a photograph. She handed it to Hope with a bright, proud smile. "It's my favorite picture." Ruby announced. "Her name was Carrie, and she was pretty, and kind, and a nurse. Daddy said she helped save lives every day. She worked at the hospital in the room where people come when the ambulance drops them off."

"The emergency room?"

"Yep, that's it."

Hope studied the photo. The woman was indeed lovely. She had long, dark, wavy hair that tumbled down her shoulders just like Ruby's was doing now. She was smiling brilliantly and holding a baby in her arms.

On cue, Ruby pointed at the baby and said, "That's me."

Smiling, she tapped her finger on Ruby's sweet little nose. "I figured."

Ruby went back to her drawing but continued chatting conversationally. "Everyone says I look like her, even though my eyes are the same color as my daddy's. But everything else is like my mom. I like that." She looked up at Hope. "Do you look like your mom?"

"I don't know." It was an automatic answer and while it was the truth, Hope hadn't meant for it to slip out so carelessly. To distract them both, she put the photo back on the table. "What a beautiful picture, Ruby. Thank you for sharing it with me."

But of course, the six-year-old wasn't distracted. "How can you not know if you look like your mom?" Then she paused, tilting her head to one side. "Did she die too?"

Hope tensed. She'd gotten herself into this, and now she'd have to get herself out. She chose the truth to get her there.

"No, I have a mom, and she's alive." Suddenly, she considered something she hadn't before. "I think. I don't actually know. The mom who raised me isn't the mom that gave birth to me."

Ruby blinked up at her.

"I'm adopted," Hope said carefully.

Awareness dawned on Ruby's face. "I know what that means! Jack, in my class, he's adopted. He's from another country, so he looks different from his parents, but they all love each other, anyway. Are you from another country too?"

"No," she said. "In fact, my mom—the mom who adopted me—looks a bit like me." Enough so that she'd clung to that resemblance as her main proof that she was indeed Audrey Morgan's biological daughter. "But I don't know who my real mom was. I never saw her. There is no picture."

After a quiet moment, Ruby sighed wistfully and said, "You're still lucky."

She set down her pencil, intrigued. "How so?"

The young girl looked up at her, a soul far older than six years looking out from behind luminous eyes. "Well, I know my mom died. And maybe your mom died too, but you found another lady who wanted to take care of you and be your mom. There isn't another lady who wants to adopt me and be my mom. It's just me and my dad." She shrugged her tiny shoulders. "And that's fine. I love my dad. But you're lucky you got another mom, that's all."

It was all said so casually, but it caused a torrent of emotions inside Hope's chest. It was like Ruby had ripped off a bandage, revealing a truth that Hope had been covering with her anger, bitterness, and shame.

She'd spent the last couple of months punishing her parents for withholding an important truth from her, feeling the weighted resentment of the betrayal, but the reality was that she had a mother. She'd been welcomed and accepted into a family of love. She'd never had to feel a single day of the kind of loss that Ruby had had to feel. And now, it was a different kind of shame that cloaked Hope.

Acting on instinct, she pulled the little girl into her embrace. Ruby crawled into her lap without hesitation.

"Oh, sweetie, I know you miss your mom," she said, smoothing the riot of wavy hair Ruby had inherited from her mother. "And that's completely okay."

They sat for a moment as silence stretched.

"Daddy says we have to count our blessings," Ruby's small voice finally said.

"That's a good suggestion," Hope replied, trying to imagine a man like Gabe counting blessings. "What are some of yours?"

"Hmm." There was a thoughtful pause. "I have a great daddy. And a cozy bedroom and lots of Barbies. And the best teachers at school. And my best friend takes me camping with her. And—"

"And you have an auntie who loves you so much she drove halfway across town just to deliver you her famous chocolate cream pie!" said a female voice from behind them, causing both Ruby and Hope to jump up out of their cuddle.

Hope gasped in shock and fright.

Ruby gasped with joy. "Auntie Lori!" She flew into the arms of the woman standing a step inside the apartment's open door.

Hope hadn't heard the door open. She must have been too engrossed in her moment with Ruby. How long had the woman been standing there?

Lori wrapped Ruby in a big hug, all the while watching Hope with sharply appraising, and now familiar, green eyes. She scanned Hope from top to bottom without revealing a single thought.

Older than Gabe, she guessed closer to forty, Gabe's sister was slim and tall, with a neat-cut, no-nonsense bob.

Lori straightened, not breaking eye contact with Hope. "Ruby, honey, are you going to introduce me to your friend?"

Ruby bounded back to Hope. "This is Hope. She's my nanny. We're drawing pictures."

Hope rose on unsteady legs and extended her hand to Lori. "Nice to meet you."

Lori took her hand and shook it firmly. "Very nice to meet you too, Hope." She went to the kitchen, set the bag she carried on the kitchen counter, and pulled out a massive Tupperware container. "So how long have you been Ruby's nanny?" she asked in a tone that would have been casual if Hope didn't know better.

She was about to have another interview.

"A few weeks now." It had been almost two months since she'd started watching Ruby, but her gut told her to keep things vague with Gabe's sister for now.

"Interesting. Gabe never mentioned that the previous sitter had quit."

"Well, um." Unsure of how much to reveal, and not wanting to get in the middle of any unfamiliar sibling dynamics, Hope settled for more ambiguous truth. "From what I gathered, she was unreliable, and it left Gabe in a bit of a lurch."

Lori dropped some utensils on the counter with a clatter. "Lord have mercy. Tell me he did not make this poor child sit in his grubby office at the back of the bar again."

"Um..." Hope fidgeted with the hem of her sweater. God, Lori sure had the whole big-sister intimidation thing down to a tee. She hadn't felt this nervous in ages.

"Well, he could have called me." Lori sniffed.

Hope knew she hadn't meant it as a slight against her, but still she found herself straightening defensively. "I was available, and more than willing to help." When Lori leveled her with a sharp, knowing side eye, her cheeks burned.

"I'm sure you were," Lori said as she finished unloading a series of containers into Gabe's fridge and turned to stare at Hope. "Look, you seem sweet." She jerked her chin in the direction of Ruby, who was seated back at the table drawing contentedly. "And Ruby clearly likes you. But if you think you can save Gabe from his own miserable self by getting to him through his daughter, you can think again. Trust me. Many have tried, all have failed."

Hope jolted back, brows raised in shock. Who the hell did this woman think she was? Okay, she was the protective older sister, but still...

Taking a deliberate step forward to show she wasn't about to be pushed around, she matched her gaze to Lori's. "I don't believe Gabe needs saving. Childcare conundrum aside, he seems to be handling his life and family quite capably from what I can see."

Lori's eyes narrowed.

Before she could say differently, Hope lifted her chin and continued. "If anyone was saving anyone, Gabe saved me. He gave me a chance when I needed one. He's been good to me both as a landlord and an employer, and never once gave the impression that he was anything but absolutely capable."

All true, she assured herself. If nothing else, Gabe Walsh needed the opposite of saving. He was always in total and utter control. The memory of how easily she'd come undone in his arms came to her. Even then, hot and heavy against each other in the bathroom, it had been Hope who'd lost it, not Gabe.

"Well," Lori said, her eyes amused and maybe even a bit impressed. "I guess that's that then."

Hope crossed her arms and nodded, hoping to convey more confidence than she felt.

With her own curt nod, Lori gathered her empty bags and headed toward the door, pausing to pop a big smacking kiss on top of Ruby's head. "Sweet pea, there is a chocolate cream pie the size of your daddy's head in the fridge, as well as a lasagna."

Ruby's face broke into an excited smile. "Yum, my favorite. Thanks, Auntie Lori." She leaned in to hug her aunt, who returned the affection by enveloping Ruby in a warm embrace.

Any resentment Hope might have been feeling dissipated at the obvious display of love between the two. Lori was only trying to protect her family, and Hope couldn't begrudge anyone that.

"Share with your daddy, okay?" Shooting a look at Hope, Lori added, "And Hope too." Then, with another kiss and a heartfelt "I love you," she disappeared out the front door as silently as she'd come in.

CHAPTER THIRTEEN

In the supply room at the back of the bar, Gabe paused counting his stock to listen to the buzz of the Thursday night crowd in the background. The sound never failed to bring him a sense of satisfaction.

Sometimes he couldn't believe that Bowie's was one of the more popular bars in town. But the noise thrumming through the supply room door was all the proof he needed. To be fair, he'd worked damn hard to build it to this point. Years of dreaming, planning, squirreling away money, putting everything he had on the line to secure that loan so many years ago.

Opening a bar was risky. Many never made it more than a few years, but Bowie's had held its own, and in recent years had even turned enough of a profit that Gabe was thinking about opening another location across the bridge.

Location was everything. He knew he'd struck gold eight years ago when he found his current one. Back then, he'd also been lucky to secure a loan by finding a bank willing to take a risk on his adolescent dream. His family had supported him. Mostly, he figured his father and sister had just been relieved that he'd managed to get his shit together enough to start building a future for himself instead of following the path that led straight to Deadbeatsville.

He had Carrie to thank for being one of the main catalysts for turning his life around. When they were in their early twenties, he'd met her at a bar similar to this one. She'd been on a girls' night out with her nursing school friends. Gabe had been with his delinquent buddies, drinking more beer than they could afford and trolling the scene to see which good-girl-gone-wild would let them into her panties that night. He'd been a colossal asshole in those days.

He'd spotted Carrie almost as soon as she'd entered the bar. She'd been laughing, and she looked so damn happy he remembered wanting to drink the sound until he was drunk on her joy. He'd made his way over to her and had been as surprised as anyone when she'd given him the time of day.

They'd been together almost five years when Carrie became pregnant. In their mid-twenties by then, and still very much in love, Gabe decided it was as good a time as any to get hitched, and by some miracle Carrie had agreed. Six months after they were married, Ruby was born.

And six months after that, Carrie had died.

Gabe shoved a case of beer back into place a little harder than necessary, and the bottles rattled ominously. He hated memory lane. Six years after the fact, he could finally admit that none of it was really his fault. Carrie's death had been an accident. A horrible, preventable accident. Still, he couldn't help thinking how he could have been the one to prevent it.

"Watch out there, Tyson. You're about to break the merchandise."

Turning toward the voice, he came face to face with his

sister. How was it Lori always managed to show up on silent feet and when he least wanted her to?

She leaned against the doorjamb and shot him her know-it-all smile.

"Tell the boss to take it off my paycheck," he said, not in the mood for chitchat.

Lori narrowed her eyes, assessing him. "What's wrong?"

Damn her. Damn her and her sisterly instinct right down to sibling hell. He hated it when she saw right through him.

"Nothing," Gabe muttered, turning back to his stock. "Just busy. Gotta get this shipment sorted for the weekend." He gestured vaguely to the cases of bottles all around him.

From behind him came a low, knowing "hmm." It was a sound that haunted his worst adolescent nightmares. It was a sound that signaled a lecture was coming.

"I saw Sean in the bar."

Shit, this was not good. When his sister got her claws into his best friend, Gabe knew he didn't stand a chance. Sean might be a six foot five martial-arts badass, but he cowered like a little child around Gabe's sister. He also sang like a canary anytime she asked him anything she wanted to know.

"He told me you got a new babysitter for Ruby. The girl who lives in the other apartment upstairs."

Gabe let his head drop between his shoulders in defeat. He should have known this was why Lori had cornered him in his supply room. Sean had told her about Hope, and Lori had come to sniff out the details.

"Hardly a girl. Hope's in her mid-twenties." He knew from her rental agreement that she was twenty-six, the same age he'd been when Ruby had been born. "That makes her a legal adult in all fifty States."

"Hmmm."

Shit. Giving up on his stock count, he faced his sister. "Christ, will you spit it out already? You clearly came here to say something, so say it."

Lori lifted her chin and crossed her arms.

"Fine," she said. "I *came here* to see if you wanted me to take Ruby this weekend, and then Sean told me that you have this new sitter who's amazing and who's really fitting in with your family. And I am thinking to myself, *Gee, why haven't I heard about this amazing new sitter?*"

Gabe sighed. "Because there's nothing to *hear about*. Hope was available to watch Ruby when I needed someone. The timing worked out well, that's it."

"So you didn't kiss her."

Fuck, he was going to kill Sean.

"That's none of your business."

"I went upstairs and introduced myself," she admitted.

His jaw went slack as he gaped at his sibling. "Tell me you did not actually do that."

Arms still crossed, Lori's expression switched from smug to defiant. "I most certainly did. I was going up, anyway. I had food to deliver."

Gabe ran a frustrated hand through his hair, trying not to yank any out as he did. "Christ, Lori. What the fuck? Why do you always think you can stick your nose into every aspect of my life?"

"Because you're my baby brother," she returned evenly.

He knew she felt it was her duty to vet any new person coming into his and Ruby's life for any reason at all. Especially a woman. Ninety percent of the time, he didn't mind. Hell, most of the time, he depended on it, but this time felt different. Hope was different. Whatever was happening between them was new and unfamiliar and, dammit, special. The last thing he wanted was his big sister making Hope feel like she was under a microscope.

"Well, as your now bigger-than-you brother, can I ask you to please, for the love of God, stay the fuck out of this one?" he pleaded, knowing his chances of success with that request were next to nil.

Lori approached, like a predator stalking its prey. "First of all, you swear altogether too much, Gabriel Walsh. And second..." His sister's eyes softened into a meaningful look. "I just don't want you or Ruby to get hurt."

He snorted. "Too late, sis."

Lori sighed, then put her hand on his shoulder like she'd always done. It was either a gesture of comfort or a reprimand. He was about to find out which.

"It's not that I want you and Ruby to be alone forever, but this girl—this woman," she corrected after Gabe narrowed his eyes at her. "You don't know her well. She's certainly beautiful, and I know you're lonely and have," she gestured toward his general crotch area, "needs."

"Jesus Christ, Lori."

"You can deny it all you want, but it's true, Gabe. It may be unbelievable for most of us, but you're still human, and like all human beings, you need a human connection. Not to mention that it's obvious Ruby craves a maternal figure in her life." Lori inhaled deeply. "I heard her talking to Hope about wanting a mother."

Gabe's heart seized painfully as his sister's words tore through his emotional weak spot. Ruby never spoke directly to him about missing a mother figure in her life. He figured she avoided it to protect his feelings, which in and of itself gutted him. But recently, he had noticed slight changes in her behavior—in her play, and in her interactions with others, especially adult women—that suggested she was starting to miss a more traditional mother figure in her life. They were subtle. So subtle he had hoped he was reading too much into them, but Lori's perceptions echoed his own intuitions. And now she'd overhead Ruby say the words, making it all impossible to deny.

For his daughter's sake, he was going to have to suck it up and deal with his uncomfortable feelings around the matter. Guilt probably being number one. When it came to Ruby, he felt guilty about so many damn things.

Guilt that he clearly wasn't doing a good enough job of fulfilling both the father and mother roles in their family. Guilt that he hadn't seen how important it was to her sooner. Guilt that his current lifestyle didn't lend itself to the time, space, or energy it took to look for, and then build a meaningful relationship with, someone who might one day fill a mother role for Ruby.

It wasn't like the perfect woman could just drop into his life, ready to fill all the gaps.

Hope came into his mind then. He couldn't deny that she'd been filling some gaps pretty damn seamlessly these days, but his sister was right. Hope was still young, and he didn't know many twenty-six-year-olds who were ready to take on a family.

Except, there was that feeling he got in his gut when they were all together that felt... right.

Gabe gave himself a mental shake. What was he thinking? Hope was his daughter's babysitter. They weren't dating. Christ, they weren't even fucking. He had no business thinking about her in that way. She'd probably run for the hills if she knew he'd been thinking like this.

"I just don't want you to confuse your feelings," his sister said, returning to her lecture, "and get into something that can't end well—for anyone."

By the look of sympathy in his sister's eyes, he knew she was trying to help, and Gabe couldn't exactly blame her. Lori had taken care of him and Ruby for so long that she didn't know how to do any different. And it wasn't all her fault. The irony was that he had spent years resisting his sister's meddling, but when Carrie had died, he'd let Lori swoop in and take over everything. He'd depended on her militant organization and dictatorial demands during that first year, and, he was embarrassed to admit, for way too long afterward.

He'd needed Lori then. He still needed her. He knew he was damn lucky to have her as a sister. But what he found himself needing more these days was a life of his own. Maybe it was time to actively look for someone to share his and Ruby's life with.

Again, Hope filled his thoughts. He might not have any business imagining what it'd be like with Hope in his life permanently, but that didn't stop his mind and heart from going there.

"Why don't you bring her to Sunday dinner?" his sister asked, deceptively casual.

Sunday dinner was a once-a-month event that Lori had been hosting at her place pretty much since Carrie died. Their dad came, he and Ruby came, and the whole family was together. There was only one rule. No guests. Ever.

Only family, a once-a-month evening where everyone could reconnect and bond—or so Lori kept telling them, because her other rule was also no cancelations. Unless you were dying, you had to be there.

So, the fact that she had just asked Gabe to bring Hope in her "no big deal" voice, was a very big deal.

"No," he replied bluntly. Automatically. This had ulterior

motives stamped all over it, and he wasn't going to play whatever game his sister was starting.

Lori planted her fists on her hips and scowled at him. "Why not?" she demanded. "Are you embarrassed by us?"

"Yes," he said, knowing full well that an evening putting Hope under the microscope of his family would be 100 percent embarrassing—for her as well as him.

"Gabriel Walsh, as I live and breathe." His sister was huffing in her haughtiest voice.

She was going to try to guilt him any second now, and he wasn't going to have it. He knew her game, and he was going to call her on it, right here, right now.

Crossing his arms, he set his shoulders back and stood at his full height. Planting his feet, he slitted his eyes in his best scowl.

Lori snorted.

"Look. Hope has been good to Ruby. Good to me," he added, knowing she was changing his world as much as Ruby's, every single day. "I'm not going to drag her to a family dinner where you and Dad will scrutinize her like she's some prize hog at a county fair."

His sister folded her arms, matching his position, and cocked her head. "First of all, I am going to do you a huge favor and not tell Hope that you just compared her to a hog. And second," she added when he let out a growl of frustration, "you *will* bring her, and she *will* enjoy herself." She put her hand on his shoulder again. "Because if she's good for you and Ruby, then maybe she'll be good for the rest of us, too. And we deserve to meet each other properly."

Gabe's shoulders sagged under the emotional weight of his sister's hand, the fight draining out of him at her heartfelt words. Maybe she was right. Hell, she was always right, not that he was going to tell her.

It had happened quickly, but Hope had come to mean more to him than he had ever anticipated, and he wanted more of her. But if he was going to pull her into his life, she was going to have to meet his family, and his family was going to have to meet her.

Just like that, having her come to the dinner became a priority. It was the next step in convincing her that she fit into his life. Now all he had to do was convince Hope that there was a space for her in it, and somehow, he knew that would be the hard part.

CHAPTER FOURTEEN

At 2:30 a.m., Gabe quietly unlocked the door to his apartment. He was exhausted, hungry, and he needed a shower, but commandeering all of that was the now familiar tingle of excitement he felt knowing he was about to see Hope.

Usually, she'd hear him unlock the door and be on her feet to greet him. Often she'd heat him a plate from dinner and they would sit on the couch and talk while he ate. Those few moments with her every evening were always his favorite, even though it never led to more. Hope hadn't mentioned their lustful encounter since it happened, probably preferring to pretend it never had. A thought that bothered him more than he wanted to admit, since the bathroom incident had been running on a loop in his brain.

Tonight, though, the apartment was silent. She was in here. He could tell by the way his body was reacting that she was close, but she wasn't up and moving around like she usually was.

Setting his keys on the side table in the entryway, he

moved into the living room, which was lit only by the soft glow of a lamp next to the couch.

And there she was, curled up on her side, fast asleep. In the dimness of the room, her usually sunny-blonde hair looked like a dark gold waterfall cascading over her shoulders. Her hands were tucked under her chin, and her chest rose and fell with the deep breaths of slumber. As he walked closer to her, his gaze caught on two pieces of paper lying on the coffee table in front of her. Two pieces of paper *and a photograph*.

Crouching, he picked up the photo. It was of Carrie, holding a six-month-old Ruby. It was the last photo he'd taken of her. The papers were drawings. One was clearly Ruby's. It was of her, him, and Carrie. She'd put wings on Carrie like she always did when she drew them as a family.

But it was the second drawing that truly captivated him. It was almost identical in design to the one Ruby had created but the rendering of each individual in their trio, meticulously drawn in pencil, was spot on. Completely mesmerizing.

Like Ruby's picture, Carrie had wings. But in Hope's, they were drawn in a way that made them look so realistic he could almost feel their softness. And Carrie looked angelic. Radiant.

Hope had captured her likeness, almost like she'd drawn her from a live portrait. Carrie's hair rioted wildly around her shoulders, and she looked so alive she almost came off the page.

Six years had passed since he'd last seen her, held her, talked to her. As he ran his finger along the beauty of her face, a sad wistfulness gripped his heart. The pain wasn't the same as it used to be. No longer sharp and agonizing. Now only a dull ache, contemplative of what had been his world so long ago. His present grief was a regret that surfaced from time to time, reminding him of all that Ruby had missed while growing up without her mother.

He missed Carrie, and the sting of frustration still hit him when he thought back to those days. He'd been so self-consumed and immersed in his fledgling business that he wasn't aware of how hard things had been for her as a new mother. If he'd known, had paid closer attention, he couldn't help feeling that he could've changed the outcome of her short life.

He'd been carrying his grief for a long time now. He'd also accepted she was gone, the role he'd played in that, and did his best to honor her by raising their daughter as best he could while keeping her memory alive in their home and family. After six years, Carrie had been gone longer than the total time he'd known her, which he found unbelievable. He still loved her, and while he knew a part of him would love her the rest of his life, he didn't long for her the way he once had.

Alone in his bed at night, it wasn't Carrie who crept into his dreams. The hard nights of longing for her had passed, and he no longer felt guilty for not needing her night after night. He hadn't needed or longed for a woman for years.

Not until recently, when his nights had filled with yearning for a certain blonde with dark brown eyes that always seemed to carry a world of sorrow and mistrust in them. A beautiful, creative, giving woman who'd fitted herself into his life effortlessly.

Gazing at Hope sleeping on his couch, that yearning now spread from his heart down to his gut, and lower still. He glanced from Hope to the beautiful drawing she created, then back to Hope again, marveling at her artistry and her caring heart.

Holding the picture of Carrie in his hands reminded him of just how precious life was. And how quickly it could all be taken away. And how much time he had wasted already being afraid of his own emotions.

Unable to go another second without touching her, he traced his finger along the soft curve of her cheek, and she sighed in her sleep. Giving in to his need, and tired of the guilt and resistance he'd been carrying around with his growing feelings, he brushed his lips against hers.

He hadn't meant to wake her, but with a soft inhale, she did just that. He lifted his lips a fraction, keeping them poised a breath above hers while he held her drowsy, fathomless gaze.

For a moment neither of them moved, they just held eye contact, as the warmth of their mutual breaths heated the air around them. Enough time passed that Gabe started to consider that she wasn't on the same page as him after all. Then in one quick, surprising move, Hope tilted her face upward, closing the space between them, her lips rising to meet his.

The kiss exploded, like the weeks of building tension between them culminated into this one moment of pure and frenzied need. Hope's lips consumed his, and when she opened her mouth for him, he dipped his tongue inside, tasting every corner. She moaned, fisting her hands in his shirt and pulling him closer. When the urge to taste more of her became almost overwhelming, he tore his lips free, tracing kisses down her jaw and onto her neck.

"Gabe," she panted, breathless.

Sweet Jesus, the sound of his name on her lips was addictive. He vowed then and there he would do anything for her, to her, just so she'd say his name like that again. He wanted her chanting it over and over as he took her. Wanted her screaming it as he made her come.

The thought of Hope naked and writhing beneath him, shouting his name, made his desire surge like a tidal wave over his entire body. Good Lord, he was a goner for this woman. Could she feel it? Did she feel the same?

Then, all coherent thought fled when she panted a needy, "More, Gabe, please." Her fingers clawed at his shirt, yanking it out of the waistband of his jeans. "I need more this time."

It was all the invitation he needed. Rising up and over her on the couch, he braced himself on one shoulder and slid his hand under her shirt and tugged down the cup of her bra. "More what, sweetheart? Do you want me to touch you here?"

When she nodded enthusiastically, he let his fingers graze her nipples, teasing them lightly until her mewls of pleasure grew into groans of desperation.

Touch wasn't enough. Not nearly enough. Nothing felt like enough with Hope. Not since the first moment he'd met her.

Tugging her shirt all the way up, he said "Fuck, you're so pretty, Hope," right before he lowered his head to her breast. A moment of relief passed through him when he tasted her. The flavor was soft and sweet under his mouth, and he couldn't remember the last time he'd wanted a woman this badly. It was more than simply spending his pent-up lust, more than wanting to lose himself in the sexual bliss of orgasm. It was all Hope. And he was coming to accept it pretty damn quickly.

Her hips lifted, rubbing against him, making him ache. Her head dropped into the cushions of the couch as soft moans of pleasure fell from her lips.

He slid his hand under the waistband of her jeans, then down under her panties, and without hesitation zeroed in on the soft flesh of her core. He stroked his fingers through her, reveling in the evidence that her lust matched his. It was such a fucking turn on, knowing that this woman—who had taken up prime real estate in his brain over the last several weeks—was as desperate for him as he was for her.

"Gabe!"

He could tell she was trying to stay silent, probably mindful that Ruby slept down the hallway. And maybe he should have stopped. At the very least, he should have picked her up and brought her to his room, where he could close the door. It would have been the reasonable thing to do, but since he was pretty much beyond reason now, he didn't move any damn thing other than his fingers as they continued to rub the slick folds between her legs.

He did want her to scream, couldn't wait to hear her unrestrained passion as he lost himself inside her. That time would come. He knew it as much as he knew his own name, but for now, he would have to content himself by making her come so hard she'd never be able to ignore this connection between them again.

He stroked her core mercilessly, while his mouth caressed her breasts with equal devotion. The panting he heard above his head drove him halfway to insanity, but he never lost focus. Not even when the pressure in his own body built until it was nearly impossible to endure. Her pleasure here was paramount. He was starving for it, and he knew she was close, could feel her muscles tightening around his fingers. Still, he could feel her holding back, not wanting to let go. Resisting her pleasure.

Not tonight, sweetheart.

He moved his lips to her ear, sucking her earlobe into his

mouth, then biting it gently. She responded with a sharp gasp that bordered on a cry.

"Give it to me," he demanded, his voice thick and heavy with his own desire. To coax her over the edge, he scooped his two fingers inside her, pressing forward and rubbing. "Give it all to me."

And at the command of his words and actions, she splintered, her spine bowed up, her breasts thrusting toward his chest with the momentum. She clamped a hand over her mouth hard, stifling a scream as she came forcefully beneath him.

Slowing his strokes, he watched her ride out the last of her orgasm. Her eyes were closed, and her chest heaved, gulping down greedy breaths. Her hair stuck to the overheated skin of her face and neck. She'd never looked more beautiful.

Dropping his head to her breasts, he enjoyed their softness against his skin, almost as much as the thud of Hope's heart racing beneath them. That had easily ranked as one of the most erotic experiences in his history and he hadn't even come. His rock-hard erection throbbed painfully against his jeans as a reminder.

As Hope's body relaxed in the aftermath of bliss, the sexy purr of satisfaction that came from her throat only made things...harder. He pressed his forehead to hers, trying to recompose himself.

"You're killing me," he growled against her cheek, and to his surprise she giggled. He leaned back to better see her face. "Didn't anyone ever warn you not to laugh at a man who's just rocked your world?"

Her eyes flashed in the dim light. "Or what?" she whispered, her smile luminous and heart stopping. She wiggled her hips against his aching cock.

He sucked in a breath. "Careful," he cautioned them both, lifting himself from her before he went off in his pants.

Hope took the opportunity of his weight being off her to switch their positions, until she had him pressed into a sitting position on the couch with her straddled across his lap. And before he knew it, she was running her hands down his chest and under his shirt, her lips parted, her blonde hair falling around her glowing golden in the soft light of the lamp, making her look like a goddess.

A goddess who knew what she wanted and was going for it.

Just when he thought she was going to devour him, her eyes met his earnestly. "Can I be honest?" She asked, her brown eyes sparkling with vulnerability.

"Always," he replied immediately, because that was what he wanted most between them. Honesty.

"I'm conflicted. About this. About us."

Gabe smoothed a lock of hair away from her face. "Yeah, I know." He felt the same. He'd been back and forth over his feelings for Hope so many times he was giving himself whiplash. She was his nanny. He had an impressionable young daughter sleeping down the hall. But he was also so fucking lonely it hurt, and he hadn't even realized it until Hope had walked into his life. Like there was an emptiness in his heart that only she could fill.

Put it all together and the push and pull of the conflict was killing him. So yeah, he got it. He knew exactly what she was trying to say.

"I want you Gabe." She pressed into him a little bit and he hissed out a breath. He was still harder than a steel rod, but he was getting used to being in that state around her. "I don't want to confuse things. I don't want to confuse Ruby.

But it doesn't stop how I feel when I'm with you. How you make me feel."

Her eyes dropped and she frowned. He hated that look on her. "Sweetheart, look at me." He nudged her chin up until their eyes met. "I know. This came out of nowhere for both of us. It's okay if we just take this slow and steady until we know where it's going."

She stared at him blankly and his heart kicked up a notch. "Or we end it here and just keep things professional." He didn't love that idea, but he wanted her to know it was an option, and he would respect it if that's what she chose.

To his relief she shook her head immediately. "I think we've proved we can't keep things professional." She eyed him coyly. "But maybe we can go for discreet and slow?" She glanced away, considered something, then looked back at him. "Gabe, in all honesty, I don't know how much or what I can give you other than," she rubbed lightly against him again, "this. I know that sounds crass. When I think about the idea of more with you, it sounds too good to be true. But I have some things I am working through, personally, and I just don't think I have the capacity to offer more right now."

Maybe this was why he was so drawn to her. They were more similar than he'd ever thought possible. They were on the same wavelength. Feeling the same conflicting feelings, just from different lenses. She got him, even without knowing his whole story. And he got her in the same way.

No wonder she'd been consuming his every thought for weeks now.

Leaning up, he kissed the tip of her nose. It had not escaped him that he had the single most attractive woman he'd ever met straddling his lap while having one of the most honest conversations with a person he'd ever had.

"I don't need more right now. I've got everything I need

right here, in this apartment. On my lap. How about we just start there for today?" He suggested before brushing his lips against hers in a kiss.

He nibbled across her mouth, feeling her smile against him. Then she opened for him, and he took, like he always did, diving deep, consuming. She matched him kiss for kiss, heartbeat for heartbeat. It was intoxicating, and within seconds they were back where they started. Grinding and grunting softly as they pressed into each other like they were trying to become one body.

Pressing her hips into his achingly stiff cock, she whispered urgently, "Gabe, when I said I want more this time, I meant it." She kissed him softly on the mouth. "I want you inside me. I need to feel you inside me. Please."

Oh. Fuck. Her words. Her body. Her hands running over the waist of his jeans. How was he supposed to resist her? He swore harsh and low, then with what he felt was monumental self-control on his end, he lifted her off him and onto the couch, before he stood up.

She lay sprawled, hair wild around her, naked breasts bared to him in all their glory. Perfection. Except for the bewildered look in her beautiful dark eyes.

"Hope..." He tucked himself in and re-buttoned his fly. When had that come undone? "I can't."

Hurt shone, vivid and painful, in her eyes. Then she blinked, and her gaze dropped, hiding from him. She sat up, pulling her bra into place and straightening her shirt, her movements jerky. "Right, no problem. I get it."

He crouched and grabbed her shaking hands, stilling them. He waited until she raised her gaze to meet his. She was trying to keep her eyes emotionless, but he could see the hurt brimming there, right below the surface.

"No," he said, shaking his head. "You don't get it."

Hope tugged her hands, but he held firm, refusing to let go until she heard him out.

"Hope, I don't have a condom," he admitted, not bothering to disguise his frustration and embarrassment. He'd never forgive himself for not being prepared for this moment with her, but sex hadn't been part of his life for a while now, and condoms weren't something he kept freshly stocked. Although he was going to change that ASAP.

Hope stared at him for a beat. She blinked several times as if trying to compute the information. After another beat, the hurt in her eyes was replaced with genuine amusement. Considering he was still painfully hard in his jeans, he could safely say she was the only one amused.

"I see," she said, biting her lip as if to keep from laughing.

Gabe held her gaze, not even smiling. "When I get inside you, Hope Morgan, we are both going to come so hard it's going to ruin us for anyone else."

She gasped and her eyes widened, all humor gone.

Good, he'd shocked her. "But I'm not going to do it without protection. Not until you know me better, and—" He paused, holding eye contact so he could be sure she was hearing and understanding everything he was saying. "Not until you trust me. You deserve better than that. Ok?"

Hope bit her lip again, nodding slowly.

"Ok." In one quick pull he got her up to her feet, then because he wanted to, he tugged her in for a long slow kiss.

When he released her, they were both breathless.

"Come with Ruby and me to a family dinner at my sister's tomorrow," he heard himself saying.

"What?" Hope asked, her stunned eyes widening as she switched gears from a searing hot kiss to a family dinner invite.

"I want you to come," he said, then admitted, "And my sister might have told me to invite you. She won't let it go until I bring you."

Hope looked at him skeptically. "Are you sure that's a good idea? Don't you think it would be confusing for Ruby?"

Of course, she would be thinking this through, considering feelings across the board. She was compassionate that way, nurturing, and suddenly she didn't seem as young or immature as his sister was worried about.

"You're Ruby's nanny. And she loves you. She'd be thrilled to have you there. You're important to her." He stopped before he said anything stupid. Something like, *you're important to me.* This wasn't the time to scare her or put too much pressure on her. Instead, he ran his knuckle down her cheek, shifting a strand of her golden hair over her shoulder. "It'd make us both happy to have you join a family dinner and meet everyone. Besides, you never know when one of them might walk in here with food, so it's probably best if you recognized them all."

She looked unconvinced, so he added a gentle "please" and saw the shift in her eyes the instant she relented. When she nodded her assent, he couldn't stop the giant smile that bloomed across his face or the relief that flooded his chest. He refused to delve into why her agreeing to spend time with all of his family made him so happy. He was afraid to know why.

"Ruby and I will come and get you tomorrow at 5:30." And all of a sudden, he was more excited about a family dinner than he had been—ever.

CHAPTER FIFTEEN

At 5:30 sharp the next day, a barely audible knock on Hope's front door made her leap from her seat on the couch like a gunshot had gone off.

Ivy, who'd been sitting beside her with her nose in a book, stared at her as if she'd finally come undone.

"What's wrong with you?" Ivy demanded in a tone that confirmed she indeed thought Hope was losing it.

Hope pressed her hand to her pounding heart and whispered, "They're here." Her excitement to see Gabe and Ruby was undone by her worry about what would happen next. Her palms broke out in a cold sweat. This was stupid. She had no reason whatsoever to be nervous. This wasn't a date. It wasn't some official meeting of the parents. It was a casual family dinner. Nothing more.

She looked to Ivy for moral support and found her grinning.

"This isn't funny," she hissed, as Ivy got up and went to the door without taking her gaze off Hope, her wicked grin morphing into an evil chuckle.

It wasn't until she opened the door that Ivy finally

turned her attention from Hope to Ruby, who stood in the doorway. "Hey, cutie," Ivy said as she bent to fist bump the little girl.

Hope's gaze shot straight to the man behind the girl, and her heart tripped over itself when his mossy-green eyes met and held hers and all the memories of last night's kiss, and orgasm, passed between them.

As they continued to stand there, staring at each other, the world as Hope knew it fell away from her. The muted sounds of Ivy and Ruby chatting faded into the background. Her apartment disappeared into a blur of objects and color that could have been anywhere or anything. All she could focus on was Gabe's presence dominating the doorway. All she could hear was the pounding of her own heart.

"Hope?"

She watched his gorgeous, sexy as hell face morph into a boyish grin, even though his lips hadn't moved to speak.

"Hope?!" came the sharp call again, wrenching her out of her reverie like a bucket of ice water on the head.

"Holy Mother of God, what planet are you on right now?" Ivy asked under her breath.

Hope's gaze snapped from Gabe, who now sported a cocky know-it-all grin, to Ivy, who looked amused.

Ivy crossed her arms. "Can you get your head out of the gutter? There are children present."

Mortified, Hope sprang into action, grabbing her purse and stepping into her shoes. Her face flushed with the knowledge that she'd just been caught lusting after her landlord slash employer slash orgasm giver with his daughter present.

"Ivy, what's it mean to have your head in a gutter?" Ruby asked, in her sweet, innocent little voice.

Oh God.

"Well, sweetheart," Ivy explained in an impressive schoolteacher tone. "It means that Hope is in a fantasy world. Has been all day, dreaming about your da—"

"Okay!" interjected Hope a little too loudly, as she grabbed the potted plant—that she bought as thank-you-for-dinner gift—from the credenza next to the door. "Let's go, shall we?"

She smiled as brightly as she could as she ushered Ruby out, and breezed past Gabe, who was still grinning at her like he'd won some competition. She tried not to inhale as she passed him, lest she further embarrass herself by drooling over his scent.

Ruby's heartfelt, non-stop chatter was the only thing that saved Hope from further humiliation as the trio made their way down the stairs and out the door to where Gabe's grey Bronco was parked just outside the building. When he opened the passenger side for Hope there was a knowing grin etched on his face, which she tried her best to ignore. Making sure not to touch any part of her body to his, she slid past him and into her seat. A low, masculine chuckle was the last she heard before he shut the door and skirted the front of the vehicle to make his way to the driver's seat.

Looking around her, she realized it was her first time in Gabe's car. Like his apartment, it was neat and no-frills. Sturdy and strong looking, like its owner. It wasn't a new car, and smelled like the perfect mix of both him and Ruby, something between cedar wood and sugar cookie. She inhaled deeply and sat back, content to listen to the little girl behind her fill the space with her random six-year-old musings, while the man beside her competently pulled out of the parking space and onto the street.

Twenty minutes later, fully caught up on Ruby's latest hot takes, they pulled up in front of a sweet little two-story house. It was already quite dark, but Hope could see a well-lit path leading past the front garden up to a cozy looking porch, complete with a swing. Behind her, she heard Ruby unbuckle her seat belt.

"We're here!" Ruby scooted out of the car, sprinted up the pathway, and disappeared inside the house.

She inhaled a nervous breath. The warmth of a big hand covered her tightly clasped ones on her lap. His heat seeped into her, spreading through her body and quieting her nerves before settling low in her belly.

"Hope," he said, his voice deep and sexy. Meeting his molten green gaze, she was suddenly aware that maybe, just maybe, she wasn't the only one affected by the simple touch.

For a moment, they merely looked at each other. When Hope licked her suddenly dry lips, his gaze shifted to catch the movement, and a low guttural sound rumbled up from his throat. He leaned forward, but the movement was too quick, and he hadn't unbuckled yet. His big chest jarred against the security lock on his seat belt, barring him from closing the distance between them.

Hope tried to stifle her giggle, but failed and it ended up coming out of her nose in a very unladylike snort.

"It's a sign." She unbuckled her own belt. Then, reaching over slowly and provocatively so that her breasts brushed his chest, she unbuckled his belt for him. "We should go in," she whispered, her mouth an inch from his. Her body thrilled when his eyes dilated and darkened. She felt feminine and powerful knowing that she, and she alone, was causing this normally controlled man to unravel before her.

Just to tease him a little more, she sucked in a soft breath, catching her lower lip between her teeth, then jumped out of the car before he could react.

Halting at the mouth of the walkway, she heard Gabe's

footsteps come up to stand beside her, then felt his palm slide down to the small of her back, rubbing lightly.

"You'll pay for that," he said, his voice a husky grumble next to her ear as his hand dipped to palm her butt.

Looking up at him, she said, "That better be a promise."

He chuckled. "You are everything I expected you wouldn't be, Hope Morgan." He guided her up the walkway. "Come on. They're waiting."

Lori stood in the open doorway, arms wrapped around herself, the shriek of children behind her. "What's taking you so long?" she demanded. "It's freezing and holding the door for you is letting all the cold air in. Get inside already." She stood back and gestured Hope and Gabe inside, shutting the door quickly behind them. She eyed them suspiciously. "What took you two so long?"

Gabe thrust a bottle of wine at his sister, ignoring her question, and shrugged out of his coat, inhaling deeply. "Smells like chicken cacciatore," he said appreciatively. "My favorite."

Lori's eyes narrowed, but she didn't push the topic. Instead, her gaze locked on the potted plant in Hope's hands. "Is that for me?" she asked, smiling prettily.

The Walsh smile had surely brought a great many to their knees, Hope mused, as she held out the plant.

"Yes. Thank you so much for inviting me. It was really kind of you to include me."

"Please," Lori replied, waving away Hope's gratitude. "It's our pleasure to get to know Ruby's ... babysitter." Lori sent Gabe a savvy side eye, then took Hope by the elbow and led her down a hallway to a living room.

On the floor in the center of the room, Ruby and a girl and a boy—who she guessed to be around eight and twelve, respectively—crowded around a cage. An older man, who

Hope recognized instantly as Gabe's father, sat on a love seat, watching her closely, his expression giving nothing away.

He had the Walsh look through and through. His head was full of the same dark hair, although his was generously infused with gray, giving him a striking silver fox look. His eyes were an identical mossy green, and though they looked older, crinkling endearingly around the edges, they were just as mesmerizing as they observed her.

Across from him, sitting on an easy chair with a beer in one hand, was a man Hope gauged to be in his mid-forties. His smile was warm and friendly, and he stood as Lori all but dragged Hope into the room.

"Eva! George! Get that rat out of here. I told you not to bring that thing into the living room," she said in a very remarkable mother-knows-best voice.

The boy rolled his eyes defiantly. "But Mom, he's in his cage. Plus, he's a hamster, not a rat."

"I don't care if it's the King of England's royal rodent. I said not in the living room, and I meant it, George."

And that was clearly that, because despite another cheeky eyeroll, the boy muttered, "Fine" under his breath before scrambling up, holding the cage precariously in one hand.

"Not so fast. We have a guest," Lori said briskly, before the children could race from the room. "This is Ruby's new babysitter, Miss Morgan. Mind your manners and say a proper hello."

Hope couldn't help but cringe at the way Lori said *babysitter*, letting the word drawl off her tongue with loaded ambiguity. Hope shot an uncomfortable look at Gabe, but he only grimaced and shrugged.

Oblivious, Ruby raced up to her and threw her arms around her waist.

"She's my favorite," she announced to her cousins. "The best."

And Hope's heart melted as she ran her hand down the little girl's riot of wavy hair.

After a polite hello and introductions, the three children disappeared up a set of stairs, hamster cage in tow.

She officially met Lori's husband when he pressed a glass of wine into her hand. "Here, you look like you could use this," he said in a friendly tone that matched his smile. "I'm Craig. I love Lori, and she's the mother of my children, but I'll be the first to say she can be a bit intense."

"Thanks," Hope said and took a grateful sip of the crisp chardonnay he'd given her.

"It comes from a good place," he explained. "She just loves so hard, it can be intimidating. I always call her the ultimate mama bear." Hope smiled, because from what she'd learned about Lori so far, that description suited her perfectly.

They fell into companionable conversation and, for the first time since she arrived that evening, she relaxed. When his sister asked him to, Gabe left Hope's side for the first time all night and wandered upstairs to get the children for dinner.

"CRAIG!" Lori bellowed from the kitchen a few minutes later, and Craig lifted his brows at Hope in a "see what I mean" gesture before obediently moving toward where he'd been beckoned.

"She has him well trained," said a gravelly, amused-sounding voice from behind her.

Hope startled, turning to come face to face with Connor, whom she'd been briefly introduced to earlier. He'd been quiet most of the evening, sitting in an easy chair sipping a drink and watching his family. But he came up to her now, his eyes warm and friendly. It was like looking at Gabe if he'd gone through a twenty-year time warp into the future.

"I'm pretty sure she gets it from her Irish grandmother, who was bossy and tenacious as hell. You couldn't say no to that woman. When she said *walk*, you *ran*. When she said *run,* you *flew*." His laugh was a low rumble that sounded identical to his son's. "Lori is the same. Can't get mad at her for it though, my girl could lead an army," he said proudly before his smile turned wistful. "She's different from her mother. Beth was as quiet and calm as they came. Subtle, but no less assertive. She had her own way of getting you to do what she wanted. Gabriel is more like her in that way."

Hope only nodded, afraid that if she interrupted, she might stop this stream of privileged insight into the Walsh family. Gabe had never mentioned his mother, although Hope knew she had passed when Gabe was still a young boy.

"There aren't many like my Beth," he went on. "She was all love and softness. It was a miracle she took on the likes of a rebel like me, but once I had her, I never let go. I held on until she took her last breath, and every day since, I guess. Not many are lucky enough to find love like that twice in a lifetime. Sure as hell not an old grump like me." He eyed Gabe who now stood in the living room doorway, shoulder against the frame, arms crossed, eyes hooded as he watched them from across the room.

Connor turned back to Hope with a twinkle in his green eyes. "Doesn't mean you should write off that possibility for both of us grumpy Walsh men. Sometimes that kind of love does strike twice in one lifetime." With a mischievous wink, he patted her shoulder and moved toward the kitchen, leaving Hope standing there dumb-struck in the wake of his words, her heart fluttering chaotically in her chest.

Dinner was a noisy, chaotic affair. The kids were loud, Lori even louder, and everyone seemed comfortable in the chaos, a conversational banter flowing easily throughout it all.

Craig worked beside his wife as they served the meal in tandem. Connor sat quietly at the head of the table, a content smile on his face as he sliced the chicken on his plate. Gabe watched Hope over the rim of his glass, with a gleam in his eye that had her wondering what he was think-ing, and if he overheard what his father has said to her.

"Dad!" Lori scolded. "You can't start eating before every-one's been served." She scowled as she dished up another plate and handed it to Gabe.

"Oh, honey," Connor said sheepishly as he placed his fork and knife back down beside his plate. "You know I can't resist digging into your chicken. It's better than your moth-er's—rest her soul."

Lori snorted a laugh, but the stress line between her eyes eased as her face broke into a smile. "It is not. Nothing beats Mom's."

A twist of nostalgia squeezed Hope's heart. She'd had this growing up. A wild and noisy dinner table with her parents and brother. Often relatives and friends were also present. Good food, good laughs, games afterward. She had loved those evenings. Sitting in on one now made her realize how much she'd missed them; how empty her life had been without them.

For the last few months, and honestly even for the years after her cousin had planted the seed of doubt, she had convinced herself that everything she'd had growing up was a carefully curated facade. Now, as she took in this family banter around her, she realized how wrong she'd been.

Across the table, Ruby laughed at something Eva had said. Ruby hadn't been adopted, but she had lost her birth mother, too. Her aunt Lori was probably the closest thing to a mother figure she'd ever known. This family was far from perfect, yet this scene wasn't fake just because pieces were missing. This was as real a family as any Hope had seen. People who loved each other, stuck it out for each other, and were there for each other through the best and the worst life had to offer.

A surge of regret hit Hope in the chest, and she pressed her palm to the center where the ache throbbed painfully. For the second time since she'd been thrust into the Walshes' world, she felt the sting of clarity. She'd let her own bitterness and hurt rob her of precious time with the only family she had.

Abruptly, Hope stood. The entire table went silent instantly. Forks paused midair. Seven sets of eyes swiveled to look at her. Her face flamed, but she couldn't move, her fist still pressed to where her heart beat wildly.

Gabe's chair scraped the floor as he pushed it back to stand beside her. "Hope?" he asked, concern etched in his tone and face.

God, they must think she was a lunatic, and she couldn't blame them, but when she glanced around the table, all she saw were looks of genuine concern.

"I—I'm sorry," she stammered. Her heartbeat was in her throat choking her words. She needed air. She needed to get out of here.

Memories of Christmas assailed her. Her father's pale stricken face, her mother's tears, her brother's quiet fury. Her own tantrum. Her inability to see the other side, to accept her parents had never meant to hurt her. She'd reacted on the wave of her anger and chosen to leave. And it wasn't until sitting here tonight with the Walsh family that she truly realized she'd made the wrong choice.

Gripping the back of her chair she said again, "I'm sorry," but this time she wasn't sure if it was to the table or to her own family back home who couldn't hear her.

Lori cleared her throat. "Gabe, why don't you take Hope out back and show her the new porch Craig put in? Kids, you help me clear the table so we can get dessert going."

And just like that, the flurry of activity and voices resumed. Gabe's fingers entwined with hers as he pulled her towards a set of French doors. Cold air washed over her flushed cheeks as he led her outside, and she closed her eyes, sighing in relief.

After a couple of deep breaths had cleared the ache in her chest, she felt stupid. She'd totally overreacted, embarrassing both herself and Gabe.

"I'm sorry," she said, wrapping her arms around herself as she stood with her back to the door, staring into the darkness.

Gabe moved behind her until their bodies touched.

He rested his chin on the top of her head as he held her tightly. Like a glutton, she snuggled against him, desperate to soak up every last drop of his warmth.

"Nothing to be sorry about," was all he said as he rubbed his hands up and down her arms, creating more heat.

She didn't know how to explain her ridiculous overreaction. How could she tell him that she had just realized she'd run away from her family because she was angry and unforgiving? How could she explain that it had taken his six-year-old daughter and his wild and boisterous family to yank her out of her own selfishness?

She couldn't. So instead, she said, "You have a great family, Gabe."

She felt him shrug. "We've had our moments. We've been through a lot over the years. When my mom died, my dad and sister tried to fill the gap." His arms tightened around her, as if he was drawing strength from her as well. "I didn't make it easy for them. In fact, I was a pretty big dick. When I met Carrie, I leveled off for a bit. Things were normal-ish. Then..."

Hope clung to him in the silence that followed. A world of unspoken pain and loss floated around them like dust that looks ethereal when caught in the moonlight but in the end is still just dust.

"When Carrie died, I went dark. Lori dragged me out of my black hole kicking and screaming, all while running my life and Ruby's like a drill sergeant. It took a couple years before I could pull my own weight. Now we are where we are. Who we are. Crazy, and loud as hell. But loyal and, for the most part, steady."

His words settled between them. Hope ran everything he'd told her through her head, trying to piece together the trajectory of his life from the broken young boy he'd been when his mom died, to the angry, rebellious teenager who pushed against his father and sister's best intentions at every turn, to his more recent past, the heartbroken father of an infant grieving the loss of his wife. He'd said his sister had to drag him back to his life, but Hope didn't think that was completely true. In the end, he'd faced reality head on. He hadn't run away in resentment like she had.

"Every family goes through their own shit cycle, Hope. No one is exempt, and no family is perfect. But they're family and in the end, it's all we got."

Tears pricked her eyes. She suddenly missed her parents

so much, yet the hurt of their lie still bubbled at the surface. When she thought back to the years she had believed that they were her biological parents, she felt stupid, embarrassed, and ashamed. Those were hard feelings to forget.

"Sometimes," she whispered, "what you thought was all you had was never really yours to begin with."

His arms tightened around her, drawing her closer. "Do you think that because you're adopted?"

Like water turning to ice in the cold, Gabe felt Hope go still against him. And since he was obviously the cold in this equation, he unwrapped his arms from around her, gently turning her so he could look into her eyes instead.

"Hope?"

"How did you know that?" she asked, hugging herself, and her vulnerability nearly killed him.

"If you're expecting my six-year-old to keep your secrets, I hate to burst your bubble, but..."

She looked down at her feet, clearly embarrassed, but he thought he saw the corner of her mouth curl up the tiniest bit. "Right."

He hated the tremor of her voice, hated that she'd started trembling, hated that she was hurting in any way. He rubbed her arms again, willing his body heat into hers. Finally, she lifted her gaze to look at him, her eyes bright in a way that told him she was fighting back tears. Then she simply sighed and leaned forward to rest her forehead against his chest.

"For most of my life, I thought I was a Morgan by blood." The sound of her voice was muffled against his chest, and he had to strain to hear her. She said something else, but he didn't catch it, so he hooked a finger under her chin and tipped her head up to face him.

Her eyes were both dark and luminous and, in that moment, she looked so open and beautiful it took his breath away.

When her lower lip quivered, he knew she was hanging on by a thread.

"I found out the truth when I was sixteen. Well, kind of." Her lips pressed together in a thin line as she struggled for control. "At my sixteenth birthday my cousin dropped the bomb, but I didn't believe it. Or didn't want to. But it was too late, the doubt was there." She paused to take a deep breath. "I spent years comparing every little detail about myself against my family, looking for similarities. Differences. It was torture. Then, this past Christmas I gave my parents a genetic test kit and, well, that did it. The truth came out."

She made a horrible, strangled sound that made him want to whisk her away to another time. Away from anything that could hurt her, that made her feel pain. But he couldn't. All he could do was let her talk, let her get out what had obviously been weighing on her heart for far too long.

"For all those years, I thought I was someone I wasn't." A big tear spilled over her lower lashes and broke his heart as it rolled slowly down her cheek. "And it hurt," she said, pressing her fist to the center of her chest like there was an open wound there, and she was trying to stifle the blood flow. "It hurt so, so much, because it felt like everything up until then had been a lie. But then I met you and Ruby, and you've both lost so much, more than I can imagine, but still, you have this." She gestured to the house behind them. "You have a family that you let fill the gaps. And I realized, I realized—" She broke off on a choked sob.

He drew her against him until not even a sheet of paper could fit between. "Family is what you make it, Hope," he told her. "We don't often get to choose how it works out, or who gets to be in it. Family isn't always about blood. It's about heart." He rubbed her back. "Did they give you love?"

"Yes," she said emphatically. "Yes. They only ever loved me. It's me who's hurting them now."

He said nothing to that, because he didn't believe it. They stood wrapped up in each other and might have stayed that way for the rest of the night, but the back door swung open, and his sister poked her head out.

"Sugar is on the table, so get inside, you two. Plus, stay out here any longer and you'll freeze your rear ends clean off."

The door shut behind her, and Gabe felt Hope shaking in his arms. For one horrible moment he thought she was crying again, but much to his relief he realized she was shaking with laughter, and when she pulled back from him, a smile shone straight through to her eyes.

Then, surprising him, she stretched up onto her tiptoes and kissed him. She didn't demand anything, simply offered him a soft, sweet kiss. Then she lifted her head and looked at him for a beat before lowering back to the flat of her feet.

"One thing is certain," she said, eyes shining bright with emotion and now also amusement. "Older siblings, biological or not, are a pain in the ass."

"Amen to that." He laughed, and slinging his arm around her shoulders, they walked back inside, together.

CHAPTER SIXTEEN

The rest of the evening passed quickly. The "sugar" that Lori had called them back for ended up being a chocolate trifle that Gabe's father had made, and Hope had to stifle a moan with every creamy bite. It wasn't as good as the dessert Gabe had dished out last night, but it sure came close.

After trifle, they played charades, during which she and Ruby were teamed up and effortlessly won round after round against all the others. Hope tried not to notice Gabe's assessing gaze as he watched the two of them whenever it was their turn.

She also couldn't help but notice how the Walsh patriarch also kept a steady eye on her and Ruby throughout the evening. Occasionally a small smile etched his rugged face, other times he was more pensive, and she recalled his words from earlier. *Sometimes that kind of love does strike twice in one lifetime.*

Was that what Gabe was looking for? A second chance at love? He hadn't indicated as much to her. Then again, she could see why he might be looking for some stability for Ruby. A maternal figure beyond that of her aunt.

And if stability was what he was after, she hated to disappoint, but he wasn't going to find it with her. If and when Gabe decided to move on he deserved to have a woman who came with far less baggage. He'd earned that after all he'd been through already, and the guilt of knowing she had more baggage that she hadn't yet disclosed to him sunk like a stone in her gut.

So, she put Gabe and his father's considering looks out of her mind.

After one particularly impressive round of charades, she and Ruby both collapsed on the couch, out of breath and sweaty from their efforts. They'd actually garnered a round of applause for Hope's correct guess of Ruby's portrayal of Beauty and the Beast.

Looking smug, and not the least bit humble, Ruby informed everyone, "We practice a lot of acting when Hope comes over. We come up with some great performances."

From his spot on the couch, Gabe cocked an eyebrow. "I'd like to see these *performances* some time, ladies."

"Okay, Daddy! Tomorrow, when Hope comes over, we'll make a play and act it out for you when you come home at bedtime."

"I can hardly wait," he said, drawing Ruby into his embrace as she climbed up into his lap.

"We'll make popcorn, so it'll be like a real show, right, Hope?" Ruby bounced excitedly on her father's lap.

Hope nodded, feeling the eyes of all the other Walshes watching her.

It all sounded so domestic, so very perfect, and she barely resisted squirming in her seat under the scrutiny. She met Lori's eyes across the living room and lowered her gaze at what she saw there. Unspoken concern emanated from Gabe's older sister, and Hope couldn't disagree with her.

It was one thing to get in too deep with Gabe, but another to raise Ruby's hopes until she confused the reality of their situation with her dream of having a perfect family.

Hope had to make sure that didn't happen. She needed to keep their attachments and boundaries clear. Unfortunately, with each passing day, that was getting harder and harder to do.

~

It was 9 p.m. when they got home. Ruby had almost fallen asleep in the back seat, but Hope had kept her talking the entire car ride to prevent it, knowing a catnap this late at night would spell disaster for bedtime.

Gabe coaxed a sleepy Ruby out of the car and pushed her ahead of him up the steps to their apartment.

She followed them, trying not to notice how very fine Gabe's butt looked in his jeans as he climbed.

She failed. His was too fine an ass not to appreciate.

Wanting him was like breathing, pure instinct and reflex. There wasn't any point in denying it. In fact, she was beyond denying it, especially after last night's mind-blowing orgasm on his couch.

She wanted more of him, more with him. It was the emotional piece that terrified her. In her heart she was still so torn over how much of herself she should or could share with him. It was tricky for her to get invested with someone emotionally. Especially a man like Gabe. A man who came family ready and needed someone steady. Someone not screwed up, confused, and aimless like her.

Opening up to him earlier had been freeing and

comforting in one. She'd shared so many of her innermost fears and anxieties, and yet their conversation had reminded her that there was a whole lot more she needed to work through in her own life before she could pretend to be a part of someone else's.

No, her brain knew she was nowhere in the vicinity of ready to play real life with Gabe. But her body—well, her body had already had its sights set on Gabriel Walsh in a very big way, and she couldn't resist jumping him much longer. She was impressed by her herculean resolve thus far.

There was also Ruby to consider. She cared for that little girl—so much. Both of them were getting more and more attached to each other every day. She didn't want to confuse Ruby or give her false hope.

Hope knew how heartbreaking it could be to wake up one day and realize that the family you thought you'd had was an illusion.

She couldn't and wouldn't do that to Ruby. If she and Gabe were going to keep giving into their undeniable attraction, it would have to be discreet. At least until Hope sorted through her endless pile of emotional baggage.

They arrived on the apartment level, but Hope was so deep in the chaos of her thoughts she hadn't noticed where they were until she ran into Gabe's back, and his very fine ass, in front of his door. She grabbed onto either side of his hips to steady herself. Gabe glanced over his shoulder and his eyes heated when they met hers. He gave her a devilish grin.

"You coming in?" he asked, although it sounded more like a statement than a question.

With effort, Hope took a step backward down the hall. Hadn't she just been giving herself a lecture on emotional distance and discretion? "Um." Stalling, she continued retreating toward her apartment.

Ruby had already disappeared inside hers, presumably heading straight to her bedroom.

"I don't think coming in is a good idea."

Gabe pinned her with an enticing look. "Or," he said, his voice husky and panty-melting. "It's a great idea." He stared at her, his eyes soft and inviting. "Hope, I'm done with this game. Come inside. Let me tuck Ruby into bed. She's so exhausted she'll be out in less than a minute. You and I can have a drink." He gave her a wicked, suggestive smile. "Then maybe, if you're lucky, I'll let you make out with me for a bit."

The problem was, she didn't want to just make out. She wanted to tear his clothes off with her teeth and finally get her hands on his magnificent body. Trying to control the surge of heat that came with her thoughts, she lowered her gaze to the floor and chewed on her bottom lip.

In any other world, she would have followed him right through his door and into his bedroom. But this wasn't any other world. This was her world, and in her world, Gabe had a precious and impressionable six-year-old girl who had lost one mother and was quickly growing a strong attachment to someone she thought could fill the gap. Hope was no one's mother figure.

If only she didn't have this darn irresistible attraction to the sexy father in this little triangle, it would be much easier to set clear boundaries with Ruby. But easy or not, bound-aries had to be set. They couldn't risk Ruby walking in on them like she had at the bar that very first night when Gabe had almost kissed her, and they especially couldn't ruin the little girl's illusion of family the way her own had been shattered.

Squaring her shoulders, Hope met Gabe's gaze. Not an easy feat, since he was looking at her with a palpable heat and promise of untold pleasure. Being with him would be combustible. Their few encounters so far had proven their chemistry was off the charts. Still, this wasn't only about the two of them, so she held firm. She was doing the right thing. She knew it.

Right?

"I can't, Gabe," she said, sounding far surer of herself than she felt. "We have to think of Ruby. It's not fair to put her in the middle just so we can scratch this... this itch."

Gabe's eyes narrowed. The look in his green eyes told her that her words had replaced the sizzle with anger and—even worse—hurt, too. He stepped into her space as he confronted her, and she tried not to cower under his cold glare.

"You think that I'm not thinking about Ruby?" He bent to meet her now faltering gaze. "You think I want to scratch an *itch*?" His voice was low and lethal. Angry.

She'd never heard him speak to anyone like this before. Shame crept up her neck and across her face. "No, of course not. I didn't mean it like that."

"Then what did you mean?" The rumble of barely contained fury in his voice kept her silent.

"Let me tell you two things about me, Hope Morgan, since you haven't already figured them out on your own. One, everything I do, every move I make, I do with Ruby's best interest in mind. Always. And two, this." He surprised her by grabbing her shoulders, hauling her up to her toes, and pressing his mouth to hers in a kiss that devoured and devastated her at the same time.

It was hot, and wet, and hard. It was all frustrated, pent-up need.

She must have been insane, given his level of anger with her, but she melted against him instantly, her body responding with a will of its own. Her nipples pebbled against his chest, and he groaned as she rubbed them against his pecs. He slanted his head, taking her mouth in a deeper kiss, his hands fisted in her hair, holding her close so she couldn't move or feel anything but the glorious heat of his mouth moving over hers.

Finally, he pulled away, his chest heaving. "This," he repeated, "is not a fucking itch." He let go of her as abruptly as he'd drawn her in, and she staggered at the loss of his touch.

Gabe ran a hand through his hair roughly, and she watched as his usual control slid back into place. "I'm going to tuck Ruby in," he said finally, then he turned to face his apartment.

"Gabe," she called after him, but her voice didn't carry any weight. She didn't know what to say, could only feel an incredible loss and emptiness as he walked away from her.

CHAPTER SEVENTEEN

A fucking itch. That's all he was to her. Gabe rolled over in his bed and tucked his hands behind his head, staring up at the ceiling like he had been for the last hour.

He should have known. A woman like her wouldn't want to get mixed up with the likes of him for anything more than a fling. He felt stupid for thinking it could be more. She might be adopted, but she was a Morgan through and through. Cultured, affluent, well-bred. All the things he was not and never would be.

Women like Hope didn't have relationships with single fathers who ran bars and got by on grit alone. No, if and when Hope Morgan decided on a relationship, it was going to be with some Harvard educated suit, with a big brain, bigger mouth, and a massive bank account.

Gabe's body burned with anger, frustration, and goddammit, unsated lust. But even as the bitterness twisted his gut, the notion that she was the vain aristocrat that he'd originally thought her to be had shattered over the last couple of months. He had seen a side of Hope that was the opposite of that.

He'd watched her interact with his daughter, unnerved by how effortlessly she had slipped into his life, filling it with a peace and fulfillment he hadn't known in years. Since she'd arrived, she'd created a routine for Ruby where none had been, leaving pieces of her calming presence all over his home.

Art—Hope's and Ruby's—hung on the walls. Delicious and nutritious food sat in his refrigerator. Laundry was getting done on a regular basis for the first time in years. There was even a goddamn lavender-scented candle in the bathroom.

To help settle Ruby before bed, she'd said. But that was Hope. She saw what needed doing and got it done, whether it was in someone's home or in someone's heart. She was a fixer. A helper. A healer.

Without them asking for it, Hope had begun to spin a web of healing and love in their lonely little world. She'd come into their orbit, bringing lightness and laughter. Ruby was sleeping and eating better and channeling all her six-year-old energy into creative, meaningful outlets.

Gabe had never known more peace. He trusted Hope with his daughter and knew Ruby couldn't be in better hands. In the last few weeks, he'd found more contentment than he'd had in years and he'd be damned if he wasn't so surprised by it all.

After losing two of the most important women in his life, he had convinced himself choosing to love someone else was too risky. He was terrified enough of losing Ruby. Willingly opening himself up to loving another person he could lose just seemed stupid.

He'd been there. It sucked. Both times.

But he couldn't stop his feelings for Hope from growing into something beyond attraction, and the fact that she'd just reduced it to nothing more than a basic physical need grated on him.

Throwing off the covers, he donned a pair of jeans and stalked out of his bedroom. He halted in the darkened hall of his apartment, not sure what the hell he planned on doing exactly, when he heard a soft thump. Cocking his head toward his entryway, he heard it again. A quiet knock on his front door.

Knowing it could only be one person, he lunged for the door, yanking it open in time to see Hope turning to go.

She froze like a deer caught in headlights, then turned slowly to face him. She wore tiny sleep shorts that showed off her milelong legs and a silk camisole that hugged her curves, emphasizing clearly that she was not wearing a bra. Her blonde hair cascaded down her shoulders in loose tantalizing waves.

His whole body responded. She looked like all his fantasies come to life, even if she was staring at him as if unsure whether to turn and run or stay and jump him. He was voting for the latter. She looked nervous as hell, so nervous she shook. It was only then, as his gaze traveled down her bare arms, that he saw a string of glow-in-the-dark condoms dangling from her fingers. The same ones he'd seen dumped from her purse on the floor in front of her apartment on that rainy day weeks ago.

Christ, he was a dead man.

This was a big mistake, Hope thought.

Huge. Enormous. Gigantic.

Gabe stood in his doorway, wearing nothing but a pair of

low-slung jeans. His abs were rock-hard, his hair was tousled, and his eyes were more than a little apprehensive.

His gaze finally rose from the condoms she held to meet her gaze again. "What are you doing, Hope?"

Excellent question. What was she doing? She didn't really know. All she knew was that she had given up tossing and turning in her empty bed, where she was only getting hotter and hornier, thinking about him and how their evening could have ended—but hadn't.

She couldn't get his last kiss out of her head. His words replayed over and over in her head. She hated that they'd left things unfinished, and more than a little acrimonious. She hated that she'd let him believe that their attraction was just some superficial physical need.

It was so much more than that. And before she could think otherwise, she'd come to stand here, condoms in hand, wanting to... What? Apologize? Jump him?

Yes, and yes.

But also, to take a chance. Part of her really wanted to believe him when he said that what was between them was more than an itch. And maybe that was why she was here.

Except now that she actually was and he was standing there watching her with guarded, wary eyes, the confidence she'd mustered in coming over slipped several notches.

"You know, on second thought..." Embarrassment heated her cheeks. "This is probably a mistake."

But as she turned to leave, his hand wrapped around hers.

"No," he said, his voice deep and rough. The sound sent a shiver up her spine. Not of fear, but lust.

He tugged her hand and she stumbled over the threshold and into his arms. "No mistake, Hope," he murmured against her ear. His throaty growl and warm breath arrowed straight through her core, and the burning hot need she felt for him snaked through her entire being. No, there was no mistake here.

He kicked the door closed behind her. Then he pushed her up against it and kissed her. It wasn't a rough kiss like it had been earlier that evening. This time, he moved his lips over hers slowly, purposefully. He was gentle, but just as thorough. His mouth moved seductively, drawing her under like he always did. Like only he could, and it was a drowning she welcomed. Grasping his shoulders, she clung to him and when he released her mouth, her body stayed against his, craving, needy.

She wanted him to take her here, up against the door, hard and fast. Right that second.

But Gabe held her steady, until her gaze lifted to his. When she saw his expression so intense and serious, she swallowed with difficulty.

"Hope," he demanded, his voice hoarse, just above a whisper. "Tell me why you came here."

In answer, she rubbed her hips over the hard length of him. Slowly. Once up, then back down. In response, he pulled away from her, just slightly.

"I need to hear you say it, Hope," he said through gritted teeth. Barely restrained lust and tested patience burned behind his dilated, dark green irises.

With stunned awe, she realized he was asking for consent. He wasn't assuming it, or counting on it, or even taking it. He was *asking* for it. Even though she was shamelessly rubbing against him, he wasn't taking her gestures as an open invitation. He wanted her to tell him outright what she wanted. And because there was no possible way that he could know the events of her past—that she was far too familiar with men who believed they could just take and not ask—a big piece of her heart melted for him.

Gabriel Walsh was a good man, and that was a gift she intended to cherish. For as long as she had him.

Cupping his jaw between her palms, she reverently kissed him. When she was done, she drew back no more than an inch and looked deeply into his darkened eyes. As clearly and deliberately as she could, she said, "I came here tonight because I want you, Gabe." She leaned in for another kiss. "I need you." Then, with one more kiss, this one not so soft, she added, "Take me to your bed, please."

"So that I can scratch your itch, Hope?" He was laying it all on the table. She could see the vulnerability flickering in his eyes. Needing to soothe, she lifted a hand to his cheek, he immediately turned his face into her palm.

"No," she whispered, before admitting honestly, "because I have a feeling one scratch from you would never be enough to make this ache go away." She paused, locking her eyes with his. "I'm sorry about what I said, Gabe. This is all new, and fast, and scary. I want to do what's right for you and Ruby. I couldn't live with myself if I hurt either of you, but— but, I just really need you tonight. And probably a lot of nights after. So I'm here to figure it out. One step at a time."

A tortured groan rumbled out of him as he bent to bury his head in the hollow of her neck, and then his hands were sliding up the backs of her thighs and under her butt, lifting her off her feet. Instinctively, she responded by wrapping her legs around his waist. When she was anchored, he walked them toward his bedroom, his lips never leaving hers.

His room was dark, only the glow from the moon and streetlights slanted through the blinds. When he released her and reached for his jeans, she slid off his body onto the mattress, enjoying her view of him pushing his jeans down his legs to reveal all of his magnificent body.

Between his jogging, the makeshift weight room set up in his apartment, and the way he fit into his clothes, all hard lines and firm contours, she knew he was fit. But she hadn't expected this. His body was sheer perfection. His broad shoulders dominated the space, and his sculpted abs formed a sexy V that went southbound and made her lose the very last of her brain cells. Lower still, his massive erection jutted out, promising untold pleasure. She had never seen anything so powerful, and she licked her suddenly dry lips.

Gabe's eyes followed the movement of her tongue. He looked a little wild and a whole lot tempting as he finished removing his clothing. Then he came over to her on the bed, his movements purposeful. When he leaned down to kiss her, she pressed her hand flat against his chest.

He immediately stilled above her. The only movement was his heart beating wildly under her palm. He watched her, waiting.

"What about Ruby?" she asked in a breathy whisper. She couldn't help it, but she couldn't fully let go, knowing that the little girl was sleeping down the hall.

Gabe's mouth twitched on one side, suppressing a smile. "I locked the door behind us." He ran his nose along the length of her jaw, then followed the path with soft kisses.

Hope lost focus, all her attention zeroing in on the pressure building between her legs.

"What if we wake her up?" she gasped between panting breaths.

Gabe lifted his head and raised his eyebrow in a pointed look.

"Ok," she said, rolling her eyes. "What if *I* wake her up?"

Smiling, he took her mouth in a slow, torturous kiss that sent arrows of pleasure firing down her body, straight to her sweet spot, which was now pulsing and throbbing with need. She rubbed her thighs together, trying to relieve some of the pressure.

Grasping her wrists, he placed them over her head and wrapped her fingers around the rails of his headboard. Holding her there, his body pressed intimately against every part of hers, he looked her in the eye. Wicked intent gleamed there, and Hope's breath caught somewhere between a gasp and a pant.

"You're not going to wake her, Hope," he whispered confidently, sliding his hands down her body, only stopping to ease her knees apart to make room for himself between her thighs. "Because," he continued, his breath tickling her as he kissed her collarbone. "You're going to be quiet."

He tugged her cami over her head and up to her wrists. A masculine groan of appreciation escaped him as he took in the sight of her bare breasts rising and falling rapidly with her erratic breathing. He sucked a nipple into his mouth, rolling it between his teeth. She gasped loudly and dropped one hand to cover her mouth.

Gabe gently drew her hand away and back around the headboard rail. He dropped his mouth to her ear and murmured, "Very, *very* quiet."

His voice was low and commanding, his movements sure and deliberate. Somewhere in the deep recesses of her brain, this seemed like a time to dissent over such a blatant display of sheer male dominance, but she couldn't bring herself to do it. Didn't *want* to do it. Everything felt so good, each nerve ending thrummed to life under his ministra- tions. She didn't feel weak or restrained, she felt alive and exhilarated. So instead of objecting, she pressed her head back into the pillow and bit her lip as his mouth continued to tease her nipples.

She was working hard on keeping quiet when his lips left her breasts, the wetness of his mouth leaving them cool to the air. Traveling down her stomach, he kissed and nipped every inch of skin he could get his mouth on.

Just when she thought she couldn't take any more of his torturous open-mouthed kisses, Gabe gripped the hem of her shorts and yanked them down in one swift motion. At the sound of his strangled groan, Hope lifted her head to see him on his knees between her open thighs, taking in the sight of her naked—and totally exposed to him.

"Beautiful," he murmured, and the intensity in his voice made her feel bold as she lifted her legs, draping them over his shoulders, inviting him closer. A growl emerged from his throat. "I bet it tastes as good as it looks."

Shocked at his bluntness, Hope gasped. No one had ever talked to her this way before in bed, but what shocked her more was that she liked it.

With a devilish smile he chuckled softly, then his gleaming eyes held hers as he brought his face down and feasted. He continued to hold eye contact as his tongue slid up and down, and then—oh God—then into her.

For all her daring confidence moments ago, she'd never actually come this way. Hadn't had much experience with it, in fact. But there was no time for a confessional with Gabe, because suddenly she *was* coming, her entire body exploding in a fire of hot, sweet sensations.

Not screaming with release took every single ounce of sanity she had left, and there wasn't much. Instead, she gasped heaving breaths, bucking her hips uncontrollably as

Gabe slowed the strokes of his tongue, letting her ride out the intense wave.

When her vision cleared, she saw him lean over to retrieve the condoms that had fallen onto the floor. Then came the distinct crinkle and tear of the foil wrapper. She shoved herself up on her elbows so she could watch him roll the condom down his length.

True to its advertising, it did indeed glow-in-the-dark.

Gabe looked up and met her gaze. Despite the pent-up sexual tension clearly visible on his face, he grinned. His erection glowed between them like an X-rated homing device in the otherwise dark room. Hope couldn't help it. She snorted out a laugh.

"Convenient," he said, before he moved over her, with his weight on his forearms.

Any residual laughter from the glow-in-the-dark cock show died in Hope's throat at the fierceness in his eyes.

A low "shh" whispered against her cheek like a final reminder from him before he pushed all the way inside her in one smooth motion of his hips.

Their shallow breaths of pleasure were the only sounds that followed.

By the time he finally began thrusting, slow and deep, Hope could already start to feel herself come undone. She didn't have many lovers to brag about, but she'd certainly never had anyone like Gabe. He was large, powerful, and potent. He filled her completely, and moved over and within as if he understood exactly what she needed and when. She whimpered and writhed under him, her legs squeezing his thighs and hips greedily, trying to urge him on, but he controlled their rhythm, creating an excruciating tension between them.

The hum in her body built until she couldn't wait any

more. She sensed him holding back, trying to draw out their pleasure, but she didn't want that. Not this time. She wanted him to move with the same desperation that was burning inside her.

"Faster," she pleaded, lifting her hips to encourage him. "Please."

Groaning her name, he buried his face in her hair. She could feel his control snapping as his breathing became harder, his skin became more slicked with sweat, his heart raced against hers.

And then he was giving her what she so desperately wanted. He pounded into her with everything he had, and she rose to meet him, thrust for thrust. When Gabe lifted her slightly, switching their angle to create an even deeper penetration, the pleasure became so acute that Hope released a sharp cry before she could stop herself.

Bending his head close to her ear again, Gabe whispered, "Quiet, Hope."

Moaning, she thrashed her head from side to side as the pressure and pleasure mounted. She'd never felt so alive. Every movement was agonizingly erotic, and her inner muscle spasmed with another impending orgasm. She didn't know how she'd get through another blinding release without uttering a sound.

The only noises in the room were their harsh breathing and the slapping of their bodies driving mercilessly into each other. Silence had never been more carnal.

Hope's legs and arms trembled around Gabe as she struggled to hang on to some control. But the weight of his body on hers, his rough rhythmic thrusting, and the way his pelvis rubbed against her core with just the right pressure pushed her to a fever pitch. It was all too much, too intense, and the tension snapped.

To stop herself from releasing the scream building inside her, she sunk her teeth into Gabe's shoulder. He hissed out a sharp breath as her orgasm consumed her, and she clung onto him for dear life.

Through the blood rushing in her ears, she heard Gabe swear viscously as his own release hit him. With a final grunt, he jerked against her, then tensed, his head thrown back as he gave himself over to the ecstasy.

Then his big body slumped over her, gasping for air

She might have blacked out after that. She couldn't be a hundred percent sure, but her next conscious thought was that Gabe was flat on his back, with his arms wrapped tightly around her, cradling her against him. His eyes were closed, his breathing slow and steady.

He looked serene and sated, more relaxed than she'd ever seen him. She ran a tentative hand down the slope between his toned pecs, then up along his arm, and over his bicep, tracing the tattoo that was etched there. A blackbird in flight.

She traced the curve of one wing, wondering what it represented.

"The song." Gabe's sleep roughened voice answered her question before she could ask it. "The song 'Blackbird.' Carrie used to sing it to Ruby when she was fussy and wouldn't sleep."

Hope's heart rolled over painfully as she pictured the young woman—from the photo Ruby had shown her—singing the melodic song in a hushed tone as her child fell asleep in her arms.

It was beautiful—and heartbreaking. She stared at Gabe's tattoo with renewed appreciation. It was more than a piece of art. It was an epitaph of what once was and would never be again. She didn't have to worry about taking

Carrie's place or erasing her memory. It wasn't possible. Carrie was etched here, on Gabe's skin forever. Never to be lost. And knowing that, seeing it, was oddly reassuring.

As if sensing her shift in mood, Gabe lifted his arm, taking the tattoo out of her view, and tugged her head down onto his chest.

The temptation to curl into him and sleep until morning was almost more than she could resist, but she knew she had to leave because there was no way in heck she wanted his daughter to eventually walk in and see her in bed with him.

No way.

"I have to go," she whispered, even as her disobedient fingertips skated against the taut flesh of his broad chest.

He tensed under her touch, then rolled over in one swift athletic movement so that she was once again under him. Nudging her legs apart, he settled between them like he was made to be there. When his hardness brushed against her, the very last of her good intentions flew out the window.

"Not yet," he whispered before claiming her mouth in a searing kiss.

CHAPTER EIGHTEEN

Hope slept like the dead. Which made sense since Gabe kept her awake long into the night. Somewhere after three in the morning, she'd lost count of her orgasms. In all her life, she'd have never thought she'd live the myth of making love through the night. But she had.

And oh, how she'd lived it. Her body felt deliciously sore and used in the very best of ways and places. Gabe was the kind of lover they wrote books about. Thorough and demanding, yet tender and patient. His stamina had been impressive.

So impressive she ended up staying far longer than she intended, and the light was starting to fall through the slats of the bedroom blinds, signaling dawn. Beside her, Gabe was asleep, but she gave a little wiggle just to make sure he was out as cold as he looked. Then, with what she considered impressive ninja-like maneuvers, she extracted herself from his embrace without moving him an inch.

Looking down at his sleeping form, she allowed herself a smug smile, knowing that she'd exhausted him as much as he'd exhausted her. She thought of their night together and shuddered with renewed lust. After all that, how could she still be ready to jump on him for another round? It wasn't a good sign. She could feel herself getting attached, and she couldn't. It was too fast, too much, and too soon. She hadn't come to Portland looking for this.

Her smile faded as she collected her clothes, put them on and tiptoed out of the room. The hall was dark and quiet. Ruby's door at the far end was shut tight. Feeling like a teenager sneaking out of her boyfriend's house at dawn, Hope crept on tiptoes to the door, turned the knob as slowly and quietly as she could. Outside, she took a moment to exhale the breath she'd been holding before sprinting across the main hallway to her apartment.

Unlike her stealth exit from Gabe's apartment, she flung herself gracelessly and frantically into her own. Shutting her front door behind her with a near slam, she pressed herself against the inside of her door, breathing hard. Once she caught her breath, she opened her eyes and looked right into a pair of confused blue ones.

Ivy was bent on one knee, tying her running shoe, her fingers still knotted in the laces as she twisted the loops. Her gaze scanned Hope, taking in her likely disheveled appearance. Hope watched the light dawn in Ivy's eyes and her jaw sag open.

"You didn't."

Hope, still plastered to the door, blew out an indignant breath, and tried her best to sound the height of offended. "Of course I didn't."

Ivy finished tying her laces and slowly rose to her feet. She was decked out in full running gear, complete with a reflective lightweight jacket. She was about to go for her insane crack of dawn five-mile daily run.

She stood, hands on hips, giving Hope the mother of all

know-it-all-looks. Hope folded under it like a cheap suitcase.

"Okay, I did." She covered her face with her hands. "All night long. I'm such a ho."

"Maybe, but you're a lucky-ass ho," Ivy said, pulling Hope's hands from her face. "Seriously. You fucked the landlord."

"Omigod! Don't say that. You make it sound so inappropriate, so dirty." As Hope stared into her best friend's eyes, her own eyes widened with worry. "Ok, so it was totally dirty, but do you think it's...? You know, inappropriate?"

Ivy's eyes lit with absolute delight, then she broke out in a loud laugh.

"Sssshhhhh!" Hope pushed Ivy deeper into their apartment, looking over her shoulder to make sure the door was properly closed.

"Oh my God, Hope. Honestly. You need to get a grip. You're ruining your postcoital glow." Ivy placed a firm hand on Hope's shoulder, her lips quirking as she obviously tried her best to morph her face back into a more serious look. "It's not inappropriate. You deserve this. Really. No one I know deserves it more."

Hope covered her friend's hand with her own. "You do," she said softly. "You deserve it more."

A silence hung between them. They both knew the unspoken meaning behind Hope's words. Hope had seen the effects of hell, but Ivy was the one who had lived through it. The past still hung like a weight around Ivy's neck, dragging her down no matter how hard she worked to become strong, or how many runs she went on to clear her head. She couldn't escape what happened. Could never let the nightmare go.

Ivy's gaze grew distant, and Hope kicked herself for

bringing the past up. Ivy did best when she didn't talk about what had occurred, when she buried the experience in the deep, dark recesses of her mind. She had never managed to go on like nothing happened, but she'd rather run ten miles in a blizzard than talk about the incident.

As far as Hope knew, only a handful of people knew the whole truth of what had happened to Ivy three years ago: Hope, Joel, the counselor who Hope had convinced/forced Ivy to see after the fact, and the college students who could rot in hell as far as Hope was concerned.

"Ivy—"

Ivy shook her head, refocusing. "That life isn't for me Hope. Besides, I quite enjoy living vicariously through you. So you need to have enough sex for the both of us." She gave Hope an impressed once over. "And by the look of things, you just did."

Hope felt her cheeks heat at the truth. "Ugh, I'm not like this. Tonight was completely spontaneous." She sighed deeply at the memory of just a few hours ago. "But geez, was it ever good. So, *so* good."

Ivy nodded sympathetically, then perked her head up. "You're gonna see him again, right? And again? And again?"

"I don't know. It's—complicated."

"Hope, that's so fucking cliché they made a movie about it." Ivy rolled her eyes as she grabbed her keys off the kitchen counter. "Look, Gabe is a great guy. One of the best. Strong and solid. Loyal and faithful. Like a goddamn Labrador. He's a sure bet. The real deal. You can count on him." She turned back to Hope, holding her gaze. "He won't hurt you," she promised. Then, with a quick hug, she left Hope standing alone in their apartment.

"No," she said to the empty space, voicing her deepest

insecurity. "But what if I'm not a sure bet? What if I hurt him? Them."

The empty space didn't answer or reassure her. Only silence filled the air around her, and this time it wasn't erotic. It was just cold and telling.

That afternoon, Gabe sat in his office behind the bar slogging through paperwork. He hated paperwork. But he was decent at the business end of things, which was part of why he'd made a success of the bar. Crunching the numbers, managing the staff schedules, and organizing product orders all came naturally to him.

But he still hated it. He'd rather be behind the bar slinging bottles, pouring drinks, and helping people enjoy themselves on any day of the week. Paper had to be pushed, though. So here he was hunched over his laptop with a stack of papers beside him, trying to focus.

And he was focused. He was focused on how hot and tight it'd been sliding in and out between Hope's thighs. She'd felt like silk. Her skin smooth and soft, her body pliant and willing. She'd done anything and everything he'd asked of her, and yet he still couldn't believe she'd actually let him touch her. But she had, and for one blissful night he'd died and gone straight to heaven.

The problem was that now he couldn't get it out of his mind, and he hadn't been able to focus on a single damn thing the whole damn day. Even more disconcerting was the fact that he knew he couldn't let it be the last time. He had to have Hope again.

She may have scratched her itch last night, but Gabe had only gotten itchier.

Hope said she wanted to take things one step at a time, and he totally got that. Agreed with her even. He just hadn't expected to wake up in bed alone. He'd wanted her to stay. He'd thought she'd wanted to stay, too.

Had he been wrong about how he'd interpreted her words? Did she want more than just sex with him?

Because he sure as hell did. He'd never been so fucking gone over a woman in his entire life. Or as confused. With Carrie everything had been clear. There had been a mutual attraction, which had led to dating, which had led to a relationship.

But with Hope, everything had started ass-backwards. And he couldn't make sense of anything other than what he felt for her. Which was more than he had anticipated feeling for anyone ever again in his life.

With a gruff sigh, he took a swig of the hour-old coffee sitting on his desk and focused on his keyboard. Lusting after Hope Morgan wasn't going to pay the bills. He needed to get his head out of the gutter.

He managed to put in another solid hour before the door to his office busted open, and Sean sauntered through carrying two big bags of takeout and a tray with two sodas on it. He was wearing a backward baseball cap, an athletic shirt, and basketball shorts even though it was fucking freezing outside, not to mention raining.

"You know," Sean said, dumping everything onto Gabe's desk before dropping his hulking body into a chair across from him. "For someone who got laid multiple times last night, you should be looking a whole lot perkier."

To show Sean just how perky he was feeling, he lifted his middle finger before reaching for one of the bags. Sean snatched it out of reach. The guy had reflexes like a gazelle.

"Oh no, you don't, princess. Not until you tell me why you're being a sourpuss."

"Fuck you."

Sean grinned, clearly enjoying this little round of *piss-Gabe-off*. "She left you to wake up alone, is that it? You didn't get your morning after snuggle."

Because Sean was unpacking burgers and fries and now handing them over freely, he decided not to kill him, but he sure as shit wasn't going to admit to Sean that he was getting way too close to the truth.

Gabe took a huge bite of his burger and a sip of his soda, feeling marginally better. He looked up at Sean over the rim of his drink. "How the fuck do you know what happened last night, anyway?"

Sean folded his arms and raised an eyebrow. "You really need to ask that?"

Ivy. Shit. If Ivy knew, that meant Hope had told her, and if Hope told her—well, what the hell did that mean? Despite having a pain-in-the-ass sister and a daughter of the same gender, he didn't speak female. He ran a frustrated hand through his hair.

"Don't worry, Hope didn't kiss and tell," Sean said, reading his mind and taking his own lunch out of the bag. "Hope did her walk-of-shame home as Ivy was getting ready to leave for her morning run. Ivy said she took one look at Hope and it didn't take much to figure out where she'd just come from. And who she'd just come for," he added with a wink, chewing on a fry.

Gabe buried his head in his hands.

Sean giggled, like a freaking giddy schoolkid. "Man, you *go*," he choked out, probably impressed that after all these years Gabe could actually still have sex. "I was starting to think that you didn't have the guts to go for Hope. I was going to make a move myself if you didn't do something soon."

Gabe stalled mid-bite and glowered at his friend.

Sean burst out laughing in response. "Holy shit, you should see the look on your face. You've got it worse than I thought if you can't clearly see I'm messing with you."

Growling under his breath, Gabe finished off his burger, then dug into the bag for the next one, knowing Sean always bought enough food to feed an army. Or a bottomless pit such as they both were.

Why had he gotten so upset at the thought of his friend going for Hope? They made more sense together. They were both friendly and kind. Amiable and genuine. Sean had a big old soft heart that a girl like Hope could snuggle right into.

They could probably live fucking happily ever fucking after.

Whereas Gabe didn't have much to offer Hope in terms of heart. He'd shut off his soft side years ago, and anything he had left was reserved for Ruby.

Great, now he was second-guessing if he could even be enough for Hope. As he'd said: ass-backwards.

He realized he'd gotten lost in thought when he heard Sean deliberately sucking the last of his soda through his straw as loudly and obnoxiously as possible.

He shot him a look, but Sean eyed him innocently and continued sucking.

"You're good enough for her," Sean said finally, when he'd sucked the last goddamn drop out of his cup. He tossed the cup toward the wastebasket in the corner of Gabe's office. It went in without hitting the rim. Then he leaned back in his chair and steepled his fingers, looking like a fucking shrink. "I know *you think* you aren't good enough, but you are."

Gabe made himself busy crumpling empty wrappers into balls and taking his own shots at the garbage. Only half went in. Sean tsked.

"I'm distracted," Gabe grumbled.

"No," Sean said. "You're afraid she only wants you for your body." He leaned forward, elbows on knees, and hit the nail on the head. "But the thing that's really eating at you is that she might actually want you for more."

Gabe wasn't in the mood for a heart-to-heart. Sean was putting words to what had just been a chaos of feelings bubbling around inside him, and he wasn't ready to hear it.

"What if she's not for me?" He pushed up from his seat. He needed to move. His chest felt tight, constricted. "I thought she could be, but maybe she's not."

"And why not, man?" Sean wasn't going to let this go. "She's beautiful, smart, funny, and can work the bar with the best of them. Ivy loves her. So does Ruby. Hope fits into your life like she's always been there. So what's the problem?"

What was the problem? Reality was the problem. She was gold. He was brass. She was fancy business school. He was community college. She was sunshine and optimism. He was pretty much the exact opposite.

But there was the undeniable. The feel of her under his hands, the way she whispered his name desperately over and over last night as he moved inside her. The way they pulled together like two magnets whenever they were in the same vicinity. The bond he could see building between her and Ruby.

If she wasn't for him, then why did they fit together like they'd been made for each other?

Christ, he was a mess. His feelings were all over the

place. The panic building deep in his chest was a physical ache, a tightening around his heart muscles, a pressure on his lungs. There was so much at stake, and one wrong move could hurt Hope, devastate his daughter, and damage the fragile stability he'd built over the last six years in an instant. Was it worth it? He'd had it all fall apart on him before, and it had been the worst thing that had ever happened.

Memories crawled out of the back of his mind like insects seeking heat as he started packing up his mess with tight, furious movements. "There's a lot to consider. It's not just me. Ruby is already attached to her. I need to be careful."

It was a very simplified version of all the thoughts rushing his head. What had felt crystal clear last night was rapidly deteriorating as the reality of waking up alone set in. Maybe going slow wasn't enough. Maybe he should quit while he was ahead.

Across from him, his friend watched consideringly as he took his sweet time chewing. Finally, he swallowed. "I get it, dude. It looks perfect on the outside, but you've been through a lot in the last few years. Switching it up isn't going to be easy." Sean wiped a napkin across his mouth before he balled up his garbage and tossed another clean shot into the waste bin. "Look, man, there's risk in everything. Risk in seeing where it goes with Hope, risk in continuing to live how you've been living—which, by the way hasn't been bad, it just kind of looked lonely. For you and Ruby. So I guess you have to decide which risk you're most willing to take."

Yeah, and wasn't that the easiest thing on his to-do list?

In the end it worked out that he didn't see much of Hope for a few days straight. He worked his usual shifts Monday through Friday, and only saw her when she arrived at his place at three, when he came up at bedtime to tuck Ruby in, and in the wee hours when he arrived home from the bar. He tried to keep their debriefs short and off the couch. Like in the entryway with the light on. He made a point of eating at the bar so she didn't have to save him a plate and sit with him while he ate.

It was self-sabotaging and he knew it, but there were no repeat performances of their night together.

It wasn't that he was explicitly trying to avoid her, he just needed some time to figure out the best way to proceed, especially if Hope was having second thoughts about them as well. Which she'd seemed to imply when she snuck out of his bed under the cover of darkness.

Waking up alone wasn't a habit he wanted to get back into without any warning. So distance seemed like the only way to protect what was left of his heart.

In the meantime, Hope continued to save his ass, taking care of household duties that he inevitably fell behind on, helping Ruby with all her schoolwork, plus all the extras. One night he came home to a cake shaped and decorated like a unicorn that looked magazine-worthy.

"Hope and I made it for the cakewalk at school to raise money for the library," Ruby had informed him proudly.

He smiled and nodded, like the fundraiser was right on the top of his list of things he'd actually remembered. Someone was looking at the school calendar on the fridge, but it sure as hell wasn't him.

On Thursday he noticed a new planter by the windowsill.

"We're experimenting growing herbs," Hope had explained, when she found him standing in front of it with a scowl so deep it made his face hurt. "It's just basil and thyme, you know, for seasoning when Ruby and I cook dinner." She looked so nervous that he figured his expression must have matched the emotions colliding in his chest. "I hope you don't mind."

He did fucking mind. He minded that every day it was getting harder to say goodnight to her, to watch her walk out his door.

Regardless, the way she'd been standing there, in the moonlight of his living room at 2 a.m., looking rumpled and exhausted after a full week of looking after his daughter and his home, made him feel like a jackass for being surly about a few herbs.

On Friday, the planter was gone. Moved to Hope's apartment because there was better light, or so Ruby had told him.

But Gabe knew she'd moved it because he'd been a jerk about it the night before.

He should have apologized. He should have asked her to bring the damn thing back, but in the end, he felt that it was probably better if she thought he was annoyed with her—and she thought he was a jerk and a jackass as well. It might help maintain the distance that he'd managed to put between them, all while making the ache in his heart dig deeper.

What the fuck was he doing?

Eleven days. It had been eleven days since Hope had experienced the most erotic night of her life. Eleven days since she'd hightailed it out of Gabe's apartment like a thief in the night. Eleven days since things had felt good between them.

Hope had wracked her brain about all the different reasons Gabe might be acting so distant. Had she disappointed him in bed? She could still feel how his body tensed against hers when he came. Could still hear the rough groan of her name tear off his lips as he finally let himself go.

No. She wasn't trying to pretend she was some vixen between the sheets, but she was sure enough of herself to know Gabe had more than enjoyed their time together.

Maybe he was mad that she'd slipped away in the early morning? But she couldn't bring herself to believe that either. They weren't a couple. They weren't even frequent lovers. It had been their first time, and Hope was sure Gabe would agree that her being there when Ruby woke up would only confuse the little girl more than anything else.

Had she done something he didn't like? The only thing

she could think of was the herb planter, but she'd removed the stupid thing the second she saw he wasn't amused about it.

She had no idea why he'd suddenly grown cold toward her when, only a short time ago, they'd nearly set his sheets on fire. Not to mention that *he* was the one who'd been adamant that whatever happened between them was more than just sex in the first place. And now he was avoiding her like all he'd wanted was a one-night stand.

What was going on in the locked vault that was Gabe Walsh's brain?

Her best guess was that for some reason he regretted their night together and didn't want to give the impression that he was ready for round two—which he most certainly had not.

That, or his version of going slow was very different from hers.

The only thing to do was to put the whole situation behind her. If he clearly wasn't interested in a repeat with her, then she shouldn't be losing sleep over wanting it with him.

Except she was losing sleep. A lot of it. Mostly because she hadn't anticipated missing him so much. She missed talking to him, hearing about his day, and telling him about hers. She missed their emotional closeness as much as their physical. It was a loneliness she hadn't predicted and couldn't dissipate.

With a sigh, she put her paintbrush in water and got up from her painting station where she'd been trying to distract herself. For the first time in forever, it hadn't worked. When painting didn't take the edge off, snacking usually did the trick. Ivy would tell her that she needed to get out, go for a run, clear her head, but right now her head was at the mercy of her stomach. Digging through the kitchen cupboards, she sighed in relief when she found the last of her Oreo stash.

Taking four cookies, she poured herself a glass of milk and headed for the couch. Besides the emotional turmoil she'd been feeling over Gabe the last few days, something else had niggled at the back of her mind and heart. Since dinner at the Walshes', it had become more acute, until it was no longer a niggle but an all-out roar.

She needed to talk to her parents.

Not just the "play-nice-and-make-peace" kind of talk, but the real "rip-your-heart-out-and-lay-it-on-the-table" talk. It was spring now. Months had gone by since the truth came out at Christmas. Years, if she counted the uncertainty she'd endured since her sixteenth birthday. The crack was a decade old. And it was enough. She wanted her family back.

Being with Ruby all these weeks had made her long for her own mother in a way she hadn't in a long time. And in so many ways, watching Gabe and Ruby interact reminded her of her childhood memories with her own father. He'd been her hero, strong and brave and hard working. The king of their castle. She missed him, too.

And frankly, she was tired of being a huge pain in her brother's ass. She was tired of hearing the wariness in Joel's voice whenever he talked to her. Or worse, his irritation. Being the go-between for her and their parents was wearing on him. He'd never admit it, and he'd never stop doing it, because he knew full well that if he didn't mediate between them, there would be nothing left of Hope's relationship with Walter and Audrey. But she didn't want to be a burden in his life.

Joel deserved happiness, a life of his own. For all Hope knew, he had one. Another reminder that she and her brother's communications revolved solely, and selfishly, around her. She had no idea where his private life stood.

It was time to forgive, make peace, and get the answers to some burning questions she'd been too angry, scared, and proud to ask. Ruby may have been only six and a half, but she'd taught Hope that life was short and relationships with your family were too precious to waste.

Licking the middle off her last cookie, she popped the chocolate wafer into her mouth and downed her milk. When she was done, she dug her phone out of her pocket and thumbed through her contacts until she found the word *Mom*.

She stared at it for a long moment.

Mom.

Audrey was that, to the core, and Hope was so lucky to have her. Whether by birth or by sheer chance, she was lucky to have a woman like Audrey Morgan mother her.

Taking a deep breath, she hit the call button.

Audrey answered after one ring. "Darling?" she said into the phone, sounding worried, which wasn't surprising.

Hope hardly phoned anymore, and never without Joel's prompting, so when she did, Audrey usually expected it.

"Hi, Mom," Hope said, trying to sound normal. Casual. Like calling your mom was no big deal.

"Hope, what's wrong?" Audrey asked.

"Nothing." But the tears that suddenly pricked her eyes and clogged her throat said differently.

Audrey must have heard it in her voice because she said, "Where are you? I'm coming."

And Hope knew she would. She could be stranded in Timbuktu and Audrey would move heaven and earth to get to her. Another punch of guilt landed right in Hope's stomach. She'd been so cruel. So hard on her parents. She'd never even given them a chance to truly explain. She had just shrouded herself in hurt and anger and froze them out. Then left.

Wiping her eyes, she shook her head. Not that her mother could see. "No, Mom, I'm fine. I'm still in Portland. Everything is fine. I just wanted..." What? She wasn't totally sure until the words were coming out of her mouth. "I wanted to confirm that I'll be home for the benefit. I'll stay with you and Dad, if that's okay."

The silence on the other end lasted so long she thought they might have lost the connection.

When Audrey spoke, her voice was thick with emotion. "Of course you can. We wouldn't have you stay anywhere else. We'll pick you up from the airport. Let Dad book you a plane ticket, and we'll send you the information."

"No." She'd worked too hard for the little she had, and she still wasn't giving up the independence she'd built. "Thank you, but I've already booked a flight," she lied. "I'll send you the details. I'd love a ride from the airport, though." She compromised, not wanting to work backward from what she was trying to achieve.

"Absolutely," Audrey promised, still sounding emotional.

Hearing the tears in her mother's voice only triggered more of her own, so she repeated that she'd send her flight information and then ended the call.

She went online and used her savings to book the cheapest ticket to San Francisco she could find. Then she emailed the information to her mother.

And for the first time in years, her heart felt a little lighter. As long as she kept the dark uncertainties about Gabe at bay, she'd be fine.

CHAPTER TWENTY

The following morning, Hope crawled out of bed early. Not run-with-Ivy early, but early enough that she caught Ivy as she was leaving the apartment to go to work. Ivy eyed her speculatively as she came out of her room in full run gear and tried to stifle a yawn.

"You okay?" Ivy asked.

"Why wouldn't I be?" she replied, trying not to feel insulted that something had to be wrong for her to go on a run.

Ivy just shrugged, gathered the rest of her PT gear, and headed out the door.

Sometimes it was really nice having a friend who'd mastered the art of being strong and silent. Other times, it was damn annoying. It wasn't until she passed the hallway mirror that she caught sight of her reflection. With hollow eyes and stress lines around her mouth, she was several shades paler than usual, bordering on gray.

She needed sleep and proper nutrition, but between her worries about Gabe and her returning anxiety over facing her family again, she'd lost her ability to sleep and consume anything other than Oreos and wine.

Maybe if she ran herself into exhaustion, she'd get some flush on her cheeks. So, she ran. She had built enough stamina to run for a full twenty minutes before she had to walk. She forced herself to walk for no more than three minutes before running again. She did the run-walk for over an hour, and by the time she got back to the apartment her legs felt like noodles.

Dragging her liquified limbs into the shower, she stood under the hot water until it ran cool. When her phone rang as she was toweling off, her heart nearly jumped out of her chest at the sight of Gabe's name on the screen.

"Hello?" she asked tentatively, feeling nervous for some inexplicable reason.

"Hope," his voice came through low and husky. He sounded like the sexiest thing she'd heard all week. Or in twelve days. Or ever. "I just wanted to let you know that I talked to Lori. She's invited Ruby for a sleepover this weekend, so I am going to take her straight there after school."

Her heart kicked up, fantasizing about all the things they could do in an apartment without a child in it.

"You don't need to come tonight," he added.

And with those words, her heart cracked so painfully in her chest she imagined she could hear it. Of course, there was now no reason to join him tonight. Because they weren't a couple.

She should be elated that she had her first Friday night off in a long time. She should be texting Ivy to make plans for a girl's night. She should be planning what sappy movies she was going to watch in her pajamas while eating her weight in carbs.

Instead, she just felt hurt, and the oddest sense of loss.

"Okay," she managed to say at last.

"So...I'll see you Monday," Gabe replied, oblivious to the gaping wound in her chest.

And even though everything in her was screaming at her to put it all on the line now, to invite herself over after his shift, or insist they talk about what was or wasn't going on between them, she ignored it and said, "Yep, Monday. See you then."

And she hung up before he could say anything else.

After Hope hung up, Gabe stared at his phone for a long minute. He shut his eyes against the wave of regret that washed over him. He was such a colossal jerk. He knew he was being an ass, and yet he couldn't seem to drag himself off his painfully slow path to self-destruction.

For the first few days, he'd convinced himself that given the situation, he was doing the only right thing. Then, somewhere along the way, he'd allowed himself to believe there was no future for him and Hope, so it was only fair to nip things in the bud and not play games. No matter how fantastically erotic the games could have been.

But as the days wore on, he had more and more trouble assuring himself that he'd made the right decision. When Lori had called earlier, inviting Ruby to sleep over, she'd alluded to the fact that he could use this time to connect with Hope.

Her actual words had been, *grow a pair and woo the girl.* As sisterly insults went, it only pissed him off more because he had to admit once again that his sister was right.

He hadn't wooed Hope. They had been making progress in their own roundabout way. Their connection and chemistry was undeniable. There was even a moment where he seriously thought they could be more, but instead of going for it, he'd run like a coward and pushed her away.

Trauma was funny that way. Just when you thought it was far behind you, it came up and bit you in the ass. It should have come with a warning: *Caution, trauma may be closer than it appears.*

Sean had been right when he'd said that Gabe had had a few rough years. He didn't think he'd be this fucking scared at the prospect of moving on.

But it wasn't just fear. More than anything he wanted to protect Ruby. The little bubble they'd created since Carrie died was safe. Lonely, but safe. Adding Hope into the bubble felt natural, but it triggered his anxiety like he hadn't anticipated.

Was it worth adding another person into their lives who they couldn't stomach the thought of losing? What had felt so blatantly clear in one moment became blurry the next.

Fuck, he wished he could turn off his brain.

Frustrated with himself and the whole situation, he decided to push it all aside for a few more hours and buried himself in work. He was neck deep in income taxes when he heard a loud bang coming from the kitchen, followed by an ear-piercing shriek. *Shit.* This could not be good.

Gabe was up from his desk and down the hallway to the kitchen in under ten seconds. The scene in front of him was apocalyptic.

Water gushed out of the industrial dishwasher, with steam billowing to the ceiling. The shriek had come from Harvey, his almost three-hundred-pound, six foot seven, normally badass, chef.

Harvey had become a man in LA's underground boxing rings in the 80s and 90s. He discovered a love for cooking after he got clocked one too many times on the side of the head, rendering him deaf in one ear.

If the scene before him could make Harvey shriek like a schoolkid on Halloween night, then Gabe knew it was worse than it looked.

"It just blew." Harvey shook his beefy finger at the blubbering dishwasher that now spewed suds. Sweat trickled down his thick neck, and his eyes were wide as saucers. "The motherfucker just blew."

"Shit. Fuck." Gabe ran to grab as many towels as he could and threw them on the floor where the water was accumulating. Then he bolted to the electrical room to turn off the main water source.

For the next half hour, he and Harvey did as much damage control as they could until the emergency plumber, who was going to cost him a bloody fortune, arrived on the scene.

The next time he looked at the clock, it was 2:30.

Shit. Shit. *Shit.* Ruby. He had to get her from school.

He let out a slew of curse words under his breath, since that was the only vocabulary he seemed capable of at that moment. It was a ten-minute drive to Ruby's school, but he still hadn't packed her sleepover bag.

He grabbed his phone and hit the redial button on his last call.

"Hello?" The apprehension in Hope's voice almost gutted him, but he didn't have time to dwell on how that was all his fault.

"I need a favor."

"Whatever you need," she said with no question as to what she was about to get into, why, or for how long. Simply a willingness to be there for him in any way he needed at the drop of a hat.

Knowing that reaffirmed what he already knew in his heart. He could trust her with what he'd not trusted anyone else with since Carrie died.

"I need you to go to my apartment and pack an overnight bag for Ruby. There's an extra set of keys to the Bronco in the kitchen drawer next to the stove. You can take those and—" He paused for a second, years of fearing this moment catching up with him. He pushed the fear aside. "Then I need you to pick up Ruby from school and drive her to my sister's for a slumber party."

"I'm on it," Hope said. She probably heard the chaos in the background and made the wise decision not to ask any questions.

But he couldn't hang up without telling her one thing.

"Hope…" Shit, this was hard. In six years, no one had driven Ruby in a car but him. Not even his own damn father. Not even Lori. "Be careful," he finally said, hoping that he didn't sound as terrified as he felt. His heart was literally seizing his chest at the thought of having the transportation of his daughter in someone else's hands. The last time that happened—

Trauma may be closer than it appears.

He couldn't think about the past. He had to trust Hope with his future.

"I'll call when I leave the school and when we arrive at Lori's. I'll drive slowly. I promise. I've got her, Gabe."

As soon as she spoke the words, he knew they were true. She had Ruby. And she had him.

And on the wave of that realization clarity washed over him, taking away any apprehension and panic he'd had earlier. Peace and certainty filled him. He was in love with Hope Morgan. His heart flooded with the feeling until it overflowed. This woman, who had become everything to his family, had his heart.

Ruby would be fine. Nothing bad was going to happen. Hope wouldn't let it. He knew it. He felt it. And the three words aching in his chest nearly left his mouth, but he heard Harvey yelling in the kitchen again, so he said goodbye instead.

~

When Hope arrived at Ruby's school, the girl squealed at the sight of her. Then she came running with her arms flung wide, launching herself into Hope's embrace with a force that nearly took them both down in a tumble.

"Whoa! Easy tiger," she said, laughing. "Although, I have to admit, it's nice to see someone so happy to see me."

"Hope! What are you doing here? Where's Daddy?" A look of alarm that no six-year-old should ever have flashed across her face. "Is he okay?"

Hope stroked her back comfortingly.

"He's fine. He asked me to come get you because something came up at the bar." Or so she assumed, judging by the clanging noises and Harvey's yells coming through the line.

Worry still etched Ruby's small face. "Daddy never lets anyone else drive me. Nobody. Not since Mommy died in a car crash."

Hope's heart stuttered at the revelation. Kneeling so they were at eye level, she laid her hands on Ruby's shoulders. Mossy-green eyes, like her father's, glittered with an uncertainty that broke Hope's heart wide open, letting all kinds of love wash in.

"Well then, this is going to be extra special, isn't it?"

Ruby's mouth cracked into a grin.

"Come on." Hope took her hand and led her toward Gabe's Bronco. "I've been instructed to drop you off at Auntie Lori's."

"What?" Ruby squealed. "Why?"

"For a slumber party."

A shout of pure joy echoed through the school parking lot as one little girl's weekend got a whole lot brighter.

Hope drove like her grandma's grandma, stopping before every white line at a stop sign instead of coasting slightly past it to a rolling stop. She kept to the speed limit, minus a few miles per hour—just in case. And finally, finally she reached Lori's.

Eva came through the front door at full speed, greeting her cousin, who'd scrambled out of Gabe's car before Hope could even unbuckle her own seat belt.

"What took you so long?" Eva asked, enveloping Ruby in a hug.

"Hope is a super slow driver. Worse than Daddy," was all Hope heard before the girls disappeared inside, the door clicking shut behind them.

Lori crossed the lawn slowly, stopping within a foot of Hope, eyeing her like she'd never seen her before. "He let you drive?"

She shrugged. "There was an emergency at the bar."

Lori continued to stare at her. "He doesn't even let me drive Ruby," she said matter-of-factly, though her look was anything but.

Not sure what to say, Hope shrugged again and tried not to fidget.

After a beat of silence, Lori nodded, as if something had clicked in her mind. "He thinks it was his fault, you know. The car accident. Carrie's death. All of it."

Hope nodded. Based on bits and pieces she'd learned over the last few months she knew Gabe's wife had died in an accident of some kind, but hearing the words said out loud sent chills down her arms.

"He never told you?" Lori asked, obviously picking up on Hope's discomfort. Playing it cool in horribly unsettling circumstances clearly wasn't her strong suit, but it seemed wrong standing on Lori's lawn discussing these things without Gabe present. Like, maybe, this was his story to tell.

"He doesn't talk about it because he thinks it was his fault," Lori went on. "It wasn't his fault, of course. Carrie didn't think she could drive herself and Ruby home one night, but when Gabe missed her call she decided to drive herself and, well, that's when the accident happened. Carrie died in the hospital three days later. Ruby, by some miracle, barely had a scratch on her." Lori stated this like it was just a fact of life and not the most heart-wrenching story Hope had ever heard. Hope dropped her gaze to the grass as she fought back tears.

"She could have called me, or Dad, or one of her friends. Not that it was her fault, either. It was no one's fault. It was a horrible, horrible accident. But Gabe..." Lori cleared her throat. "Well, he's never forgiven himself. And he's never let anyone drive Ruby anywhere since then. Until today."

A gentle palm nudged Hope's cheek, and she looked up, her wet gaze meeting Lori's knowing one.

"Until you," Lori added.

They held eye contact for a long moment. Then Lori nodded approvingly and turned to face her house.

"We'll keep Ruby till Sunday. I'll touch base with Gabe about pickup," she said, her back to Hope, as she walked off.

With this new insight, Hope got into the Bronco and fumbled for her phone. She had promised to call Gabe before she left Lori's, and she now understood how absolutely important that would be for him, but when she clicked open her phone, her battery was down to one percent.

How had that happened? She could've sworn it was at thirty percent when she'd called him from the school. Or maybe it was at thirty percent this morning.

A slight panic swelled in her chest as her fingers flew to type out a text to Gabe, in case the blasted thing died on her while she tried to call him.

Hope: *Just dropped Ruby off at Lori's. All is well. On my way home.*

She pressed send, then she hit dial on his number and sent up a silent prayer that her battery would last.

"Hel—" was all she got of Gabe's voice before her phone went silent. And dark.

Quickly, she searched the Bronco to see if there was a charger she could use. Of course, she didn't find one. Murphy's-freaking-Law.

Ooookay, well, at least she got the text off. He'd know Ruby was safe at Lori's. He could call Lori if he wanted to double-check.

Easing out of Lori's driveway, she had a renewed appreciation for the car. It made total sense now why he'd drive a vehicle like this. It was basically Fort Knox on wheels.

She drove for a while, feeling humbled that he trusted her enough to drive Ruby. Maybe if they could build on that trust, they could work toward bridging the gap that had grown between them during the last week.

Because she wanted to. She wanted to fill in the gaps that still existed between them and create something special. If he could trust her with the most important thing in his life, she would do her best to be worthy of that trust, and maybe she could trust him too.

She only wished she'd taken the time to charge her darn phone.

"Well, it's too late now," she muttered to herself and turned onto the highway. She'd be home soon enough, anyway.

But ten minutes later, a loud bang pierced her ears, and killed her hope of *soon enough*.

CHAPTER TWENTY-ONE

here the fuck was she?

Gabe paced his office like a caged animal, trying his best not to lose his shit. Apparently, wearing a path in his office floor wasn't helping.

It had been over two hours since he'd got her text. Over two hours since he'd answered her call and got cut off before he could even say hello.

He'd called back about eighty times, and got her voice mail every single time. He'd called Lori and, sure enough, Hope had dropped Ruby off around 3:30. No one had heard from or seen her since. It was going on six now. His bar was filling up with the Friday night crowd. The plumber had fixed the dishwasher disaster. He should be out there running his bar.

Instead, he'd put Carter in charge, and gone out looking for her. He'd borrowed Sean's car and driven to his sister's house, re-tracing the few routes he thought she might have taken. There had been no sign of a vehicle collision, any extraordinary traffic delays, or Hope. After a while he'd had nowhere left to go but back to the bar, where he was now locked in his office trying, unsuccessfully, to rein in his panic.

This couldn't be happening again. Fate wouldn't be so fucking cruel.

Would it?

He tried to be logical. When he'd been out searching for her there'd been nothing to indicate the worst had happened, and yet... the anxiety building in the pit of his stomach seemed to have a direct link to the negative thoughts in his head. Every possible dark outcome played itself out in vivid detail in his mind.

He scanned his office for something he could punch or destroy. His gaze fell on a beer bottle sitting on the edge of his desk. In a desperate attempt to let off some steam, he hurled it against the far wall and watched it shatter.

He shouldn't have sent Hope. He could've left Harvey in charge of the kitchen disaster. He could've called Lori and asked her to get Ruby. He could've done a thousand different things to spare Hope from the curse that was his fucking life.

If something happened to her because of him—

Hunching over his desk, he gripped the edge ferociously, bowed his head, shut his eyes, and gritted teeth. All the anger, and pain, and injustice of his lifetime culminated in this one gut-wrenching moment of reckoning. All the hurt from the losses he'd endured burned a path through his core and emerged in a guttural roar that echoed through his very soul.

When had she become so vital to him?

He hadn't meant to let her in, but she waltzed in anyway. He hadn't meant to fall in love again, but he'd done it. And now he was paying the price. But even worse, Hope was paying for it.

He walked over to the couch in his office and sank into it, then dropped his head into his hands, fighting the reality that he might need to call the police if he didn't hear from her soon. A flashback of the two officers showing up at his bar the night of Carrie's accident invaded his thoughts. Nausea roiled in his gut.

He couldn't stay here another second. He had to find Hope. Making the split-second decision to go out and look for her again he made a beeline for his office door. The knock on it stopped him.

It was so soft, almost apologetic. He shook his head, incredulously, not sure if what he was hearing was real.

The knock came again. The doorknob turned. The sounds of his bar in full swing roared into his office. His heart slammed into his throat, the past dissolving as she appeared.

Hope.

She slipped into the room and shut the door behind her, shrouding them in silence. He could only stare at her standing there, alive and beautiful in front of him. For a brief moment, he thought she might be a mirage. Then she spoke.

"Gabe, I'm so sorry."

~

Across the room from Hope, Gabe stared back at her like she was a vision he couldn't trust. The hollow look in his usually vibrant green eyes told her what she'd cost him beginning with one careless moment of not charging her phone. For the millionth time in the last couple of hours, she mentally kicked herself for how the afternoon had unfolded.

She'd finally flagged down a driver and gotten them to call for a tow. Roadside service had changed her tire, and off she went, but the whole process had taken a lot longer than she anticipated. And before she knew, it was *a lot* later than she imagined.

Now she was here, looking into Gabe's haunted eyes, and a renewed regret bloomed in her chest. She should have tried harder to get a hold of him.

When he dropped down on the couch and hunched over his knees with his face in his hands, Hope rushed to kneel on the floor in front of him. "Gabe," she said and was met with silence.

His broad shoulders remained rigid, his entire body unmoving.

Tentatively, she reached for him, wrapping her fingers around each wrist. "Look at me," she pleaded.

Finally, he lifted his face and his green eyes burned into hers. She inhaled a shocked breath at the raw emotion she found there.

"I'm so sorry," she whispered again. "My phone died. Then I had a flat tire. I tried to wave someone down, but it was harder than I thought, and..." She drifted off, the words falling flat even though they were true. She knew it wasn't her actions that had caused him pain, but the past she had brought back to haunt him. She lifted her shoulders, then let them drop. "I thought if Ruby was safely at your sister's, that you'd—"

He cocked his eyebrows in the universal look that said, *go on*.

"She's okay, Gabe." Hope reminded him softly.

He jerked back, but she held firm. He could've easily moved away from her or pushed her away from him, but he didn't. She took some reassurance in that.

"You think I was only worried about Ruby?" he finally said, his voice gravel. Lethal. "I knew she was safe."

Hope swallowed painfully.

Gripping one of her wrists, he pressed her palm to his chest. Beneath the hard ridge of muscle, she could feel his heart pounding wildly. "I didn't know where *you* were. I couldn't find *you*." His voice was deep and steady, but his eyes held a world of anguish. She could see the fear in them too, and it told her the truth.

He'd thought she'd been hurt, maybe even killed. His mind had taken him to the worst-case scenario because it had happened to him before. Heartache sliced through her, and suddenly she felt the weight of his grief as if it were her own. He'd believed he was reliving his nightmare, and she'd as good as let him believe it.

"I'm so sorry," she whispered, her throat tightening. The impact of how much they were coming to mean to each other settled over her. "I didn't mean to scare you." With her free hand, she ran her fingers along his cheek, feeling the coarse stubble along his jaw. Remembering what Lori had divulged to her earlier, she murmured, "The accident wasn't your fault, Gabe."

She watched his face harden and his eyes grow cold, but he didn't pretend to misunderstand her. "How would you know?"

"Lori told me what happened that night," she said quietly. She wedged herself closer between his splayed knees, needing to be as close to him as possible. To let him know she was there. Right there, with him.

His eyes narrowed. "Did she?"

"Don't—don't be—mad," she stammered, suddenly uncertain.

"What exactly did my sister tell you, Hope?"

"She said that the night of the accident, Carrie called to ask you for a ride, but you missed the call." Hope watched him closely, but his steely gaze gave nothing away. "So she went, and on the drive back there was an accident and—and —" She couldn't bring herself to say the words out loud.

Gabe laughed darkly. "My sister doesn't have her facts right." He scrubbed a rough hand down his face and blew out a breath. "I didn't miss her call. I ignored it. I saw that call come in, but I was in the middle of something at work that couldn't wait." As he spoke his tone was mirthless, his eyes increasingly distant, like he wasn't here with her but somewhere far away. "I hit 'ignore' thinking I'd call her back in a minute, but of course that minute never came. Next thing I knew, two cops were in my bar telling me that there'd been an accident and my wife and baby were at the hospital."

Hope murmured his name, unsure of what else to say or do. She felt so helpless, watching him relive the worst of his life through the reflection of his eyes.

"Carrie was an ER nurse. Shifts. Brutal ones. Some twelve hours long. Some longer. Often through the night. Those were the worst. She went back to work three months after Ruby was born when her mat leave ended. She was still breastfeeding, so when she worked nights I'd bottle feed Ruby the milk she pumped."

Hope listened, the story unraveling in her mind like a live action film. An exhausted mother pumping breastmilk during breaks at work so her husband could feed their baby on nights she wasn't home.

"The bar was less than a year old. I was always there. It took up all my time. During days when Carrie wasn't at the hospital, she was with Ruby. She was doing everything. Burning the candle on both ends. But I didn't see it. I just didn't fucking see it. I was too wrapped up in making the bar a success thinking it was the only way I could provide for my new family. And she never complained. She never—so I didn't see how tired she was. How worn out. I was so fucking blind."

Something in his voice caught, and tears immediately spilled over Hope's eyes in response. Watching a man like Gabe become emotional—it was gut-wrenching. But it was also the most she'd ever heard him speak about his wife or her death. She didn't want to interrupt him.

He brought a knuckle to his eye and dug it in. "Ruby was in a daycare twenty minutes away from the house we lived in at the time. That evening—that evening after a twelve-hour shift Carrie called me. She wanted me to come pick her and Ruby up because she was so fucking exhausted she didn't trust herself to drive." He dropped his hand to his lap, eyes lost in the past. "The phone rang and I was in the middle of something, so I let it go to voicemail. She left a message. I just thought I'd listen to it later, whenever I was done with whatever the fuck I was doing that I thought was more important at the time." A muscle popped in his jaw, and Hope guessed he probably couldn't even remember what he'd been doing at the time he'd missed his wife's call. "I must have listened to that message a thousand times afterwards."

Silence sat between them like an uninvited guest, glaring and awkward.

Then Gabe's eyes refocused on Hope's as he slowly came back to her. "So, you see, Hope. I ignored my family, and my wife died thinking that this goddam bar was more important to me than her life. She died knowing that I wasn't there when she needed me."

If he'd sounded cold before, he sounded utterly without

emotion now. But she knew that wasn't the case. She could feel the anguish, remorse, and despair rolling off him in waves.

Tears flooded her eyes as she shook her head. Had he really thought that for all these years? "No, Gabe, she didn't think that. This bar was your family's livelihood. You were in it together. I'm sure she understood that. If she had really thought she couldn't handle it, she would have tried harder to get a hold of you. Or called someone else."

"It wasn't her fault," he said grimly.

"You're right, it wasn't." Still squatting in front of him, Hope reached up and ran her palm along the curve of his jaw, holding his gaze so she could be sure he was really listening to her. "But it wasn't yours, either."

There was no stopping the tears that streamed down her cheeks, mourning the loss of life, the years of anguish, the woman who never got to truly experience motherhood, the child who never got to know her mother, and the man in front of her who'd spent every hour since blaming himself for it all.

"Gabe, at some point you're going to have to stop living your life like lightning will strike twice every time you let a little bit of trust in."

She found she couldn't stop touching his face, running her fingers over his eyes, his mouth, his jaw, wanting to soothe the pain away, but he lifted his hands now to cover hers, stilling her movements. For a moment, they just stared into each other's eyes. Deep brown against molten green.

"I'm scared," he admitted, and by the way the words came out, like there was just a thin passage in his throat for them to escape, she could tell he was being as vulnerable as he'd ever let himself be.

"Give some of it to me. Let me help you carry the fear." It

was all she could offer him. "We'll calm it together." It was all she could promise.

When he finally released her, it was only to envelop her face between his hands and crush his lips against hers. Spreading his thighs wider, he dragged her even closer, pulling her up on her knees so her torso came flush with his. Then, weaving his hands through her hair, he simply devoured.

Hope wasn't sure she'd even call what was happening a kiss. It was raw and greedy, possessive and frantic, as though he were pouring every last ounce of emotion into this one all-consuming connection. She could only loop her arms around his neck and hold on as she met each stroke of his tongue with one of her own. The fire built between them until the heat they were creating became explosive.

Finally, Hope pulled away, gasping for air as she looked at him. His eyes were dilated and dark. The misery that had lived in them a moment before was replaced by a hunger. A hunger they both needed sated.

With unhurried movements, she got to her feet, knowing they were about to close one door and open another. The moment was powerful, significant, and she had never felt closer to him. Their gazes held while Gabe reached forward and curled two fingers into the waistband of her jeans. With a growl he tugged her forward until she was back in the space between his legs, so close she would have felt his breath against her skin were it not for the inconvenient clothes she was wearing.

As if he could read her mind, Gabe reached for the button of her jeans and flicked it, letting out a groan when it opened with an echoing pop. Slowly, he slid the zipper down, then tugged it, so she came closer again—this time his breath heated the skin just above the pale blue silk of her panties, and Hope felt a burst of feminine pride when he muttered a curse.

She sent a silent prayer of thanksgiving to the wardrobe gods that she'd done laundry the day before. This underwear reveal could have gone very differently twenty-four hours ago.

"Take them off," he ordered, his voice hoarse.

Part of her, the part that was always desperate and aching for his touch, wanted to rip her clothes off and jump onto him for a hard and fast ride that matched the desperation coursing through her.

But the other part of her, the part that wanted so much more than that with him, was intent on savoring the moment. A moment that seemed all the more pivotal given how he'd just opened himself up to her. So she took her time sliding her pants down until they fell to her ankles. Toeing off her shoes, she kicked the last of her jeans off.

"Take off your shirt," Gabe commanded next.

Once again, she obeyed. Then, without being asked, she unsnapped her bra and let it drop to the floor along with the rest of her clothes. She stood before him now, wearing nothing but a pale blue silk thong.

"Hope." He uttered her name like a prayer, his tone reverent.

Hooking his fingers into the seam of her panties, he dragged them down her thighs and past her knees. Gabe groaned as his gaze feasted on her. Palming the backs of her thighs, he ran his hands up until he cupped her ass. He squeezed her cheeks then slid his hands between her legs until his fingertips grazed her center from behind—and released yet another appreciative growl.

"Open," he demanded, nudging her legs farther apart.

Gabe's gaze, intense and focused, zeroed in on the center

of her femininity, and Hope couldn't believe she'd once felt self-conscious to be bared so fully in front of a man. With Gabe she felt exhilarated when he stared at her like this, a powerful sense of thrill firing through her when he looked at her naked and wanting in front of him. She felt the opposite of self-conscious. She felt proud and bold.

And when his tongue stroked over her swollen center, she sucked in a breath and felt nothing but the exquisite pleasure of his flesh on hers. There was nothing, *nothing* that could accurately describe the sensations that arrowed through her when he set his mouth on her. He licked and sucked until she had to clutch his shoulders to stay upright. Her pants turned to desperate pleas. She sobbed his name over and over. When he slid his finger inside her, matching the rhythm of his wicked tongue, she lost it—and exploded against his mouth.

Her legs refused to hold her up. She collapsed to straddle him still sitting on the couch. Reeling from the intensity of her release, she watched Gabe quickly unzip his own jeans and free himself. He rolled on a condom and guided her onto him.

As she took him inside her, she watched, awed, as he closed his eyes and sheer relief washed over his face—like he'd been hanging off a cliff by his fingertips and she'd just thrown him a rope. His broad chest rose and fell in deep breaths as he held her, the rest of him unmoving. Whether he was savoring the sensation of filling her or trying to get a grip on his control, she couldn't be sure. But she knew that in this position, he was at her mercy. She only had to move, and he'd be unable to resist. Buoyed by the sexual confidence and desire that raced through her, she slowly rolled her hips forward, then back.

His eyes opened, and the intensity in them made her own fill instantly.

"Do you have any idea how much power you have over me?" he growled through gritted teeth as he raised his hips fractionally.

She caught her breath, not knowing how to acknowledge this revelation. She didn't want to feel its weight or the pressure it carried. She didn't want to have *complete* power over him, or anyone, not when there was still so much he didn't know about her. So much she wasn't sure she could ever share with anyone. She might never let Gabe in the same way he'd let her in tonight. She wanted to share in his pain but she still wasn't sure how or if he could ever fully share in hers.

So she took the coward's way out and ignored his impassioned words. Instead, she gave him the one thing that was hers to give freely. Rolling her hips over him again, she squeezed her inner muscles. His satisfied groan spurred her on.

She lifted her hips then bore down again and again, running her hands down his chest and through his hair and anywhere else she could, the need to be as close to him as possible consuming her.

Gabe stroked his tongue over her nipple. She moaned appreciatively when he nipped her pebbled skin, then blew on it. His fingers moved to her over-sensitized flesh where they were joined, rubbing and stroking as his mouth continued its lick, nip, blow staccato.

At this rate, she wasn't going to be able to hold out for long. As much as she wanted to hurtle toward her release, she desired something more.

"I want you to come," she gasped.

He laughed against her breast. "Trust me, sweetheart, that's not gonna be a problem."

She shook her head. "No." Her body started to tighten and shudder, so she tried to still the rhythm of her hips, but he only bucked into her harder. "I want you to come with me," she panted, raking her fingernails down his washboard abs. "Together."

"Hope," Gabe growled. "You're killing me."

"Please! It's starting, Gabe." She moaned. "I want to feel you coming inside me while I do." She undulated with abandon now, racing toward her orgasm, its pressure building inside her.

Gabe surged to his feet, gripping her hips as his mouth came down on hers madly. His tongue pillaged as he hammered into her, rebounding her off his hips with each hard thrust.

When the delirium of passion threatened to overwhelm her senses, she tore her lips from his and dropped her gaze between them. Her breasts were bouncing, their skin slapping as he moved in and out of her, his biceps bulging as he held her to him. But it was the sight of his length disappearing inside her, over and over, that made her let go with a cry.

"Oh God, I'm coming," she sobbed, as her climax flooded through her. "Gabe! Please!"

Through a storm of erotic sensation, he kept her close for one last powerful thrust, and then he came with her.

He collapsed back onto the couch, taking her with him, his chest heaving against hers, their heart beats pounding in tandem, reassuring her. She wasn't the only one with this demanding, insatiable need burning inside. Dropping her head onto his chest as she worked to catch her breath, Hope relished the feeling, and shifted so she could lay a palm over his racing heart.

Gabe ran his hands down her spine to cup her backside, keeping her tucked against him. She felt cherished, warm and protected. It was a long while before the world around them slowly came back to focus. The thrumming sounds of the bar on Friday night vibrated through his office walls.

"You probably need to get back to the bar," she said, into the crook of his shoulder. She felt bad keeping him from his work obligations for so long already.

"It's been running fine without me all night. I'm good right here." His arms remained locked around her hips, anchoring her to him—with him still inside her and the aftershocks of her orgasms still rippling over him in little spasms. Hope sighed contentedly.

Only after a chill from the room sent a shiver down the length of her body, did Gabe slowly draw her back. "I'll get in there to finish the shift and close the bar, but after—" He stared at her intently. "I want you to spend the rest of the night with me."

The way he was looking at her made her wonder if he feared she might say no, as if she'd want to be anywhere else tonight. "I want that, too," she whispered.

Warmth swamped her heart when the first real smile she'd seen in days broke across his rugged face.

Lifting herself off him, she gathered her clothing from his office floor. When she was finally dressed, she smoothed her hands down her front in a vain attempt to feel less rumpled. Then she caught Gabe leaning against his desk looking gorgeous and composed and decidedly unrumpled as he watched her with gleaming eyes.

"I'm sorry," she said, doing her best to sound cavalier, because dammit, she hated feeling flustered and out of her element while he looked totally comfortable and in control. "Is something amusing?"

When his crooked half-smile turned into a full one, her haughty stance melted a fragment because, God, he was irresistible when he smiled. Gabe pushed away from his desk and came to her, threading his fingers into her hair as if they belonged there. Then he leaned in and kissed her crazy. She dove right in, because apparently her body was loath to resist him. They only pulled apart when their need for oxygen demanded it.

"Nothing amusing, Hope. You're so damn beautiful, inside and out. You make me happy. You put a smile on my face." He tipped his forehead to hers, looking into her eyes deeply. "Is that okay with you?"

And there, in the back office of a bar in the Pearl District in Portland, the last part of her heart opened and handed itself to him. She was a goner. She'd fallen for him completely, which was beyond scary, because she was still hiding part of herself from him. She wasn't lying to him exactly, because he hadn't probed. But one day, when he inevitably asked about her past, she'd have to lie because it wasn't altogether her story to tell. And a man like Gabe wouldn't stand for lies.

Which left her completely head over heels for him and desperately afraid it would all be taken away at any moment. *Poof.* A dream that she could have sworn was real but wasn't.

It was all too big and overwhelming, a fear she couldn't confront right now, so instead she leaned into him and whispered, "It's more than okay."

CHAPTER TWENTY-TWO

Normally, a Friday night at Bowie's flew by. The flurry of movement, the sound of laughter and conversation threading through the beat of the live music, the scented heat from the dancing bodies on the floor, not to mention the steady stream of drink-a-long-week-off Portlanders usually made the hours burn through to last call.

This Friday night, however, was dragging on for so long, Gabe found himself checking the time on his phone every five minutes—and cursing each time the numbers didn't reflect what he wanted. Twice he had almost convinced himself to shut the bar down early. All he wanted to do was pick up Hope and haul her off to his apartment, like a fucking caveman, so he could spend the rest of the night buried inside her.

After she left his office, she ran up to her apartment to shower and change clothes, insisting that she wanted to spend the evening helping him at the bar. So she was now wearing black-and-white Converse sneakers, a Bowie's shirt that she'd tied under her breasts in one of those knots that gave a peek-a-boo view of her stomach, and the shortest, tightest skirt he'd ever laid eyes on. She'd spent the last several hours bussing tables or covering staff breaks by waitressing or tending bar as needed. Watching her work the place, *his* place, like she'd been there for years, had turned him on to the point of discomfort.

From behind the bar—where he'd been ogling Hope like some horny teenager for hours, hard as a fucking rock —he glanced at the clock. Almost midnight now, thank Christ.

He finished mixing a Moscow Mule for one of the suits from the law offices down the street, snuck a peek at Hope again, then set the drink in front of the suit—whose gaze darted to where Gabe had just looked and landed on Hope as she leaned over a table collecting empty glasses, her tight little ass on full display. The suit let out a low whistle, swiveling his gaze back to Gabe's with a nod of companionable appreciation. Gabe nearly ground his molars into dust as he leveled the shitbag with a look of his own.

The suit suddenly became as smart as he was dressed. He grabbed his drink and disappeared into the bar—in the opposite direction of Hope.

Christ. There'd been a time when he actually thought he could have a casual fling with her and then move on. Then tonight happened, and every moment they'd had together in the last several months flashed through his brain like one of those romantic movies she loved to watch with Ivy and always told him about.

Seeing her outside her apartment, vulnerable and crying, draping his jacket over her, needing to protect her even then.

Having her show up to help him over and over again. Watching her play Barbies cross-legged on his daughter's bedroom floor while she dropped her voice and pretended to be Ken.

Memorizing the way her cheeks blushed the prettiest pink when he complimented her.

Bringing her along to dance recitals and elementary school spring concerts like it was the most natural thing in the world.

Sitting with her, night after night, eating food she'd made for him, listening to her go on about all the little things that were happening in their lives. *Theirs,* because without even trying they'd become so interwoven that it felt like she'd always been there. In his apartment, in his daughter's life, in his heart.

The only way out of the grief and crushing guilt he'd been trapped in for so long had been her. Hope.

He'd tried to slow things down, put on some breaks, keep things less intimate, but he'd been kidding himself. A Hope-less life had never even been an option.

If he hadn't fully understood that before, he'd had the rude awakening tonight, when she'd scared the living daylights out of him. In all his life, he hadn't known that level of fear, not even when Carrie died. He'd been blindsided then, and there hadn't been time for fear when the cop showed up at this very bar to tell him there'd been an accident. He'd only felt a cold numbness and dread for the three long days before they made the decision to take Carrie off life support. Then there'd been crushing grief. Bucket loads of guilt and apprehension about his future as a single father. But not fear. It'd been too damn late for fear.

But tonight, when Hope hadn't come home, when he couldn't contact her, when he couldn't find her, when no one he'd called knew where the fuck she was—he'd suffered a panic unlike any he'd ever known. He'd never felt so helpless and terrified, imagining every godforsaken scenario over and over until he thought he'd go insane.

Then she'd walked through his office door and all he could feel was a relief and love so fierce he'd nearly collapsed at her feet.

Yeah, there'd be no getting Hope Morgan out of his system now.

After what seemed like days but was really only a couple of hours, he finally signaled to Carter that it was time to escort the drunk stragglers out and lock the front door.

He spent another twenty minutes on the shutdown routine, then asked Carter if he could cover for him tomorrow night.

Carter gave him a look like he'd grown a second head. And Gabe couldn't blame him. It wasn't like he made a habit of leaving anyone in charge on a Saturday night at the last minute, what with his trust and control issues and all. But Carter was his right hand at the bar, and Gabe did trust him. And after tonight's scare, he was renewing his vow to focus on his priorities.

"Something came up," he said by way of explanation.

"By something, do you mean Hope?" Carter asked as he casually dried a glass with the bar towel that had been slung over his shoulder.

"By something, I mean none of your damn business," Gabe bit out, and Carter snorted a laugh. "Can I count on you, or do I have to put fucking Harvey in charge?"

This only made Carter laugh harder.

Not in the mood for dramatics, he said, "You know what? Forget it." He turned to leave, but Carter grabbed his shoulder, stopping him.

"Man, relax. I've got the bar tomorrow." His tone was now serious, but his baby blues were still alight with amusement. "I've got your back. Go get your girl. You deserve more time with her."

Gabe grunted in acquiescence and went to find Hope. She was in the staff room, shrugging into a short jacket, when he found her.

He propped his shoulder on the doorjamb and enjoyed the view of her body as she moved to put on her jacket. The lift of her arms that pulled her t-shirt up to expose more of her smooth skin. The way her breasts strained against the t-shirt. The pretty fall of her hair as she removed it from of its ponytail.

She was gorgeous. In every way a person could be. And she was just about everything he'd assumed she wasn't when she'd first appeared in his world.

Hope was hooking her purse over her shoulder when she noticed him, and a smile spread across her face that lit up his whole night.

"Where do you think you're going?" he asked gruffly.

"Hey," she said sweetly, but he could feel the heat of desire behind her casual acknowledgment. He could feel it because it mirrored his own. She wanted him every bit as much as he wanted her, and he was done making either of them wait for what they wanted. "I don't know. I thought maybe you'd want to go out for a drink or something."

He moved toward her, reveling in the way her tongue darted out to wet her lips as she watched his approach like he was a long cold drink and she was dying of thirst. He threaded his fingers into her soft, golden hair and tipped her face up to look up at him.

"The only place I want to go with you is home," he said. Fuck, it felt like he hadn't touched her in days, not hours.

Her dark brown eyes melted as they locked on his.

"Good," she said, her voice breathless. "Because I want to go home with you too."

Then he dragged her to him, so that every inch of her was touching every inch of him, and kissed her. She moaned, completely undoing him, and when she wrapped her arms around his neck, rubbing her whole body against his, she set his blood on fire with desire.

He had to have her, would have had her right here on the staff room floor if he could have, but he'd already taken her like a desperate animal tonight, and she deserved a lot more finesse for round two. So when those bewitching fingers crawled their way beneath his t-shirt, he summoned the dredges of his control and held her away from him.

"Not here, Hope."

A look of disappointment flashed so quick in her eyes he almost missed it, but it betrayed her need. She was as desperate as he was.

"I want you upstairs, in my empty apartment, in my bed, under me, screaming my name so loud you'll be hoarse for a week."

Her eyes went from chocolate brown to near black as her pupils dilated.

He offered up a wicked smile as he added, "Empty apartment this time. No reason to be quiet." He grabbed her hand and led her out of the staff room and up the back staircase in less than a minute.

In front of his apartment door, he fumbled with the keys like a shaky virgin, almost dropping the damn things when she pressed against his back to run the tip of her tongue along the curve of his earlobe.

Shit, if she kept this up, he was going to come in his pants—and he hadn't done that since he actually had been a fumbling virgin.

By the time he'd shoved his keys into the lock and pushed open the door, he was sweating. He had the door shut and Hope pressed up against the inside of it in under a second. His mouth found hers and he kissed her with all the desperation that'd built inside him throughout the torturous night.

He all but ripped off her jacket and shirt. Rearing back, he stared at her for a minute, taking in the sight of her chest heaving as she sucked in air, her beautiful breasts straining against the lace of her black bra. Then he claimed her mouth like a man starving.

It was alarming how desperate she made him feel. How he lost control with her every fucking time. He wanted to lift her skirt, shove away her panties, free himself from his jeans, and be inside her. He didn't care that he didn't have a condom on hand, and he didn't care what the consequences would be.

And suddenly, there it was. The image of Hope pregnant with his child lodged in his mind and a feeling of rightness enveloped his heart, flooding him with warmth. He jerked away from her, more than a little panicked at where his thoughts had gone. It was too soon to be thinking those things—she was still so young. Too young. He'd been her age when he'd had Ruby, and while his daughter was the single most important thing that had ever happened to him, he also knew how many other things he could have done and experienced if his life had taken another path.

Hope deserved a chance to live out whatever dreams she wanted. Especially the ones that had brought her to Portland.

Which, he was pretty sure, did not include getting knocked up by him.

Oblivious, Hope used the space between them as an opportunity to undress him.

"Off," she panted, her fingers tugging at his shirt as she tried to find purchase.

Shaking off the shocking realization that he wanted a real future with Hope Morgan that involved commitment and family and white picket fences, he yanked off his shirt in one fierce tug. When he refocused on her, he caught her staring wide eyed at his chest, running her gaze up and down his torso, her lips parted. The look of sheer feminine hunger brought him fully back to his desire, and he chuckled under his breath as he pulled her down the hall to his bedroom.

"Come with me if you want to see more," he rasped as he waggled his eyebrows.

Behind him, she laughed, a sound that never failed to chip away at the darkness ghosting his heart.

In his room, he edged her to the bed and cupped her face as he gazed intently into her eyes, needing her to know the joking was over. "This is more, Hope," he said, praying she could read the truth of that statement in his tone and his eyes. "This is so much more than I thought it ever could be. And I don't know where it's going, but I know I'll never be ready for it to stop."

The way she stared back at him, her eyes dark and unreadable, made his heart pound in his chest, because for a moment he thought she might actually turn away from him. It would crush him if she did, but he was prepared to take it like a man. He'd never take from her what she wasn't willing to give.

When she danced her fingertips softly over his pecs, lighting his body with a fire of sensations, he shuddered with a wave of relief.

"I'm not ready for it to stop, either," she whispered.

With one nudge he toppled them both onto the bed behind her, and she gave a startled cry, then a giggle, which died in her throat when he hooked his fingers into the top of her skirt. He tugged it, and her panties, down the length of her killer legs. Then he hovered above her for a moment and just looked at her.

He wasn't sure how the hell he got so lucky to be given this second chance with another amazing woman, so he wasn't going to ask too many questions. He was just going to be damn grateful.

Leaning over, he ran his tongue lazily across her nipple. He loved her breasts. Loved the sound she made when he licked them. Loved the way her hands clawed at his back, trying to bring him closer. She was so responsive, turning to fire under his caresses, and he dipped his fingers between their bodies to run them along her core, groaning hungrily at how wet and ready he found her.

She called out his name. Not quietly this time, but loudly, urgently. The sound of it tearing from her lips made him feel like he had a superpower.

Quickly, he shucked his jeans and boxer briefs, grabbed a condom from the nightstand, and ripped it from the foil. Hope yanked the condom out of his hands. Then, gently, carefully, she slipped it over the tip of his erection, her eyes so focused that she looked like she might be conducting an elaborate science experiment. Any laughter he had at the studious look on her face died in his throat when she smoothed the condom over his length with her long, delicate fingers.

"Holy shit, Hope," was all he had to offer as sensation coursed through him.

After she finished with the condom, she stretched her

arms up over her head, lifted her knees, and opened them wide, exposing herself to him in the most intimate way.

"You can make me scream now," she said, a devilish smile gracing her gorgeous face.

He couldn't get enough of this woman. In the outside world, she was sweet, smart, gentle, calm. But in the bedroom, in *his* bedroom with him, she was turning out to be quite the little vixen. And he loved it.

Accepting her sassy challenge, he drove into her with one powerful thrust. Satisfaction and pleasure shot through him when her back arched off the bed to meet him halfway.

Pulling back out, he rolled his hips forward, slamming into her again.

"Gabe!" she cried.

Christ, she was hot, and tight, and felt so fucking perfect he could have lost himself inside her right then and there. Gripping her thighs, he held her legs tight at his side, forcing himself to exercise some control over his movements.

Within moments, she was writhing under him, calling out unintelligible words that he understood intuitively. She spoke to his heart, which understood every word, knowing exactly what she needed, and how hard she needed it. Together they set a rhythm that had them barreling straight to ecstasy at a record speed. Reaching between them, he thumbed the spot he knew would tip her over the edge and proved himself right when his name tore from her throat— half pant, half scream. Again. And again, and again.

When she came down from the high, he hoisted her legs over his shoulders. Thrusting in at this new angle got him about as deep as he could go. Below him, already spent from one orgasm, Hope moaned.

He urged her on, sliding in and out of her in measured

thrusts. His body tightened almost painfully in the desperation for release, but he kept his rhythm controlled. One more time. He wanted to make her come *one more time.*

"More?" he asked, his breathing increasingly ragged.

"Yes!" she said frantically, lifting her hips to meet him. "Yes, please yes."

He shifted, pinning her legs to his chest with one arm as he pounded into her.

She got louder the closer she came to her release, but when she dropped her hands to roll her nipples between her fingers, her neck arching into the pillows under her, it was Gabe who lost it.

Control went out the window. It always did with Hope. Every damn time.

Bucking wildly, incoherent grunts escaped his mouth like a caged animal come loose. And when she reached her climax moments later, her muscles squeezing him even harder and tighter than the first time, he roared her name as his own release slammed through him.

CHAPTER TWENTY-THREE

When Hope woke the next morning, the first thing she heard was the faint rush of water. *Shower,* she thought, stretching her body and moaning in pleasure as she savored the delicious pull of muscles that hadn't seen this kind of action in years. Sex truly was a most excellent workout. She was pretty sure she'd burned a zillion calories through the night. And this morning.

Buoyed by the memories from a couple of hours ago, when dawn was cracking through the shutters and Gabe nestled low between her legs to gently lick her out of slumber, she kicked the covers off her heated body and followed the sound of running water into a small ensuite.

She took a moment to appreciate the sheer masculine beauty of his tall, broad form behind the fogged glass of the shower door.

His head was bowed as he leaned into the spray, hands braced against the tile, water pouring down his head and over his toned back.

She felt herself go damp at the mere sight of him. She had no idea when she'd developed a ravenous sexual appetite, but she knew it had everything to do with this man. Quietly, she slipped into the shower, looped her arms around his torso, and pressed her body against his back.

Gabe froze for a beat, then expelled a harsh breath when she ran her fingertips down his ripped abs to her favorite appendage, which was already deliciously hard. She shivered with the memory of how good it felt when he'd been deep inside her.

She reached up on tiptoe to kiss him. "Morning." She smiled against his lips, before slowly sinking to her knees on the floor of the shower.

"What are you doing?" Gabe asked, his voice a gruff rumble.

Hope ran her hand along his length in one long stroke.

"Hope." His tone was a warning, which she ignored with a smile.

Instead, she did what she'd wanted to do since she woke to the sound of the shower running. She bent her head, taking him into her mouth as far as she could, running her tongue along his smooth skin.

She had to clench her legs tight when a rough growl tore from his lips, his hands tangling in her hair in a firm grip. She loved the sound of his passion and was pretty sure she could come from that sound alone, but she'd had her turn earlier. This time, she wanted to get her pleasure solely from giving him his.

~

Later, as they toweled each other off, Gabe casually said, "So I thought we'd spend the day together."

Hope stilled. They'd talked briefly last night about this thing between them being *more*, and her heart had sung at the idea. She wanted more with him so badly she could taste it.

But she was apprehensive. There were things he didn't know about her past. Things she didn't even know how to share with him without betraying Ivy. Things that were complicated and painful, and quite frankly things she didn't really want to relive again—but knew she had to. For him, she had to.

She just hadn't quite worked out the how or the when yet. Which made her feel like they were starting off on the wrong foot and he didn't even know it. And that didn't sit right with her.

As if sensing her hesitation, Gabe stepped forward, his damp body towering over hers, his slightly too long hair—made even longer by the weight of the water—curling at the nape of his neck and around his ears. He took her towel from her, dropped it on the floor, and pulled her into his arms.

"Hope, last night was..." He dipped his head until he held her gaze fixed on his. "Last night was the closest I've been with anyone since Carrie died. Both physically and emotionally. I told you I wanted more, and I meant it. I want more of you. I want to learn more about you. I want to explore this thing between us." He looked as serious as she'd ever seen him, and she realized he was putting it all on the line for her. "I know I'm not always easy, and I come with a shit load of baggage and—" He halted when she lowered her gaze.

Little did he know she also came with a shit load of baggage.

"And Ruby..."

"I love Ruby," she said adamantly, her gaze flying back to meet his.

His eyes burned into hers, searching for the truth. After a moment, he must have found what he needed because he relaxed.

"So," he repeated. "Spend the day with me. Just us. We can keep going slow if you want to. I just don't want us to stop."

With his damp body pressed against hers, his words soft, enticing, and most of all, honest, she had a hard time reminding herself of the reasons she should be hesitating.

She needed to trust that when the time came and her past came out, he would understand. He would understand because he knew about sacrifices better than anyone. He would recognize why she'd made hers and support her. She had to stop second-guessing him—them.

With that thought in her head, she looked up at him, a small smile breaking free, a sense of peace flooding her heart. "Does the day start with breakfast?"

Gabe grinned, and his green eyes shone. "It does." Then he tossed her over his shoulder as she shrieked and headed back to the bed. "But first, dessert."

They spent the day together, just the two of them, and it felt so good and so right that Hope let all her worries about her past and the secrets that lived there fade away. She gave herself permission to enjoy this time with Gabe, holding hands as they strolled through the city, exploring the amazing street art that poured life and color into every district, and popping into local shops on a whim. She enjoyed hearing him describe the city from his perspective as a born-and-raised local, feeling closer to him with every story he told, every location he brought her to. She reveled in seeing this carefree side of him that she'd rarely seen before.

It got to be evening, and though it was March, at five o'clock it was still quite dark. Still, it didn't feel as bleak as it had when she'd arrived all those weeks ago. Or maybe it was that she didn't feel as bleak as she previously had.

So much had changed in such a short time she didn't even feel like the same person she'd been back then, frustrated and desperate to break away from her family. For the first time in years, she felt like she'd found a sense of what she really wanted out of her life, and it looked much different from what she thought all along.

She wanted peace with her family, the only family she'd ever known. More than ever, she wanted to put the past to rest. She wanted to look to the future, a future that she wanted to build here in the City of Roses.

She'd come to appreciate her independence and the new parts of herself she'd discovered over the last few weeks. She was diving deeper into her art and was excited to see where it would take her. She wanted to spend more time with Ruby and be inspired by her fresh perspective on life. She wanted Gabe, for as long as he would have her—which undoubtedly would be only until he found out about the cheating scandal at USC, or at least the version that had been made public.

"Why Portland?" Gabe asked casually, breaking her out of her reverie.

They were sitting on a bench by the river, looking out at the water and sipping coffee from biodegradable to-go cups.

She turned to face him. "Why do you ask?"

"You looked pensive," he said with a shrug. "I assumed you were missing home, and it got me thinking that you never really told me what brought you here."

When she stared at him, stunned that he'd read her thoughts so easily, Gabe's mouth kicked up on the side, and he looped his arm around her shoulders and cradled her against his chest.

"So, tell me how a well-bred California girl like you ends up in a cramped apartment above a bar in Portland, far away from her family mansion?" His voice was lighthearted, but she knew it was a serious question. A valid one too.

She was as misplaced in this city as pickles on peanut butter.

"It's not cramped," she said, snuggling into him a bit more. "I find it quite spacious actually."

He snorted but said nothing. Waiting her out, she mused. He wouldn't push, but he wouldn't let it go either. She knew this about him now. She sighed, deciding that she could offer him a nugget of truth, if nothing else.

"I was heartbroken." When she felt him stiffen, she hastened to add, "Not like that. My family." She'd never talked about the complex feelings that had lived inside her since she'd learned about her adoption. "It's not easy, thinking you're one thing for so many years, then realizing you're not that at all. That you don't know what or who you are." She took comfort in the fresh air off the river gusting against her cheeks and the feel of Gabe's arm around her. "When I found out, I felt an incredible anger, but I also suddenly felt even more pressure to prove myself as a Morgan. Like I needed to justify that I still had a place in the family. It doesn't make a lot of sense, I know."

Gabe's arms tightened around her. "It makes sense to me," he mumbled into her hair, and once again she wished things between them could include the guarantee of a future.

"Before I even found out about being adopted, I felt this

need to prove that I deserved to be a part of the family, a part of the business, but I wanted to do it without any of their help and none of their money." She laughed mirthlessly. "It's kind of like I knew all along. I just didn't want to admit it. So I went to the USC to study business, not loving it but feeling like I had to. To prove that I could be what they wanted." She was silent for a while, her years at USC playing through her head at super speed. "They never pressured me outright. Never told me I had to—but growing up, it was always there. Morgan Construction is my father's legacy. It was built up by my father to be handed down to my brother and me. There was no question. For Joel, it was all he ever wanted. The first thing I thought when I found out I was adopted was—" She paused, hating this part of herself. "I thought, *now it all makes sense.* Joel's drive, his innate ability. It was because he was a biological Morgan. It came naturally to him. The wanting. The desire to be a part of the family business. For so long, I wanted to want it too. Like it would prove I was meant to be there."

She shrugged. "In the end, I was tired of trying to be who I thought everyone wanted me to be, and when I found out at Christmas that I was adopted, it felt right to come here, to be who I wanted to be instead of who I'd been molded to be. And do what I wanted to do, instead of what I was expected to do. I wanted to be independent. Myself." She let her words hang there. Hoping they would be enough for him for now.

"So, what you wanted was to come here and become a nanny?" he asked, and she couldn't help it—she laughed.

"No! Well, yes. I love Ruby, but it wasn't what I expected when I arrived. Ultimately though, it was exactly what I wanted. Needed," she amended and meant it. "When I came, I applied for a bunch of business jobs I thought would make my family proud but be different enough that I'd feel a sense of accomplishment. But I didn't get any of them, which is just as well, because if I had gotten them, I wouldn't have been doing what I wanted."

"Is there anything else that you want?" he asked quietly, his voice right by her ear as she snuggled closer.

She didn't have to think about it. The answer sprung out of her in a burst of relief.

"I want to paint. I love creating art." She took a deep breath. What the hell, no point in holding back now. "And I want to continue watching Ruby. Being with her makes me happier than I've been in a long time." There, she admitted it. It wasn't ambitious, or the high-flying lifestyle she'd been raised to lead, but it was what she wanted, plain and simple. Family and space to be creative.

She held her breath. She couldn't bear it if he told her that she wasn't living up to her full potential. Or worse, that he felt weird about her admitting spending time with his daughter made her happy. But he didn't say any of those things.

Instead, he said, "Then you're living your dreams, Hope."

It stunned her to hear it so plainly, because she hadn't really thought of it like that.

"You can be pretty damn proud of yourself." He leaned over and kissed her softly on the lips. "I am."

How she was supposed to not fall totally in love with him at this point, she had no idea. But she knew she had to stay strong, because this couldn't last. When he found out about what happened at USC, he'd leave her so fast he would be the one who'd feel like he'd been living a dream.

CHAPTER TWENTY-FOUR

When Hope let herself back into her apartment on Sunday morning, her body was still warm and buzzing with the aftershocks of bliss. She'd spent two whole uninterrupted nights in Gabe's bed and she felt more relaxed and lighter than she had in forever.

He'd left to pick Ruby up from her sleepover, and it felt strange that she'd have to wait until three o'clock to see him again. Back to their routine: bar, work, and Ruby. Still, she knew nothing would be routine for them again. Gabe had made that clear not half an hour ago when she'd been writhing beneath him as he gave her her thousandth orgasm of the weekend.

Their last time this morning had been a desperate kind of mating, and he'd been more dominant, more possessive than he'd ever been with her before, whispering demands and assertions over her, as though he was afraid she might not return if he didn't claim her. As though he was branding her as his. Little did he know she was already counting down the hours until she could be back in his arms again.

For as long as he'd take her, she'd always come back. She just couldn't tell him that, especially if it couldn't last.

As soon as she stepped inside her apartment, she spotted Ivy standing in the kitchen, wearing leggings and a sports bra that highlighted her very impressive abs. Witnessing Ivy's metamorphosis over the last few years was still incredible to Hope. Ivy had gone from being downright skinny and self-conscious to a strong, toned, resilient warrior.

Even now, as she leaned against the counter, her bicep flexed smoothly as she lifted her coffee cup to her lips. She eyed Hope with her sharp crystal-blue gaze as she sipped.

"Hey," Hope said casually, tossing her keys in the bowl by the front door.

"Hey, yourself," Ivy replied, expression neutral. "Haven't seen you all weekend. You look...flushed."

She knew it was stupid, knew she was acting like a sixteen-year-old rather than the twenty-six-year-old she was, but she couldn't stop the goofy smile that cracked her face.

At the sight of it, Ivy's eyebrows disappeared beneath her dark-brown bangs. "He's that good, huh?" Pouring another cup of coffee, she gestured with her free hand for Hope to sit on the couch. She added a dollop of milk, just as Hope liked it, then brought the steaming mug to Hope as she flopped down on the couch with a tortured sigh.

"Ivy, he's more than good." She accepted the cup and drank deeply. As much time as she spent in bed the last two days, very little of it actually involved sleeping, and she needed the caffeine kick. "He's attentive, interesting. He's the strong and stoic type for sure, but not in a macho, dominant way." She paused, considering. "Although he's that too. But in a good way, not a loser way," she rushed to correct, knowing how unattractive macho and dominant sounded, especially to someone like Ivy. "It's more like he's a man who knows what he wants. But he won't take anything I'm not ready to give. He's... considerate, but not weak. Does that make sense?" Explaining the many sides of Gabriel Walsh wasn't simple.

Ivy looked at Hope with equal parts humor and sympathy. "He's good people, Hope. I told you that myself. Anyway, in this case I take macho and dominant to mean confident with a great set of abs and an even better butt. Both of which are definitely a plus in a bed partner."

Hope sipped and sighed. "I like him," she admitted. "A lot." Her tone wasn't thrilled, because she was less than thrilled that she was letting herself fall for this man when she knew very well it was all going to come crumbling down eventually. And Ivy was the only one who would really understand why falling for a man like Gabe was less than ideal right now.

Ivy set her cup down on the coffee table and took a deep breath. "Hope, are you going to tell him?" Apparently, Ivy could now read her mind.

"No!" she said emphatically, watching the telltale apprehension creep into her friend's eyes. "Ivy, no," she said again. "No way." To signal the conversation over, she stood abruptly.

She hadn't quite worked out how to bring up her past with Gabe, but she knew she'd have to do it in a way that didn't betray her soul sister.

Ivy grabbed her wrist and yanked her back down to the couch, reminding her again of how strong she'd gotten. She let go immediately. "Hope, I've taken enough from you over the last few years. I wouldn't blame you if you did tell Gabe."

"Ivy, stop." She shouldn't have said anything, should

have known Ivy would somehow find a way down the rabbit hole of blame which was typically followed by self-loathing. "From the beginning, you've said that you didn't want anyone to know. That you wanted to look forward, not back."

"Yeah, Hope, but that was before you fell in love with a drop-dead gorgeous, single father who's been through hell already, and doesn't deserve to be lied to by the woman who he thinks is his second chance. He deserves to hear the truth —before he hears the lie, and you both get hurt for no good reason."

"But there is a good reason, Ivy. *You're* a good reason." Hope turned to her friend and took her hand in hers. "You've worked so hard to put the past behind you. I'll be damned if it's dug up again because I can't control my emotions around a man."

Ivy sighed. "Hope, my past will always be with me, whether Gabe knows or not. And," she went on before Hope could say anything to that, "you're not supposed to control your emotions when you're falling in love."

"First of all, who said anything about love?" Hope ignored Ivy's dubious look and went on. "Second, Gabe doesn't need to know anything beyond what's public knowledge of what happened three years ago. I can handle this without bringing you into it." She stared pointedly at Ivy, making sure to hold her gaze. "Besides, if anyone *deserves* to know the truth, it's Sean."

"Hell. No." Ivy stood up, yanking her hand out of Hope's, breaking their connection. She wrapped her arms around herself and took several long steps backward.

Okay, conversation obviously over.

Or so Hope thought, until Ivy said, "Look, all I'm saying is that Gabe is the best thing that ever happened to you.

Gabe *and* Ruby. I see how you've changed in the last few months. You're painting and drawing more than ever, and don't even think I haven't noticed you opened an Etsy account, by the way. I put in an order for the meadow painting, FYI." Ivy gestured to the painting that was propped by the window in the far corner.

It was true, Hope had opened an Etsy account a couple of weeks ago—out of sheer necessity, she'd told herself. She had an overabundance of paintings piling up and selling them made sense, given her current fiscal situation.

"That man and his adorable daughter have wrapped themselves around your heart and gotten your creative juices going in a way I haven't seen—ever. And if you lose that, or worse, walk away because of some fucked up lie that wouldn't exist if it weren't for me, I'd never forgive myself, okay?"

Ivy was shaking, and her eyes looked suspiciously shiny. Hope moved toward her carefully, knowing better than to make any sudden movements when her friend was emotional like this.

"Ivy, you listen to me," she said in a low, even voice. "You're right. Gabe and Ruby have come to mean something to me in a big way, but whatever happens between me and Gabe will never be your fault, okay? Either he falls for me as I am or he doesn't. I've given him plenty of opportunity to get to know the most important parts of me, and if he lets some rumors from my past change the way he feels, then he's not the man I want, anyway."

She held her breath and hoped that Ivy thought her reasoning was accurate. After a long moment, Ivy gave a single nod, and Hope breathed a sigh of relief.

It was all a huge load of crap, of course. If she let Gabe believe a lie about herself, then he wasn't falling for her as she truly was. He was also falling for an incomplete version of her. When he found out that she'd nearly been kicked out of USC for cheating, and that the only reason she'd been exonerated was because her brother and father had to bail her out, he'd hightail it out of her life so fast her head would spin.

But for now, Ivy seemed to be buying what she was selling, and she'd take that win. As always, Ivy's well-being had to be her priority.

"I love you," she said softly.

And Ivy nodded again. She never said it back. Hope was used to it by now. She didn't need the words because she knew Ivy loved her.

She held open her arms, and when Ivy ran from where she'd retreated and dove into them, Hope felt it, too. Ivy Harrington was full of love. She just needed a gentle and patient hand to coax it out of her.

As she held on to her best friend, she marveled at all that Ivy had lived through and emerged from so much stronger than before. She was so brave, and she'd worked so hard to arrive at this place in her life. Hope wasn't going to be the one to compromise it. Even if it meant losing the best thing that had ever happened to her.

For now, Hope was resigned to the fact that when it came to what she had with Gabe and Ruby, she was going to be selfish. She was going to indulge in her time with them and soak up every precious second. She vowed to pour all of her love and care onto both of them, because a time would come when they would both be out of her life. And when that time came, she needed them to know she'd loved them with everything she had.

CHAPTER TWENTY-FIVE

"So I went and did this pretty big thing," Gabe admitted, standing behind Sean, spotting him while he sprawled on a workout bench, lifting nearly twice his body weight without so much as a grunt. He figured if he broke it to him now, while Sean was sweating and preoccupied, he might be able to avoid being sucked into one of those fucking heart to heart chats Sean loved to have.

Sean was six foot five, weighed a solid 210, was MMA trained, and grew up in one of the roughest neighborhoods in Chicago. The only family he had left was a brother who was serving time in prison somewhere, and yet Sean was still one of the biggest softies Gabe had ever known. As his best friend, Gabe had warned him many times that his trusting heart was going to ruin him one day. It was just a matter of time.

"Oh yeah?" Sean grunted as he pushed a rep up, then brought it down again. "What's that? Did you adopt that kitten Ruby's been after?"

Gabe snorted. "You mean the damn kitten you've been

after? Ruby hasn't mentioned it since Christmas. You, on the other hand—"

Sean chuckled but didn't lose pace lifting.

"I bought a house," he spat out. Saying it out loud didn't make it seem more real. He still couldn't believe what he'd done.

The opportunity came up several weeks ago when one of his regulars at the bar, who was also a friend on his rec basketball league and a real estate agent, had sent him a listing for a home in the Northwest Heights area. It was close to Ruby's school, on a quiet street, fairly central, and had a decent-sized backyard where he could set up a trampoline or a treehouse for Ruby.

It hadn't been totally spontaneous. The idea of giving Ruby a more solid foundation and space where they could truly plant roots had been ruminating for months. And, yeah, he could admit Hope had a lot to do with it. She'd breathed new life into his future—one he'd never thought he'd get a chance at again. One he hadn't even realized he'd wanted again.

Of course, he didn't expect her to drop everything and move in with them, but he liked the idea of, down the road, maybe one day settling into the house with her there and building a home.

It's nowhere he'd thought he'd be a year ago, or hell, even six months ago, but there it was. He'd signed the papers that morning.

Sean lifted the weight and placed it in its rack. He sat upright on the bench, so he faced Gabe. For a moment, he just sat there, sweat dripping down his face with a look that Gabe couldn't decipher.

"What?" he demanded.

Then a slow grin cracked Sean's face. "Did you pick out a

pretty ring too?" he asked, clearly trying to hold back a laugh—and failing miserably.

Gabe gave him a not-too-gentle shove off the bench. Any other time Sean wouldn't have budged, but he was so busy laughing, he landed on the floor on his ass. Gabe hoped it left a big fat bruise. He lay down on the bench and began lifting before Sean could get into position to spot him.

"Man, I'm sorry," Sean choked out, not sounding sorry at all as he got behind the bench. "A house, dude, that's huge. It's great. I mean, it's about fucking time you got Ruby out of that tiny-ass apartment. The girl deserves a yard for the puppy I'm gonna get her as a housewarming gift."

"Fuck you." Gabe grunted, pushing through his reps.

"Seriously," Sean went on. "This is a real good thing, Gabe. Real good. Does Hope know?"

Sweating bullets, Gabe didn't say anything until he completed his reps. Sean helped him guide the bar back onto its rack, then he lay there for a second, trying to catch his breath. He'd forgotten to take a weight off the bar before he started and wasn't used to lifting herculean weight like his best friend, who was also, apparently, Superman.

Finally, he was able to sit up. "Not yet." Sean raised a single eyebrow so high it almost popped off his forehead. "Timing hasn't been right," he added, but Sean's eyebrow only got higher, and fuck it, his friend was right. If he was having dreams of Hope one day living at his house with him and Ruby, he was going to have to tell her about it sooner than later. "I'll do it soon."

Sean provided a snort in response, and Gabe acknowledged the doubt lingering in his heart.

Over the last couple of weeks, since they'd spent that solitary weekend together, there'd been an obvious change in his and Hope's relationship. They spent time together on weekends, made love every night when he got home from his long shift at the bar. She'd come to another dinner at his sister's place. They attended Ruby's school spring concert together. As far as everyone around them was concerned, they were a couple. And even though Hope was still careful not to spend the night when Ruby was there, Gabe could tell his daughter had already accepted Hope as a part of their unit.

Yet Gabe couldn't shake the feeling that Hope was still holding something back. In his bed, during her time with Ruby, with their friends, and with his family, she gave everything. But when they were alone together, and not tearing each other's clothes off, he felt a distance. He couldn't put his finger on it, wasn't sure what it was, but it was there, like a thin sheet of glass between them, and until he could break through, he knew there was no real relationship. Not without honesty, not without trust. Both of which he needed from Hope.

"So, about your apartment then," Sean said, snapping him back to reality. "Whose gonna live there when you move out?" he asked as he lowered himself back down onto the bench and adjusted his grip on the bar.

He sounded casual, but Gabe knew better. For the last three years, his friend had some kind of weird tension going on with Ivy. Both were too damn stubborn to admit it or put a name to it, but in times like these, Gabe knew that something was definitely there.

"Actually, Greg Lewis is coming by this weekend to take a look at it."

Sean almost dropped the weight bar onto his neck. Luckily, Gabe grabbed it in the last second, lifting it back onto the rack.

"What the hell's wrong with you?" Gabe demanded,

after ascertaining his friend had survived. He'd never ever seen Sean lose control during a set like that.

Sean scrambled to a sitting position and eyeballed Gabe with a look of horror. "What's wrong with me? You want fucking Greg Lewis to move into your apartment, and you're asking what's wrong with me?"

Gabe frowned, confused. He thought Sean liked Greg. He was a personal trainer who had rented training space from Sean in the gym.

"Dude, you want a player like Lewis living across from your girlfriend?" Sean said, totally incredulous. "He'll be on those two like butter on toast in under a week unsupervised."

First of all, he was still counting on the fact that he could break down the final barrier between him and Hope, whatever it was, and convince her to move in with him and Ruby sooner rather than later, and second—

"Ivy would gouge out Greg's eyes with a kitchen spoon before she'd let him make a move on either her or Hope," Gabe said.

It was true, and they both knew it. Ivy mostly distrusted men, and if there weren't this obvious tension burning between her and Sean, he would have guessed she batted for the other team. She especially hated guys like Greg. Smooth, confident, boyishly good-looking, sun-streaked blonde surfer types.

Sean, however, didn't look convinced.

"He's a decent guy, if not a bit of a Casanova. Plus, he's willing to pay rent. Who else do you know is ready to move above a bar on short notice?" Gabe asked.

"Easy." Sean selected a weight and began doing bicep curls. "Me."

Hope sat on Gabe's couch, waiting for him to come home while she worked on her laptop doing upgrades to her Etsy site. Her art had been more popular than she imagined it'd be, and her impromptu business was taking off.

She wasn't making thousands per painting, choosing instead to keep her prices purposefully low so she could draw a wider range of customers. Her new Instagram account was also a work in progress. She was only just mastering Reels and still felt a rush every time her followers shared one in their stories.

But whatever she'd been doing was working, because she'd sold more than a dozen paintings since she opened the site, and even had a few commissions.

And then there was the other thing. The thing where she'd received a message from a gallery owner in Detroit. He had found her through Instagram and liked what he saw, so he'd kept researching her background. When he'd discovered her business qualifications, he'd asked her to interview for the manager position at his gallery.

She'd ignored his request at first, but when he reached out again, she figured there was no harm in interviewing via an online meeting. So, last week, she'd done just that. It'd gone very well. The owner was a lovely middle-aged, art-loving man, with very few business skills. He'd taken a leap opening his gallery in Detroit. And against the odds, it had done well. Now he wanted a manager to help him with the business end of things.

When she'd left home, this had been the exact opportunity she'd been looking for. But now, the thought of moving to Detroit held little appeal, and that rested solely on the fact that Detroit was missing a few people she realized she'd have a hard time living without.

And that was probably the very reason she should take the job if she got it. Her goal when she'd come here was to find a purpose, an identity all her own. Not to leave one family and latch straight on to another. No matter how much they felt like her true home.

In any case, maybe it was all a moot point because she hadn't heard back since the interview. She also hadn't told Gabe about it, figuring there was no point bringing it up until official decisions had to be made.

At two in the morning, she heard a key unlocking the door, signaling Gabe's return home. As always, her nipples hardened, and she felt the familiar tingle between her legs. The man turned the key in the lock and her body responded like clockwork.

She slapped her laptop closed.

"Hey," he said, joining her on the couch and immediately nuzzling the sweet spot under her ear.

Aaanndd she was aroused.

She wondered if her instantaneous reactions to him would ever stop. Or when this ended, how she was going to walk away from him and move on. Every day they were together made it harder to imagine leaving, even if it was to a dream job in a new city. She pushed the thought out of her mind. The past hadn't caught up with her, and the future lay ahead of her. She still had time.

"This place smells like heaven," Gabe murmured as he kissed her neck.

"Roast chicken," she murmured back, her body catching fire with the embers his lips were stoking. When he kissed her like this, she had no chance. "There's some left in the fridge if you're hungry."

"Oh, I'm hungry, Hope," he murmured, and instead of sounding cheesy, it turned her on even more. "I might even want seconds," he continued as he pulled her onto his lap to straddle him and guided her shirt up and over her head. "And thirds." He unhooked her bra and caught her breasts in his hands. "Maybe even fourths." He bent his head, teasing a nipple into his mouth, and her head fell back with a sigh.

After that, it was just the sounds of their desperate moans, whispered pleas, and strangled cries as they reached their peaks in tandem.

It was always what felt best for her, coming with him, clenching around him as her release fed his. Secretly, she sometimes thought about a day where she could welcome him inside her without a condom. She wanted to feel him come inside her, the wetness and heat of his passion. When she really let herself dream, she'd imagine one day holding a child that resulted from their union, but she knew that this was a dream too big for her and Gabe. Maybe too big for her ever. Jury was still out.

Pushing that thought away, along with so many others that she'd had that evening, she curled against him on the couch and sighed as he drew her into the curve of his body. For now, she'd take what she could get for as long as she could get it.

Gabe tugged a blanket that was draped off the back of the couch and pulled it over them, nuzzling the back of her neck. His warm breath sent renewed shivers of awareness down her body. They lay in silence, still coming down from the wave they'd just rode, even as every touch and rub of their bodies started the inevitable climb to the next one.

"I bought a house," he said quietly into her hair, stunning her out of her afterglow bliss. "It's not too far from here." He paused, obviously waiting for her to say something.

Well, he could wait because she was speechless. What could she say when her throat was constricting to the point of pain?

"Three bedrooms." Another pause. "It has a decent backyard. The fence is falling apart, but I can fix it. It's got space."

The insinuation was clear—it would have enough space for her, too.

Seconds ago, she had been daydreaming about this very thing: having a baby with this man, building a family, and now he was talking that dream to life. So why did it suddenly feel like it was something she couldn't have?

Maybe because you're still keeping a huge part of your past from him. The thought that had been plaguing her for weeks invaded her brain in a full-frontal attack, stealing her breath and constricting her chest.

There was no way she could continue to play house with Gabe when she knew there was a big piece of her he was missing.

Until she found a way to tell him, she wasn't a part of this family and she couldn't pretend to be. The gut-wrenching pain of realizing that her time with Gabe and Ruby might run its course before she found a way to tell him the truth without hurting Ivy came barreling down on her, and she was powerless against it.

Suddenly hot, her chest tightening with a clawing sort of heartbreak, she struggled into a sitting position. Gabe easily followed her up, watching her closely.

Bending to pick up her discarded clothing, she avoided eye contact. It was her last means of defense. "That sounds amazing, Gabe," she managed to say, as she shrugged her shirt over her head and stood. "Does Ruby know? I bet she'll be thrilled."

Gabe remained sitting, calmly watching her. "I was going to tell her this weekend. Maybe take her to go see it." He reached out to still her hands, which were shakily trying to do up the snap of her jeans. "I'd like you to come see it, too."

And because those words sounded less like, *You should come see where your new place of employment will be*, and more like, *Come see this home I bought for us to build a family in*, Hope's dread morphed into full blown panic.

Her heart was in a free fall toward being totally in love with this man and his daughter. Who was she kidding? She had already fallen, and the pain of the landing was soul crushing. There was no way she could stand in a house that in another dimension could be a home for them and pretend that it wasn't tearing her apart.

In this dimension, she was keeping a big detail of her life hidden from him. A detail that wouldn't have him painting white picket fences so fast. Regret, heartache, self-pity, and all the other good stuff pooled in her gut.

"I can't this weekend," she said, sliding her hand out from under his touch. Which wasn't a lie. It was the weekend she was due back home for the hospital benefit. The timing had worked well because Ruby had another sleepover planned at her aunt's house. She'd mentioned the trip to Gabe a while back in passing, and was going to remind him tonight, but then she'd gotten distracted by the removal of clothing and blinding orgasms.

Now the timing of her trip seemed even more serendipitous as it offered her a chance to create some much-needed distance from this man and all the feelings he was making her feel.

"You can't?" he asked, moving behind her as she made her way to the door to leave. "Why not?" He'd clearly not remembered her quick visit back to San Francisco, and sounded disappointed, a little annoyed, definitely confused, and, the part that triggered a defensiveness in her own heart, hurt.

She whirled on him. "Because I'm going back to California this weekend, Gabe." She was whispering, aware that they were in the hallway now, Ruby down the hall. Gabe was standing in front of her in unbuttoned jeans, bare chest and feet, hair tousled from the sex they'd just had. He looked like her very own dream come true, and the ache the sight of him caused only fueled the balking anger brewing inside her.

She resented the fates for putting something so wonderful in front of her, only to remind her she could never have it. Why did he have to back her into this corner right now, when she wasn't ready? "Believe it or not Gabe, not everything in my life revolves around you."

Her words flew out. Mean, brutal, and unfair, rocking Gabe back on his heels. He couldn't have looked more shocked if she'd actually hit him. Hope was breathing hard, trying to keep her tumultuous emotions in check while simultaneously trying to keep from throwing herself into his arms and admitting that going to see the house with three bedrooms and a dilapidated fence was what she wanted more than anything in the whole world. Then begging to stay there with him forever.

Instead, she steeled herself and turned to the door, wrenching it open.

"I have to go. I'll be back on Tuesday by three to watch Ruby for you." And with that, she shut the door behind her and fled to her apartment without looking back at all she was leaving behind.

CHAPTER TWENTY-SIX

Hope stayed in her bedroom until almost noon. After she'd left Gabe standing in his doorway, with a look of shocked hurt and confusion on his face, she couldn't sleep, alternating between tossing and turning and getting up to pace her room.

She couldn't face the day—or worse, face Ivy, who would instantly recognize that something had gone terribly wrong and would likely find a way to blame herself for it.

That wasn't going to happen, not again. Silently, she vowed that she wouldn't leave her room until she had her emotions totally under control. When she faced the world again, she'd need to present as totally normal. And normal didn't include puffy red eyes and blotchy cheeks.

It was Friday, and Ivy was still at work, so Hope figured she still had a good four or five hours to get her shit together before having to face her best friend and the rest of the world.

Her mother had texted confirming Hope's flight details, and for the first time in years she found that she wanted nothing more than to go see her mom, wrap herself into her warm embrace, and soak up all the comfort and unconditional love only Audrey could give her. Had always given her.

It had taken a lively little girl and her strong and steady father to show her the truth about what family really meant. It wasn't all blood ties and lineage. The legacy of love was built in the heart, not in the bloodline. And above all else, Hope's family had always loved her.

Just after noon, she got a text from Gabe.

Gabe: *The bed felt cold without you this morning. When can we talk?*

Her finger hovered over her screen to reply, but she couldn't find the right words, so she tucked her phone under her pillow and forced herself into the shower. Then she spent the next few hours doing laundry and packing enough to get her through the gala and the weekend.

By four she was painting by the window overlooking the city street below. Totally caught up in her therapy session of art and imagination, she lost track of time until Ivy came slamming through the door with her pile of foam rollers and exercise bands.

"Tell me it's actually Friday and not my brain playing tricks on me, because I've been thinking it's Friday since Tuesday, which has made this the longest week ever. Please don't let it still be Tuesday." A few thuds and crashes later, Ivy and all her physical therapy equipment were inside the apartment. She blew her bangs out of her eyes and let loose a long-suffering sigh.

"It's Friday," Hope said, setting down her paintbrush and turning to face her friend. This was the test to see if she had perfected her acting skills enough to fool her best friend.

Ivy stood in their entrance way, head cocked to one side, hands fisted on her hips. She studied Hope carefully. Hope tried her best not to swallow hard under the scrutiny, and mentally crossed her fingers.

"Shouldn't you be with Ruby?" Ivy eventually asked.

Hope breathed a huge sigh of relief and managed a thin smile. "Slumber party at the cousins this weekend."

Ivy nodded sagely. "You know what this means."

"Um, pajamas, wine, and romcoms on the couch?" she guessed.

"Wrong!" Ivy shouted with glee as she skipped down the hall toward Hope's room. "It means four-inch stilettos, red lipstick, and a blowout."

Resigned, she followed Ivy into her bedroom, where she found her friend with her head already buried in Hope's closet. Something red and shiny came flying over Ivy's shoulder.

"Did you pack all your best stuff for your trip back to Cali this weekend? Where's that cute little black leather skirt? And the heels?" Ivy tossed a look at Hope. "The necessity heels, you know the ones."

"I'm not going out tonight," Hope said firmly. It was honestly the very last thing she felt like doing. Especially to Bowie's, where she'd have to face Gabe and watch him work behind the bar, which never failed to turn her heart to mush. She could not afford a mushy heart. She needed to stay strong now more than ever.

Ivy abandoned the closet and walked toward her. Slowly, purposefully, determined. "Yes, you are going out. It's been a long week for both of us. I can see it on your face. And these days you and I get a Friday night together exactly never. In fact, the last time Ruby had a sleepover, you spent the whole weekend having your own sleepover at Gabe's." She flexed her fingers in quotations around the word *sleepover*, then crossed her arms, and gave Hope a look. "You owe me a girls' night."

Hope sighed. Ivy was right. They hadn't spent much quality time together since Hope met Gabe. Still, she gave it one last shot. "I won't be good company tonight," she warned.

Ivy shrugged and moved back to Hope's closet. "You will be once you have a couple of drinks in you. But if it makes you feel better, I'll text Sean. He had a shit day, too. He'll be looking for some distraction." She threw a slinky black blouse at Hope. "Come on, it'll be fun."

Yeah, famous last words.

Bowie's was alive with some pretty hard-core Friday night vibes. It was as busy as Hope had ever seen it. She sat on a bar stool at the table Sean had been lucky enough to snag earlier and sipped on a fruity red drink Carter had brought her. As she watched the growing crowd, she did her best to keep her gaze from wandering to the bar where Gabe was working.

This was an awkward mistake, and yet here she was. And even though she'd spent the last few hours telling herself that she could never make a relationship with Gabe work, just being in his proximity made her heart feel whole.

Sean and Ivy stumbled back to the table, laughing. They'd torn up the dance floor to an Ed Sheeran dance remix, and Hope couldn't help but smile. Seeing Ivy relaxed and having fun was a relief. There'd been a time when Hope thought she'd never see a glow of joy around Ivy again, but coming to Portland and starting her PT clinic at Sean's gym had been a huge turning point.

Sean had been another one. His gentle and patient friendship drew Ivy out of her dark little shell and brought light back into her eyes.

"It's crazy busy tonight," Ivy exclaimed as she pulled her small frame back onto her stool and downed a gulp of her beer.

"Double bachelor party," Carter said, loudly over the noise. He was sitting on the fourth seat at their table, taking a break from bar duty. "Gabe tries to never book more than one at a time, but somehow another one slipped in tonight." His sharp gaze assessed the crowd. "It'll be a shit show tonight. Guaranteed. The boss is already fit to be tied." He tossed a nod in Gabe's direction. "Came in this afternoon pissy as ever. None of this has helped his mood."

Giving up her sorry attempt to not stare at him, she turned her gaze to the surly man in question. He stood behind the bar in his black Bowie's t-shirt with a matching bar towel slung over his shoulder. His brow was furrowed in concentration as he poured shots into a row of glasses in front of him. His scowl should have made him appear less handsome, but to her, it only added to his raw, potent masculinity. Her insides melted with desire even as guilt swamped her.

She'd said callous, thoughtless things, and she'd hurt him. On top of that, she hadn't replied to his texts or calls today. She knew she had to apologize, but she was feeling vulnerable, too. And the truth was, she wasn't ready to face him because she didn't know what she could say to explain herself.

But none of that changed the fact that she'd reacted poorly, and she'd been raised better than that. Truth be told, recently, she'd reacted poorly more often than she'd care to admit. Her response to finding out the truth about her adoption was something she'd come to regret. Running away instead of staying and fighting for her family wasn't something she was proud of. Her reaction had been purely emotional, but she was going back to Cali this weekend to fix all that. Unfortunately, she wasn't exactly sure how to fix this mess with Gabe. Or if she could.

As if he sensed her looking at him, Gabe lifted his head and his molten green-eyed gaze collided with hers. His expression was grim, his lips drawn in a tight line, and his eyes looked tired—like he'd gotten about as much sleep as she had. Even from across the room, she could see the lingering pain and confusion in them.

Meanwhile, she was dressed up and drinking with their laughing friends—like nothing in the world was wrong. She broke eye contact and turned to face Carter.

"Yeah, seems rowdier than usual," she agreed, not even sure if they were still talking about the same thing.

Ivy sauntered back to their table. When had she left?

"Line up at the ladies was insane." Ivy wiggled back onto her seat. "I bailed when the chick in front of me started drunk dialing every ex she'd ever had—which was a lot, by the way—and went up to our apartment to pee. That's why I took so long. In case anyone noticed I was missing." She glanced at Hope with an arched eyebrow and a smirk.

Hope had most definitely not noticed Ivy was missing, or anything else in her surroundings other than the tall, dark, and broody man behind the bar.

"I always notice when you're missing," Sean announced, and every head at their table turned to face him.

A much-needed smile tugged on Hope's mouth, and her mood shifted instantly. Sean was so good for Ivy, in so many ways, and it made Hope feel good knowing her friend was cared for by such a decent human being.

Carter snorted a laugh. "I'm cutting you off, dude."

Ivy turned beet red.

And Sean shifted uncomfortably in his seat, suddenly becoming very interested in the golden liquid that remained in his beer glass as he muttered, "I always notice shit people do, okay?"

"Right," Carter said, chuckling, but he had enough self-preservation not to push this particular issue. Instead, he hopped off his chair and made a show of stretching his arms above his head and cracking his knuckles. "Whelp. Sorry to love you and leave you guys, but my break's over. Anybody want another bevy before I head back behind the bar?" He pointed his finger at Sean's face. "Not you, Romeo."

A muscle in Sean's jaw twitched, and Hope wasn't sure if he might clock Carter or dump his beer over his head. But Sean never had a chance to do either because his death glare was interrupted by a slurred voice coming up far too close behind her back.

"Well, fuck me. If it isn't little Miss Ivy Harrington and her cheating friend, Hope fucking Morgan."

It'd been three years since she'd heard this voice, but it was the one that haunted her nightmares ever since. She'd know it anywhere.

Adrenaline flooded her body, making her heart pound wildly in her chest. She leaped off her bar stool and spun to face the owner of the voice, clenching her fists so hard her nails bit into her skin.

Beside her, Ivy went completely and utterly still. Around them, everything—music, people, the sounds of the bar—melted away. And for a long, blinding moment, the two of them were transported back to that one terrible night that changed both of their lives irrevocably.

She knew that if she looked at Ivy, she'd see blind fear

on her friend's face. She already felt it emanating from Ivy in cold, shivering waves. But she couldn't take her eyes off Adam, didn't dare to so much as even blink.

He looked the same as he had that night three years ago, eyes glassy from too much booze, a sheen of sweat on his brow, classy business shirt unbuttoned at the neck, sleeves rolled up to his forearms. He appeared casual, handsome even, but she knew better. She knew the faint scar that reached from eyebrow to temple was a clue to the demon that lived inside Adam Reed.

Sean must have picked up on the tension choking her and Ivy, because out of the corner of her eye, she suddenly saw his full intimidating height standing in front of Ivy, protectively blocking her from Adam's view. Sean had no idea what Adam meant to either of them, but he was never one to ask too many questions. He'd sensed something was off and gone into Guardians of the Galaxy mode.

"Do we have a problem?" Sean demanded in a low voice.

Adam grinned, copious amounts of alcohol and arrogance fueling his audacity. "A problem? No problem, man. Hope, Ivy, and I go a way back," he said, sounding innocent, non-threatening, like he wasn't actually the devil himself.

Nausea turned in Hope's stomach as he spoke. Her body grew cold and sweaty as her past collided into the present.

Adam glanced from Sean back to Hope. "Don't we, girls?" The bastard had the guts then to lean sideways and try to peer around Sean's massive torso to stare down at Ivy. "We're old pals. Right, Ive? So why don't you call off Goliath here? I think we're long overdue for a good catch up." He paused, his smile evil, his glassy eyes leering. "You look good, Ive. Real good."

Beside Hope, Ivy shot out of her chair so fast she knocked the glasses off their table. They crashed to the floor, spraying beer and glass everywhere. Ivy would have gone down with the crash, but Sean quickly steadied her, guiding her securely behind his body. Ivy clutched to the back of his shirt like it was her only armor, and Hope moved to stand beside Sean, shoulder to shoulder—forming a double-barricade between Ivy and Adam.

Something brushed her arm. Hope glanced sideways to find Carter flanking her other side. In a low voice, she said to him, "Get her out of here."

Carter didn't hesitate, but he also didn't move fast, probably sensing that might spook Ivy. Slowly and very carefully he took Ivy's hand in his. "Come on, Ivy, let's bounce," he murmured. And with a gentle but firm tug, he led Ivy away.

Before she could take another breath, the space where Carter had stood beside her was filled by Gabe. The crashing glasses must have alerted him to the altercation. Casually, like this wasn't a gut-wrenchingly tense situation, he put his arm around Hope's shoulders and held her close.

"Problem, babe?" he asked her, eyes on Adam.

After a long, wide-eyed beat, Adam tipped his head back and laughed loudly. A howling, evil kind of laugh.

"Babe?" Adam's gaze met hers, but his eyes weren't sparkling with amusement, instead they held the dark gleam of anger, resentment, and—worst of all—revenge. "That's rich, *babe*," he said with exaggerated drunken slowness.

He turned to look at Gabe, who'd come to full attention beside her. Braced and ready. But Adam only gave him an amiable once-over before his gaze shifted back to her, and the darkness returned to his eyes. "So you found someone to give a shit about you after all. Does he know the truth, Hope?" He popped the *p* in her name as he glared at her.

She knew exactly what Adam was asking.

But Gabe didn't know.

She clenched her teeth hard, trying not to react, but it was unbearable being near Adam again. A headache pounded behind her eyes. Her nails continued to bite into her fisted hands. The sting centered her.

But the truth must have been in her eyes, and Adam could see it. Neither of the men flanking her knew Adam's truth or the real truth. And no matter how badass—and capable of handling any truth—that they looked, she wasn't going to tell them. Not ever. Not her. Just like she didn't tell anyone three years ago, and she knew that gave Adam all the power.

Adam knew this—must have seen this truth in her eyes or her stance—because a slow smile of victory spread across his face. "It's been a long time." His gaze slid down her body, and she fought the bile churning in her stomach. "You still look good as ever."

Beside her, Gabe growled, low and threatening, his body straining like he wanted to pounce. She grabbed his hand, threading her fingers through his, gripping hard, holding him back.

Adam craned his neck to stare up at Gabe. He didn't seem disturbed by the violence emanating from Gabe. With a disdainful expression, he scrutinized Gabe, taking in his day-old stubble, his too-long hair, and his tattoos.

"Not your usual type, is he, Hope?" Adam mused. "I remember you used to like them cleaner. You know, the white-collar types." His gaze cut to her and slithered down her body again. "Like me."

Gabe shot forward and seized Adam by the collar of his own crisp white shirt.

Adam jerked back, raising both hands in mock surrender. "Whoa, whoa, whoa. Easy there, Tarzan. I'm not the one you need to worry about." He canted his head to indicate her.

When Gabe didn't loosen his grip but instead tightened it, Adam gasped in disbelief and started talking faster than ever with spit shooting out of his mouth.

"Come on, Hope, are you really going to throw me under the bus again? Why don't you tell lover boy here what you did to me and the others? How you cheated, then lied, and got us all kicked out of college. How daddy and your brother had to bail you out, while you watched from your high horse as the rest of us burned."

Under Gabe's fierce grip, Adam started sputtering and wheezing from lack of air. His eyes went dark, almost black, and his lips curled into a sneer. "I lost everything," he gasped. "Because of you. You're a liar. A cheating bitch. And you still fucking owe me."

Fury rose in Hope, unlike any she had experienced in three years.

"You fucker," Gabe growled. Then he yanked Adam into the crowd that had gathered to watch the spectacle.

Pushing through the throng, Hope followed close behind Gabe as he dragged Adam toward the front door of the bar. Sean opened the doors for Gabe as he dragged Adam through and onto the street.

Hope let her storm break once they were outside.

"You're the liar, Adam," she screamed, a burning rage flooding her body and face. "You know the truth. I never—"

"The truth?" Adam choked out, still under Gabe's relentless grip. "Come on, Hope, tell him the truth. Tell him what really happened. I dare you. See if he believes you. If anyone believes you!"

Slamming Adam up against the brick wall on the side of the building and pinning him there, Gabe growled, "You stay the fuck away from her. You stay the fuck away from here. If you ever talk to her, or so much as look her way again, I will fuck you up. Understand?"

Adam had turned a little blue under Gabe's hold on his collar. But Gabe's eyes were nearly black with violent intensity. A tick jumped in his jaw. The muscles in his shoulders and biceps bunched as they strained.

She had never seen him so consumed with anger. A thinly checked violence vibrated off him. And as much as it pained her, she knew she had to intervene and end this, before Gabe did something he couldn't take back.

"Gabe. Let him go," she said quietly as she put her hand on his shoulder, the muscles hard as steel under her touch.

Adam choked out a noise of distress, his eyes bulging.

"Gabe. Please. He's not worth it. Trust me."

In the tense moment that followed, the only sounds around them were Adam's gurgling gasps, and the whoosh of a passing car. She opened her mouth with another plea on her lips when Gabe finally reacted.

He thrust Adam away from him, and Adam staggered sideways, almost comically, before regaining his footing. Rubbing his neck and gasping for air, he doubled over heaving in rasping breaths. Hands braced against his knees, he glared up at Hope.

"You'll pay for this, you lying fucking bitch. You fucking ruined my life, you cheating who—"

Before he could finish the word, something snapped inside of her, and she hadn't realized she'd moved until her fist collided with Adam's face. Fury tore through her in red hot bolts of rage. Three years of carefully hidden anger, pain, and resentment flooded out of her in a flurry of violence she didn't even know she was capable of.

"You son-of-a-bitch," she shrieked, as she hit and clawed

and kicked anywhere and everywhere on Adam that she could make contact with. She pulled out every move she'd ever learned at the kickboxing classes she'd taken. Her knee came up full force to Adam's groin, and she heard his satisfying groan of pain as he fell to his knees. She continued her attack, not caring that he was down.

She heard herself scream unintelligible words as memories intertwined with reality feeding a storm inside of her—filling her with a power she could've never imagined. She wanted nothing more than for Adam to finally pay for all the hurt he and his friends had caused, all the lies they'd told.

Behind her, steady arms wrapped around her waist, dragging her away from Adam. She protested, struggling against the force, but it was too persistent, too... calming. A familiar voice, deep and steady, rumbled in her ear.

"Hope. Sweetheart. Come with me." Gabe's words broke through her rage.

She felt her body being spun around, away from Adam and closer to the warm and reassuringly firm wall of Gabe's chest. He held her there, cradling her body to his, as she struggled to catch her breath.

"Go inside," Sean instructed from beside them, his baritone voice controlled but also lethal. "I'll deal with the trash."

She glanced up from Gabe's chest in time to glimpse Sean giving Gabe a hard, level look that must have communicated something between them, because Gabe responded with a curt nod before he glared down at her. His eyes were dark and his mouth was set in a grim line.

And Hope knew—now that Adam had been handled like the trash that he was—her own time of reckoning had come.

CHAPTER TWENTY-SEVEN

Grabbing Hope's hand, Gabe pulled her into the pub, dragged her past all the partygoers—who paid them no attention, having apparently already forgotten about the evening's excitement—and down the hall where he pushed her, not too gently, into his office.

He shut and locked the door, then spun to face her.

"What. The. Hell," he growled.

She had to agree. From where she was standing, it truly did feel like hell all over again. Lost for anything to say, she wrapped her arms around herself. Her body still shook from the whole encounter, and she needed to get her emotions under control for what was still coming.

She'd known that the past would eventually catch up with her. She just hadn't expected to be confronted by it in the flesh. Seeing Adam had shaken her more than she could have imagined.

Gabe inhaled deeply, shutting his eyes for a long moment, and she realized he was struggling for control, too. When his eyes opened again, he seemed more composed, his anger in check.

Slowly, he moved toward her and gently placed both hands on her shoulders. He took one final step into her space and dropped his forehead to touch hers. The connection was intimate—and soothing.

"You okay?" he whispered.

She nodded but didn't unwrap her arms from around herself—afraid if she did, she'd completely unravel. She nodded again, hoping to convince herself. But there was no convincing anyone, so she shook her head slowly, letting the tremors starting inside her roll over her in waves.

"Not okay," Gabe confirmed, as he wrapped his strong arms around her, rubbing his hands up and down the length of her spine.

He did this for several long minutes until his body heat seeped into hers, moving up through her back into her chest and down to her toes. Eventually, she unwrapped her arms from between them, and locked them around his waist, hanging on tightly, pressing into every part of him until she felt like they were one. She buried her face in the crook of his neck, rubbing her nose into the spot where his skin met the collar of his t-shirt.

Then and only then did she allow herself one long, shuddering sob.

Gabe held Hope tight. Considering he had no fucking clue what was going on, it was all he could do. What he did know was that he'd just watched Hope go batshit crazy on some evil fucker, and while he'd been confused as hell, not to mention terrified of her getting hurt, watching her pull out her moves had been pretty damn impressive.

She'd beat up that dirtbag pretty good, and he'd never felt prouder.

But none of that could erase the fact that something was very, very wrong. And neither of them was leaving this room until he found out what it was. Not that Hope looked like she was in the talking mood. A better man might have given her the time and space to recover from the confrontation before badgering her with questions, but his better side flew out the window the second he'd heard glass crashing in his bar and realized it'd come from her table.

When he'd approached and seen the barely veiled fear in Hope's eyes, and a normally laid-back Sean in an offensive position, any thought of diplomacy or decency had gone right out the window. He'd almost choked a stranger with his bare hands inside and then outside his own goddamn bar. So whether it made him an asshole or not, he wanted—no, he *needed* to know what the hell was going on.

When he felt her body finally relax, he led her to the couch in his office. Then he gently hooked a finger under her chin and lifted her face until her dark gaze met his.

"Hope," he began, carefully, trying to temper his tone to gentle. "Who the fuck was that?" Fuck. Why the fuck had he said *fuck*? Okay, maybe he wasn't all that good at gentle. He inhaled a breath and tried again. "Can you tell me who that was and what just happened out there? Please."

Her deep-brown eyes were shining. Despair was so vivid in her gaze, he wondered how he'd ever missed it. Had she suffered all this time and he'd never seen it? Was he so blinded by his own lingering grief and anger? Or had she hidden it so well under her many layers she made sure no one saw it?

Whatever the case, Hope wasn't talking. She just looked

up at him with all those secrets swimming in her eyes, threatening to spill over. He had to tap in, had to find a way to get her to open up to him, to share this one last part of herself with him.

This was the missing piece. He knew it.

"Okay then, twenty questions it is." He stood, walked to his desk, and turned to look at her.

She sat mutely, hands folded in her lap, head bowed, looking like she was preparing for an execution.

Shit, she was threatening his resolve with her naked vulnerability, but if he wanted to protect her, really protect her, he needed to know.

"The fucker out there. You know him?"

Nod.

"From college?"

Another nod.

"He hurt you." Not a question.

No nod. Nothing.

The tick in his jaw picked up again. "He hurt you," he repeated, still not counting it as a question. It was clearly fact, and he curled his hands into fists as the truth became clearer.

His gut clenched tight at his next question, fearing he already knew the answer and not sure how he was going to handle it.

"Did he hurt you physically?" Because one thing was non-negotiable. If that asshole laid so much as one fucking finger on Hope, he was going back out there to finish what she started.

But Hope was quick to shake her head. No? He hadn't touched her. He should have felt relief. Instead, inexplicably, his dread kicked up a notch.

Shoving his hands into his pockets, he did a quick pace

of his office, thinking back over the last twenty minutes. What was he missing? He'd heard the crash, told Nala to watch the bar, went over, saw Hope standing with Sean at her side, tension pouring off both of them, facing a visibly drunken stranger in front of them. The usual noise and movement of a typical Friday night at the bar buzzing around them. And—then it hit him.

"Where was Ivy?" She'd been there earlier. He'd seen her dancing with Sean, clinking glasses with Hope and Carter who'd been at her table, but when Gabe had arrived at the scene, Ivy hadn't been there.

On the couch, Hope's entire body stiffened.

"Does Ivy know that guy?" he asked slowly. "Does she know what happened?"

Suddenly, Hope sprung to her feet. "Forget Ivy!" she yelled. Scrubbing a hand down her face, she took a deep breath, looked him in the eye, and said, "Leave her out of this, Gabe. Let it go. Let all of it go. Please, I beg you."

He shook his head and took a step toward her. "That son-of-a-bitch came at you, guns blazing tonight, Hope. He threatened you, insulted you. I'm not going to fucking let it go. So start talking before I get Ivy in here to tell me what she knows."

Hope gave him a pained, pleading look, and he almost broke under the agony he saw in her eyes.

Fuck it. Causing her more pain wasn't worth it. He just wanted to hold her. They'd figure out the rest later. He moved toward her, but she suddenly started circling his office at a caged tiger's pace.

"His name is Adam Reed, and I went to college with him. Everything Adam said to you about me tonight was true." She stopped pacing to stand a good two feet away from him.

Far enough that he couldn't touch her.

She looked radiant, her blonde hair like a halo around her, her skin luminescent under the soft glow of his desk lamp. Her drawn and hollow eyes only added to her ethereal beauty. In that moment, she looked otherworldly. So far removed from the villain Adam had claimed her to be.

"He said you ruined his life. That your father and brother bailed you out after you got caught cheating, while he and his friends took the fall. He called you a liar."

Silently, he willed her to defend herself. To tell him that Adam was the liar. But she only looked up at him, eyes glistening, her expression stricken. It was a long moment before she spoke.

"In my final year at USC I got caught up in a scandal. Adam and I, and three of his friends, were implicated in a cheating scheme that involved our final exams." Her words came in a rush of breath, like she was trying to force them out of her mouth.

And even though he was hearing her very clearly, his brain refused to compute the information. *Cheating.* It didn't fit. Hope wasn't a cheater. She worked hard. She showed up. She had a determined spirit. And he had admired that about her. Had loved it. Loved her.

"When my father found out," she went on, "he flew my brother Joel down to rescue me. Joel made the allegations against me disappear, but the others were found guilty of cheating and were expelled. Afterward, I couldn't stay at the school anymore. I was," she paused, her voice cracking, "too ashamed. So I went home. And finished my degree at a nearby college."

At some point in her confessional, she'd started pacing again, her voice getting tighter as she spoke, her words more clipped and fragmented. "I don't know what happened to the others after I left. But obviously the scandal ruined their lives judging by Adam's outburst tonight. It's the first time I have seen him or any of them in three years."

Finally, she turned to face him. Her eyes unreadable, emotionless, while every feeling under the fucking sun screamed through his veins. Of all of them, betrayal beat the loudest.

His mind reeled as her words registered. He thought he knew her, but after all this time there was this huge piece missing. "Why wouldn't you tell me this before, Hope?"

He came off more accusatory than he'd meant to, and she recoiled at his tone before she said, "I didn't think it mattered."

She was lying. He could see it. There was more to this story. Something wasn't adding up, and frustration simmered when he couldn't put his finger on it. Everything she'd just told him sounded so unlike her it was laughable.

Look, he got it. People did stupid shit when they were young. He knew that better than anyone else. But Hope was a Morgan. Morgans didn't cheat. Fuck it, Hope wouldn't cheat. There had to be more.

"I didn't not tell you on purpose," she rushed to continue. "It was more of an—omission, than anything else." She chewed her bottom lip as she watched him. But only one word sunk in.

"Omission," he repeated numbly. It still wasn't registering in his head. He ran a hand through his hair trying to grasp at understanding. "Is there anything else you're *omitting* here, Hope? Anything else I should know?"

He was met with silence as she looked down at her open palms. Little blood red crescents lined the base of her palms, as if she'd clenched her fists so tight her own nails had drawn blood. She stared at those bloody crescent marks, as if in another world.

Her silence killed him more than any omission ever could. He thought they'd built a foundation of communication over these last few months. He'd opened up to her in a way he hadn't opened himself up to anyone in a damn long time.

From the moment she'd arrived in his life she'd been her most authentic self—open and loving, optimistic and determined. Caring. He'd never once thought she wasn't being one hundred percent herself.

When she had confided in him all her confusion and turmoil over finding out about her adoption, she had shared herself so beautifully with him it had encouraged him to do the same. And now...

Silence.

And, *fuck,* that hurt. He let his anger bubble to the surface and dull the ache. Her omissions, as she called them, beat against his trust. What else had she not been fully honest about? Could he trust what he'd come to believe about their relationship? Did she truly want all the things she seemed to want? A life with him, with Ruby? Was that why she freaked about the house the night before? Was she omitting the very important information that maybe, just maybe, he and Ruby weren't what she wanted?

If there was more she was not telling him he wanted to know. *Needed* to know.

The last time communication had broken down between him and a woman he loved, she'd gotten behind the wheel of a car and died.

"What else?" he asked again into the deafening silence.

When she continued to say nothing, he slapped his palm down on his desk, making her flinch.

"What else, Hope?" He knew he had no right to demand anything from her, but dammit, her silence was like pouring vinegar on an open wound. He inhaled loudly through flared nostrils, a frustrated sound. "I want to understand, Hope. I feel like there's a black hole between us right now. I thought we'd created something stronger than this, this—silence." He gestured between them.

Hope dropped her hands and raised her eyes to meet his. Her gaze was shiny with unshed tears.

"Why would you cheat?"

That was the part that made no sense. She was bright and hardworking; he couldn't imagine she'd have to cheat for anything.

"I—" She started to speak then abruptly stopped. Her eye contact faltered, and in that moment she looked so helpless.

He watched her closely, unable to shake the feeling that something wasn't right. Something beyond that fact that she'd just yanked the rug of dreams out from under his fucking feet.

But she stood still, saying nothing, sharing nothing. And the hurt that had been at a simmer started to boil.

"Tell me there was a good reason," he urged, leveling his gaze with hers, searching for any sign that what they had was salvageable. "Tell me there was a good reason that you had to cheat. A good reason that your family came to bail you out while others had to face the consequences. A good reason you kept it from me, when you knew all I wanted was your honesty. Tell me."

He realized that he sounded like he was begging, but the desperate part inside of him, the part that ached for her— for what they'd had that felt so goddamn real he could taste his future in it—needed her to throw him a lifeline.

"I did have a good reason," she whimpered half-heartedly.

The tension coursing through him pulled his patience tight, and it took great effort not to shout his next words. "What was it, Hope? What reason did you have for any of that?"

For a long time, she just stood there, a longing so vivid in her eyes that for the first time since she'd told him what had happened, Gabe's heart lifted. Maybe she would open up to him. Maybe there was a way back to her.

But then her shoulders slumped, and her gaze fell with them. "I can't tell you. I'm so sorry." The words were no more than a ripple of air in the room, but he'd heard them clear enough.

He exhaled a rush of air that he hadn't realized he'd been holding. She didn't trust him. She'd rather keep the truth from him than trust him with it. And with a gut-wrenching sorrow, he accepted the reality—there could be nothing between them if she didn't trust him enough to be honest. How could he protect her from men like Adam, and God knows who else, if she didn't trust him with the truth? He'd been in a situation before where the woman he loved wasn't open with him, and it ended tragically. He couldn't risk that all over again. "Then I'm sorry too, Hope."

Suddenly, the room shrunk around him, sucking all the air out of it. His chest tightened as walls closed in on him. His past pushed memories mercilessly against his present. Memories that reminded him of all the reasons he never should have let himself trust again. He needed to get out of there.

He let his resentment take over, lacing his words with venom.

"You know, you should do yourself a favor," he said as he

opened the door to leave. "Just accept who you are. Embrace it. Live your golden life, in your golden castle, and save all the rest of us the heartache of feeling like a pawn in a game."

He walked out without looking back, leaving her and every dream he'd had for them alone in his office.

CHAPTER TWENTY-EIGHT

"So you just left her there?" Lori's voice chastised over the phone, reminding Gabe why calling his sister was the worst idea he'd had since walking out on Hope.

He'd tried calling Sean first, but his best friend wasn't answering his phone. Multiple shots of whisky later, he caved and called his sister. He'd been hoping for some sympathy, maybe even a bit of advice. What he got was screeching recriminations in his ear.

"I knew you'd fuck this up. I knew it! Gabriel Walsh, nobody, and I mean nobody, self-destructs quite like you do."

"She's the one who lied to me, Lori," he mumbled, caught between misery and exhaustion.

After he'd left Hope in his office, he walked the streets of Portland for hours, but it did nothing to loosen the knot in his chest. Now, after a sleepless night spent becoming intimately familiar with the bottom of his whisky bottle and drunk dialing his sister at six in the morning, he was still no closer to processing all that Hope had told him.

"Maybe she lied because she was afraid her past would

screw up her future with you? Maybe she was scared? Maybe she rightly believed you'd judge her based on her past? Maybe she was trying to put it all behind her? Maybe there's more to the story, Gabe, but guess what? You'll never know because you're a fucking moron."

"Christ, will you stop swearing? It sounds weird, you never swear."

"You know what's weird, Gabe? You abandoning the love of your life, then getting drunk and calling your sister to *bail you out* of a bad situation. Are you and Hope really that different?"

Jesus. He hated when his sister was right. He'd been an asshole for walking away from Hope. He'd been hurt because he'd trusted her, and thought she trusted him. It hurt to know she'd kept something so big from him, and at the height of his shock and anger, he'd wondered what else she'd kept from him.

"Go find her, you idiot." His sister's voice was like a drill in his head. Or maybe that was the hangover starting. "Before it's too late."

"I liked you better when you were nice."

She snorted. "I was never nice." Then in a softer tone, she asked, "You love her, don't you?"

He did. So much he couldn't imagine life without her in it anymore.

"Go find her. Talk to her, Gabe. Find out the details." Lori sighed heavily on the other end of the phone. "I know it's a foreign concept to most men, but it's called communication, and if you do it right, it usually works."

"I'm an idiot."

"Yes. You are."

"Christ, I said that out loud?"

"Yes, you did."

Shit. He needed to stop drinking. "I gotta go, sis."

"Yes, you do."

After he hung up, he hit the shower, then pulled on fresh jeans and a shirt, then headed across the hallway, not even bothering with socks.

After a few seconds of Gabe's non-stop knocking, Ivy opened the door. He thought he'd looked like hell after his sleepless night walking the streets and drinking, but Ivy looked like death, barely warmed up.

"You okay?" he asked, his voice hoarse from lack of sleep and too much whisky.

"She's not here," was the answer he got in return.

"What?" He was too late. Always too fucking late.

Ivy turned and walked back into the apartment. "She went home to Cali. Took the first flight on standby. She figured you wanted space, so she left."

"Jesus Christ."

"He's not here either," Ivy muttered as Gabe followed her to the sofa where they both flopped down, exhausted.

He was immediately assailed by the scent of Hope. Her paintings were propped all over the living room. The fucking herb planter she'd rescued from his place was thriving on her windowsill. "I'm such an asshole."

"Yeah, you are," Ivy said, but her voice was so thin and desolate that it was hard to take offense.

"I've got to go." If there'd been seconds to spare, he would've stayed to ask what had put the hollow look in Ivy's eyes. He'd have to call and tell Sean to check in on her later. He raced for the door.

"Wait," Ivy called after him sharply, making him stop and face her. "Did Hope tell you?"

"It doesn't matter," he said and meant it. He no longer cared about the past, he only cared about now. And he'd been an asshole for not realizing and saying so when he'd had the chance.

"Did she tell you?" Ivy demanded, her voice forceful and her eyes urgent.

Confusion assailed him, curiosity brought him a step closer to Ivy. "She told me about the cheating, but it doesn't matter. It's the past." His feet once more moved toward the future, toward Hope. "Look, Ivy, I've gotta—"

"She didn't cheat," Ivy whispered. "That's a lie." Those words froze him in mid-stride.

"What are you talking about?" he demanded.

Ivy wrapped her arms around herself, much like Hope had in his office last night. She moved to the window. "She's protecting me. Like she has been for the last three years. Keeping my secret because I asked her to, but she's too loyal for her own freaking good."

"Ivy?" It was all starting to feel too much like the *Twilight Zone* for his liking. He was a person who liked to have control in any and every situation. He'd surrendered control before, and it hadn't gone well. But in this situation, with these two women, he was at a total loss, caught in their tide.

Inhaling deeply, as if bracing herself for a blow, Ivy angled her slight frame to face him. "Back in college, I—" She made a choking sound, like the words she was about to say were trapped in her throat. "Shit." She returned to the couch and sat down. Then almost immediately stood again and rubbed her fist against the center of her chest.

"What happened back in college, Ivy?"

But she only stood there looking like she was either going to pass out or throw up.

"Just take a deep breath and start from the beginning. No rush." Which was bullshit, of course. He'd already wasted far too much time being an ass with Hope. But he didn't want to be an ass with Ivy, too. And something told him that whatever Ivy was trying to say was the key to helping him piece together what had happened in the bar earlier.

"Hope and I were roommates in college, and it was a classic situation of opposites attract. She was well off, outgoing, and popular. Obviously, I was the opposite in every possible way." Ivy twisted the hem of her shirt so hard that Gabe thought she might rip it. "Anyway, in the end, we bonded over our mutual desire to study our asses off and get what we came for. Which was our respective degrees."

She continued to torment her shirt as she paced the room. Gabe leaned against the doorjamb, striving for calm despite the storm building in front of him.

"For the most part, it was all work and no play. But by our last year, Hope decided we couldn't graduate without having had at least a taste of a social life. Our peers were partying every weekend, and most weekdays, while we dried up our best years, and body parts, in the dusty library studying."

Gabe tried to imagine Hope hunched over books in a library, working tirelessly trying to get a degree she had no desire for, just to prove something that didn't need proof.

"Hope, being Hope, got invited to parties all the time, but she never went. Then one night, at the end of midterms, she came home and said *we* were going to a party at one of the frat houses where her friends lived." A flash of pain crossed her pale blue eyes.

Dread dropped into Gabe's gut like a dead weight. He pushed off the doorjamb he'd been leaning against.

"Business school friends?" he guessed. "Adam?"

"Yes. He was one of them. There were four that hung out like a pack. They did everything together." By now, Ivy had fidgeted with her shirt so much it was wrapped tightly around her fingers, probably cutting off circulation. "That night at the party, one of them, Ethan, he got friendly with me. Had a few drinks with me. Complimented me. Paid me real attention. It was unusual, because no one ever noticed me, and I... liked the attention. So, when he invited me up to one of the rooms, I—" Ivy swallowed so hard he could see her throat work with the effort. "I went along gladly."

"Oh shit." Suddenly, he could see the end of this story. And by the dread, agony, and remnants of terror visible in every angle of Ivy's face, he knew it was killing her to relive it. "Ivy, you don't have to say more."

She nodded. A flicker of relief passed over her features before they fell into a loaded silence. Finally, she looked over at him resolutely.

"What you really need to know is that Hope saved me that night. When I was in that room, Adam was at the door, making sure no one could get in." She wrapped her arms tightly around herself, as if trying to hold herself together. "He got the brunt of Hope's rampage. I mean, he got some shots in. He shoved her against the door, I think. I remember hearing Hope cry out, I think he slapped her. She was holding an ice pack to her cheek when we got back to her place. I don't—I don't remember all the details." Staring at the floor, Ivy rubbed the spot between her brows that had been etched in a frown. Then she looked up at him, the blue of her eyes were haunting in their clarity. "She fought him so hard, Gabe. Once she got her knee up between Adam's legs she busted through that door screaming like a banshee, throwing anything she could find. She ripped a lamp out of the wall and threw it at the mirror. It was enough of a distraction that I could get out from under Ethan, the one who was—" She rolled her lips, silencing the memory.

Gabe said nothing. Hope had lied to him. That asshole *had* hurt her—in more ways than one.

The thought of someone laying hands on Hope... He clenched his fists at the visual. So much rage was coursing through his system in that moment he was sure he was going to explode. And what good would that do now? Ivy had been through enough, she didn't need him flipping his lid in front of her.

"Adam always had it out for Hope after that. I think he was embarrassed that she got the best of him. She clawed him pretty good, you know? Left a scar on his face." A small smile twitched against her mouth. "There was nothing good that happened that night, but I didn't mind seeing the blood dripping off his face when we left."

He remembered seeing that fucking scar. He hadn't known Hope had put it there while she tried to save her friend. Pride filled his chest at her bravery. *That* was the Hope he knew. The one who went to battle for the people she loved. "Why didn't she just tell me the truth?"

"Because of me," Ivy said, her voice small. Fragile. "Hope busted through that door that night, like something out of a movie. Shrieking, throwing things, cursing, hitting, punching. You name it. She pulled me out, brought me home, showered me, wrapped me up in her arms, and held me as I cried."

He let the image paint itself in his mind. Hope, the caregiver, sheltering her friend, soothing her, supporting her after she survived an unimaginable horror.

"I made her promise to never tell anyone," Ivy said weakly. "She wanted me to go to the police, but I—I didn't."

It was hard to keep the emotions out of his features, to keep his inside voice inside. He didn't know much about the thought process of a person who survived what Ivy had, and he was certainly in no position to be advising anyone on the topic. But he did know how his own thought process worked. It was simple: actions must have consequences. Crimes needed to be punished. Asshole touches someone against their will, violates their body, asshole hangs until his eyes bug out of his head. Justice served.

Knowing that Ivy kept silent meant that justice was not served in this case, at least not Gabe's brand of justice, and that picked at something in the very core of him that took every ounce of his focus not to project onto Ivy. Because above all else, above justice, above retribution, above consequence—there was free will. That had been taken away from Ivy once. It wasn't his place, or anyone else's, to take it a second time.

"That's why they almost got away with accusing her of cheating. She could never really defend herself because they knew she'd never go against my wishes." Ivy sighed, her breath fluttering her bangs. "The whole cheating thing was so stupid. I'll let her tell you that story in her own words if she wants to, but you've got to know she'd never cheat. I mean, honestly, we're talking about Hope. Anyone who believes that is an idiot."

He was. He was the idiot. He hadn't believed she would cheat—that had sounded so wrong the moment she'd said it. But he hadn't believed in her. Hadn't believed in them. Not enough, certainly not the way she deserved, and *that* made him the worst kind of idiot.

She'd been carrying these burdens completely alone,

thinking they would keep her from having a future with him. And he'd gone ahead and proved her right by walking out on her. If she ever looked his way again, it would be a miracle. Still, he had to try. He had to get to her.

But first there was something he needed to say to Ivy.

"It's not your fault, Ivy," he whispered, looking directly at her until she met his eyes. "Not one part of what happened, or will happen between Hope and I, is your fault."

Instead of looking reassured, she looked wary—and a little apprehensive.

"There's... one more... thing," Ivy said hesitantly.

Christ, he thought. *What more could there possibly be?* He was afraid to know.

"It might not be my place to say anything, but I really think you need to know. Last night, Hope got a message on her phone. It was an offer for a job she interviewed for a while back, for the position of manager of an art gallery in Detroit."

Blood rushed to his head, then pounded there mercilessly.

It was Ivy's turn to consider him carefully. "I'm guessing by the fact that you don't seem to be breathing, you didn't know about it."

With great effort, he forced his mouth to move. "I did not."

"I don't think she had any plans to take it, but then last night happened and, well..."

"Well, what?" he asked, through teeth clenched so hard he was pretty sure they were cracking.

Ivy studied her feet for a moment before meeting his gaze. Her expression said it all.

"I have to get to her." He just hoped he wasn't too late.

CHAPTER TWENTY-NINE

That evening in San Francisco, Hope pushed open the doors of the pavilion at the children's hospital and walked out into the cool evening air. She'd just given her welcome speech to officially kick off the benefit and needed fresh air before going back inside to mingle with the deep pockets who were currently plowing their way through a six-course meal.

Every year the hospital transformed its largest meeting room and pavilion into a chic, chandelier lit ballroom and white tablecloth dining room. And every year, the very upper crust of Northern California society was invited to attend this elite event that, under her mother's experienced hand, had become one of the most exclusive—and successful—charity events in the state.

It brought in millions of dollars each year to fund the hospital's extra costs and grow its services annually. The children's hospital had always been a part of Hope's life. Her family had been long-time benefactors and contributed not only financially but with volunteer hours. The hospital had been close to her heart in a way she could never explain.

This year she could. This year, she felt an even greater tug to the cause.

Spending time with Ruby, knowing that at six months old she'd relied on hospital services after the car crash that killed her mother, had only cemented Hope's desire for every child to have access to the best possible health care regardless of prognosis, financial status, or opportunity.

At the thought of Ruby, her heart squeezed painfully. A familiar feeling since Gabe had left her in his office. Totally alone.

It gutted her, knowing he believed she was who he'd thought she was when he first found her crying in the hallway so long ago. But what choice had she had? She'd vowed never to tell Ivy's secret.

She'd be lying if she said she wasn't feeling a little angry about it all, too. It was true she hadn't been totally above board, but she'd hoped when the time came he would have fought for her a bit more, had a little more faith in her. Instead he'd just left. How could he just leave?

And what she'd come to realize, after hours and hours of thinking of nothing else, was that in Portland with Gabe and Ruby—and Ivy as well—she hadn't found independence. She'd only replaced one family with another. She'd opened herself up to love and gotten burned.

That was why she'd immediately accepted the Detroit gallery job when she received the official offer after she arrived in San Francisco for the gala. She needed a fresh start away from everybody she knew. Detroit would be her chance to truly be independent. Instead of latching herself onto another family she didn't belong in. Just her.

It was for the best. Her heart just hadn't accepted it yet.

"There you are, darling."

She turned to see her mother approaching her on the balcony.

Audrey was stunning in her floor-length emerald gown with a Queen Anne neckline sparkling with gemstones. She was an ageless beauty. She was always elegant and refined, but on these occasions that required her to dress up, her mother came across as regal, untouchable. "If you stay out here much longer," Audrey said with no criticism, "you'll miss the main course altogether."

Hope glanced over her shoulder at the bright lights of the city beyond. "I needed to get out for a moment. It's such a beautiful night."

All day, she'd done her best to hide her raw emotions from the previous night's events. Catching the earlier flight, she'd arrived at dawn, needing to put as much distance between her and Gabe as possible.

Since her arrival, she'd had the best day with her parents that she'd had in a decade. Even though a part of her heart was totally and utterly broken, another part had been healed. It was ironic that Gabe had a hand in both.

Her mother's footsteps halted beside her. "You know, darling, the very first night I held you in my arms I was here at this hospital, and I brought you up to this very balcony to show you this beautiful world you'd arrived in."

Hope's throat tightened. They hadn't discussed her arrival into the world, well, ever. She looked at the face of the only mother she'd ever known. "You've never talked about my birth before."

Audrey's gaze dropped but Hope still caught the shame that fell across her lovely features. "I did so much wrong in how I handled that. So many things I can never take back." She raised her gaze to meet Hope's—brilliant blue eyes facing deep brown. "Having you here today, so open with us for the first time in—" Audrey cut off, her voice thickening with emotion. "In far too long. It's given me the courage to now tell you all the things I should have said so long ago." She gathered Hope's hands in her. "If you'll hear them?"

Hope studied her mother. She appeared so hopeful, yet so afraid at the same time. And even though her heart was threatening to beat right out of her chest, she squeezed Audrey's hands reassuringly and nodded her consent. The time for truth was long overdue.

Audrey's eyes shone with tears on the verge of spilling over. "The night you arrived, I was here at the hospital, coming off a volunteer shift in the NICU. I was walking out with one of the nurses when I spotted a bundle of blankets. As I moved closer, I realized the bundle was a baby. Someone had dropped off a baby on the front steps of this very hospital."

"Abandoned," Hope breathed the word, realization dawning. She'd been abandoned at the hospital.

Audrey shook her head, causing a tear to slip down her cheek. "Abandonment insinuates a callousness. Neglect. But your birth mother, whoever she was, cared about you enough to find a place that cared for children."

At the revelation, Hope didn't know how to feel.

"There could be a thousand reasons why she felt unfit to keep you. Those answers, my darling, we will never know. But what we do know is that she loved you enough to leave you in a place that had the resources and capability to care for you." She squeezed Hope's fingers in her own. "You weren't abandoned. You were found. Just as the woman who gave birth to you wanted you to be."

What her mother was saying made sense, but the feelings jumbling around inside her – not so much. She didn't feel any anger or resentment, but she still felt the sting of hurt, and the hollowness of loss. There was no way to track her birth mother at this point. Hope would never know her story, never fully understand why she'd felt compelled to give her child away.

"The doctors said you couldn't have been more than a few hours old. Less than a day," Audrey added, her voice laced with emotion. "As you know, Joel was already five years old when you came along, too young to question the difference of how you arrived. Your father and I had been trying to grow our family for years, and..." She gave a helpless shrug of her elegant shoulders. "The doctors called it 'secondary infertility.' There was no reason they could find as to why we couldn't conceive. I was heartbroken, devastated. Your father said we had to move on, to find enjoyment in the blessing we had. But I had this longing in my heart. An empty space aching to be filled." She reached up and cradled Hope's face.

Hope leaned into her mother's touch, taking comfort from it for the first time in a long time.

Audrey smiled. "Then that night, you were there. I never thought we'd be able to adopt you. There was a process, a system—but somehow, by some miracle, you became ours. Not just in our hearts, but legally ours. And I never looked back."

Both mother and daughter were crying now, soundless tears tracking down their faces. The hollowness inside of Hope filled with a long overdue sense of gratitude.

Audrey breathed a sigh of relief. "Just when I'd lost all hope, I found it again—in you. My Hope."

Hope let out a choked sob and threw herself into her mother's arms. The only mother she'd ever known. The only mother who mattered, now and forever.

As she released the decade's worth of tears inside her, Audrey ran soothing hands up and down her back.

"Families don't always come together in the exact way we imagine," Audrey whispered into Hope's hair. "But when they do, we should hold on to them with everything we have." Audrey's hold on her tightened. "We should fight for them always, because family is the most precious gift we are given." Audrey released her and brushed away the last of Hope's tears. "I'm sorry I let you down, darling. But please don't let my mistakes ruin your chance at happiness. You were never meant to be alone. Not on this hospital's steps or in Portland or where you go next."

She stared at Audrey, confused. It was like her mother could see into her mind, could read what had all happened in the last few days—months. Then Audrey leaned in to give her one last hard and fierce hug, before turning Hope to face the pavilion doors.

The sight in front of her made her gasp and stagger back in shock. Gabe stood there, which was one thing to wrap her head around, but he was also decked out in a formal black suit, looking so handsome she almost couldn't believe he was real. The man cleaned up nicely.

"A family is precious, darling," her mother whispered into her ear. "No matter how it comes to you. Don't ever let go."

Then, with a regal nod in Gabe's direction, Audrey slipped back into the pavilion, leaving her alone with this man who had both ruined her and blessed her in ways that were beyond her wildest imaginings.

He approached her slowly, his eyes dark and unsure, yet in their green depths she saw relief. A relief that echoed in her own heart. She'd missed him. It had been less than a day, but her heart ached for him and seeing him here, even with all the uncertainty, relieved the ache.

"What are you doing here?" she asked, appalled at the wobbly sound of her voice.

"I wanted to see you. Needed to." He halted in front of her, so close that she had to tip her head to look up at him. "I shouldn't have left you last night, Hope. I screwed up, and if I could do it all again, I would've never left that office. Never left you." He lifted a hand and brushed a strand of hair away from her face.

The touch was so familiar it made her heart ache.

"Then why did you?" She wanted to know. Wanted to hear why he *had* walked out of her life so easily. Her anger bubbled dangerously just under her hurt.

"Everything that happened last night—" He broke off, his voice rough. "Seeing you threatened like that—by some asshole who'd clearly threatened you before." A muscle clenched in his jaw. "Then what you said after, about the cheating. It didn't make sense, but at the same time, it triggered all kinds of shit inside me. All kinds of fear. It brought back memories, and all the reasons why I promised myself I'd never trust anyone again, because in the end you were keeping things from me. Getting out of there felt like the only way I could protect myself from totally losing it. Turns out that was my biggest mistake."

As far as heartfelt monologues went, that one made it pretty impossible to stay mad at him. After all he'd been through, she couldn't blame him for reacting as he had. She'd had the opportunity to tell him the truth, and she'd delayed until it was too late. *Because the truth wasn't an option*, she reminded herself.

"I went to your apartment this morning, but you were

gone. Ivy told me you'd gone home." He paused, his eyes poignant. "Ivy told me everything."

The air in her lungs evaporated. What did that mean? There was no way Ivy had told him *everything.*

He must have read the apprehension in her eyes because he nodded, his expression grim. "She told me what happened that night at the frat party. What happened to her. What happened to *you.* What you did to save her." He leaned closer to her, smelling like he always did—like spice and cedar, all male.

She inhaled him like she would a breath of fresh air, deeply and greedily. She wanted to close the distance between them as well, but she needed to clarify something first.

"Ivy couldn't have told you. She's never—"

Gabe's eyes darkened murderously, and in that moment, she knew it was true. Ivy had told him.

"I understand why you kept her secret, I can even understand why she decided to make it one, even if I don't necessarily agree with it because it means those fuckers got away with what they did. But I understand it's her choice." His eyes softened marginally. "What I don't understand is why you'd lie about the cheating. Why would you go along with what Adam said about you?"

So Ivy hadn't told him everything then. She whirled away on a sigh, moving closer to the balcony's railing where the city beyond glistened brightly against the backdrop of the ocean.

"Well, I couldn't tell you about Ivy. Not without her consent. And it wasn't a total lie," she admitted, turning back to him, wanting nothing but the truth between them now. "But I need you to know I never cheated. I would never do that."

He nodded. "No more omissions, Hope. Tell me what happened."

Hope sighed again. "Toward the end of the first term in our last year, after the rape, Adam and Ethan got caught cheating. I guess all their partying had finally caught up with their GPAs, and it was either cheat or fail. They were cocky as hell, so they never thought they'd get caught. When they did, they accused me of helping them cheat, telling the administration that I supplied them with test answers and copies of the exams. They figured if I took the brunt of the blame, the department would be more lenient on them." The memories of that horrible time filtered into her mind. It had been so long since she'd let herself think about it.

"At first, I told them to go to hell. I worked my ass off to get to where I was, and there was no way I was going to let them get away with it. But my words held no weight. They knew they'd just gotten away with rape since Ivy hadn't reported it and that I'd never betray her. They were cocky fucks who thought they could get away with anything. Who *did* get away with anything. So I had absolutely no leverage against them. Then they threatened to spread rumors about how easy Ivy was. Threatened to tell more of their friends that she'd give them what they wanted. That she liked it rough." Her voice grew thick as the memories assailed her. "They said such horrible things. And they were so arrogant and conceited I was sure they'd follow through."

With a growl, Gabe dragged her to him, and she went willingly, taking his warmth and his strength to help her get through the rest. "So, they blamed me for supplying them with material to cheat. I was so flabbergasted that it was even happening, I couldn't figure out a way to defend myself or clear my name. Without telling me, Ivy got a hold of my brother, and the next thing I knew, Joel was on campus armed with lawyers and the Morgan bankroll. Within hours, he'd cleared my name." She'd never forget how her brother had dropped everything to come and help her. "He didn't stop until Adam and Ethan were expelled, and it was vindicating, that small victory, after everything they'd done." She released a sad sigh as she walked through the memory, step by step, for the first time in a long time. "I thought it was over and I was told I could resume my studies, but that was naive. My reputation was ruined. And even though they were gone, those guys still had friends. Friends who believed I was guilty and proceeded to make my life a living hell on campus." The cruel names she'd been called and not-so-hushed gossip that followed her everywhere, the constant cloud of Ivy's grief and guilt, the weight of her brother's protectiveness thereafter, all flooded back at once. "In the end, I couldn't take it, so I came back home to finish my degree at a local college."

"Ah, Hope, I'm so sorry you had to go through that on top of everything else." He kissed her forehead as he wrapped his big arms around her. "You're so fucking brave. So loyal. I'm sorry I wasn't there for you then, and I'm sorry I wasn't there for you last night."

She clung to him. "You didn't know."

"Yeah, but what I did know, what I've always known, is that you're strong and courageous. You work harder than most people I know. You're creative and loving. You've given my daughter the maternal affection she's craved, honoring her real mother while you do it. Do you have any idea what that means to me, Hope? What you mean to me?"

Her insides burst at the words coming out of Gabe's mouth. They sounded so much like all of her dreams coming true. She snuggled closer, looping her arms around his waist, keeping her arms beneath his suit jacket. She felt so good right there in that moment. Safe, free from all the secrets she'd carried, and, most of all, loved. Even though he hadn't said it, she sensed it flowing out of him and straight into her. She never wanted to be apart from him and the life they had.

And then she remembered. Detroit. She curled her fingers into the fabric of his shirt and pressed her forehead against his chest.

"What's wrong?" Gabe asked, rubbing his hand reassuringly along her back.

"I did something," she groaned. Regret and uncertainty snaked through her.

Gabe gently lifted her chin so her gaze met his. His green eyes glinted in the moonlight. "You took a job in Detroit."

"How did you—?" She stopped when she suddenly realized the answer. "Ivy. Hasn't she just become the regular blabbermouth?"

"She's worried about you. She loves you," Gabe murmured. "Why didn't you tell me?"

She sighed and once again turned away from him to face the balcony railing. "I wasn't going to say anything at first, because the opportunity came so fast, and I wasn't really considering it. When I didn't hear anything back, I assumed it wasn't going anywhere. But then we argued. And when I got home, there was a message offering me the job to manage the art gallery—where I could also show my paintings. So I accepted it."

Gabe's arm brushed hers as he took his place beside her. When she looked up at him, he was staring straight ahead out at the ocean.

"Do you want the job?" he asked, his voice giving no hint of what emotion he might be feeling.

"I came to Portland to distance myself from the heartbreak and betrayal I felt my family caused me. I wanted to find independence and the knowledge that I could make it on my own." She turned to Gabe, her heart awash with agony. "After our argument, it hurt so much when you left me standing there. You just left, Gabe. It felt like someone tore my heart out. Again. And in that moment, I realized I hadn't achieved independence. I had just given my heart to another family who broke it."

A tortured sound ripped from Gabe's throat. "If I made you feel that way, I'm so sorry. I lost sight of what was most important for one fucking second and I'll never forgive myself for walking away from you. But you're wrong. You are independent and strong, and you don't have to be alone to be those things. You can have the life you want, the life you dream of. You do have it. It's right here." The crack in his voice echoed in her heart. "With me. Not De-fucking-troit. But in Portland with me—and Ruby."

Gabe reached for her, cradling her face in his palms. "Hope, you are a brilliant, talented artist. If you want to show your work in the world like it deserves to be shown then I'll do everything in my power to make sure your paintings are in every fucking gallery in Oregon. In the whole world. Just stay. Stay. This is your home Hope, right fucking here." He thumped his fist against his heart.

She choked back a cry, because he was saying everything she needed to hear, and the weight that had settled in her heart suddenly released and flew away like a balloon. Needing to be close, she curled her fingers into the lapels of his suit jacket and pressed against him. Gabe's arms came around her instantly, holding her tight.

The soft and luxurious material of his suit reminded her of something she'd wondered when she'd first laid eyes on him that evening.

"How did you know to bring a suit?" she asked, her fingers brushing the smooth fabric.

Gabe leaned back an inch and grinned down at her, his green eyes twinkling with mischief. "Ivy gave me your parents' number, and I called them before I hopped on the first flight I could get. I figured they should know who I was before I came to convince their daughter that she was meant to be in Portland with me and Ruby."

She gasped at his presumptuousness, even knowing her father probably respected his boldness and her mother appreciated his candor. "What did they say to that?"

When Gabe drew her up against his chest, lifting her off her feet, she gave into the shiver that rolled through her, not of cold, but of electric heat. Heat and lust and love for this man. She could admit it easily now. She loved him.

"They told me that if I wanted to convince you to forgive me and take me back, I should arrive wearing my best suit." He rained soft kisses along her jaw. "Will you, Hope?" His voice was husky with emotion.

"Will I what?" she asked, distracted by the feel of his firm muscles under her fingertips as she ran them across his chest.

Without taking his mouth off her skin, he murmured, "Forgive me." Then he leaned back so his gaze bore into hers earnestly. "I need you. My daughter needs you. You're our home now. I love you, Hope."

A gasp escaped as his words registered and fell into place inside her heart, like Scrabble pieces on a board. "I love you, too." On a wave of relief, her own words freed themselves from her soul. "I love you and Ruby so much. And I need you both, too."

The words were barely out of her mouth when his lips descended on hers. Their kiss was deep and heated. Familiar.

She wrapped her arms around his neck, her body melting under his embrace, eager for the future. "Take me home," she managed when his lips released hers.

Gabe's answering chuckle vibrated between them.

"Trust me, I am counting down the minutes until I can peel this dress off you." He kissed her again, until she was all longing and need and desperation. "But I believe you still have many more millions to raise tonight, and I don't think your parents will view me favorably if I drag you out of here right now—just so I can have my wicked way with you."

She rubbed her body against his and purred into his ear, "But what if *I'm* the one who drags you out of here?"

Groaning, Gabe claimed her mouth in one last hard kiss, then led her back into the pavilion before she could make good on her version of what they both wanted.

CHAPTER THIRTY

Somehow, Gabe made it through the rest of the night without having his tie choke him to death. What he really wanted was a long drink of a cold beer, and/or to whisk Hope away so he could peel that sexy as hell dress off her inch by inch.

In the stunning white gown that hugged her curves just right, with her hair swept up and diamonds sparkling on her ears and neck, she looked every inch a bride.

His bride. She didn't know it yet, but he planned to ask her to marry him as soon as he could.

He couldn't believe it. How he'd gotten so lucky—when he'd nearly succeeded in totally shutting himself off from any form of intimacy ever again—he'd never know. But he did know he'd spend the rest of his life being grateful and giving his family the very best of himself every day.

Watching Hope work the room, laughing and chatting with the ultra-rich until they all but emptied their pockets into her hands, filled him with pride. She was special in so many ways. She could engage with anyone and would step up to help anyone.

Sitting back in his white-satin covered chair, he took a long drink of the golden bubbly that a passing waiter had offered him and took pleasure in simply watching her.

Beside him, he heard a chair scrape up.

"So, word is you're here to steal my baby sister from us."

Gabe continued to stare over the rim of his glass, watching Hope as she tipped her head back and laughed at something a middle-aged, rotund woman—wearing a tight blue velvet dress and sporting brightly-dyed red hair—had just said.

"I'm no thief. She's coming willingly." At the deep chuckle that followed his statement, he turned to make eye contact with Hope's brother, Joel.

Joel held two bottles of beer. Gabe's preferred drink, and a drink that no one else in the pavilion had. He'd never met the man before, but he knew Hope had a deep-seated respect for her brother. So Gabe swore he'd aim for the same. Joel was, after all, the man who saved both Ivy and Hope from the grim aftermath of that assault in college. He owed him for that.

Joel stared at him for a long moment, his gray eyes intense and assessing. And Gabe, recognizing when he was being sized up, held Joel's gaze.

He might not be as rich as Hope's brother, but he had nothing to be ashamed of, nothing to hide. He loved Hope, and he was going to give her everything he had. If Joel couldn't see that, he wasn't as smart as his sister thought.

Joel continued to stare until it was a second away from being uncomfortable. Then, as if he'd come to a conclusion, he gave a curt nod and handed Gabe one of the beers. Gabe accepted it warily.

Joel smiled, his eyes warming, and lifted his glass to Gabe's in a toast. "In that case, here's to you, brother. I'm glad Hope's your problem now." He spoke in a humorous tone, grinning as he took a long drink of his beer.

But Gabe was no fool. He saw that all the things Hope had said about her brother were true. Joel's backbone was made of honor and grit, and he was loyal to the core, especially to family. Gabe knew without a shadow of a doubt that if anyone hurt Joel Morgan's baby sister, the man wouldn't hesitate to eat them for dinner.

"I'll never hurt her again," he vowed.

Joel nodded. "I know you won't."

There was a moment of silence as both men watched Hope move from donor to donor.

"Because you understand what's at stake," Joel said after a while. "You loved someone and lost them. Then you almost lost Hope by being a dick. You'll move heaven and earth not to feel that soul-gutting pain a third time," Joel added, surprising Gabe with the depth of this heart to heart. "I once had something special, too. I let it slip through my fingers, and I've regretted it every day since. If I got my second chance, I wouldn't fuck it up." He stared at Gabe pointedly. "That's how I know you won't either." Then he took sip of his beer and fixed his attention back on the crowd. "Also, you're planning to open a second bar, and you've bought a house. You're looking toward the future. A future my sister deserves."

Gabe's jaw dropped. He hadn't told his own family the plans he had underway for opening another Bowie's across town. He'd assumed Joel had a lot of power and influence, but this?

"You spied on me?" he asked, not sure if he was mad as hell or impressed.

Joel's features remained affable as he shrugged. "Not spied. Vetted. I vetted you." Then he met Gabe's gaze head on again. "Did you really think I would let my baby sister ride off into the sunset with just anyone?"

No. And understanding what he did about Joel Morgan, he wasn't surprised he'd go the distance to make sure his sister would be safe and happy. Still, the balls on this guy were fucking unbelievable.

"You're one hell of a determined bastard, aren't you?"

Joel tossed his head back and laughed. "Don't worry. You passed my tests. The vetting is over. We're on the same side, Gabe." Joel downed the rest of his drink, then sighed. "We do have one problem, though."

Gabe raised a questioning eyebrow.

"You're a fucking Trail Blazers fan."

By the time the mingling, schmoozing, drinking, and eating was done, it was well past two in the morning, and Gabe had shoved his tie into his pants pocket hours ago. But the hospital had raised more than a million dollars, and Hope was glowing with excitement as she led him into the private room in her family home where they were staying, so he considered it all a win.

"Tonight was our most successful fundraiser yet," she said as she moved toward a door on the other side of the palatial room.

He halted just inside the room, rendered immobile by the massive space—unlike any bedroom he'd seen. A four-poster king-sized bed on an elevated platform rose regally to over ten-foot ceilings, while a full-length white couch sat in another section of the room, in front of a fireplace that had floor to ceiling bookshelves on either side. And beyond multiple sets of French doors, a balcony decorated with exotic plants and luxurious patio furniture—visible even in the darkness—revealed a multi-million-dollar view.

As he took in another reminder of Hope's immense family wealth, a ridiculous insecurity washed over him. The modest three-bedroom house he bought suddenly seemed inadequate for someone who'd been raised in a California mansion.

Gentle hands ran up his back and across his shoulders to loop around his neck.

"All I need is you, Gabriel Walsh," she said, reading his thoughts with uncomfortable accuracy. "You and Ruby." She pressed herself against his back, her breasts snug against his shoulder blades as she brought her delectable lips to his ear. "That's all I want; that's all I need," she purred. "So stop thinking whatever you're thinking and come unzip my dress." When she kissed the sensitive skin on the nape of his neck, his body responded in anticipation.

Then her heat and softness were gone. He turned to watch her sexy figure sashaying once again toward the mystery door, and he was helpless but to follow her. He'd always be helpless for her. His body would always want hers. His heart would always work to match the beat of hers. More than any of that, though, he would always trust her. He trusted her with his bar, his heart, and his daughter. He also trusted her words, so if she said she didn't need or want this life of extravagance, he knew she was telling the truth.

When he arrived at the door, he halted to lean against the doorjamb and watch indulgently as she stood inside an equally palatial ensuite, carefully pulling pins from her hair, letting the golden mass fall over her shoulders in soft, gorgeous waves. Her gaze caught his in the mirror, her dark eyes dilating with desire.

He moved close behind her, taking her hair in his hands

and scooping it around her shoulder so her neck was exposed. He bent to kiss her there, his body shuddering in response to the gasp that escaped her lips. He watched her in the mirror, her eyes closed in trust and surrender, needy little pants puffing through her parted lips, head angled to the side, exposing her neck for him.

She was perfect, inside and out. And she was his.

For the millionth time that evening, his heart swelled with gratitude, and he suddenly felt like the Grinch from the classic Christmas story, his heart too big for his chest. She had done that. She had reawakened his heart and his soul to the miraculous gift of love.

Again, he bent his head to nuzzle the length of her neck. "You will be mine, and I will be yours."

"Always," she whispered, making him realize he'd spoken out loud.

He opened his eyes and caught her staring at him in the mirror. Everything in his heart was reflecting back at him in her warm chocolate-brown gaze, and he was overcome by a hunger for her so powerful he felt he might die if he didn't have her in that moment. It was a kind of desperation that stole his breath and made him shake.

Gripping her waist, he pressed his aching body against hers. Hope responded by pushing her hips back, maximizing the contact, until he throbbed so hard and tight, he couldn't take it.

"Hope." Her name tore from his lips, half plea, half prayer. He couldn't imagine life without her, couldn't believe he'd come so close to losing her forever.

Abruptly, the need to claim her, to brand her and make her his in every way possible, became paramount. It was primitive, completely primal, and made no sense, especially since he'd already had her—several times over. But being with her in this moment felt different. *He* felt different. He wanted to bind himself to her in the most permanent and basic way possible. He didn't want barriers between them anymore. He wanted, more than anything, for their love to create something even more beautiful. Something lasting.

"I don't want to use a condom." He murmured the words before he could even think them through. Yet he knew as soon as he said them that he didn't want to take them back. He meant every word.

Then she went very still against him. *Shit.* His fucking timing—perfect as always.

He turned her in his arms and held her close, so she could feel his heart beating wildly in his chest. He prayed she could read the morse code of the beat, that she would understand the truth of his words, see the promise and commitment in his eyes. He held her face between his palms and drew her up until their foreheads touched.

"Hope, I love you. I want you." He bent to kiss her, devouring her mouth in a hot, devastating kiss that he hoped reinforced the sincerity of his words. He pulled back a fraction, his lips still whispering against hers. "I want a life with you, and I want the works on that life. You, Ruby, me, the house, a dog—and more children."

Hope closed her eyes, swallowing a sob. Panic rose in his chest. The last thing he wanted to do was scare or pressure her.

"But more than anything I just fucking want you, Hope. Everything about you, just the way you are. And the rest will happen whenever you're ready." He pressed his lips into her forehead, praying he wasn't screwing this up. "I know you're still young. You have a whole world ahead of you. I don't ever want to be what slows you down. I just really need you to know..." What? What were the right words to follow up on *I don't want to use a condom*? "As long as we're together, as long as you let me love you every single day, all will be well in my soul—everything else is just a bonus."

She let out another strangled sob.

He held onto her face and prayed it was a good sob, and that he hadn't just undone everything they'd fought so hard for. But, Christ, if there was more for him to say he couldn't say it. Emotion clogged his throat. He preferred words and actions to displays of emotion, but tears burned his eyes now.

When Hope finally opened her eyes, they were shimmering, and to his immense relief it wasn't with sadness or anger or despair. There was only joy brimming in them, and Gabe slowly released the breath he hadn't realized he was holding.

"I want that too," she whispered, a tear escaping her pretty brown eyes and rolling down the soft creamy skin of her cheek. In his chest, his heart erupted. Yet he still needed the words.

"Want what, sweetheart?"

"The works. You, Ruby, the house, the babies."

He might have looked a fool, but as soon as the words left her mouth he couldn't have stopped the ridiculous grin that burst across his face to save his life.

"Are you sure?" His voice backlogged as his forehead found hers again.

Hope nodded, then smiled too, choking out a watery laugh, and in that moment their love was so alive and vivid he could imagine Hope painting it on a great big canvas.

She reached behind her, pulled the zipper of her dress down, lifted the straps off her shoulders and let the white silk fall to her feet.

"Make babies with me, Gabriel Walsh."

His gaze dropped with the fabric, then rose again—taking her in, standing before him in a lacy white bra and a next-to-nothing white silk thong.

"Christ, you're perfect," he muttered. He gripped her hips, turning her abruptly, so she faced the mirror. "Look. Look how fucking gorgeous you are." He ground his aching erection, thick and bulging in his pants, against her, relishing in the gasp that tore from her.

"Gabe!"

"That's it," he growled, hunger and need consuming him. He lifted her arms around his neck. "Say my name *just like that* when I make you come."

He took in the sight of her in the mirror wearing nothing but a bra and thong, her arms raised and clutching the back of his neck. He ran his hand down her belly and under her panties. Delving his fingers into the depths of her core, he couldn't suppress his groan of appreciation.

"I love how fucking ready you are for me," he rumbled as he stroked her. "Tell me how that feels."

"So good!" she gasped as she writhed against him. She squeezed her thighs against his fingers, increasing the friction, as needy whimpers and unintelligible pleas fell from her lips.

"Open," he demanded, using his free hand to pull one thigh away from the other. "I want to see you spread out for me. And Hope..." He stilled his hands, savoring her moan of frustration. "Open your eyes too sweetheart." When she kept them shut tight, he nipped her earlobe. "I want you to watch yourself come."

Only after she obeyed and met his gaze in the mirror, did his fingers pick up rhythm again.

He trailed his left hand from breast to navel and watched as her glazed eyes followed his movement until they were trained to the spot where one hand was splayed low on her belly, and his right hand disappeared beneath her now dampened panties.

He licked the length of her neck up to her ear, then blew gently on the wetness he left behind, enjoying the feeling of her trembling with need against him.

"And I want you to watch while I fuck you with nothing between us."

With a long moan, she bucked against his hand. *"Yes."*

The sound of her desire-roughened voice turned him on beyond reason, and he worked his fingers mercilessly over her, while plunging two others inside her, rubbing her sensitive flesh, until she was panting his name like a litany. He growled in victory when her body tightened a second before she threw her head back against his shoulder and screamed her release to the ceiling.

She started to sag against him, but he bent her forward and wrapped her fingers around the cool, marble of the bathroom sink. He curled his fingers over hers to make sure she had a firm grip.

"Don't let go," he instructed, holding her sex-glazed gaze in the mirror. Then he stepped back only enough to divest himself of his clothes, letting out a groan of relief when he unzipped his pants and his desperate cock sprang free.

Finally naked, he unhooked Hope's bra, catching her breasts as they fell into his hands. He rolled her nipples until she was mewling again in that way that drove him mad.

When she rocked her ass back against his throbbing length, he abandoned her breasts. He would be sure to worship them later, but right now, he needed to be inside her. He slid her thong down her legs, then gripped his erection and pressed it against her entrance.

She met his gaze in the mirror. The frenzied need in her eyes matched that beating through his own body.

"I need you now, Gabe," she said, then pushed back against him, taking in his tip and breaking the last of his restraint.

With a rough grunt, he bucked into her with one hard thrust, and she cried out as the force of it launched her up on her tiptoes.

Oh God, she was tight and warm and everything about being with her was amazing.

"Please," she begged, and he began to rock into her with an intensity that matched his sense of urgency. Soon they found their perfect rhythm, and the bathroom echoed with the sound of their heaving breaths and jumbled pleas.

Then he felt her inner muscles contract until she squeezed so tightly around him that the friction against his engorged flesh became overwhelmingly intense.

"Yes! Harder!"

Driven by the demand of her shouts, Gabe let loose the animal that had been caged within him.

He pumped his hips into her with a passion that had come undone. His thrusts were no longer controlled, his motions harsher and jerkier the tighter she got, the closer his body climbed to its release. He took in the sight of Hope's bowed head as she watched him pumping into her from between her legs. She had a white-knuckled grip on the counter as her own sounds and breathing became more and more erratic. Her breasts bounced erotically with each thrust. Reaching around her waist, he slid his fingers along the sensitive folds between her legs.

She lifted her head on a gasp, catching and holding his gaze in the mirror.

Seconds later, they hit the peak together. Hope let out a

cry as she pushed her hips hard against his pelvis. He threw his head back, bellowing her name as she contracted forcefully around him, drawing his release up and into her body.

It was the most intense sexual experience he'd ever had, and as he slowly came back to earth, he draped his body over hers, wrapping his palms around the hands that were still clasped on the marble counter. He was breathing like he'd just run a bloody marathon.

Beneath him, Hope was gasping, murmuring words he couldn't quite understand. The blood in his ears still roared with his climax. Slowly, he withdrew from her, and she moaned in protest. When he turned her and scooped her up, she wrapped her arms around his neck and burrowed her face in the crook of his shoulder.

With their slowing breathing the only sound between them, he carried her to the bed, lifting the blankets and tucking her in. Then he crawled in behind her, the cool sheets feeling good against his heated and damp skin. Immediately, Hope curled herself against him.

"I love you," she whispered, and he ran his palm down the soft skin of her torso, settling low on her stomach, taking in her words, letting them settle in his heart along with the dreams he had for the two of them from that day forward.

CHAPTER THIRTY-ONE

A week later, Hope stood in front of the house Gabe had bought, staring in disbelief. With its well-manicured lawn and charming French shuttered windows, the English-style cottage was far more beautiful than he'd originally described. She could see the balcony peeking out from the back, and knew that if she were standing on it, she'd see the city of Portland from all its best angles.

Gabe came up beside her and draped his arm around her shoulders. "What do you think?" he asked, bending to press a kiss to her temple.

The last week had been one of the best of her life. Since their return from California, they'd spent a lot of their spare time together with Ruby. When they were alone, they made love and talked. True, she did more of the talking, but she was coming to appreciate all Gabe could say in his silence.

Over the last few months, she'd gotten to know him well, but in the week that had passed, with everything finally out in the open between them, their feelings made clear and viable, a deeper connection had grown between them. He was letting her in fully, and in return, she was doing the same.

Every moment with him, every conversation, every time they made love, revealed more of who he was, confirming all the reasons she loved him, and adding even more.

Of course, she'd had the awkward conversation with the art gallery owner in Detroit. She'd been nervous when she'd called to retract her acceptance of the position because she couldn't make the move to Detroit after all. But the call had been surprisingly easier than she'd thought, and the gallery owner had been understanding. He'd still expressed interest in showing her artwork, and she'd agreed to meet with him in the coming month to discuss that arrangement further. But for now, she was content to soak up every moment she could with Gabe and Ruby.

Turning to him, she stared up into his handsomely rugged face. "It's absolutely beautiful." She elbowed him lightly in the ribs. "As if you don't know that it's the perfect house."

A smile tugged his lips, his eyes lighting and crinkling in the way she loved so much because it told her he was perfectly content in this moment as well.

"There are floor to ceiling windows in the living room. The natural light will be ideal for your painting."

A surge of love filled Hope when she realized he'd considered what might be best for her painting when he'd bought the house.

"Do you want to go in and take a look?" he asked.

"Of course," she replied, and one of his strong, warm, hands enveloped hers and tugged her forward.

He opened the door to reveal a lovely hallway with hardwood floors that led to a bright living room beyond.

Behind them, Ruby ran in, squealing in delight. "Daddy, are we picking bedrooms!?"

Gabe grinned at her mischievously. "Yes, in a minute. First, let's show Hope the living room and the gift we got for her." He winked, and Ruby grinned as well, revealing her double-tooth gap from the teeth she'd lost.

"Ooooh, right!" Ruby grabbed her other hand and together they pulled her into the living room that was, indeed, full of perfect natural light.

She couldn't help her gasp of delight. "Oh, Gabe," she breathed, crossing the room to stand in front of the windows. The view of the garden below and the city beyond stole her breath.

Ruby crossed to a table and picked up a long ceramic tray. Balancing it carefully, she brought it over to Hope. "This is for you, Hope," she said, her normally boisterous voice suddenly hushed and unsure. Her gaze darted to her father, who'd come up beside her.

Tears immediately filled Hope's eyes as Ruby presented her with a small herb planter, similar to the one she'd tried and failed to bring into Gabe's apartment a few weeks ago.

And there, nestled between the basil and the oregano, was a tiny velvet box. The tears that had filled her eyes to the brim, spilled over.

Her hand flew to her mouth. "What's this?" she whispered against her fingers, her heart hammering against her rib cage.

"Daddy," Ruby whispered, sounding worried. "She's crying."

Gabe ran his hand down the length of his daughter's hair reassuringly. "It's okay, baby. They're happy tears." Then he removed the tiny box from its perch and glanced back at Hope, the first signs of nerves awakening in his eyes. "I hope," he added under his breath before he sunk onto one knee in front of her.

"Oh—" she breathed.

"Hope." Gabe swallowed, emotion thickening his voice. "I know we haven't known each other all that long, and I know I haven't always made the time we have had easy. I know that you deserve a million times more than I could ever give you. But I also know that I don't want to go another day without knowing you'll be mine. I know I can't think about the future without you in it. I know I can't imagine this house if you're not here in it with us, breathing life into every corner. Bringing life into it." His eyes burned earnestly into hers. "And I know I love you, Hope Morgan, with my whole heart. Will you marry me?"

Beside him, Ruby dropped to both knees and pressed her palms together, prayer style. "I love you too, Hope Morgan. I want to marry you, too." Her big green eyes shone brightly.

A watery laugh escaped Hope as she took in the sight of the two of them on bended knees before her. Her very heart living outside her body. She wondered how she'd gotten so lucky, then decided it didn't matter as she opened her arms wide and gathered them both into her embrace.

"Yes," she cried, her voice muffled against Gabe's shoulder. "Of course, I will. You know I will."

It was all Hope needed. Gabe and Ruby, wherever they were was her home. The three of them together, maybe even four. Her hand fluttered down to her belly at the thought. She would know in a few weeks. But for now, she had all she could have ever imagined and more.

Everything else was just a bonus.

Thank you for reading *Finding Home!* Keep reading to see how writing a book review can mean the world to an indie author like me!

I hope you enjoyed Hope and Gabe's story. If you did, please consider posting a review and telling all of your friends who like heartfelt, contemporary romance with plenty of steam.

Review wherever you purchased *Finding Home* or on Goodreads, BookBub, or social media.

Leaving a positive review is a quick and easy way to support an indie author and they mean so much to us. Every time I read a positive review from a reader it fills up my whole bucket.

Don't be a stranger! Let's keep in touch. For exclusive updates and content, join my newsletter at ValentinaBurns.com

Valentina

ALSO BY VALENTINA BURNS

THE ROSE CITY SERIES

Finding Home – Book 1

Finding Freedom – Book 2

Finding Forever – Book 3

For a complete list of Valentina's books, visit ValentinaBurns.com

ABOUT THE AUTHOR

Valentina Burns is a contemporary romance author living on Vancouver Island with her husband, two children, and a multitude of pets. When she was fifteen, she picked up her very first romance novel at her high school fall fair, and has been devouring the genre ever since. She's long dreamed of writing her own romance books and is inspired by stories with strong female protagonists and their swoon-worthy, well-muscled heroes. She loves to create believable and relatable characters that readers can connect with. Drawing upon her own life experiences, Valentina writes books that are genuine, emotional, and entertaining, with more than a little heat served on the side.

For exclusive updates and content, join Valentina's newsletter at ValentinaBurns.com

Where to find Valentina:

amazon.com/Valentina-Burns/e/B0C3Y7JN3J

goodreads.com/valentinaburns

bookbub.com/authors/valentina-burns

instagram.com/valentinaburnswrites

facebook.com/valentinaburnswrites

tiktok.com/@valentinaburnswrites

x.com/ValentinaBurns_

ACKNOWLEDGEMENTS

It feels like an impossible task to try and name everyone who has supported me throughout the process of writing and publishing this book. It has been such a journey and I am so incredibly grateful for all the friends and family who have been there for me along the way.

I want to begin at the beginning, and thank my dear friends Drea, Lindsay and Izobell, who read this book word for word, page for page, long before anyone else knew it existed, when it was a completely unedited manuscript and 135,000 words long. Not only did you read it, you loved it (or maybe you just loved me enough to love anything I wrote, but regardless...) Without your initial enthusiasm for this book and these characters I would have never forged ahead.

My life and this novel changed radically when I met my mentor Kathleen Lawless, and there are simply not enough words to thank you for all the hours you poured into me over the last three years. Thank you for always being there, having the perfect advice, and pushing me to keep going. Thank you especially for introducing me to the myriad talent that exists in our little Vancouver Island Romance Authors group. What would I have done without you?

A very special thank you to Kate, who was the first to take a red pen to this book in any way, shape or form. Your work and feedback was invaluable.

To my editor Jacqui Nelson, who is the real hero here. You did things to this story that I didn't know were possible.

You asked all the right questions, and made all the right suggestions. You are patient, you are kind, you are the best editor a girl could find.

Elizabeth Vidulich, my proofreader, you took me on when I came to you desperate and frantic because of course I left everything until it was last minute. You put the finishing polish on this story. I will always be grateful for your talent and your generous spirit.

To my very own cheerleading squad, the Supper Club Moms, your friendship and endless encouragement over dinner and drinks is something I will always cherish. Especially Jane, whose pom poms have been in the air from day one—your relentless excitement for this project kept me going through the dark days.

And, of course, I cannot pass up the opportunity to thank my beta readers, especially Jackie from @bookroomaddict and Melissa from @bruhasbookshelf. You have been my online champions since my early days on social media and I Iove, love, love you. Your insightful comments only added to the depth and flavor of this book. You are stuck with me now, I'm afraid.

This has been a three-year journey. Three years of me stealing away to write any chance I got, three years of throwing a frozen pizza in the oven so I would have more time to edit in the evening, three years of me crying that I'll never make it one minute, only to be giddy with elation when things finally come together the next. I have been a rollercoaster, and my family has been taking the crazy ride I created for three long years. I am nothing without their support. Everything I have done is because they made space for me to do it. Matt, I love you more than all book boyfriends combined. To me you are perfect, and I couldn't do any of this without you. And my children, seeing your proud faces when I talk about this book just fills my heart to bursting. You have no idea what lies between these pages but you are proud of me anyway. You are the love I imagined I'd see in the world.

And finally, to everyone who reads this book—you are making my dreams come true. Thank you for taking a chance on this story, a chance on these characters I created, and a chance on me. My heart is laid out there, between every line, and sharing it with all of you is one of the most frightening and exhilarating things I have ever done. Thank you for sharing this moment with me.

xo Valentina